THE KIN
EL

"Double Tro... by Chet Williamson
We all know that Elvis had a twin brother who died at birth.
What if Jesse had lived? Chet Williamson creates an alternate
universe that will knock your socks off . . . and maybe your
blue suede shoes.

"Bubba Ho-Tep" by Joe R. Lansdale
A resident in a Southern nursing home just might be Elvis, and
he's got a problem. Not only doesn't anyone believe him,
there's something sinister going on in the lonesome nights that
only Elvis can solve.

"The Pale Silver Dollar of the Moon Pays Its Way and Makes
Change" by Harlan Ellison
Another version of the what-if-Jesse-had-lived tale, but in the
hands of master storyteller Harlan Ellison it becomes a literary
tour de force—and a brilliantly realized portrait of Elvis's dead-at-
birth twin.

"The Sacred Treasures of Graceland: Excerpts from the
Sanctioned Museum Catalog" by Nancy A. Collins
The author of the cult vampire novel *Sunglasses After Dark*
writes a droll catalog of the revered items left behind by, and
created in memory of, The King. Some, it should be noted, like
the Elvis vibrator, are real.

When Elvis Died: "Epilogue" by Neal and Janice Gregory,
In an excerpt from a new edition of their book *When Elvis
Died,* the authors explore Dead Elvis's extraordinary influence
on our culture.

DON'T MISS THE LATEST SIGHTING . . .
RIGHT HERE IN . . .
THE KING IS DEAD

THE KING IS DEAD

Tales of Elvis Postmortem

edited by

PAUL M. SAMMON

Delta

A Delta Book
Published by
Dell Publishing
a division of
Bantam Doubleday Dell Publishing Group, Inc.
1540 Broadway
New York, New York 10036

Copyright © 1994 by Paul M. Sammon

All rights reserved. No part of this book may be reproduced or transmitted
in any form or by any means, electronic or mechanical, including
photocopying, recording, or by any information storage and retrieval
system, without the written permission of the Publisher, except where
permitted by law.

The trademark Delta® is registered in the U.S. Patent and Trademark
Office and in other countries.

Library of Congress Cataloging in Publication Data

The King is dead : tales of Elvis postmortem / edited by Paul M.
    Sammon.
        p.   cm.
      ISBN 0-385-31253-9
      1. Presley, Elvis, 1935–1977—Death and burial—Fiction.
    2. Fantastic fiction, American.   I. Sammon, Paul.
    PS648.P65K56   1994
    813'.0108351—dc20   94-6048
                                                                   CIP

Interior design by Jeannine C. Ford
Manufactured in the United States of America
Published simultaneously in Canada

September 1994

10 9 8 7 6 5 4 3 2 1
BVG

The King Is Dead—copyright © 1994 by Paul M. Sammon. All rights reserved.

"Introduction"—copyright © 1994 by Paul M. Sammon. All rights reserved.

Burnin' Luv—copyright © 1994 by Robert Zasuly. This is an original story first published in *The King Is Dead*.

"Damaged Goods"—copyright © 1994 by Lou Reed. This is an original essay first published in *The King Is Dead*.

"Elvis Lives"—copyright © 1990 by Lynne Barrett. First published in *Ellery Queen Mystery Magazine* 1990.

"Backstage"—copyright © 1994 by Del James. This is an original story first published in *The King Is Dead*.

"Double Trouble"—copyright © 1994 by Chet Williamson. This is an original story first published in *The King Is Dead*.

"Someone You Never Forget"—copyright © 1992 by Greil Marcus. First published in *Interview* magazine May 1992.

"The Burglar Who Dropped in on Elvis"—copyright © 1990 by Lawrence Block. First published in *Playboy* magazine April 1990.

"Elvis Is Dead: Why Are *You* Alive?"—copyright © 1994 by The Ontario Review, Inc. This is an original story first published in *The King Is Dead*.

"The Shoemaker's Tale"—copyright © 1994 by Lewis Shiner. This is an original story first published in *The King Is Dead*.

"Want" by Christopher Fahy—copyright © 1994 by Christopher Fahy. This is an original story first published in *The King Is Dead*.

"Limited Additions"—copyright © 1994 by J. S. Russell. This is an original story first published in *The King Is Dead*.

"Bubba Ho-Tep"—copyright © 1994 by Joe R. Lansdale. This is an original novella first published in *The King Is Dead*.

"This Is Elvis"—copyright © 1985 by Roger Ebert. First published in *Roger Ebert's Movie Home Companion*.

"Elvis Meets Godzilla"—copyright © 1994 by Michael Reaves. This is an original story first published in *The King Is Dead*.

"The Pale Silver Dollar of the Moon Pays Its Way and Makes Change"—copyright © 1992 by The Kilimanjaro Corporation. All rights reserved.

"The Sacred Treasures of Graceland: Excerpts from the Sanctioned Museum

The King Is Dead—copyright © 1994 by Paul M. Sammon. All rights reserved.

"Introduction"—copyright © 1994 by Paul M. Sammon. All rights reserved.

Burnin' Luv—copyright © 1994 by Robert Zasuly. This is an original story first published in *The King Is Dead*.

"Damaged Goods"—copyright © 1994 by Lou Reed. This is an original essay first published in *The King Is Dead*.

"Elvis Lives"—copyright © 1990 by Lynne Barrett. First published in *Ellery Queen Mystery Magazine* 1990.

"Backstage"—copyright © 1994 by Del James. This is an original story first published in *The King Is Dead*.

"Double Trouble"—copyright © 1994 by Chet Williamson. This is an original story first published in *The King Is Dead*.

"Someone You Never Forget"—copyright © 1992 by Greil Marcus. First published in *Interview* magazine May 1992.

"The Burglar Who Dropped in on Elvis"—copyright © 1990 by Lawrence Block. First published in *Playboy* magazine April 1990.

"Elvis Is Dead: Why Are *You* Alive?"—copyright © 1994 by The Ontario Review, Inc. This is an original story first published in *The King Is Dead*.

"The Shoemaker's Tale"—copyright © 1994 by Lewis Shiner. This is an original story first published in *The King Is Dead*.

"Want" by Christopher Fahy—copyright © 1994 by Christopher Fahy. This is an original story first published in *The King Is Dead*.

"Limited Additions"—copyright © 1994 by J. S. Russell. This is an original story first published in *The King Is Dead*.

"Bubba Ho-Tep"—copyright © 1994 by Joe R. Lansdale. This is an original novella first published in *The King Is Dead*.

"This Is Elvis"—copyright © 1985 by Roger Ebert. First published in *Roger Ebert's Movie Home Companion*.

"Elvis Meets Godzilla"—copyright © 1994 by Michael Reaves. This is an original story first published in *The King Is Dead*.

"The Pale Silver Dollar of the Moon Pays Its Way and Makes Change"—copyright © 1994 by The Kilimanjaro Corporation. All rights reserved.

"The Sacred Treasures of Graceland: Excerpts from the Sanctioned Museum

For my father
PAUL ALOYSIUS SAMMON
November 6, 1925–November 9, 1991
Who preferred Hank Williams

Like Elvis and the Jordanaires (the gospel/country vocal group dubbed "The Sound Behind the King"), this book wouldn't be the same without its backup band.

First, my sincere thanks to the various writers, agents, and editors whose work is represented herein; The King Is Dead was your concert, and you put on a helluva show. I'd also like to thank Charles Ardai, for services above and beyond the call. A further tip o' the hat to John Jakes, William Kotzwinkle, Greg Bear, and Lucius Shepard, who at least tried, and to Tom Wolfe, Katherine Dunne, Elmore Leonard, John Waters, and Clive Cussler, who at least replied. To Peter Straub/Stephen King, apologies for the onslaught. To John Skipp; grazie for the story, man! All praise to Clive Barker for finding the time, and to Joe R. Lansdale for the Texas mafia connections.

I also appreciated the help of Shirley Sonderegger, Harlan Ellison, Greil Marcus, Sylvia Reed, Craig at Sister Ray, Marlene Gelfond, and John Morthland. To Charles Ardai, Ray Garton, Phil Nutman, Kathleen Goonan, Gorman Bechard, T. Winter-Damon, Rex Miller, Ed Gorman, and Doug Winter—Elvis 2!

Penultimately, may Allah shower blessings on the heads of Jeanne Cavellos (my editor at Dell) and Lori Perkins (new mom and agent; Hi, Max!).

Finally, a second The King Is Dead dedication definitely belongs to Sheryl Edith Sires Sammon. Wife, confidante, soulmate—eighteen years now, and still going strong—Sherri is the Good Woman alluded to in the "About the Editor" section.

She has saved my sorry ass many times.

For that and all else:

Thank you, sweetheart.

Always, and for everything.

Elvis was on leave, sleeping at Graceland, when Vernon called with the news. Cousin Billy Smith took the call and told the boy his mother was dead. He fell apart. Accounts of his emotional state as he grieved are almost unbearable to hear. He threw himself on her coffin, weeping over her tiny feet, calling her by the baby-talk names they had used in private conversation. He caressed her lifeless body, combing its hair, wailing laments as he clutched her pink housecoat (the one he had given her) to his chest. He talked to the corpse, telling it which visitors had come to pay their respects. No one, no relatives or friends, not even his father, could penetrate the delirium that engulfed Elvis in his moment of abysmal pain.

—On the death of Elvis's mother, Gladys Presley
From *Elvis World* by Jane and Michael Stern

Contents

INTRODUCTION
by Paul M. Sammon

The passing of a simple Southern singer on August 16, 1977, spawned a strange and shining beast.

A powerful, mythic creature whose sullen/smiling face has been branded onto politics—culture—art.

His name?

Dead Elvis.

And He is everywhere.

On postage stamps and CD's. Films. Tapes. Books. On television, newspapers, clothes.

Even, God help us, on commemorative pillboxes.

Leading to one inescapable conclusion:

Dead Elvis is now more popular than the Living Presley ever was.

For proof, witness the following—

- "Elvis Sightings" generate headlines in the press.
- Space shuttle astronauts get their wake-up calls via His greatest hits.
- Troops scrawl "I Saw Elvis" on Kuwaiti walls during the Persian Gulf war.
- Legions of His impersonators surround us.
- An American president refers to "Elvis Economics" during his nomination acceptance speech.

Strange manifestations which make up only *part* of the World Of Dead Elvis.

A World that fueled this book.

Here is a work of both fiction and nonfiction, of stories and essays.

One whose main theme is that Elvis Presley has so permeated our lives,
He is capable of turning up anywhere. In any*thing*.

In short stories, articles, or reviews.

In satires. Mysteries. Mainstream fiction.

In comedy. Horror. *Science* fiction.

All of which will be found herein.

You are now holding a star-studded anthology, a showcase for celebrities like Roger Ebert, Clive Barker, and Lou Reed. A book that is also an introduction to a host of lesser-known, equally gifted talents. All of whom were required to follow the same two, simple guidelines before submitting to this work:

1. *Each entry must include Elvis Presley in some way, shape, or form, and,*
2. *Elvis must be dead.*

So prepare yourself.

You're about to begin a most unusual trip.

Its paths are many. Its landmarks, numerous.

Its final destination?

A funeral that just won't quit.

Because rock 'n' roll may never die, but—

The King Is Dead.

ROBERT ZASULY is a fledgling fictioneer from Denver, Colorado.

And if there's any one story in this book which encapsulates Elvis's satirical potential, it's probably Bob's.

Fat Elvis. His tacky taste. The garish Vegas spectaculars.

It's here, folks. All here.

Not to mention overzealous fans and jelly doughnuts.

Zasuly's biography states that for several years "He made a living designing, writing, and editing publications for huge corporations that couldn't possibly have survived had it not been for the assistance of government contracts. Fed up, tired, and overpaid, Zasuly quit the corporate world in May 1991 to concentrate on more honest fiction.

"His first sale, 'Corporate Culture,' appeared in the horror anthology Chilled to the Bone. Currently Zasuly is trying to place several other stories and is researching his horror novel The Dark Deep. He also spends a considerable time in the mountains spotting vast amounts of nature and falling into most of Colorado's rivers, as he chases the elusive Great White Trout."

Zasuly may not yet have netted that evasive aquatic beastie, but "Burnin' Luv" is a prize-winning catch. For beneath its humorous surface lies a wickedly barbed gaffe, hooked deep into the gills of decomposing careers.

"Burnin' Luv" also features a concert.

One of The King's last, I would think . . .

BURNIN' LUV
by Robert Zasuly

Nobody called the bar the Fusileer; everyone in Drheemy, Tennessee, knew Rupert owned it and that was good enough. The backstage "dressing room" at Rupert's was nothing more than a large storage closet. In fact, Rupert still kept mops, buckets, extra lights, and whatnot in there. Beneath the odor of sour sweat and cigarette smoke you could smell the pine cleaner. All Rupert did to convert it into a dressing room was toss in an old card table, a couple folding chairs, and a mirror he got at a yard sale.

Jimmy Lee paused outside the room and looked at the rusty door latch. *This ain't spit,* he thought. There was a time when he felt going to Rupert's was an affair, somewhere to go on Saturday night, but that was changed now. Drheemy wasn't big enough to hold Jimmy Lee anymore, and Rupert's was nothing more than a backwater feed store with a bar stuck on it.

Isn't spit, he corrected himself. *In Memphis, the doors'll be gold and there'll be deep carpets and the bathrooms'll have waiters in 'em.*

He smoothed his black hair back behind his ears, and his hands came away sticky with gel. Rubbing them on his polyester slacks, he reminded himself that tomorrow they'd be "on the road," as those in the biz said, and he'd get some styling mousse in Bolivar.

He wiped the sweat off his upper lip and opened the door. "How's my boy?" he asked, smiling broadly.

Elvis didn't answer, didn't even register Jimmy Lee's entrance. He was slouched in the metal chair, staring darkly at the painting on the wall. His huge bulk struggled to pull free of its fabric confines and spill to the floor like so much liberated dough. The singer's sagging girth enwrapped the small metal chair so that all Jimmy Lee could see were the four spindly legs, which looked slightly bowed out under the weight.

Mounted inside the chrome picture frame was a black velvet painting of Elvis. The velvet Elvis was dressed in white bell bottoms and jacket with a wide collar, and Hawaiian leis hung around his neck. He was sitting on a cloud, city lights far below, and sitting next to him was Spock. He had one arm around Elvis's shoulder and the other hand cradled the King's palm in some sort of a brotherly Vulcan hold. A full moon backlit the pair in a heavenly nimbus.

Jimmy Lee beamed. "Ed Wyler, fellah down at the slaughterhouse, hung that up this mornin'. Loaned it to us special for closin' night."

Elvis's upper lip lifted slightly in a somewhat distasteful sneer as he regarded the velvet artwork, one hand fingering the wide lapel of his own jacket. Still contemplating the painting, he raised a meaty hand to his mouth and popped a couple more of the whites.

Jimmy Lee hissed. "Shit, piss, and coruption! I thought I told you ta lay off those things. Where'd you get *these* ones?"

The singer took a moment as he worked to clear enough room in his mouth to speak. "Rhhumbuth," was his response. He sounded like a liposuction vacuum backflushing its contents, but Jimmy Lee's trained ears heard the oily gargle well enough.

"Well, Rupert don't give diddly about you. You keep messin' with those and they'll kill you sure as cows blow farts."

The two looked at each other.

"Well, anyway," Jimmy Lee amended, "those donuts are from his sister's bak'ry, which means they're three days' old if a minute." He grabbed the box of powdered donut balls off the table and flung it into a nearby pail.

Elvis continued to chew, methodically working at the donut bolus like a cow chewing its cud. His cheeks hung in pale, flaccid jowls, and they quivered as he chewed. Sugar dust covered his pouty lips, and the white on his nose made it look as if he'd been inhaling some of the donuts as well. He allowed his gaze to fall on a spot on the floor, once again becoming lost in dark thoughts.

Jimmy Lee sniffed and wrinkled his nose. "Little ripe in here," he said, and took a bottle from the table. "This here's what does it for me," he grinned, "Stud Son Cologne." He dribbled the green liquid around

Elvis's collar, then poured some into his palm and wiped it under his own armpits.

Elvis twitched his nose once as if shooing away a fly, and Jimmy Lee took another sniff from the bottle. "Anyway," he said as he eyed the container suspiciously, "we'll get some of the Hollywood stuff once we hit the city."

He set the bottle back down on the table, then checked himself out in the mirror. "Place is fuller than a fat whore's girdle," he said over his shoulder. The mirror had a silver plastic border with señoritas in colorful Mexican dresses painted on each side, and a wad of gum was stuck in the center of the mirror with a happy face drawn in it. He picked out a piece of leftover dinner from between his teeth, then smoothed down his eyebrows.

"We'll give 'em twenty minutes. Seein' how this is the last night an' all, might as well let ol' Rupe sell as much liquor as he can," Jimmy Lee said, grinning.

His companion cocked his head, as if listening to the air whisper secrets in his ear. He looked at Jimmy Lee and shook his head. "They're ready for me," was all he said.

Jimmy Lee nodded, his grin slipping. He could see fear working around the man's eyes, perhaps the beginning of a tic at the corner of his mouth.

Jimmy Lee smacked his hands together and stepped toward the instrument in the corner of the room. "I done work on your guitar," he said, trying to sound cheery. "I took off the—Sheee-ite *Mus*lims!" he yelled and lashed out with his foot, sending a bucket hurling through the air and clanging against a wall. A rat squealed and scurried behind some boxes.

"Pardon the French," he said, "but those suckers are gettin' closer every day. They give me the creepin' bajeezus."

His moody associate didn't flinch, didn't show any sign that he'd heard anything. He was staring out beyond the door, lost in contemplation.

"Anyway," Jimmy Lee continued as he grabbed the guitar out and brought it over, "I took the strings off it. That way we won't have no more trouble."

The singer stirred in his chair. The movement started a series of seismic waves rippling under the red silk shirt stretched across his enormous belly. The shock waves rolled from the epicenter of his gut and flowed out to his arms, legs, and neck, then seemed to rebound and collide with each other. "Yit's time," he said, and cocked one hand up, splaying his fingers like a knockwurst fan.

Jimmy Lee sighed, "Yeah, okay." He reached for the roll of athletic tape, and with the dexterity of a professional trainer quickly stripped off six-inch pieces and stuck them along the table's edge.

"Now, remember," he instructed as he began wrapping the strips around the two bigger joints of the man's fingers, "nice an' easy. Not too much dancin' around. I want ya to keep balanced, feet shoulder's width apart, knees slightly bent, but not too much or you might get in trouble."

Using the roll of tape, he deftly wrapped around the thumb and across the palm. "Hand," Jimmy Lee said when he was finished, and Elvis lowered his hand and raised up the other, his eyes still staring into space.

"They'll try ta make ya move," Jimmy Lee continued, "but ya gotta face 'em square. Ya get sideways outta position and you'll have ta twist and turn and we might have trouble. I can't save ya once you're out on the floor."

Jimmy Lee finished taping the other hand, except for the middle and ring fingers, which were missing half their lengths. Leaning over into his partner's line of vision, he pointed at him and said solemnly: "And do not. Whatsoever. Do the Shake."

Elvis lifted his puffy eyes to Jimmy Lee and looked at him helplessly.

"Just don't," Jimmy Lee answered.

"Yit ain't that easy . . . they want it."

Ignoring the comment, Jimmy Lee knelt down by the singer's feet. He laced the ankle braces and zipped up the blue suede boots, carefully tucking in the beefy legs under the zipper as he went. The boots were a compromise: the blue suede was for them, and the over-the-ankle design helped support the singer's overstressed joints.

Jimmy Lee stood. "Jiminy Cricket!" he yelled, slapping the last bit of jelly-filled roll from Elvis's hand. The pastry splattered on the floor with a liquid sound, and Elvis just stared at the red and white mess as if it were a lost opportunity.

"Now look an' see what happened!" Jimmy Lee said, removing a handkerchief from his pocket. He dabbed at the red jelly leaking from the hole below the man's Adam's apple, careful not to pull off any more tissue with it. Then he pulled one of the silk scarfs from the pile on the table and arranged it around his performer's neck.

"Why do ya keep eatin' that stuff anyway?" Jimmy Lee asked. "Ya can't taste it, can ya?"

"Ah can still feel it," Elvis said quietly, raising his left hand toward Jimmy Lee. "Better do this one, too." A ragged smile arched across his purplish wrist.

Jimmy Lee frowned.

"Ah didn't do it," Elvis explained in his roller coaster cadence. "Yit just happened when Ah was . . . rrreachin' for a little sumfin' ta eat."

Shaking his head, Jimmy Lee grabbed another scarf and tied it around the torn wrist.

"Ah . . . Ah godda go," Elvis said nervously.

"We don't have your truss on," Jimmy Lee argued, but even as he said it he was helping the giant to his feet.

Getting him up was always a tricky moment, because it involved so much stress in so many awkward angles. The metal chair squealed under the shifting weight as the man ponderously rose up. Jimmy Lee moved about the singer, holding here, pushing there, ready to catch this or that, until his star was up and steady.

"Don't forget this," Jimmy Lee said, and grabbed the immense white belt off the back of the other chair. It was easily two hands across at its widest, tapering down to the metal buckle. Huge rhinestones, opals, rubies, diamonds, and other assorted jewels sparkled on the belt so that hardly a spot was left uncovered.

Jimmy Lee fitted it around Elvis and buckled it from behind, making sure it was good and tight. He was barely finished when Elvis lurched toward the door.

"Godda go," Elvis repeated.

Jimmy Lee grabbed the guitar and followed after his performer. "If a man's gotta go, a man's gotta go," he said a little nervously. "Just remember now what I said. Nothin' fancy."

Rupert's stage was nothing more than a cleared area against the back wall of the bar. At Jimmy Lee's insistence, Rupert had constructed a frame of two-by-fours and chicken wire to separate the stage from the audience. A six-foot-high cardboard partition decorated with poorly spray-painted bonsai trees blocked the view of the dressing room door and served as the off-stage area. In the back corner, the front half of a stuffed cow stared at them with big blank eyes.

When they stepped out of the room, Jimmy Lee handed Elvis the guitar and motioned for him to wait behind the partition.

A car battery rested against the wall, and two black cables ran from its posts to the ceiling, where they were connected to two car headlights. Jimmy Lee bent down and touched the loose cable to the post, sending sparks jumping. The headlights shot double beams onto the stage floor, and instantly the crowd roared with renewed life. He touched the cable to the post three times, blinking the lights, and each time the crowd boiled over with cheers and whistles.

Elvis staggered forward in response to the crowd's noise, but Jimmy Lee jumped up and restrained him.

"Ho now, son. Let's let 'em simmer just a tad more," he said, pushing his star back against the wall. He straightened his shirt, slicked back his hair, and walked out onto the floor.

The bar was the fullest it'd been all week. During the last five days, word had spread about the show at Rupert's, until all of Drheemy and more knew about the boy wonder. Monday and Tuesday nights hadn't turned many people, a couple regulars and the odd traveler or two. But as word quickly spread business picked up, so that by Saturday night Rupert couldn't squeeze any more customers inside his tiny bar.

It looked like Rupert had dug up five extra tables, making it about fifteen all together. Stools, chairs and crates, each occupied by at least one person, covered every remaining inch of floor space. More people lined the walls so that the bricks appeared to undulate, and the bar top had become a makeshift bench for five.

Jimmy Lee recognized some of the faces as those he'd grown up with. Others he recognized as people he'd seen at the show earlier in the week —truck drivers, salesmen, several road-tripping college students with a Frisbee, a couple lost Shriners—people who happened to be passing through Drheemy on their way somewhere else. They'd been passing through, but once they saw the show, most changed their plans and stayed for another look.

Still others in the crowd he recognized as complete strangers, newcomers who'd heard about the event and made a pilgrimage to the small town.

He could smell the ozone of anticipation in the air. The crowd was excited, agitated. Its boundaries flowed and pulsed; its center was a hive of movement, mixing images and sounds. To his left he saw an old woman mouthing something at him, while on his right he heard a man's harsh voice yelling.

It was a carnival atmosphere and Jimmy Lee was at the center of it. He knew what they wanted, and it was his to provide.

He tapped the mike and bent to it, the twin spot on his right illuminating one side of his face in a ghostly hue while casting the other side in shadow. The crowd quieted just enough to allow his voice to be heard.

He was going to say something special. A few words and observations for closing night that would sum up the purpose of their being there into a neat, poignant package they could take home with them and cherish in their hearts for the rest of their lives.

"I guess y'all know what we're here for . . ." he began, and the crowd erupted. Their sound quickly unified, coalescing into a rhythmic surf that started as an undercurrent and surged with each utterance until it was a demonstrative tidal wave: "Elvis . . . Elvis . . . Elvis," they chanted. Whatever Jimmy Lee was going to say was washed away in their enthusiasm.

He looked over to the partition. Elvis had that look again, the mixture of humiliation, surrender, and resignation that he got when he tried to fight the fever. To Jimmy Lee, it looked like Elvis was about to puke.

Jimmy Lee watched the man struggle with himself for a moment, but it was a lost battle. As the crowd chanted, the performer looked apologetically at Jimmy Lee and started from behind the partition.

Seeing the inevitable, Jimmy Lee scrapped the remainder of his speech and yelled into the mike. "Ladies and gentlemen . . ." he said, gesturing grandly with his arm, "long live the King!"

His intro was swallowed by the crowd, though, because the main attraction was already on the floor and the modest speaker system was no match for their roar.

Jimmy Lee bowed out and skipped by his boy, smiling and yelling to him as he passed by, "No Shake! No Shake!"

From the wall Jimmy Lee watched and held his breath as Elvis raised the guitar above his head in his classic greeting to the audience. He executed the maneuver a little slowly, pausing halfway through so that Jimmy Lee feared the worst, but he completed it nonetheless. The crowd was oblivious to the less-than-perfect salute, and they roared a greeting to their beloved entertainer.

Relieved that his star had passed his first hurdle, Jimmy Lee began picking his way through the people to the bar in the rear, thinking that they'd probably have to scrap that salute pretty soon.

By the time he reached the bar, the crowd had quieted enough to allow the their superstar to be heard.

"Uhh . . ." Elvis said in his low, syrupy Tennessee drawl, "thangyou . . . thangyouverymuch. Uhh . . . Ah jus' wanna say . . . yyyits goodtobebag."

The sound system was bad, the acoustics awful, and it was obvious to Jimmy Lee that the new tear in his singer's throat was changing his voice once again. That uniquely Elvis sound was still there, but the strain over the past week had taken its toll so that it sounded as if the singer's throat were still crammed with those damned jelly donuts.

The audience didn't notice. They roared and screamed passionately at the superstar's words, words they'd missed hearing all those long years.

Jimmy Lee grinned broadly and slapped his knee. "My boy still gots it!" he shouted over his shoulder to Rupert.

Grinning from ear to ear but working with the fanatical concentration of a weight lifter, Rupert was grabbing fists of beer bottles from the cooler and passing them over the bar to his wife as fast as he could. What meager resources he had in the way of liquor and drink mixes were already strewn all over the back counter as a result of the bartender's frenzied efforts to keep pace with his customers' demands.

Turning his attention back to the stage, Jimmy Lee stuck his hand out behind him. Instantly he felt the cold wet weight of a bottle in his hand, and he brought the beer around to his lips. *This is the way it'll be from now on,* he grinned to himself.

Music flared, the crowd cheered again, and Elvis started singing "Welcome to My World."

Jimmy Lee listened to his singer for a while. Annie Filton's organ work was bad even by Sunday church standards; her husband Homer played a dead snare, and the acne poster child himself, Darrell Lykes, needed to reconsider his commitment to the guitar. But none of that seemed to matter to the audience, so it didn't matter much to Jimmy Lee. Besides, he'd fix the band situation when they hit Memphis.

Despite it all, there was no denying that Elvis was still The King. To say he was overweight was like saying Tammy Faye Bakker dabbled in cosmetics. Megaweight was probably a better description, and as far as Jimmy Lee could tell it was due entirely to donuts.

That's how he discovered the superstar, just off U.S. 45. Stuffing down a couple gross of jelly donuts at Earl's Pastry & Ammo at two in the morning. The singer was dazed, dressed in a mechanic's jumpsuit filthy with car oil and grease—and of course he was dead, so his complexion wasn't the best—but beneath it all remained whatever intangible element it was that made him Elvis, The King of Rock and Roll. Afterward, Jimmy Lee would guess that maybe it was some kind of weird virus that explained Elvis's posthumous comeback. Or maybe it was a one-in-a-million combination of all those pharmaceuticals he was crammin' down his throat—Jimmy Lee had heard tell that The King was a goddamn walking drugstore toward the end. But it wasn't in Jimmy Lee's nature to concern himself with a lot of the hows and whys. The financial opportunities, however, weren't lost on him and he hadn't hesitated to sit right down and begin talking to the lonely singer.

Toward the end of Elvis's song, Jimmy Lee felt a tapping on his shoulder. He turned to find Rupert smiling at him from behind the bar. Rupert was in his fifties, had a beer belly and skinny arms, and his brown toupee didn't come close to matching his gray sideburns.

The bartender wiped the sweat from his red face with a rag and yelled something at Jimmy Lee. Jimmy Lee couldn't hear amid the noise, so he shook his head and leaned over the bar. Rupert leaned into his face and said again, "One more week."

Jimmy Lee smiled and shook his head. Rupert held up his index finger imploringly. "One," he mouthed.

Jimmy Lee shook his head and pointed east, toward Memphis. He took the gum from his mouth, dropped it into his empty beer bottle, and pushed it toward Rupert. "One," he mouthed smugly, indicating the beer.

Frowning, Rupert pulled out another bottle from the cooler, popped off the top, and slammed the longneck down on the counter.

Jimmy Lee took the beer and turned, sloppily sucking off the overflow. During the past week he'd given Rupert more business than the bar normally did in two months, and Rupert knew it. He wiped his wet chin along his arm, and he reminded himself that a man would be a fool to water a field during a storm.

This last week had been just a warm-up, a stage check to iron out any wrinkles in the act and rebuild the singer's confidence. It was also a chance for Jimmy Lee to enjoy his new status as Drheemy's top dog. But Memphis was the big show.

During "Bossa Nova Baby," "Witchcraft," and "Got a Lot o' Livin' to Do," Jimmy Lee kept one eye on his singer and one on the crowd. He was watching Elvis to make sure he kept to the routine. The "fever," as Jimmy Lee called it, was hard for his boy to resist, and he had to constantly monitor him to make sure he didn't try something beyond his limits.

That's what had happened the other night during "Jailhouse Rock," when Elvis couldn't fight the fever anymore and he started thrashing his hand across the guitar strings, actually trying to play the instrument. The guitar was supposed to be strictly for show, but they wanted him to do it, wanted to see their superstar slap at that guitar just like he had so many years ago. So Elvis had flashed his hand across the strings in a showy uppercut—the result being that two of his fingers arced into the audience like a drummer tossing his sticks out at the end of a show.

Jimmy Lee could appreciate the entertainment value in allowing someone to take home a physical piece of rock and roll history. After all, entertainment that had to be left at the door was the cheapest kind. And hell, losing a couple fingertips certainly wasn't going to bust the act. But it was obviously a feat of limited duration, and that was where Jimmy Lee's job as a manager came into play, protecting the product. Removing the guitar strings and taping Elvis's fingers was Jimmy Lee's solution, just like the supports and the large belt, which was actually a weight-lifter's belt that Jimmy Lee had done up with a few bucks' worth of spray paint and costume jewelry. The trick, he waxed philosophic, was in seeing possibilities where others couldn't.

Jimmy Lee was amusing himself by watching old Widow Gruddle dancing in front of the chicken wire to "Rock-a-Hula Baby," when Darci Anne Tyler pushed up against him.

Darci wore her black hair short and straight, one long bang slashing across her right eye. Her skin was pale and she used almost no makeup, but despite this she was attractive—no, she was flat drop-dead gorgeous. Darci Anne Tyler was the epitome of "wet dream" as far as Drheemy was concerned, and that included Jimmy Lee.

At the age of fifteen she left Drheemy for New York City, only to return a year later with a wardrobe of black clothes, music from groups with names like "Electric Puke," "The Meat Puppets," and "Pompous Hairchild," and a baby girl. Darci mostly kept to herself these days, and normally she wouldn't give Jimmy Lee the time of day. Tonight, however, he discovered her squeezing his arm affectionately and wrinkling her nose at him in a very inspiring way.

He looked into her dark brown eyes, and then let his gaze fall to the substantial cleavage line that her black spandex halter was unabashedly presenting. Darci allowed Jimmy Lee to look a good long time, then she snuggled herself against him and raised her lips to his ear.

"I wanna meet him, Jimmy Lee," she said, somehow managing to tickle his ear with the tip of her tongue at the same time.

Jimmy Lee took a long pull on his beer. He knew what she wanted, and it wasn't just to meet him. Darci's idea of "meeting" Elvis was like the Good Bible's idea of "knowing" someone: begetting was the primary thrust of it. He took another deep pull from his beer while he summoned up his courage. Then he turned to her and yelled over the crowd noise, "Me first."

Her eyes narrowed into hateful slits and the smile dropped from her face. "Screw you!" she yelled back at him.

Jimmy Lee nodded and grinned. " 'Xactly." He turned to the stage and reached in his shirt pocket for another stick of gum.

Elvis had started in on "Shake, Rattle, and Roll." That was a potentially dangerous piece, and Jimmy Lee quickly gauged the crowd's mood. Several fans had joined Widow Gruddle in front of the wire, but he decided that there wasn't any danger yet.

Elvis was keeping it down to small movements of his belly and an occasional twitching of his shoulders at the appropriate moments. Jimmy Lee marveled. Despite being dead and grossly overweight, the man still had an incredible sense of timing.

Then Darci poked him in the ribs.

"Second!" she yelled at him.

He just shook his head slowly and continued watching the act.

A moment later he felt something hit his head, and a stirring straw fell off his shoulder. Darci had walked around the corner of the bar and was standing by the door that entered into the feed store part of Rupert's. She nodded for him to follow her.

Jimmy Lee swallowed big and looked at Rupert, who was too busy hustling beers to notice. In quick movements like a baseball coach giving signals, he wiped the sweat off his upper lip, slicked his hair down, adjusted the belt on his hips, and followed Darci Anne into the feed store.

They stood just behind the door, letting their eyes adjust to the darkness of the closed store. Jimmy Lee placed his hand on her hip and began sliding it down the side of her short black leather skirt.

"Wait," she said, walking back to the door.

Before Rupert had added the bar, this door had been the back exit of the feed store. It held a little window in its center, and Darci peeked back through it into the bar. The crowd noise was much quieter in the feed store, but Jimmy Lee could hear the twisted sounds of Annie's Wurlitzer as she opened up the next song.

Satisfied with the view, Darci pulled her black panties down around her ankles and spread her hands against the door as if she were assuming the position for a police frisk. "Okay," she sighed, "let's go."

Jimmy Lee shrugged: a gift horse and all. He fumbled his pants down to his feet and then lifted Darci's skirt.

Darci passed the time adoring Elvis through the window while Jimmy Lee strained and groaned behind her. Jimmy Lee started out in rhythm with Elvis, matching the slow beat of "Love Me Tender" while he loved Darci, although not quite so tenderly. But before Elvis could finish the opening verses, Jimmy Lee stepped up his own beat, and in a crescendo of strangled ecstasy he quickly reached chorus.

Pulling her panties back up into position, Darci turned to him. "Okay, Stud Puppy, when and where?"

Jimmy Lee finished buckling his belt. "Sure, sure, Darse," he said, clutching his throat as he realized he'd swallowed his gum in his passion.

"What do ya mean *sure*?" she snapped.

"I mean sure," he said as he smoothed back his hair. "I'm sure we're gonna be back ta visit sometime and you can meet 'em then."

"You fucking shit!" she yelled, launching a vicious kick to his crotch. But Jimmy Lee was ready and sidestepped the attack.

"Now, Darci Anne," he grinned, "you're just a little too much woman to be messin' with him. A firecracker like you could injure a man in his condition."

She kicked at him again but he deflected the blow. "I'm his manager, and it's my duty to keep him together. Already fell to pieces once," he said as he popped another stick of gum into his mouth. "The world of show biz . . ." He ducked a right hook to his head. ". . . is fast and furious. I'd've thunk a girl who's been to New York . . ." He dodged a sweeping hook and twisted around to her blind side. ". . . would be more understandin'"

He opened the door and walked back into the bar. Darci Anne's yelling was washed away as the crowd noise exploded around his ears.

Jimmy Lee rapped his knuckles on the bar and collected another beer from Rupert. The audience was beginning to quiet a little as the magic of Elvis's love song took over. His voice seemed a little worse now. It had a congested, phlegmy resonance on the long notes, as if he needed to cough something out.

Jimmy Lee frowned. He'd have to check after the show to see if the dislodged piece of cartilage or flesh could be removed from his singer's throat. *The duties of a manager . . .* he sighed to himself.

Jimmy Lee cleared his own throat with a swig of beer and looked around the audience. No one seemed bothered by the singing. On the contrary: although the noise level had lowered, Jimmy Lee could sense the crowd's mounting fervor as they fed off the emotions that the famous song was rekindling. This was good; it was what the crowd wanted, what it demanded. But Jimmy Lee knew it could also be the quiet before the storm. This was the largest crowd they'd played to, and the line between entertainment and disaster was that much finer now.

As the song ended, many of the women—and a couple men, Jimmy Lee noticed with satisfaction—were wiping away tears as they yelled and applauded. Even at the table with the hippie Frisbee twirlers, one of them raised a respectful thumbs-up.

A few more people had moved in front of the cage now. Widow Gruddle was pushing a purple scarf through the wire, imploring Elvis to accept it. That didn't bother Jimmy Lee much, though, not just a few people begging for personal fulfillments like that. It was when they all got together that it was more serious.

"Thangyou," Elvis said in ragged breaths. "Thangyou very mush . . . yurboooful. Thangyou Iluvya." He paused, then continued in his halting rhythm. "Uhh . . . Ah'd like ta . . . gonna do wa song for ya now . . . called . . . uhh . . ."

Jimmy Lee waited as his singer hesitated. The next piece in the routine was "Pocketful of Rainbows," it had been every night, but Elvis seemed lost. The singer raised a hand to his temples as if to squeeze the confusion from his head.

Jimmy Lee tried to silently mouth the title across the bar to his struggling singer, but Elvis turned his head to his three-piece backup and said something. Annie and the others nodded, and Elvis turned back to the mike.

"Gonna do wa . . . little thang here . . . song Ah haven't done for a bit. Hep me, fellahs," he said, and Annie smashed out a troubled sound on the Wurlitzer as Elvis began singing "I Want You, I Need You, I Love You."

Jimmy Lee set his beer down. That song wasn't in the routine; they hadn't even practiced it. But even as the shock hit him he knew the reason for it. He looked over the audience, saw the enraptured expressions, the heaving chests, and clenched fists. It was obvious the crowd wanted the song; they had requested it.

Elvis was having trouble remembering the opening lines. Several times his voice just trailed off into unintelligible mumbling until he'd pick up the words again.

The crowd didn't care, though. Their faces were flushed and beaming as they watched their superstar perform one of their favorites. Some were reliving the specific moment when they'd first heard that song, the very actions, colors, and smells of that memory preserved by the song's amber-like resin. Still others reveled in the renewed power and vigor that the song and its messenger lent them.

By the end of the opening verses, the old lyrics had come back to Elvis as if he'd never stopped singing them. Jimmy Lee sat back and hoped that things didn't get out of hand. He didn't sense danger, but he clearly could feel the crowd's energy now. It stood invisible in the empty corners and sat weightless on shoulders and laps. It had become a third party, separate and autonomous from performer and audience.

At the song's conclusion the crowd seemed to pause. Its collective sound was somewhat unfocused, almost ruminative as it basked in the song's pleasing aftertaste. Elvis turned to his band again and quickly started another song.

"Return to Sender" wasn't in the routine either, although Jimmy Lee liked the selection. The crowd liked it too; however, this time Jimmy Lee noticed a slight hesitation as the audience took a moment to taste the sound, digest it, and voice its approval. This song was Elvis's choice, and despite his tattered vocal cords he sang it with an element of feeling.

Elvis finished the song in a rasping, wheezing voice. However, rather than rebuffing the crowd as it truly seemed the singer was attempting to do, the song aroused it. The audience responded with heightened enthusiasm, and before the gasping star could say anything he was singing its next request, "Teddy Bear."

The surrounding enthusiasm was intoxicating, and Jimmy Lee found himself getting caught up in the ardor despite himself. What the hell, he reflected. Show biz was a game of ever-changing demands and conditions, and the mark of a true professional was adaptability. As long as they remained flexible, he and his boy could handle anything. He slugged down some more beer and tried to indicate his approval to his singer by showing him the "okay" sign.

Elvis countered that song with his choice of "I'm So Lonesome I Could Cry." To Jimmy Lee it almost seemed like a personal statement to the crowd, and he realized that he was witnessing a sort of dueling medley of wills between the star-struck audience and its beloved performer. It was the ultimate show, the pinnacle in performance in which audience and star shared roles, each alternating between ringmaster and mastered.

The crowd insisted on "Hound Dog" next. It was a dangerous song, a song that had the potential of harming the singer, and Jimmy Lee's newfound enthusiasm melted away as quickly as it had come. If the audience wanted it done to its fullest, Elvis would have to make moves more than common sense and physics allowed.

Jimmy Lee waited and hoped for the best. His singer was on a roll and there was nothing either of them could do. As Elvis attempted to gyrate and shake with the song, Jimmy Lee suffered sympathetic contortions, using body English to help his singer through the routine. He was relieved when Elvis was brought ever so near to the knee-twisting, hip-jerking move but not forced to actually execute the maneuver.

As the song ended, the floor in front of the cage filled with people, obscuring any boundary between the audience and the stage except for the tenuous wall of chicken wire.

Elvis's plea was to launch into a strangled and mournful version of "Don't Be Cruel," but despite the impassioned appeal for mercy, the fervor of the crowd only increased as the song progressed.

Jimmy Lee decided it was time to protect his investment. It didn't take ESP to figure out the crowd's next choice, and if the situation was allowed to build any further, there'd be a whole lot a trouble going on.

He turned to Rupert, who'd stopped serving now and was enjoying the performance with the rest. Yelling at the bartender, Jimmy Lee frantically signaled him to stop the show, but Rupert just smiled and held up his hands in a helpless gesture.

Jimmy Lee turned and pushed someone out of the way as he made for the stage. He figured he could disconnect the battery cable and turn off the spot. Cutting the lights usually was a good way to calm things down.

Pushing through several people, he got to within perhaps twenty-five feet of the cage, but beyond that it was hopeless. By this time most of the crowd was standing, and a wall of frenzied bodies prevented him from getting any closer to his stranded singer.

Suddenly, a hand wrapped around the back of Jimmy Lee's neck and pulled his face down. Something warm and moist smeared across his right cheek, and he caught a whiff of lilac laced with commercial bathroom deodorizer. Little Mrs. Kosekie smiled up at him and said something that was lost in the noise.

The thick glasses inflated her cataract-clouded eyes so that they seemed to take up most of her face, which was so wrinkled it looked like a wadded-up pink tissue. Heavy red lipstick was smeared across her lips and mouth, and when she talked he could see she had lipstick on her dentures as well.

In the crook of one arm, she held her grizzled poodle. It had a white satin bow on its head, and its eyes showed the same smoky look as its owner's. The dog was impassioned too, but with an altogether different zeal from that which gripped Mrs. Kosekie. Lips curling, it menacingly bared little yellow teeth at him.

"What?" Jimmy Lee yelled down at her through the crowd noise.

She yelled, pushing her lemur eyes toward him again. "Heal us! I want Elvis to heal me and my Mitzy."

"Heal *you*," he screamed in astonishment. "Piss and coruption! Who's gonna heal *him*?" But the old woman couldn't hear him, so he just humored her by nodding.

Grateful, she tried to kiss him again, but the poodle reached him first, administering a death grip to his shirtsleeve. The befuddled old lady tried to pull her enraged pet away, but the dog held on tenaciously, ripping Jimmy Lee's sleeve. Jimmy Lee flattened out his right hand and popped the dog sharply on the top of its head. The animal immediately released the shirt and curled back into the crook of its owner's arm, regarding Jimmy Lee with wide, watery eyes. Just then the amoeba crowd undulated and several people were shoved between them, mercifully separating Jimmy Lee from the geriatric tag team.

By this time the crowd had already demanded its next request, and all Jimmy Lee could do was moan as the notes filled the small bar. "Jailhouse Rock" was the song they'd dropped from the act earlier in the week. But tonight the crowd was much bigger, impossible to control. Critical mass had been reached.

Unable to get to his singer and unsure what he'd do even if he could, he retreated back to the bar, where he could see better.

As the song's intensity rose, so did the crowd's excitement. It was a tangible thing now; Jimmy Lee could all but touch it, a collective energy that affected audience and entertainer simultaneously. It was a vicious cycle between the crowd and its performer, each feeding upon the other for energy while at the same time trying to impose its own will upon its counterpart. With every move Elvis made, he both enslaved and energized the crowd. And with every demand the audience made on the superstar, it empowered the singer while enslaving itself.

It was a cycle, but not an equal one, and the singer was losing the battle. His bulbous body shook like gelatin under the strain of his movements, threatening to burst with every shake and twist. His voice was harsh and ragged, the dead flesh within his throat undoubtedly torn from its original structure.

Jimmy Lee watched the singer become more and more animated as the music's intensity mounted. With every pelvic thrust and shake, disaster was that much closer.

For a moment, just before it happened, Jimmy Lee recognized a brief plea for help in his singer's expression. Elvis seemed to look out into the audience, as if searching for his manager's aid. But even before Jimmy Lee could process the thought Elvis had already done it.

Actually, Jimmy Lee would've guessed it'd be worse than it actually was. With the music and the crowd noise, he couldn't hear the brittle bones breaking. Instead, he saw a kind of pantomime set to rock and roll music in which Elvis, as he had done so many times alive, attempted to bend his knees out and teeter on his toes as the song reached the critical juncture. The high boots and the ankle supports must have helped a little, because for a moment Elvis actually did it, balancing on the tips of his toes, but then the weakened bones and tissue gave way and the ankles went out on him.

Fortunately, Jimmy Lee noticed, both ankles snapped almost simultaneously, lending some sort of grace to it all. And, eternal pro that he was, Elvis stayed up, hardly even missing a beat. He finished the song standing more or less on his ankles, his feet at right angles to the floor.

Exhausted and broken, Elvis sank to his knees. It was a slow, painful process, the dead man forcing his dried and corrupted joints to do what they had done so easily as living, supple mechanisms. The singer's body settled in its new position like a huge red and white bean-bag chair. Clasping the microphone with both hands in front of his belly, Elvis dropped his head to his chest, forming multiple strata of chins. Then he stopped moving entirely.

The myriad arms and faces of the crowd continued to flail and shriek their adoration. Eyes bulged and cried, painted lips like bloody wounds opened and let yellow teeth gnash and chomp, and hot, beery breath and saliva filled the small bar as the crowd screamed their undying love for Elvis, the King of Rock and Roll.

Jimmy Lee watched and waited, wondering whether his performer had just sung his last. He was beginning to see his plans for Memphis crumbling right along with his singer's decaying body, but then he heard the sound that was not part of the crowd. It was very low at first, and it sounded like the gargling noise Jimmy Lee's sump pump made when it was broken. But it slowly rose above the roar of the people, becoming clearer as the singer channeled his energy, until Jimmy Lee recognized it as another song.

Jimmy Lee smiled and hooted with relief as Elvis raised his head to the jubilant audience and filled the bar with the lyrics to "Release Me." The band wasn't prepared to play along, but at this point it didn't matter. Although it really wasn't possible to increase its hysteria short of mass collapse, the crowd seemed even more incensed as Elvis begged for mercy.

As he watched, Jimmy Lee realized that what he'd mistaken for Elvis's half-cocked, playful sneer was actually caused by a small piece of the singer's upper lip being missing. During the strain of the last few songs, the piece of decayed flesh must have torn off. But that and even the broken feet were trivial concerns compared with what happened next.

As Elvis's pleading became more impassioned, the crowd responded with reciprocal energy, their enthusiasm demanding even more from their star. And during the painful climax, when he cried to be released, Elvis arched backward in a desperate gesture to satisfy the crowd.

Jimmy Lee knew that Elvis would never be able to stop himself once he'd started his considerable mass moving in that ill-fated direction. He knew the man was doomed to fall onto his back. But as Jimmy Lee jumped onto the bar to see his collapsed singer, he could tell serious damage had been done as well.

The twist in the huge man's body was subtle, but it was enough to tell Jimmy Lee that something had torn. A red smile began to crawl along the white polyester just below Elvis's sparkling belt. The huge weight-lifting sash had done its job, but it couldn't stop the weak flesh around the singer's lower waist from giving way under the stresses of the back-breaking arch.

Jimmy Lee popped in a fresh stick of gum and assessed the damage. Missing a couple fingers was one thing, and he decided the effect of the torn lip really wasn't all that bad. Even the broken feet weren't insurmountable. But this?

He looked at his singer, who was facing the ceiling, motionless. Red jelly oozed from the broken waist, and with it leaked Jimmy Lee's fame and fortune. Jimmy Lee was struck with a sense of profound remorse. He'd have to call Geraldo and cancel.

He was standing there, lost in somber reflection as he tried to remember if Sammy Davis, Jr., had died, when to his shock and amazement he realized that Elvis was finishing out the song. The crowd went insane with jubilation.

He shook his head and smiled. "Boy's a pro," he said, and snapped his gum. "Adaptable as hell. Flexibility and adaptability," he mumbled. "Flexibility and adaptability."

Jimmy Lee paused and scratched his chin for a moment. A smile slowly inched across his lips. Hell yes, that was the key! For a few bucks he could pick up a wagon in town. Better yet, he could probably get one of those mechanic's boards with the wheels on it like the one down at Jake's garage. And with the help of some expertly placed duct tape . . .

Of course his boy'd be shorter, he figured, but then they wouldn't have to worry about all that damn moving around anymore!

"Shitfire!" he yelled, and slapped the bar top for another bottle. Jimmy Lee stamped his feet on the bar and whistled his delight as the crowd chanted, "Encore, encore!"

"Encore!"

There are rock stars and musicians.

And then there's LOU REED.

Reed first gained attention in 1966, after forming the Velvet Underground. A tough, anarchic band, the Velvets reveled in the wild side. They also predated/influenced the entire punk movement (by a full decade) and forever altered the face of rock.

A solo career then saw Reed moving effortlessly among mutating images; glam-rocker (Transformer), *heavy metal wailer* (Rock 'n' Roll Animal), *experimental noisemaker* (Metal Machine Music), *comedic performance artist* (Take No Prisoners), Top 40 hit maker (Sally Can't Dance). *Throughout this metamorphosis, Reed displayed a fiercely intelligent, ruthlessly honest talent. One drawn to the iconoclastic, the seamy, and the outlaw.*

Yet it wasn't until Reed's 1982 album The Blue Mask *that mainstream critics noticed Lou's writing.*

Perhaps it's because Mask *included a tribute to poet Delmore Schwartz, Reed's friend and mentor. Whatever the reason, words like "sensitive," "sharp," and "uncompromising" were lavished upon Lou's lyrics.*

In point of fact, however, Reed had been demonstrating an ongoing commitment to serious, deceptively simple verse as early as 1967, with the Velvet Underground and Nico.

Leave it to the critical establishment to wait a good fifteen years before suddenly noticing Lou Reed could write.

In any event, let's say it plain; Reed is a poet. Of the urban variety. One whose latest projects—the withering social critiques of New York, the AIDS-themed Magic + Loss, the Andy Warhol anecdotes comprising Songs for Drella—have attracted as much attention for their words as they have for their music.

The purest distillation of Reed's words can be found in Between Thought and Expression, *a 1991 Hyperion collection of Lou's lyrics from 1965–90. This recommended book clearly demonstrates Reed's fascination with life on the fringe; it also rings with passion and wit, cynicism and sentiment. Self-contradictions that echo Walt Whitman's classic observation on human contravention:*

"I am large, I contain multitudes."

An attitude typifying "Damaged Goods," Reed's bristling rumination on the contradictions teeming within Dead Elvis.

DAMAGED GOODS

by Lou Reed

I was thinking of you, Elvis, not that I think of you all the time, but I was thinking of you, your pout, your sneer and how feminine they were. How you didn't scare small children, and I was wondering if that meant you were soft. You were like a male Sharon Stone. Cartoon sexy. You looked so much like Priscilla. They say you loved your mother so much you threw yourself on the coffin. Who throws themselves on a coffin. I don't personally know anyone who does things like that. Were you serious or out of control or was the camera on.

They say you died with $5 million dollars in your account. The rodent Colonel certainly took you for a ride. Management knows how to mine insecurity. I'm in the music business so I certainly know what that's about. You probably did too. Did it . . . dawn on you? The money was in the song publishing Elvis! Everybody knows that. All the songwriters were getting screwed. How come it didn't say written, produced, arranged by E. Presley? At some point in the haze of it all why didn't you say, "What the hell is going on here, who do you think you are you fat fuck, I'm Elvis Presley—I don't need you." Or were you scared to leave, so crippled by adulation and insecurity (failure—just look at those movies—you couldn't possibly have had that in mind as a career goal if, indeed, you had one), Maimed By Fame! crippled emotionally, crippled by drugs, and desperately trying to medicate yourself into one quiet night. Marlon Brando and Orson Welles also gave up their bodies to weight, bulbous fat grafted inexplicably to their person, so attractive and then suddenly so fat as though to say, "This is what I really am. Look at what I really am. Love me now knowing that that early beauty was an apparition no more real than this talent I possess and don't think much of." Or were you as gaudy on the inside as Graceland is on the out, the talented pig syndrome, is that it? Elvis, the lower taste to this day exhibits a need to debase and degrade their betters. Witness this joke that appears on the "genius" line of a computer bulletin board:

"Why was the 'King of Rock and Roll' buried in his backyard like a pet hamster?"

Answer: "Because he was too big to flush down the toilet."

Now I don't know if anyone's researched this but I don't know anyone else legally named Elvis at birth. Your life has become part of everyday knowledge. The white man who sings black. The dead twin, Aaron. The Colonel. Sun records. Sam Phillips. Jerry Lee and Carl P. Johnny Cash. The things of myth. Mother's Day demos. The Memphis sound. Truck driving. Harley. The Sweet Inspirations. James Burton (who's never said a bad word about you by the way). I met an engineer once, a union engineer just to demonstrate how untalented he was, who said he'd recorded you. Said you couldn't sing a note, they had to splice together every word. Such bullshit from the technoclass. It must have been HELL. You let them get you.

There's no in depth interview with you. Early on you said you wanted to be Dino and you weren't being sarcastic. What are we to think. A lack of a certain knowledge leaves things in a pure state. We have your work. The movement from the exciting to the most mundane. A movement from polar opposites. You became exactly what we had all imagined you despised. But maybe you didn't. Maybe you wanted to be a crooner. You say you wanted to really "act" and you became the Flying Nun. No wonder you wanted out. Everything you touched as time went on showed lack of commitment and caring for the talent you had. And you did have a talent. That excitement. We know the effect you had on future singers and players. I ran out and bought a guitar after I saw you. No more classical fucking piano! But it seems as though once you got your foot in the door you dropped the ball and were either corrupted or did what you'd really wanted to do in the first place, i.e. become a crooner. At least you didn't sing the national anthem at the Super Bowl or appear on Broadway in "The Will Rogers Follies." What can we make of all this. You could have made any record you'd wanted. Who said no. Why did you follow when it was so obvious you could lead. For that matter why did Jack Kerouac die drunk sitting in front of a TV set, drinking beer, living with his mother. But I could never read him and I never bought another record of yours. The best was the first.

What was your mental age I wonder. At what point did you stop developing. Were you unaware of what you had, what you'd done. Did you think about it at all for that matter. Did you think it was easy, too easy that it was bullshit and that anyone who liked it was an asshole. Did that make you think you were stupid. A thief in the night riding out of town on the rock and roll express with the family jewel clutched under your spandex jump suit. How could you sing "My Way." Did you really just want to be an entertainer like Frank and Sammy. If you couldn't do what you wanted what was it you wanted to do. Or is it that you were an average cracker (like some idiot lounge singer from Jersey who dresses up in camouflage outfit with mud on his face, drunk and ready to hunt BEAR!) with dreams of Vegas—if you had any dreams—and your nirvana would have been a TV variety show replete with gospel choirs, bears on unicycles and a cooking lesson—the art of cajun cooking—grits on the rock.

I think you saw every dream vanish in a flurry of money and that you were so scared and so much tied up with being Elvis that whoever you were never had a chance and that all you knew was that you were terribly unhappy and that if Elvis—the Elvis you played at being—couldn't be happy well then who could. I figure you thought you had less talent than a coon hound, cryin' all the time. I think you thought they'd find you out one day and that you were safer with sychophants and thieves than anyplace else in the outside world. Better to be with young girls as any older man will tell you. They haven't heard the stories before and they're easily impressed. Better to ride the wave until it crashes to the shore than jump off and try to swim—where? Where could you go. And do what. In some way you were like Ali. You took too many punches and I think some of them were there before you got in the ring. I'm Elvis Presley you'd say, and I still can't do it. The child in you was scared and mean and probably tortured you with visions of what it thought you should be. Some fantastic version of a child's reality ricocheting through your adult brain like a searing spoon of poison. Some blue moon consciousness that made you feel as useless as a night clerk in a hotel without any rooms. And that's when your heartbreak begins. When the realization of a dream demonstrates more amply than you'd like to know just how barren and forsaken your reality is. And how foolish the dream was. How undeserving the dreamer. In dreams begin responsibilities but that's how your nightmares begin. Are you lonesome tonight. Are you lonesome tonight. Oh yes. Oh yes. I'm down at the end of lonely street. I'm on Lonely Avenue. And my bucket's got a hole in it. Can't work no more.

LYNNE BARRETT lives in Miami. She has taught in that city's Florida International University as well as the International Women's Writing Guild Conference at Skidmore. Her stories have appeared in Ellery Queen Mystery Magazine, Redbook, *and* Carolina Quarterly. *In 1988, Carnegie Mellon University Press published a collection of Barrett's short fiction; it was titled* The Land of Go.

That bare-bones biography pretty much sums up my knowledge of Lynne Barrett's life. Except for the following.

On February 21, 1992, I telephoned Barrett to finalize a few details regarding her story. During our chat she professed a great interest in the ongoing Elvis phenomenon. Then Lynne mentioned this:

" 'Elvis Lives' was the first story where I killed anybody. It immediately won a prize. There might be a lesson there."

Indeed there might—Barrett's prize was the coveted Edgar Award for 1990's Best Mystery Story.

As for the killing . . . well, "Elvis Lives" takes a rather gimlet-eyed look at a particularly bizarre breed of entertainer—the Elvis Imitator. Those well-intentioned but basically parasitical performers who, with the passage of time, have become perversely endearing cultural artifacts.

Although the bad ones remind me of legless puppies trying to sit up and beg.

In any event, and based on the evidence presented in "Elvis Lives," Lynne Barrett is not amused by their antics.

Not at all.

Welcome to Las Vegas, folks.

And the ultimate Dead Elvis act.

Featuring not one, or even two.

But three—count 'em, three—Elvis Impersonators.

ELVIS LIVES

by Lynne Barrett

"Vegas ahead—see that glow?" said Mr. Page. "That's the glow of money, babes."

Lee looked up. All the way from Phoenix he'd ignored the others in the car and watched the desert as it turned purple and disappeared, left them rolling through big nothingness. Now lights filled his eyes as they drove into town. Lights zipped and jiggled in the night. Ain't it just like humans, he thought, to set up all this neon, like waving fire in the dark to scare away the beasts, to get rid of your own fear. Lights ascended, filling in a tremendous pink flamingo. There was something silly about Las Vegas—he laughed out loud. "What's so funny, man?" the kid, Jango, asked with that flicker in the upper lip he'd been hired for, that perfect snarl.

Lee shrugged and leaned his cheek against the car window, studying the lights.

"He's just happy 'cause we're finally here," said Baxter. "Here where the big bucks grow and we can pick some, right?" Baxter was a good sort, always carrying Lee and the kid. A pro.

"Just you remember, babes, we're here to collect the bucks, not throw 'em down the slots." Mr. Page pulled into the parking lot of the Golden Pyramid Hotel and Casino. On a huge marquee, yellow on purple spelled out E L V I S, then the letters danced around till they said L I V E S. The lights switched to a display of Elvis's face. "They do that with a computer," said Mr. Page.

Lee, Baxter, and Jango were silent, staring up. The same look came over them, a look that spoke of steamy dreams and sadness women wanted to console. The face—they all three had it. Three Elvises.

It was surely a strange way to make a living, imitating another man. Sometimes Lee thought he was the only one of them who felt its full weirdness. As they moved their gear into the suite of the hotel provided for Talent, the others seemed to take it all for granted. Of course, Baxter had been doing Elvis for ten years. And the kid thought this was just a temporary gig that would bankroll a new band, a new album, where he'd be his punk-rock self, Jango. But Lee had never been in show business before. Maybe that was why it kept striking him as something horrifying, bringing the dead to life.

He threw his suitcase on a bed and went out to the living room where the bar was stocked for Talent. He poured himself a whiskey and carried it back to sip while he unpacked. Or maybe, Lee thought, he was just getting into the role, like Mr. Page said to, understanding Elvis Presley's own hollow feeling. He played the sad, sick Elvis, after all. Maybe his horror was something the man had had himself in his later years as he echoed his own fame.

Lee snapped open his old leather suitcase, the same valise his mamma had forty years ago when she was on her honeymoon and getting pregnant with him. "Why buy something new?" he'd said when Cherry pestered him before their trip to New York that started all the trouble. "This is leather, the real thing—you can't get that anymore."

Cherry admired fresh vinyl, though. Her wish for new things was so strong it tore her up, he could see. Game shows made her cry. She entered sweepstakes, stayed up late at night thinking of new ways to say why she should win in twenty-five words or less. There was so little he could give her, he *had* to let her enter him in the contest the Bragg *Vindicator* ran. New York wanted, as part of its Statue of Liberty extravaganza, dozens of Elvis Presley imitators, and Bragg, Tennessee, was going to send one. Cherry had always fancied he resembled Elvis—she used to roll around with delight when he'd sing "hunka hunka burnin' love" to her in bed. She borrowed a cassette deck and sent a tape of him in, along with a Polaroid taken once at a Halloween party.

When he won, Lee said he didn't have the voice for it, that great voice, but they said no one would notice, there'd be so many others up there, he could mouth the words. He could too sing, Cherry said—oh, she still loved him then—he sang just beautifully in church. There was little enough Cherry was proud of him for anymore. They still lived in the trailer on his mamma's land, and now that he'd put it on a cement foundation and built on a porch it seemed all the more permanently true that they were never going to have it any better. He was picking up what jobs he could as an electrician since the profit went out of farming and their part of the country got depressed. A free trip to the Big Apple was maybe what they needed.

And it was fun. Lee liked the pure-dee craziness of the celebration, a whole city in love with itself. Cherry bought one of those Lady Liberty crowns and wore it with a sexy white dress she'd made with just one shoulder to it. When they were riding on the ferry he heard a man say, looking at them, "Duplication is America's fondest dream," and the man's friend laughed and answered, "Such is identity in a manufacturing nation." Lee glared at them. *I ain't a duplicate,* and anyway, he noticed, they both had the same Fifties' sunglasses and wrinkled jackets as everyone in soda-pop commercials. But when he got to rehearsal with all the other Elvises, he knew that, yes, it was hard to see them as real men instead of poor copies.

Because he had some age and gut on him, they put him toward the back, which was just fine. He didn't even feel too embarrassed during the show. After, he and Cherry were partying away when a white-haired man, very sharp in his Western-tailored suit, came up and said Lee was just what he needed. Lee laughed loudly and said, "Oh, go on," but Cherry put Mr. Page's card inside her one-strap bra.

And when they were back home and Cherry sighing worse than ever over the slimy thin blond people on *"Knots Landing,"* Mr. Page showed up, standing on their porch with a big smile. Cherry had called him, but Lee couldn't be mad—it meant she thought he was good for something.

Mr. Page's plan was a show like a biography of Elvis in songs. And he wanted three impersonators. For the kid Elvis, who drove a truck and struggled and did those first Sun sessions and Ed Sullivan, he'd found Jango, a California boy with the right hips and snarl. He had Baxter, who had experience doing Elvis at his peak, the movie star, the sixties Elvis. And he wanted Lee to be late Elvis, Elvis in gargantuan glittery costumes, Elvis on the road, Elvis taking drugs, Elvis strange, Elvis dying. "It's a great part, a tragic role," said Mr. Page. "The King—unable to trust anyone, losing Priscilla, trapped by his own fame—lonely, yes, tormented, yes, but always singing."

"Have you heard me sing?" Lee asked. He was leaning against the fridge in the trailer, drinking a beer.

Mr. Page beamed at his pose, at his belly. "Why, yes," he said. "I listened to the tape your lovely wife sent. You have a fine voice, big whatchacallit, baritone. So you break up a bit now and then or miss a note—that's great, babes, don't you see, it's his emotion, it's his ruin. You'll be beautiful."

And Cherry's eyes were shining and Mr. Page signed Lee up.

"Check, check, one two three," Baxter said into the mike. His dark Presley tones filled the Pharaoh's Lounge, where they'd spent the morning setting up.

"Man, what a system," Jango said to Lee. "If they'd let me do my stuff, my real stuff, on a system like this, I'd be starsville in a minute."

Lee looked over at the kid, who was leaning against an amp in the black leather suit he'd had made after they played Indianapolis. Jango wasn't saving a penny, really—he kept buying star gear.

"Yeah, one of these nights," Jango said, "when I'm in the middle of a number—'All Shook Up,' I think—I'm just gonna switch right into my own material. You remember that song I played you, 'Love's a Tumor'?"

Lee grinned and finished his can of beer. Worst song he'd ever heard in his life.

"Yeah, they'd be shook up then, all right," said Jango.

Mr. Page came over to them. "Go hit some high notes on there, kid," he said, "let's check out the treble." While Jango went over to the mike, Mr. Page said to Lee, "How you doing?"

Lee squatted down by the Styrofoam cooler they always stashed behind the drummer's platform, fished out a Coors, popped it open, stood drinking.

"You seem a little down, babes. Can I do something?"

"You can let me out of the contract so I can go on home," Lee said.

"Now, why should I do that? I could never find somebody else as good as you are. Why, you're the bleakest, saddest Elvis I've ever seen. Anyway, what home? But let me fix you up with a little something— some instant cheer, you know?" Mr. Page leaned over and put some capsules into the pocket of Lee's Western shirt.

"What home?" is right, Lee thought. He dug out one of the pills and washed it down with beer. Why not?

"Yeah, babes," said Mr. Page, "party. Here." He gave Lee a twenty. "After you get through here, go take a shot at the slot machines. But don't bet any more than that, right? We don't want you to lose anything serious."

"Oh, right," said Lee. He moved downstage to where Jango and Baxter were hacking around, singing "Check, Baby, Check" and dancing obscenely.

"My turn," said Lee, and they went off so he could do his sound check.

He looked out into the theater filled with little tables set up in semicircles. Looks like a wedding reception, he thought, and laughed and then jumped back—he was always startled when he first heard his voice coming out through the speakers, it sounded so swollen and separate from him. It made him feel shy. He'd been so shy and frightened, he'd had to get drunk as hell the first time they did the show, and he'd been more or less drunk ever since. He started sweating as the men up on the catwalk aimed spots at him. They always had different lighting for him because he was bigger than the others. He squinted and went through his poses, singing lines for the sound check. The band took their places and swung in with him for a few bars of "Suspicious Minds," and then he was done and they started working on the band's levels.

He toured around the theater a bit, nodding to the technicians. Everywhere they went, Mr. Page hired local crews and Lee had found they were the only people he felt comfortable with. He'd always been good at electronics, ever since they trained him in the service, and hanging out with those crews the last few months he'd learned a lot. The Golden Pyramid had the most complicated system he'd seen. Up in the control booth, a fellow showed him the setup, talking about presets and digital display. The show always had the backdrop with pictures suggesting what was happening in Elvis's life. Up until now they'd done this with slide projections, but here it would be computerized, same as the sign outside. Lee looked out at the stage and the fellow tapped into a keyboard and showed him Graceland all made of bits of light and then the blazing THE KING LIVES! that would come on with his finale.

He said thanks and made his way back down behind the set. Might be computers that were the brains of it, but there was a whole lot of juice powering the thing back here. Usually, he could stand behind the scrim backstage and follow what was going on, but now he faced a humming wall of wires. He knelt down by a metal box with power cables running out of it and held out his hands. Seemed like he could feel the electricity buzzing right through the air. Or Mr. Page's party pills, maybe.

Lee went through the backstage door and found his way into the casino. Bright? The place made his head whirl. He changed his twenty and the cashier gave him a chit. If he stayed in the casino an hour, he got a free three-minute call anywhere in the country.

He got a waitress to bring him a drink and started feeding quarters into a slot machine. He had a hard time focusing on the figures as they spun. He was buzzed, all right. He tried to go slow. If he made his money last an hour, who would he call?

When they began rehearsing in Nashville, he called Cherry every Saturday. Cherry would put on the egg timer so they'd keep track of the long distance. Mr. Page was giving a stipend, but he said the real bucks would have to wait till they were on the road. Lee, Baxter, and Jango shared a room, twin beds with a pull-out cot, in a motel. Mr. Page drilled them every minute, made them walk and dance and smile like Elvis. They practiced their numbers all day and studied Elvis footage at night. To Lee, it was a lot like the service, being apart from Cherry and having all his time accounted for. In '68, when Lee was drafted, Cherry was still in high school—too young, her daddy said, to be engaged. He remembered calling her from boot camp, yearning for the sound of her but terrified when they did talk because she seemed so quiet and far away. Just like she sounded now.

They'd barely started on the road, trying out in Arkansas and Missouri, when Cherry gave him the axe. She'd filed papers, she said when she called. She was charging him with desertion—gone four months now, she said.

"I'll come right back tonight," said Lee.

"I won't be here. You can send the support money through my lawyer." She said she'd hired Shep Stanwix, a fellow Lee knew in high school and never did like. He'd grown up to play golf and politics.

Cherry was still talking about money, how they wanted compensatory damages. "I gave up my career for you, Lee Whitney," she said.

She'd gotten her cosmetology license when they were first married, but she'd never gone past shampoo girl. She always said it was hopeless building up a clientele out there in the country, anyway—everybody already had their regular. Only hair she ever cut was his. She said she liked its darkness and the way it waved up in the front, like Elvis's.

"You can come along with us," Lee said, his voice breaking. "I'll get Mr. Page to hire you on as our hairdresser—he's spending money on that, anyway, dyeing us all blue-black and training our sideburns."

"There's no use talking. It's desertion and that's that."

"But, Cherry, this was all your idea."

"Oops, there's the timer," Cherry said. "Gotta go now."

"Wait—we can keep talking, can't we?"

"Save your money," Cherry said. "I need it." She hung up.

When he called back, he got no answer, then or all night. In the morning he called his mamma and she said Cherry'd been going into town till all hours since the day he left and now she'd taken everything out of the trailer that wasn't attached and moved into Bragg.

Lee went to Mr. Page—they were playing the Holiday House in Joplin, Missouri—and said he quit. That was when Mr. Page explained that Lee'd signed a personal-service contract for two years with options to renew and no way out. "Anyway," said Mr. Page, "what's one woman more or less? There's plenty of them interested in you—didn't you hear the sobbing over you last night? You were sad, babes, you were moving."

"Ain't the right woman," said Lee.

The women who came to the show only depressed him. Every night, die-hard Elvis Presley fans, women with their hair permed big and their clothes too girlish, were out there sighing, screeching, whimpering over Jango and Baxter and him. They'd come back after the show and flirt—hoping to get back their young dreams, it seemed to Lee, trying to revive what was in truth as lost as Elvis. Baxter took a pretty one to bed now and then—he considered it a right after so much time in the role. But then sometimes Lee wasn't sure Baxter fully realized he wasn't Elvis. Jango confided he found these women "too country." He waited for the big towns and went out in his punk clothes to find teenage girls who'd want him as himself. Lee slept alone, when he could get drunk enough to sleep.

When they were in Oklahoma, he got the forms from Shep Stanwix. He sent Cherry monthly checks. He had more money now than ever in his life and less to spend it on that mattered. Now and then he bought things he thought were pretty—a lapis lazuli pin, a silver bracelet made by Indians—and sent them to Cherry, care of Shep. No message—no words he could think of would change her mind.

One night in Abilene Jango said he was going crazy so far from civilization and good radio and tried to quit. When he understood his contract, he went for Mr. Page in the hotel bar but Lee and Baxter pulled him off. Why? Lee wondered now. They dragged Jango up to his room and Baxter produced some marijuana and the three of them smoked it and discussed their situation.

"It's two years' steady work," Baxter said. "That's hard enough to find."

Lee nodded. He lay back across the bed. The dope made him feel like he was floating.

"Two years!" Jango stood looking at himself in the big mirror. "When two years are up I'll be twenty-three. Man, I'll be *old.*"

Lee and Baxter had to laugh at him.

"Thing is," Lee said, "he tricked us."

"Not me," said Baxter. "I read the contract. Why didn't you?"

Lee remembered Cherry's hand on his shoulder as he signed. Remembered Mr. Page saying what a sweet Miss Liberty she made. And he felt Bax was right, a man's got to take responsibility for his mistakes.

Baxter passed the joint to Jango, who sucked on it and squinted at himself in the mirror.

"Mr. Page is building something up here," Baxter said. "What if we were quitting on him all the time and he had to keep training replacements? As it is—do you know he's hiring on a steady band? They'll travel in a van with the equipment while we go in the car. And he's upgrading the costumes. Not long, he says, till we'll be ready for Vegas. It's like what Colonel Parker did for Elvis."

Jango swiveled his hips slow motion in front of the mirror. " 'Colonel Tom Parker was a show-biz wizard,' " he quoted from his part of the show. He laughed. "Page wrote that, 'He guided me. And I' "—Jango's voice deepened into Memphis throb " '—I came to look upon him as a second father.' Shit. Isn't one enough?"

"My daddy died when I was a boy," said Lee dreamily.

"Mine's a money-grubbing creep," said Jango. "Just like Page."

"Course, Elvis should have broken with him in the sixties," Baxter said. "That was his big mistake—he kept doing all those movies exactly alike because the Colonel was afraid to change the formula. No, at the right moment, you've got to make your break."

Jango snarled at the mirror. "I'm gonna save every dollar, and when I've got enough I'm going to rent the best recording studio in L.A. and sing till I get Elvis out of my throat forever."

Lee circled quarters through the machine till they were gone. He hailed a waitress and while buying a drink asked her the time. Four o'clock here. It would be suppertime in Tennessee and darkness falling. Darkness never reached inside the casino, though—there were no windows, no natural light. Could you spend your life here and never feel it? He went and turned in his chit and they let him into a golden mummy case that was a phone booth.

He dialed his mamma. When she heard it was him, she went to turn down the pots on the stove and he was filled with longing for her kitchen. So far off. She exclaimed all right when he told her he was calling from a Las Vegas casino where he was to perform that night, but he could tell it didn't mean much to her, it was too strange.

The telephone glittered with gold spray paint.

"I only have a minute here, Mamma," he said, "so tell me straight—how's Cherry?"

"She was out here the other day. Kind of surprised me. Listen, Lee, you coming back soon?"

"I don't see how I can. Is something wrong?"

"It's Cherry. I know you're legally separate and all, but I don't think she's as hot on this divorce as she was. I was talking to my friend at the grocery, Maylene, she said to say hey to you—"

"Thirty seconds," said the casino operator.

"Mamma—" Lee's heart was pounding.

"Well, I mentioned Cherry stopping by for no good reason and Maylene said it's all over Bragg that Shep Stanwix dropped her to chase some country-club girl and—not that she deserves you, honey, after how she's acted—but maybe if you get back here right now, before she takes up with anyone else—"

Lee fell into a night with stars in it. When he came to, he was slumped in the golden mummy case and the line was dead. A lady from the casino leaned over him. "I'm fine," he said, "I just forgot my medicine." And he took a pill out of his pocket and washed it down with the last of his whiskey.

The lady was tall and half-naked and concerned. "Is it heart trouble?"

"That's right, ma'am," said Lee. "My heart."

They ate dinner in their suite, at a table that rolled into the living room. The hotel sent up champagne in a bucket, for Talent on Opening Night. After they knocked it off, they ordered up some more to have while they got into costume in the mirrored dressing room off Jango's bedroom. Jango was ready first, in black jeans and a silky red shirt.

"Uhwelluh it's one fo the moneyuh," he sang into the mirror, warming up. "Uhwelluh it's one," he sipped champagne, "one fo the moneehah." He looked sulkier every day, Lee thought.

Baxter leaned into the mirror opposite, turning his head to check the length of his sideburns, which weren't quite even. He plucked out a single hair with tweezers. Beside him on the dressing table was a tabloid he'd picked up that had a cover story about how the ghost of Elvis got into a cab and had himself driven out past Graceland, then disappeared. Baxter read all this stuff for research.

"Uhwelluh it's two fo the show, damn it, fo the showowhuh," sang Jango.

Lee, who was drunk but not yet drunk enough to perform, confronted his costume. Hung up on wooden hangers, it looked like a man he didn't want to be—the vast bell-bottoms, the jacket with shoulders padded like a linebacker's, the belt five inches wide and jewel-encrusted. The whole deal heavy as sin. Lee sighed, took off his shirt and jeans, and stepped into the pants. The satin chilled his legs. He wrapped a dozen scarves around his neck to toss out during the show. He held out his arms and the others lifted the jacket onto him. The top of the sequined collar scratched his ears. He sucked in his stomach so they could fasten the belt on him, but just then Mr. Page breezed in, all snappy and excited.

"You know who we got in the audience tonight, babes? You know who?"

They all just looked at him.

"Alan Spahr!" he crowed. "I'm telling you, Alan *Spahr*. The Dealmaker!"

Baxter said, "What kind of deals?"

"Hollywood deals, babes. Hollywood. The Emerald City. We're talk-ing moolah, we're talking fame, we're talking TV movie. What's this, champagne? Yeah, let's have a toast here." He filled their glasses. "Las Vegas to Hollywood—westward ho, babes, westward ho!"

"The Emerald City," said Lee.

The champagne was cool and sour. He poured some more and flexed his shoulders.

"Listen, man," Jango said. He still held Lee's belt in his hands. It flashed in all the mirrors. "I am not going to Hollywood. There's no way I'm going to play Elvis where anyone I know might see me."

"You won't be playing *in* Hollywood," said Mr. Page. "In fact, if we make this deal I'm going to see to it that the script is expanded—you know, do the whole life, filmed on location. Might even find a child, you know, to play Elvis at six, seven."

The poor kid, thought Lee.

"But a TV movie is on everywhere," said Jango.

"You betcha." Page drank champagne.

"I won't do it." Jango sneered. "Sue me—I don't have anything to lose."

Page leaned close to him. "Oh no? A lawsuit lasts a long, long time, babes, and I would own all your future work if you quit me. Any albums, any concert tours, I would own your damn poster sales, babes, get it?"

"Mr. Page," Lee said, "you don't need me and Jango for a TV movie. Baxter is the real talent here. On film they can do everything with light and makeup—Baxter can go from twenty to forty, can't you, Bax?"

Baxter looked up from his tabloid and said, "I know I could do it. It'd be my big break, sir."

"Babes, I can see you wouldn't be anywhere without me," said Mr. Page. "That there's three of you"—and he gestured at the mirrors where, small in his white suit, he was surrounded by ominous Elvises—"that's the whole gimmick. The three stages of the King. And with a TV movie behind us, babes, this show could run forever."

The show was on downstairs. Lee had finished the champagne and switched to whiskey. He had to find the right drunk place to be. The place without thought. Like in the Army. Which he never thought about. Stay stoned, don't think. He checked the clock—lots of time yet. He was in full costume, ready to go. Lee avoided the mirrors. He knew he looked bad. When he was young, he was dark and slim—like an Indian, Cherry used to say. Cherry had loved him. Cherry—better not think about Cherry. Where were his pills? In his shirt, on the floor of the dressing room. He tried to bend, but the belt cut into him, stopped him. He had to kneel, carefully, and then, as he threw back his head to wash down the pill, he saw. Who was that? Down on one knee, huge and glittery, his hair dark blue, his chest pale and puffy, his nose and eyes lost in the weight of his face. He looked like nothing human.

He had to get away. He took the service elevator down. It was smothering in there, but cold in the corridor, cold backstage. Sweat froze on his chest. Jango was on, near the end of his act. Off stage left, Lee saw Baxter talking to Mr. Page. He started toward them, then stopped.

Baxter had Mr. Page by his bolo tie. He pulled him close, shook him, then shoved him onto the floor. Baxter moved through the curtains, going on just as Jango came off with a leap, all hyped with performing and sparkling with sweat. Mr. Page was on his hands and knees, groggy. Jango did a swiveling dance step behind him and kicked out, sending him sprawling again. Then Jango saw Lee, shrugged, snarled, and flashed past.

Lee came forward and Mr. Page grabbed onto him and helped himself up. The old man was flushed—his red scalp glowed through his puffed white hair. He pulled at the big turquoise clasp of his tie and squawked. Baxter was singing "Love Me Tender." Lee shushed Mr. Page and led him behind the back wall, where the music was muffled. Page kept shaking his head and squinting. He looked dizzy and mean.

"I got contracts," he said. "There's nothing they can do." He started brushing his suit—dust smeared the white cloth.

Lee held out his shaking hands. "Look—I can't go on."

"Oh, babes, you're a young man still," said Page. "You just gotta cut down on the booze some. Listen, I'll get you something that'll make you feel like a newborn child."

"When I get too old and sick to do this, will you let me free?"

"At that point Baxter'll be ready for your job. And Jango for Baxter's." Page patted his hair.

"And you'll find a new kid."

"That's the way this business goes, babes. You can always find a new kid."

Lee's heart was pounding, pounding. He had to look away from Mr. Page, at the wall of wires, lights, power.

"Yeah, kids are a dime a dozen. But I'll tell you what, babes," said Mr. Page, "you were my greatest find. A magnificent Elvis. So courtly and screwed-up. A dead ringer."

Lee looked away, listening to the noise of his punished heart.

"A dead ringer?" He remembered the first pills Mr. Page handed him, just after Cherry—don't think about Cherry—and Lee knew he would die, would die as Elvis had and never again see his wife, his mother, Tennessee.

"Magnificent," said Mr. Page, "we gotta get that look on film! It's gorgeous, it's ruinous—I tell you, babes, it's practically tragic."

And Lee struck him, with all his weight and rage. Mr. Page fell onto the metal box where the power cables met. Lee bent over him, working fast. Green sparks sizzled around them.

Onstage, Lee was doing the talk section of his last song, "Are You Lonesome Tonight?" He was supposed to get lost, say what he liked, then come back into the lyric with a roar. "Tell me, dear—" he murmured into the mike and remembered Cherry when she was just out of high school. "You were so lovely." Wrapping a towel around him with a hug before she cut his hair. "And I know, I know you cared—but the—" Oh, what went wrong? "What went wrong? You sent me away—"

He stood still and looked out at the people sitting at little tables like they were in a nightclub. *Well, it is a nightclub,* he remembered, *a hot spot.* And he laughed. "Watch out." He shook his head. "Gotta get straight," he muttered and, looking out, saw tears on faces. "Don't cry for me," he said, "she's waiting." And then the song came back to him as it always returned, the band caught it up, and behind him the wall of light blazed and then ripped open with a force that cast him out into the screaming audience.

Breakfast was cheap here. Even in the diners they had slot machines. Lee drank black coffee and scanned the newspaper. He read how Liberace's ex-chauffeur had plastic surgery to look more like Liberace and about the tragic accident backstage at the Golden Pyramid. The manager of the "ELVIS LIVES" show had been caught in the electrical fire caused by the new computer system. Now, days after the accident, the newspaper was running follow-up stories about past casino fires.

The first day or so, there had been investigators around, in and out of their suite, but they mostly left Lee alone. He'd been onstage during the fire, when the finale display overburdened the wires, causing a short and an explosion. And there'd been so much emphasis on how complex the system was, digital this and that, no one imagined a hick like Lee could understand it. Even to him, his own quick work seemed now beyond himself, like something done by someone else. Lee supposed the other two thought they'd contributed to Page's death—left him woozy so he passed out backstage and got caught in the fire. But they accepted the explosion as the dazzling act of some god of electricity looking out for them. The second night, when Baxter came in with their contracts, they ripped them up without a word.

A new three-Elvis act was opening soon—Mr. Page had owned *them,* but anyone could use his gimmick. Baxter was staying on in Vegas—he'd pitched himself to Alan Spahr and they were talking about cable. This morning Jango was heading west, Lee east. Wasn't everyone better off? Except Page—better not think about Page. Already he seemed far back in time, almost as far back as things Lee'd done in the Army. Anyway, Lee blamed the pills. He'd sweated himself straight in the hotel sauna and meant to stay that way.

Lee paid for breakfast, picked up his old leather valise, and went outside. This early, you could smell the desert. The sun showed up the smallness of the buildings, their ordinariness squatted beneath their flamboyant signs. Lee stuck out his thumb and began walking backward.

The trucker who picked him up was heading for Albuquerque. At the truck stop there, Lee drank some beers and hung around till he found a ride through to Memphis. He had resolved to cut back to beer only until he saw Cherry again, but in the middle of the night in Texas he felt so good, heading home, home, home, he wanted to stay up the whole way and bought some speed for himself and the guys who were driving him, and knocked it back with some whiskey the driver had. Home, home, home, they tore along Route 40, through the darkness, listening to the radio. When Elvis came on, they all sang along.

"Hey, Lee, you sound like Elvis. Look a little like him, too," the driver said. He nudged his buddy. "What do you think? Have we picked up Presley's ghost?"

"Naw," said Lee. "He's dead and I'm alive and going home." Sipping whiskey through the night, song after song, he felt so happy he just sang his heart out.

DEL JAMES *spends much of his time on the road with Guns N' Roses, a phenomenally successful hard-rock band. Why? Because he's currently writing GNR's authorized biography.*

Yet Del's not some newly arrived journalistic buzzard circling the Guns N' Roses gravy train. He directed the rock video for GNR's single "The Garden," co-wrote that song as well, and has basically "known the band since Day One." Del James is also a staff songwriter for Virgin Songs and has collaborated on tunes for other bands like Testament and The Almighty; furthermore, he's senior editor for the rock magazine RIP *and will see his first collection of short stories (*The Language of Fear*) published in 1995.*

So it's safe to say that Del's an insider.

A rock insider.

One whose vivid description of the "Backstage" life found at most concerts reverberates with seductive, bitter truths.

Did I mention this is also a Dead Elvis story? Which infers how He got that way?

Along with too many other Dead Rockers . . .

BACKSTAGE

by Del James

Since death is said to be the most pleasurable sensation known to man, it is easy to understand why so many people are walking, blue corpses.

A casual observation of the wasteland indicates that urban decay is at a hazardous level. Much like the Surgeon General, graffiti warns the educated. Yet so few take note. Another body bag is filled as one more endangered species checks out while desolate zombies rejoice at the sight of other jonesing corpses.

The ability to self-destruct will always be what separates mankind from animals.

The euphoria from injecting heroin is the closest sensation to death one can experience without actually doing the whole nine-yard stroll. Families are ruined by powders and black tarlike goo with scarred-up arms being the trophies of addiction. Everything from entire paychecks and promising futures to babies' milk money is spent on trying to die temporarily. But there is an even more expensive price being paid for feeling so good, so dead. . . .

Oh, the perils of rock 'n' roll decadence.

The backstage areas of every major arena all look the same; dressing rooms filled with road cases of hip stage clothes, stained carpeting, generic white walls, musical instruments, some sort of catered food, tattered couches, public toilet stalls, and eager little girls waiting patiently. This is where the postconcert hysteria begins. It's the fabled land where booze flows endlessly and no rules other than those of pleasure apply. All of the stories about Led Zeppelin orgies, Van Halen groupie scouts, and Guns N' Roses hot tub parties are true.

But in order to actually get backstage, you must have an ALL ACCESS pass.

To get that accessibility you must earn it.

There are several ways to wind up backstage. The first requirement is physical beauty. Good girls may go to heaven but the horny ones will eventually wind up backstage. Fat chicks and double baggers need not apply since even the most coked-out member of the road crew won't fuck a hound. There's no need to when there are plenty of pretty chicks to go around. Knowing someone involved with the band is another way of getting past the security guards. It's amazing how many relatives or friends of friends wind up partying with the band, but if you don't know someone and you don't have the proper pass, drugs are a final resort.

Sex and drugs have always been the bottom line when it comes to getting backstage.

Being backstage was nothing new to Janey McKellar. She'd done this scene before with the likes of Skid Row, The Cult, Alice In Chains, and just about any other band she enjoyed that came to play the Knicker-bocker Arena in Albany, New York, as a part of their tour's itinerary. Albany was a part of the secondary market and although the venue held over ten thousand, it was not nearly as prestigious as playing Madison Square Garden or the Nassau Coliseum. To most bands, playing Albany was just another night to forget, another dollar earned.

Janey's tiny waist naturally made men want to lift her off the ground. She had the appeal of the girl next door that everyone wants to fuck and she knew how to bring out the beast in even the mildest of men. Her innocent, unblemished face was a work of art that belonged sculpted somewhere. Thin cheeks and a small chin accented her thick red lips. Silky blond hair danced past her shoulders and rested comfortably on her pert breasts. Her pale flesh was irresistible. Her wide blue eyes were strong and noble, but sexy in their own right.

It was these blue eyes that made most men melt. She could be virginal and seductive in the same breath. Janey had the beauty and grace of a woman who, if she so chose, would never have to work a day in her life.

There was only one problem; she was only fifteen.

While other fans waited patiently in a makeshift hospitality area for the members of Faux Paw to come out, Janey was walked right into the band's dressing room.

Jon Black wanted to meet her.

Jon was an American outlaw of the finest gypsy pedigree. Faux Paw were synonymous with decadence but it was Jon who was usually at the center of every controversy. Fortunately, Jon's penchant for chaos was matched by his undeniable talent. A flash in the pan he was not. He was the embodied spirit of rebellion and thus the singer most parents loved to hate.

And most girls wanted to fuck.

His anemic frame looked natural in leather. One music critic said Jon reminded him of Keith Richards and Jim Morrison rolled into one person who was having a very bad day. Unbuttoned silk shirts, expensive silver jewelry, and snakeskin boots were all a part of his usual attire but with Jon anything was possible. He had the ability to create trends just by wearing something once. In the eyes of most critics, Jon Black was style.

His jet black hair was naturally unkempt and fell past his shoulders. His attractive brown eyes always looked tired and Jon was always a day late when it came to shaving. High cheekbones and a slack jaw were his two most photogenic features, although everyone had an opinion.

It was no secret in the music community that Jon had a three-hundred-dollar-a-day heroin habit.

After shooting up in the privacy of a locked bathroom stall, Jon swaggered out to meet Janey. Most of the members of Faux Paw had cleared out of the dressing room and this was fine with Jon. Only Mookie, the bassist, remained. Mook was scarfing down a slice of shitty pizza and fighting with a pair of boots.

"You're gonna drop that." Jon informed him in a very low tone.

"Wha?" Mookie asked as the pizza slid out of his hand. Janey tried holding back her laughter but couldn't. Jon and Janey broke up as Mook pulled on his boots and left grumpy.

"You want a drink?"

"Got one," she replied nervously. She held up a quart-sized bottle of Jack Daniel's that one of Faux Paw's security men had handed her. She'd already drunk quite a bit and had no intentions of slowing down. The booze had loosened her up considerably.

Jon slowly walked over to his date. Without even knowing her name he knew that she would be his tonight. That is, until he grew bored.

Music, burning incense, and atmosphere candles set the proper mood. It took Jon quite a while to get hard; it was the dope, but Janey didn't mind. In fact, she rather enjoyed making him go from soft to hard inside her mouth. Her hungry mouth throated as much of his prick as possible.

Once he was fully erect, he'd stay that way for hours. Again it was the dope.

Tongues and fingers danced over each other's bodies. He took a pert breast and sucked, flicking the nipple with his tongue until it was erect. A slight moan escaped from her as he lovingly pinched the nipple with his teeth. She felt herself go wet with excitement as she stroked his cock.

She couldn't believe she was actually going to fuck Jon Black!

Jon rubbed his eyes and tried figuring exactly where the hell he was. He remembered screwing that little cutie. He remembered smoking cigarettes and drinking whiskey with her afterward. He remembered fixing up again in the bathroom and winding up on a couch, holding Janey. Maybe he'd passed out and the party had returned to the dressing room? It was dark enough for it to be the dressing room but there were too many people here. And they didn't look right.

A spiky-haired punk rocker with a lock and chain for a necklace walked away from a small circle of people.

"I think your music sucks," the lanky punk spat out in a thick English accent before belching at Jon.

"At least I write my own shit."

"Fuck off, wanker," Sid Vicious declared before moving to rejoin his dead pals Stiv Bators, Johnny Thunders, and Jerry Nolan. The four of them standing there were quite possibly the greatest punk band of all time.

Darby Crash, the lead singer for The Germs and another punk rock casualty, came up to Jon.

"Don't worry about Sid, he's always a little hard on the new guys."

Jon looked at Darby bewildered. Was he trying to tell him that he was dead?

"Nah, you ain't dead yet. But you ain't well either."

Philip Lynott, the lead singer and bassist for the Irish hard rockers Thin Lizzy, came up beside Darby.

"He's right, mate. I had several warnings during my time and never took heed. If you don't get it together soon then your number will be up too," Lynott explained in his own particular flair of black Irish cool.

"What is this place? A Betty Ford clinic for the damned?"

"No, a clinic is a place you check into. The only way to get here is to check out . . ."

Lynott and Crash left Jon thinking about what they had said. Disori-
ented, Jon started wandering about. He didn't know if he should be
scared or asking for autographs. Everywhere his eye searched, another
one of his dead heroes stood. Brian Jones stood next to Steve Marriott,
Randy Rhodes, and Jimi Hendrix. Lynyrd Skynyrd plane crash victims
Ronnie Van Zant and Steve Gaines were making conversation with
another Skynyrd alumni, Allen Collins, who died of pneumonia. Two of
the greatest drummers ever, Keith Moon and John Bonham, were making jokes at each other's expense. Andrew Wood from Mother Love
Bone was talking to Freddie Mercury and both men stopped to watch as
Jim Morrison walked by. Even in death, Morrison was a show-stealer.
AC/DC's Bon Scott was putting the moves on Janis Joplin.

After watching the stranger fumble around the room for long enough,
Duane Allman decided to let Jon in on a little secret. So he walked over.

"There's all kinds of beasts in hell," explained the guitarist in a thick
Southern accent. "Don't let them fret ya none. It's the ones on earth
you shoulda' paid attention to."

Allman backed away and began laughing. First softly then louder and
louder. Then others followed his cue. Stevie Ray Vaughn, Ron "Pig-
pen" McKernan and Brent Mydland of the Grateful Dead, T. Rex's
Marc Bolan, Def Leppard guitarist Steve Clark, Bob Marley, Free
guitarist Paul Kossoff, Tommy Bolin, and others were all viciously laughing at Jon. He had never been the subject of such disdain and it was
killing his feelings as well as his ears but try as he might he couldn't block
it out. Never before had he heard such vile tones as rubbery mouths
stretched open way beyond their normal capacity. Gnarled teeth and
tongues became more and more visible as dead eyes glowed wildly. With
each passing second, the hideous laughter became more and more hys-
terical.

Then Jon spotted a dead version of himself standing in the corner
alone, and all the laughter stopped.

"NOOOOOOO!" he groaned, as his head butted Janey's face.

The groupie recoiled, holding her nose. What little was left of the
whiskey spilled in her lap and she almost fell off the couch.

"What happened?" the drunk girl asked, quite confused.

"Weird, weird dream."

He nervously stood up and looked around the room as Janey slipped
back off into her whiskey slumber. Jon wasn't dead and it was going to

take a lot more than a dream to make him quit smack. He silently excused himself and for the third time in three hours, prepared to shoot up.

The underweight frontman locked the bathroom door behind him. He ran tap water through the syringe to make sure it would draw. It did. He placed his smack in the spoon, added water, and cooked it until it cleared up. Then he dropped a tiny dab of cotton from a cigarette filter in the spoon and drew the smack up into the syringe. He pumped up his arm, getting a vein in his forearm to rise. With an expert's accuracy, he popped the skin and blood surged into the syringe's clear cylinder. Then he pushed the bulb down with his thumb and the dope was in his vein. His frail body sagged into opiated comfort as his eyelids drooped down. Once again, he found peace of mind in a needle. Then he noticed something odd.

Rising out of a barely visible smoky mist from the cooked spoon, a crystalline dragon began to take form. Infinitesimal at first, it rapidly reached two feet in length. It was crystal white, the color of cigar smoke, only more brilliant and its scaly skin appeared to be made of fine glass. Fins rose from its back. Ran all the way down to its tail. The tail was almost as long as its muscular twelve-inch body, writhing with every movement it made. Jon fumbled with the door and fell out of the bathroom, staggering back into the dressing room. Hallucination or not, the dragon was following him.

The glossy dragon rose, floating three feet away from the rock star's face. Jon did not quite understand what was going on and was too high to care. He tried to move but couldn't. His arms and legs refused to lift. The dope had paralyzed him. Only his stoned eyes seemed to function and even they were betraying him. Out of the corner of his eye, he noticed that Janey was drooling in her sleep.

"*This is fuckin' strange,*" Jon thought, unable to move. After all the time he'd spent shooting up, sniffing powder, and chasing the dragon, the roles were now reversed.

When it finished circling the room for the second time, the dragon stopped and reared up like an excited horse. Standing on its two hind legs, the glassy dragon raised its front arms, claws extended, and opened its mouth, showing two rows of jagged, razor teeth.

Then it charged.

Maneuvering rapidly through the air, the dragon quickly cut off the distance between Jon and itself. Its powerful jaws were stretched as far as they would go. A forked tongue fell out of its hungry mouth. With every passing inch, velocity increased and the crystalline beast began evaporating. Its magnificent features became dull, difficult to discern. Its snout melted into the dissolving face. The monster's rigid body conglomerated into a shapeless mass, its tail losing definition with each movement. By the time the dragon was less than two feet from him, it was completely invisible.

But the singer felt the impact.

Savage talons sunk into his shoulders and ripped downward, getting a firm grip in his chest muscles. Three sharp pains hit each side of his upper torso. The searing pain of blades through flesh pried its way to Jon's breastbone. He felt himself being shredded by the invisible entity. In the same motion, powerful jaws clamped onto his chest, sinking their jagged teeth. Soft flesh was ravaged, chewed, and ground into nothing as exposed nerve endings throbbed. He grabbed his chest and fought desperately but nothing would work. Desperate, he felt himself being overpowered, falling backward in slow motion, until razor teeth gnawed his pounding heart, killing him instantly.

There was no blood. There never is. The coroner's medical report would read *heroin-induced Overdose*. Only Jon would know any different. But whom could he tell?

Janey opened her sleepy eyes and found her loverboy lying on the ground. Very tipsy and feeling no pain, she looked down at her prone idol and wondered how he'd gotten so damn high? She shrugged her slender shoulders. She felt just fine. Another, wider smile crossed Janey's face as a new thought registered itself.

Maybe Jon would want to fuck again?

Janey stumbled off the couch and crawled across the floor to where Jon lay. She kissed his cold cheek and whispered softly, "I'm gonna go freshen up. When I get back you better be ready to party."

As Janey made it to her feet, the room started spinning. She was quite smashed but that was cool, at least she was awake again and hanging out with Jon Black. With feet that wanted to betray her she stumbled to the bathroom door and opened it.

This night was too unbelievable she thought to herself as she immediately recognized two of the men standing there. You had to be a brain-dead rock 'n' roll fan not to recognize Jim Morrison and Jimi Hendrix. Behind them were a bunch of famous hippies that her mom probably could've identified.

"Hello," said Hendrix, dragging off a cigarette. Jimi, as always, was dressed to the nines.

"How's it goin', beautiful?" Morrison piped in. He looked just as good as he ever had. Janey was mesmerized by his physical appearance as she slowly backpedaled away. Bewildered and afraid, she was back in the dark dressing room. Then she tripped over Jon and landed on her ass.

"Are you ok?" Hendrix asked, genuinely concerned.

Slightly embarrassed, Janey nodded yes.

"Sure?" Morrison added as he helped her back to her feet.

"I'm ok . . . Aren't you guys, like, dead?"

"Yeah, but as long as our music lives then so will we," Morrison explained as he put an arm around the underage beauty. She didn't resist. Actually, she instantly snuggled up next to the dead musician.

"You can help our music live on," Morrison explained in a sexy tone that could convince a girl to do just about anything.

"How?" she asked, smiling like a vamp and reading his mind. After all, she had been backstage before.

"You know, baby, just take care of us like only you can," Hendrix explained, trying not to grin.

"But I'm here with Jon," Janey explained, slightly depressed. She wanted to make it with Morrison and Hendrix and opportunities like this didn't happen every day.

"I'm sure he'll still be there when you get through," Morrison said knowingly. Janey looked down at Jon and nodded. He was still out cold.

Janey's blue eyes glimmered as the hunter captured another trophy. Smiles spread all around the room as the sexy girl made herself comfortable on the couch. Jim Morrison slowly undid his leather pants. Hendrix was second after him. After Jimi was Bon Scott, then Johnny Thunders, then Brian Jones, then John Bonham, and after Bonham was a line that appeared to go on forever.

All the way at the end of the line was the King of Rock 'n' Roll himself, Elvis Aaron Presley.

He hoped that Janey remembered who he was when his turn finally came around.

What if Elvis hated rock 'n' roll?

A rhetorical query, of course.

But "What if?" questions are the backbone of science fiction.

Robert Heinlein asked himself, "What if the next Messiah came from Mars?" The answer was Stranger in a Strange Land.

William Gibson thought, "What if our computerized society produced an outlaw subculture of cyberpunk cowboys?" Presto! Neuromancer.

Which brings us to CHET WILLIAMSON, who isn't known for writing science fiction at all.

Chet has written over sixty other mystery and horror stories, however, for the likes of Playboy and Esquire. Critically praised and affably bent, Williamson resides in Elizabethtown, Pennsylvania, with his wife Laurie and son Colin. Two of Chet's more solid novels are Reign and Ash Wednesday.

Unfortunately, despite mountains of glowing reviews, Williamson's work can't seem to break through its own cult barrier. Too bad; it deserves a wider audience.

"Double Trouble" might change that, since Williamson here tackles two of the ultimate "What if?" questions.

One concerns Elvis Presley. The other, rock 'n' roll.

And both take place within that most difficult of science fictional constructs:

A fully detailed, well-thought-out, totally convincing alternate universe.

One I never hope to visit.

DOUBLE TROUBLE

by Chet Williamson

I can't go into detail about *how* I was able to travel through time. No-body would believe me, and I scarcely remember myself. No, there's no evidence except the changes that only *I* know are changes.

Not a helluva lot of proof that I changed the world, is it? Except for maybe the ten to twenty years that going back will take off the far end of my life. Or would have.

But going back is what I had in mind from the beginning, going back and making things different, making them *better*. It's what I wanted to do ever since I was seventeen years old and Elvis died.

I became a fan on December 3, 1968, when I was eight years old. That was the night of the Singer Special, the night when Elvis became something more than the doofus in those dumb movies that my mom dragged me and my dad to ever since I could remember. Up until then I had always thought the guy was a jerk, racing sportscars and riding water skis on rear-screen projection so phony a five-year-old in the backseat could see through it. Sometimes the movies had some funny parts, but I thought the songs were dumb, and this Elvis guy had a lot blacker hair than anybody *I* ever knew.

In fact, about the only time I ever saw anything more than a singing window store dummy was during one of the worst songs Elvis ever sang. It was at a drive-in triple feature of *Tickle Me, Spinout,* and *Girls! Girls! Girls!,* and Elvis was singing "Song of the Shrimp," and after he finished a verse he just gave his head a little shake and closed his eyes for a second, and in that gesture there was the unmistakable sense of *Jesus, I can't believe I'm singing this piece of shit . . .*

I guess that was the first time I ever felt respect for Elvis. And a little pity too.

But the Singer Special nailed me to the floor and sent me through the roof, if that's not too contradictory. That demon in black leather made me forget *Frankie and Johnny* and *Double Trouble* and *Harum Scarum*, "No Room to Rhumba" and "Cotton Candy Land." Instead I saw a guy who was cooler than the Beatles or the Doors or Jefferson Airplane.

So I became an Elvis fan. Oh, I was mocked and reviled by my friends who claimed that Elvis wasn't cool or hip with his capes and American eagles and his handshakes with Tricky Dick Nixon. But the more I learned about Elvis, what he had done to pop music, and what he was still doing (now that those asshole movies were over), I realized that there was nothing hipper or cooler than Elvis. He had *created* cool with that withering sneer of his, and anybody who said Elvis wasn't cool was like a rebel priest denying the God that gave him life.

I started buying the records that Mom didn't have, and went to my first live concert in 1972. It didn't take a lot of effort to get Mom to drive the two of us across the state to see The King, but it wasn't long before we started to appreciate him on different levels. Mom dug him like a regressed teenybopper, while I worshiped him like a force of nature.

To me, the capes, the spangles, the rhinestones weren't tacky and vulgar displays, but the vestments of a Sun King, the man who had brought rock and roll and rebellion to America, who, despite his antidrug stance, had made the sixties and what followed possible, had molded an entire society in his image.

You think I'm exaggerating?

Okay, he got fat and tired and old before his time. But a mere mortal was never intended to bear the burden of love and history that Elvis bore. A single man was incapable of dealing with the force of so much devotion. I was at the concerts, I *know* what it was like—a palpable force that swept across the audience to the stage in waves, a chinook wind of adoration, burning the man out, wearing him down.

Until he died.

I was seventeen when it happened. I loved Elvis. I was a top student. And I had read a lot of science fiction, and even more science.

See where I'm heading? If not, you can look around and see what it got us.

I attended MIT and did in five years of schooling what it took most people eight, because I was driven. I had a purpose. I knew that bending time was attainable, and I had a reason to do it.

I worked on the problem while I was in school, and after I got out. Even with the resources of one of the world's finest research facilities, it took me another eight years of twelve- to sixteen-hour days before it became a practical reality. Not practical for most people, since the radio-activity involved guaranteed cancer in ten to twenty years. But by then it had become too much of an obsession for me to worry about what might happen a decade or two away. The exposure and a certain type of brain wave activity were all that was needed. Simple in retrospect, in-credibly difficult to develop. Getting back there was the hard part, but returning was easy—it was actually harder to stay back there than it was to return.

So what did I do once I knew it worked? What was worth cutting years off my life? Maybe go back and keep Lincoln from being assassi-nated? Hardly. I'm an Elvis fan, not a Lincoln fan. My biographer of choice is Jerry Hopkins, not Carl Sandburg.

Kennedy then? Hah. Who would I go to who wasn't already in on it? And how could I stop three or four different shooters? Besides, *Elvis* was who I was concerned about. And God knows he was more important than any four- to eight-year officeholder.

The first thing that most Elvis fans would have done was go back to August 16, 1977, try to get through Graceland security and keep Elvis from OD'ing, then get him to lose fifty pounds and cut out the cheese-burgers and peanut butter and banana sandwiches. That would have been futile. If it hadn't been then it would've been later. No, what concerned me wasn't death. It was birth.

I costumed myself from antique clothing stores, bought three thou-sand dollars' worth of currency dated before 1935 (which cost a lot more than three thousand dollars), and an old suitcase. Then I flew into the little airport at Tupelo, Mississippi, rented a car, and drove to the area that was once known as Shakerag. I parked in an alley, changed into my old clothes inside the car, and then, to make a long story shorter and a good deal less complex, I went back.

There was no transition, no dream-sequence vortex like you see in the movies. I was just there, a well-dressed white man holding a suitcase in a field about fifty yards from the nearest tumbledown house.

A quick glance around showed me that no one had seen me appear, and I walked away from the small, black community a quarter mile east into the tiny town of East Tupelo, then north across the Birmingham Highway, and onto Old Saltillo Road, where I recognized the humble, one-story, two-room shotgun shack that I had visited a dozen times in the future as a shrine.

It was the house where, six months later, Elvis Aaron Presley would be born alive, and his twin, Jesse Garon Presley, would be born dead.

Unless I did something to change it.

Ever since the day I had learned of Elvis's twin, the possibilities had haunted me. It was almost too early to be sure if Elvis and Jesse were identical, but Vernon and Gladys thought they were. What if Jesse had survived and grown up? Then there would essentially have been *two* Elvises, twin brothers with the same looks and talent and voice, that deep, syrupy timbre that changed the world.

What would *two* such voices do? Dear God, it would be the greatest brother act since Romulus and Remus.

But beyond aesthetics, there was also the question of Elvis's spiritual strength. With his twin alive, he would no longer be half an entity, but a psychic and cosmic whole. Together they could survive, giving each other the strength that either one individually would lack. And if Elvis died on Graceland's bathroom floor in 1977 or 1982 or 1989, Jesse would still be there to carry on. The voice would not die.

But in order to ensure the health of both boys, I would first have to ensure the health of Gladys Presley.

I had read that it was a difficult pregnancy, and that Gladys was not able to work during it. With that already against Jesse, I planned to see that Gladys received the best of care. So I walked toward the house, praying that my lies would sound like truth.

I introduced myself to Gladys, a rather plain young woman whose pregnancy was already obvious in her full face and figure, as Luther Smith, a distant cousin on her mother's side, and told her that I'd come to the Tupelo area to set up practice as a doctor. She told me that Vernon wasn't home, but was, as I had suspected, delivering milk for the Bean dairy farm. Then I said I was looking for a place to stay, and asked her if she could recommend one.

She suggested a hotel on Tupelo's Main Street, then expressed surprise that I was able to find their house, since they had only moved in a short time before. But other than that niggling point she swallowed my story whole. A friendly, salt of the earth woman, she seemed none too bright. But Madonnas don't have to be geniuses.

I asked if I might stop by when Vernon was home for a longer visit. She said that would be fine, and we made a date for after dinner the next night.

So I checked into the hotel Gladys had suggested, and spent the rest of the day and the next walking around a different time, getting acquainted with the place where I would spend the next few months. Before I went to the Presleys' that evening, I stopped at a grocery and bought several dollars' worth of food, including vegetables, fruit, whole grains, eggs, and only a few pounds of fresh meat, since I knew from my research that the Presleys had no icebox.

That evening I took the food to the house, offering it as a house-warming present. Vernon, whose old eyes looked at me from his un-seamed, eighteen-year-old face, seemed suspicious and puzzled by my generosity, but accepted the bags. I helped him carry them through the front room, which served as their bedroom, and into the kitchen, where we stored them in the single cabinet, and then sat down around the kitchen table. I answered any questions about relatives with vague gener-alities, explaining that I'd been up North for the past five years.

I spent most of my time telling them about New York City, which Gladys seemed anxious to hear about, trying to cast my perceptions of the city in terms of the thirties. My stories were derived more from black and white movies than from my own memory, but Gladys sat entranced just the same, while Vernon, a frown on his face, watched his wife and the wall.

Finally the topic came around to my practice, and I mentioned that I was a general practitioner with a specialty in prenatal care. The word was new to them, but when I defined it, Gladys looked at her husband, her eyes bright, and Vernon finally looked at me.

"Glad's gonna have a baby," he said quietly, leaving a space in the conversation into which I was all too eager to jump. But I held myself back, looked at her, and nodded sagely.

"Well," I said, "although I don't actually deliver babies, maybe I could be of some help, make sure everything's going all right."

Vernon shook his head. "We really can't afford no doctor, least till the end."

I smiled. "Vernon, you and Gladys are family. I wouldn't take a penny of your money. It'd be a pleasure to help your . . ." I was about to say *sons,* but bit it off. ". . . your child come into the world healthy."

"Well," Vernon said slowly, "if it's okey with Glad, it's okey with me."

It was that easy. I lost no time in ingratiating myself into the little family, and spent a great deal of time with Gladys, whose warm personality quickly grew on me. I saw to it that she ate right, and talked her out of her dreadful habit of dipping snuff, at least until she delivered. I also made sure that she did no heavy work, and became both nurse and majordomo in the tiny household.

At first Vernon seemed to resent my attention toward his wife, but when he saw in what esteem I held her, and how solicitous and respectful I was, he eventually accepted my presence as one of the family. And a large family it was. I met most of the Presley and Smith clan over the few months I spent in Tupelo. Most were pleasant, like Vester, Vernon's brother, and a few were not, like J.D., Vernon's father, a thoroughly nasty man.

It wasn't long before Gladys suspected that she was carrying twins, a suspicion I confirmed with a brief press upon her abdomen and a knowing nod. Like Prissy in *Gone with the Wind,* I didn't know nuthin' 'bout birthin' babies, but I had studied prenatal care meticulously enough to give an authentic, cursory examination. Too, I felt certain that I could keep Gladys in good health until her delivery. The fact that her legs did not swell was proof that my care was having positive effects, since most of the Elvis biographies had remarked on her badly swollen legs and continual tiredness.

So the summer passed into fall, and the fall into winter, and my excitement increased as January 8 drew near. I spent the days caring for Gladys, the nights in exhausted sleep in my hotel room. Two weeks before she was due, I called on Dr. William Hunt in his office over a jewelry store, and told him about the Presleys, and how I would be responsible for any fees he charged for the delivery, and that if all went well, he would get a large bonus besides.

Gladys went into labor in the early evening of the 7th, I drove over to the doctor's house at 1 A.M., woke him up, and drove him back to the Presleys' house. Finally I can settle the question of who was there that night, something the biographies differ on—there was Dr. Hunt, Vernon, Minnie Mae, Vernon's mother, and myself, assisting Dr. Hunt.

The first child was born at four in the morning, and I grew tense as the head came into view. Dr. Hunt swept it out and up, and I saw it twitch and shudder, and then the doctor whacked its backside and it let out a healthy yowl, and I nearly passed out from joy.

Jesse Presley was alive and well. Now Elvis remained.

A half-hour later, the King was born, screaming even more lustily than his brother. Two babies, identical twins as far as my tired eyes could see, alive and healthy, cradled in their mother's arms, their grinning father kneeling by the side of the bed, his rough fingers touching each one tentatively, then soothing the hot brow of his wife.

Dr. Hunt and I stepped onto the porch, washed our hands in the cold water of the basin, and shivered in the chilly night. I paid him the fifteen dollars he asked for, and gave him another ten as well, which made him grin as widely as Vernon had, seeing his two sons. Then I drove him home.

It was on the way back to East Tupelo that I knew I couldn't stay any longer. My work was done. There was nothing else to keep me there, and I was anxious to see the results of the change that I had made in the life of Elvis.

I was *too* anxious, for one moment I was driving east, watching the sun rise through the windshield, thinking about Sun Records and wondering if they'd call themselves the Presley Brothers, and the next moment I was sitting in my office in my apartment in 1992. I realized then that my conscious brainwave activity had finally fallen below the point needed to keep me back in 1935. But it didn't matter. Now I was home, mission completed. I felt like Zorro, or the Scarlet Pimpernel, or Batman after he caught the Joker.

But what I looked like was Perry Como on a 1956 album cover. What the hell was I doing in a cardigan sweater, brown wool slacks, and a polo shirt buttoned to the neck? Where were my sweatshirt and jeans? And what were wing tips doing on my feet instead of my usual Nikes?

I scratched my head in confusion, only to find that there was a lot less hair there than there had been before. And it was set tightly into place with the kind of grease I hadn't used since I was six.

Hell with it, I thought. Not important now. What was important was Elvis.

I stood up, crossed the deep shag pile carpet (where was my hardwood floor?), and scanned the Elvis bookcase that held, not the first editions, but my working copies that I read over and over. There it was, Jerry Hopkins's *Elvis*. But his follow-up, *Elvis: The Final Years,* was nowhere in sight. Success! I thought, pulling out the paperback. But as I started to open it, I saw that there was something different about the front cover photo.

No guitar, no white, high-collared leisure suit, no mike.

Instead, Elvis, his hair dark brown instead of lacquered black, dressed in white tie and tails, just like when he sang "Hound Dog" on the "Steve Allen Show." But there was none of the self-mockery and discomfort that he had shown then. Instead he stood against a black background, looking as though he had been born into such finery, rather than in the two-room shotgun shack in which I'd seen his infant self in what seemed only minutes before.

And now he had a beard, dark brown and bushy. What the hell was this, *Charro II?*

Jesus.

I flipped the book open to the photo section. There, instead of the photo of Elvis at the age of two, was a photo of *two* little boys, and the caption "Elvis at two with brother Jesse (right)." There was the picture of the birthplace, and the Lauderdale Courts apartment where the Presleys lived in Memphis.

Then things went crazy.

There were no photos of Priscilla or Sam Phillips or Scotty Moore or Colonel Parker; no movie stills with Michelle Carey or Richard Egan. Instead there were shots of Rudolf Bing and Leontyne Price and Luciano Pavarotti and Plácido Domingo; a photo of a breathtakingly young Elvis as Rodolfo in *La Bohème* in his La Scala debut in 1956; another of him with Maria Callas in his 1957 Met debut as Cavaradossi in *Tosca;* another with Joan Sutherland in *Rigoletto;* and the last showed him darkly made up for the title role in Franco Zeffirelli's film of Verdi's *Otello.*

Opera. Elvis was an opera star.

I tossed the book aside and tore into my living room, where I scanned the ranks of CD's and LP's. The single jewelboxes had been replaced by fat boxed sets of operas and librettos, whose sides read:

"Wagner: *Lohengrin* Presley—Norman—Randova—Nimsgern—Sotin—Fischer-Dieskau—Solti"

"Boito: *Mefistofele* Samuel Ramey—Eva Marton—Elvis Presley—Hungarian State Orchestra—Giuseppe Patane"

Frenzied, I turned to the vinyl. *The Sun Sessions* was missing, and in its place was *The Angel Recordings: Elvis Presley Arias, 1954.*

My soundtracks of *Roustabout* and *Fun in Acapulco* were gone, replaced by *Presley Sings Puccini* and *Verdi Duets: Sills and Presley.*

My laser discs of *Jailhouse Rock* and the Singer Special had become a Met Marathon and a San Francisco Opera Company production of *Turandot.*

My dear God, what had I done?

Where the hell was Jesse? Why hadn't he done something to keep his brother from this . . . this strange fate?

I grabbed my first edition of Hopkins's *Elvis* from the shelf and frantically went through it, finding that this version, unlike the other, had an index. I quickly looked up "Presley, Jesse Garon," and found three subentries: "relations with Elvis," "influence on Elvis," and "death."

I ripped my way to page forty-three, and there I read:

On July 29, 1949, Elvis was witness to a terrible tragedy in which his twin brother, Jesse Garon, drowned while saving Elvis's life. On an outing to the Mississippi River, Elvis swam out too far and was swept away by the current. Jesse swam after him, caught him, and was able to lift him high enough to grab a tree branch, to which he clung until help came. The effort to save his brother had exhausted Jesse, who was caught by the river's strong currents. The boy's body was never recovered.

Elvis has referred to this as his most influential experience. "It taught me the value of life," he said. "Jesse died for me, and that made it doubly important that I never throw my life away. I take care of myself today because of the way that my brother took care of me then. To do anything less would be to betray his sacrifice."

I read on then, about Elvis's participation in Gilbert and Sullivan productions in high school, about his voice training, his scholarship to Juilliard, his studies in Paris, his first European successes, and finally his 1956 appearance on "The Ed Sullivan Show," where his "Nessun dorma" from *Turandot* electrified the country. That night, Elvis's good looks, sex appeal, and miraculous voice made every woman in the country—and most of the men—immediate opera buffs.

Opera, at first mostly Elvis's arias and duets with fortunate divas, began to be played on the radio, sharing pop programming with Patti Paige, Dean Martin, and the Ames Brothers. Within five years, every small town had its own opera company, teenagers formed vocal ensembles in their parents' garages, and Elvis Presley's recitals and performances were consistently at the top of the charts.

On and on the book went, a breathy list of opera after opera, with side jaunts into German *lieder* and oratorios, and, when Elvis was in a playful mood, the occasional Gilbert and Sullivan. Thirty-six years later he is still "the King," performing in concerts and operatic extravaganzas in arenas all over the world, looking as fit and trim as when he began.

Goody for opera. But where the hell was rock and roll?

There was none on my shelves, no U2 or Janis or Jimi or Guns N' Roses. Nothing except for a few LP's in something called the *Recorded Anthology of American Music: Negro Rhythm Songs, 1956–64,* and *Soul— America's Lost Music, 1961–63.*

I couldn't take any more. I had to get out of my apartment into some fresh air, maybe have a drink at the Hard Rock a few blocks over. I grabbed at the hook where my leather jacket always hung, but instead came up with a pale blue coat with a ribbed collar, the kind of thing my father used to wear. I slipped it on with a shudder, and took the elevator down to the street.

And walked into 1954.

The styles, I mean, not the year itself. It was 1992 all right. I could tell that from the newspaper I bought at the corner, the same newspaper whose headline read, "EISENHOWER PREDICTS VIETNAM VICTORY BY CHRISTMAS." *David* Eisenhower, that is. There was a picture of him and Julie waving on the steps of *Air Force One.*

Everybody on the street looked like their parents. There were square clothes, butch-waxed haircuts, horn-rimmed glasses, and big round cars, like whales in pastel shades, driving down the streets. The gay bookstore was a Christian Science Reading Room, and the Hard Rock was, God help me, a Howard Johnson's restaurant and "cocktail lounge."

They still served drinks, but I couldn't bear to go in after I'd peered through the window. It looked like a casting call for *What Makes Sammy Run,* all thin-lapeled suits and briefcases and stemmed glasses with cherries in front of each person. I nearly puked.

I went to the library instead. I had to know everything, and it didn't take me long to find out.

The world, as appearances suggested, was different. Rock and roll was an underground music, tolerated by society and centered in "Negro" (as they were still called) communities. All the changes that had come about in the sixties had never occurred. We were still in Nam, civil rights was nothing but a dream for blacks, gays still hid their inclinations, and the Cold War was iced over so hard it would never thaw out.

People didn't know how to rebel. And the only conclusion that I can draw is that it was because they never had an Elvis Presley to teach them, to show them how to sneer, and how to assault their elders with music.

But how did Elvis change? How did the King of Rock and Roll become a super-Caruso? Could the death of his brother have had that much of an effect on him?

Thoughts started coming randomly then, and I remembered that movie of *Otello*. I didn't know much about opera, but I did recall that Plácido Domingo had once played Otello, and Domingo was a tenor.

So how, I finally wondered, heading back to my alien home, could Elvis, that creamy baritone, become the world's greatest tenor? Once that thought hit me, I knew something was fishy, and when I got home I took Hopkins's book and started going straight through from the beginning.

It didn't take me long to find it, to confirm what I suspected had happened, probably only minutes after I left the little house in Tupelo in 1935.

Vernon and Gladys named their babies. Only they named them the *opposite* of what they had before. The first time they had called the dead baby Jesse as a backhanded tribute to that old bastard J.D., and the live one, the *second* baby, Elvis.

But this time, the time *I* had caused to be, they had named the first baby Elvis and the second Jesse. It said it right there in the book.

And that meant that the real Elvis, the future King of Rock and Roll, had, under an assumed name, drowned and fed the catfish in the Mississippi River back in 1949. Leaving the stage open for his older brother, his twin, identical in every way, except for voice register and musical taste.

And the ability to change the world. The ability that I too had, and used, God help me, to incredible effect.

I let the book fall to the thick carpet, and then I cried for Elvis and for that world we had both left behind. There was no going back either.

The company I still worked for was too busy trying to shrink the ozone hole to mess around with time travel. Besides, I realized that I could barely remember how I had done it in the first place, and that was when I knew that the time I was in was going to eventually erase my memory of the other time, that rock and roll time that never existed in this white bread world.

That's why I wanted to get it all down, so that I'll remember even when I forget. I guess I could write down the lyrics to "Heartbreak Hotel" and "Jailhouse Rock" and even "No Room to Rhumba" while I still remember them, but it wouldn't be the same without his voice singing them.

I'll finish by telling what I did after I stopped crying. I put Elvis/Jesse Presley's "Nessun dorma" on the CD player, and listened.

I melted. And I wept again, but this time at the beauty of it, of that deep, bathed-in-the-bayou voice, but now higher, richer, trained to take advantage of its strengths and bury its weaknesses, a voice filled with self-confidence and command, and with unparalleled sensitivity as well. I didn't know what the words meant. I didn't have to.

As I sat there, eyes closed, the music washing over me like a cleansing stream, I started to think that maybe it was for the best. In this world that I had made for myself, for Jesse, for everyone, there was less crime, no drugs, and the churches were full. Business went on as usual, people knew their places, and if they weren't content, they didn't say so. It was much easier to forget about things and just relax, relax and listen to the music, the lovely music I'm hearing now.

What I've done I've done. I can't change it. I might as well accept it. And if I didn't, who would care?

Goodbye, leather jackets and protests and marches and drugssexrock-androll. Goodbye, Elvis.

And hello, Elvis.

You know, you give it a chance, this opera stuff grows on you.

GREIL MARCUS *is America's greatest living Elvis critic.*

"Elvis critic" is too restrictive a term, however, for a man who's also written thoughtful essays on pop culture and world events for Rolling Stone, Artforum *and* The Village Voice. *Greil's an editor, too; he hammered together* Psychotic Reactions and Carburetor Dung, *an essential collection of rock critiques by the late, still-relevant Lester Bangs.*

Yet Elvis continues to be Marcus's primary passion. For the past twenty years, Greil has obsessively charted every shifting color reflecting off the multifaceted metaphor Presley has become.

Nonfiction books like Lipstick Traces: A Secret History of the Twentieth Century *and* Mystery Train: Images of America in Rock 'n' Roll Music *collect those colors. They also illustrate Greil's unique method of treating Elvis Presley as an incredibly versatile springboard (for example, one essay might begin with an examination of Presley's roots before ending with an overview of Deep South social mores). But whatever direction Greil's vaulting off in, you can always be sure it'll be an intelligent, unexpected one.*

Take Greil's latest book. Dead Elvis: A Chronicle of a Cultural Obsession *contains eighteen previously published articles detailing E.'s unprecedented impact on contemporary culture. Its topics range from Elvis spin-off merchandise to "you are there" tours of Graceland, and it is so comprehensive, so beautifully written that it could be called the Mount Everest of Marcus's Elvis Presley books.*

His own Presley pinnacle, if you will.

By the way, Dead Elvis *was also the original title for* this *anthology. A title I'd coined years before I was aware of Greil's book.*

But that's another story.

So is the following article, which recalls the 1992 European press tour Marcus undertook to promote Dead Elvis *itself.*

This junket eventually placed Greil in Ireland during a nationwide abortion debate.

An experience that involved drug addiction, Elvis Presley, Irish intellectuals and the always-controversial Sinéad O'Connor.

What was that I said about Greil Marcus launching off in unexpected directions?

SOMEONE YOU NEVER FORGET

by Greil Marcus

In late February and early March 1992 I went from London to Dublin to Amsterdam to talk about a book on the culture that's grown up around Elvis Presley since he died—you can say promote, or flog, but most of the time that's not what it felt like. The breaking stories included the *National Enquirer*'s Dee Presley explosion: HIS OWN STEPMOM REVEALS SHOCKING TRUTH AT LAST—ELVIS AND HIS MOM WERE LOVERS. The U.S. Postal Service announced a primary season vote to decide which of two Elvis head shots (more or less '56 vs. '73, both healthy) would be chosen for the long-awaited Elvis stamp. (With the *Washington Post* calling Bill Clinton "Elvis Presley with a calculator on his belt," Molly Ivins rating Paul Tsongas "minus-zero on the Elvis scale," and George Bush singing Presley's praises on a campaign stop in Memphis, the timing of *this* election was sublime.) Meanwhile, an Irish high court judge refused to allow a fourteen-year-old girl, who, her family told police, had been raped and impregnated by her best friend's father, to travel to England for an abortion.

The theme I carried in my head was "That's Someone You Never Forget," a 1967 Elvis number I'd heard for the first time a week before, on the radio—a ghostly, passionate, infinitely more personal version of his 1955 Sun recording "Blue Moon." "It's credited to Elvis and Red West—you know, one of his bodyguards," said Ger Rijff, former head of the Dutch Elvis Society, in Amsterdam. "Elvis came to Red West with the title and asked him to write a song from it. About his mother, it's said"—Gladys Presley, who died in 1958, at forty-six, after, if Dee Presley is right, years of bliss with Elvis in her bed, or she in his.

"It makes sense," said Adrian Sibley of the BBC's "The Late Show." "America has brought Elvis up to date—now he needs therapy just like everybody else. Don't they have twelve-step programs for incest survivors?" "It makes sense," said Jip Golsteijn, pop critic for the *Amsterdam Telegraaf.* "It's what I heard again and again in Tupelo, years ago. Nobody meant it as a condemnation. Given the way Elvis and Gladys were about each other, it was simply the conclusion everyone drew."

In Dublin, Joe Jackson of *Hot Press* looked over the Elvis-stamp choices, noted that Elvis was still being shot from the waist up, and mentioned that among Irish intellectuals it was only the news that Elvis, too, was a drug addict, like Charlie Parker or Chet Baker, that made him cool. The day before, Sinéad O'Connor had told a Dublin abortion-rights rally that as a mother she herself had had two abortions—and that if there were to be a new referendum on Ireland's nearly absolute ban on abortions, passed by a two-to-one vote of the populace in 1983, only women of childbearing age should be allowed to take part.

Just as in Amsterdam it was strange to be in a great city without people sleeping in doorways or begging on every corner, in Dublin it was strange, after months of listening to our candidates evade the political crisis that is turning the U.S.A. into a nation of scapegoaters, to be in a city in the grip of a moral crisis, where it really made no sense to talk about anything else. People had their radios on for bulletins on the Irish Supreme Court's hearing on the fourteen-year-old's appeal; as the government spoke of possible exceptions for this "special case," one heard the story of another raped teenager, who had hidden her pregnancy from her family, and who died along with the baby, giving birth in a churchyard, alone.

The papers read tensely. The *Irish Times* alternated hard news with a series of riveting editorials, superbly reasoned, carefully worded. The tabloid press played up accusations by antiabortion leaders that the raped girl had almost certainly seduced whoever got her pregnant, while a Catholic priest claimed that abortion-rights groups had conspired with the girl to create a "test case" to overturn the abortion law. There were marches in the street, and biting satire on television. RAPED? read a cut-in on "Nighthawks," an interview show filmed in a studio made over into a crowded Dublin pub: PREGNANT? DISTRESSED? IRISH? FORGET IT. With a cut back to the pub, a woman spoke into a pay phone. "Yeah, this is Sinéad O'Connor," she said, in a good imitation of O'Connor's thick snarl. "You tell the Prime Minister I'm hangin' on this line until he picks it up—I don't care if I stay here all week." O'Connor was taking a lot of heat in Dublin—for pop-star arrogance, for "divisiveness"—but people missed the point. Singing or talking, she stands up to say what she thinks, to piss people off. Like Madonna, she means to make everyone uncomfortable in their turn. She's a punk, not a politician.

So was Elvis, in a different way, in the clothes he wore, the way he moved, not in what he said. No, you can't imagine him in Sinéad's shoes, even if he helped put her in hers—and that's why it remains so easy to write him off. "American history doesn't look the slightest bit different for the presence, or the art, of Elvis Presley," I read in the *London Review of Books* when I arrived in the U.K. "Presley is a distraction, a placebo," the writer went on, unlike the "feral" Howlin' Wolf. The pictures of Elvis in almost every London newspaper and magazine, noting a fine William Eggleston retrospective at the Barbican Art Gallery —"Colour Photographs Ancient and Modern"—were not an answer. Every publication used the same Eggleston shot of Graceland: the only one that included a portrait of Elvis himself. But the reference was to nothing. This Elvis was less a recognizable symbol than a symbol of recognizability.

So I tried to talk through such ciphers, and I was lucky to get back more than I gave. Ger Rijff had been at one of Elvis's winter 1976 concerts, and remembered it with horror: "I knew it couldn't go on." Jip Golsteijn had met him after being ushered up to his Las Vegas suite with presidents of various international fan clubs. "I got his ear somehow," Golsteijn said. "I said, 'Was this your ambition? Did you ever think you'd get so far?' He just looked at me. 'If I had any ambition,' he said, 'it was to be as good as Arthur Crudup' "—the bluesman who wrote "That's All Right (Mama)," Elvis's first record. " 'I wanted to be as good as Arthur Crudup when I saw him, back in '49. Arthur Crudup —you know that name?' "

Yeah, he knew it.

LAWRENCE BLOCK *is a popular, much-honored mystery author who has written over forty books. Equally adept at novels, short stories, and nonfiction, Block also was a columnist (for thirteen years) at* Writer's Digest, *for which he contributed an ongoing examination of the art and craft of fiction writing.*

However, Block's most famous creation is Matt Scudder. Ex-detective, recovering alcoholic, and unlicensed investigator, Scudder has appeared in eleven novels, including Eight Million Ways to Die *and* The Devil Knows You're Dead. *And like John D. MacDonald's Travis McGee series or Ross Macdonald's Lew Archer books, Block's Scudder stories are not so much detective capers as they are ongoing chronicles of American society, ones shaded by interior portraits of believable human protagonists.*

For Block, this usually means portraying Scudder's ongoing battles with the bottle. Or detailing the bleak, lower-depths world of violence and inhumanity through which Scudder walks.

"The Burglar Who Dropped in on Elvis," however, is not a Scudder story. And it's anything but bleak.

In fact, this one's downright cheerful.

Although I'm sure certain parties aren't going to be happy that Block's devised such a detailed blueprint for breaking into the second story of Graceland . . .

The Burglar Who Dropped in on Elvis

by Lawrence Block

"I know who you are," she said. "Your name is Bernie Rhodenbarr. You're a burglar."

I glanced around, glad that the store was empty save for the two of us. It often is, but I'm not usually glad about it.

"Was," I said.

"Was?"

"Was. Past tense. I had a criminal past, and while I'd as soon keep it a secret, I can't deny it. But I'm an antiquarian bookseller now, Miss, uh—"

"Danahy," she supplied. "Holly Danahy."

"Miss Danahy. A dealer in the wisdom of the ages. The errors of my youth are to be regretted, even deplored, but they're over and done with."

She gazed thoughtfully at me. She was a lovely creature—slender, pert, bright of eye and inquisitive of nose—and she wore a tailored suit and a flowing bow tie that made her look at once yieldingly feminine and as coolly competent as a Luger.

"I think you're lying," she said. "I certainly hope so. Because an antiquarian bookseller is no good at all to me. What I need is a burglar."

"I wish I could help you."

"You can." She laid a cool-fingered hand on mine. "It's almost closing time. Why don't you lock up? I'll buy you a drink and tell you how you can qualify for an all-expense-paid trip to Memphis. And possibly a whole lot more."

"You're not trying to sell me a time share in a thriving lakeside resort community, are you?"

"Not hardly."

"Then what have I got to lose? The thing is, I usually have a drink after work with—"

"Carolyn Kaiser," she cut in, "your best friend. She washes dogs two doors down the street at the Poodle Factory. You can call her and cancel."

My turn to gaze thoughtfully. "You seem to know a lot about me," I said.

"Sweetie," she said, "that's my *job*."

"I'm a reporter," she said. "For the *Weekly Galaxy*. If you don't know the paper, you must never get to the supermarket."

"I know it," I said. "But I have to admit, I'm not what you'd call one of your regular readers."

"Well, I should hope not, Bernie. Our readers move their lips when they think. Our readers write letters in crayon, because they're not allowed to have anything sharp. Our readers make the *Enquirer*'s look like Rhodes scholars. Our readers—face it—are D-U-M."

"Then why would they want to know about me?"

"They wouldn't, unless an extraterrestrial had made you pregnant. That happen to you?"

"No, but Bigfoot ate my car."

She shook her head. "We already did that story. Last August, I think it was. The car was an AMC Gremlin with a hundred and ninety-two thousand miles on it."

"I suppose its time had come."

"That's what the owner said. He's got a new BMW now, thanks to the *Galaxy*. He can't spell it, but he can drive it like crazy."

I looked at her over the rim of my glass. "If you don't want to write about me," I said, "what do you need me for?"

"Ah, Bernie," she said. "Bernie the burglar. Sweetie pie, you're my ticket to Elvis."

"The best possible picture," I told Carolyn, "would be a shot of Elvis in his coffin. The *Galaxy* loves shots like that, but in this case, it would be counterproductive in the long run, because it might kill their big story, the one they run month after month."

"Which is that he's still alive."

"Right. Now, the second-best possible picture, and better for their purposes overall, would be a shot of him alive, singing "Love Me Tender" to a visitor from another planet. They get a chance at that picture every couple of days, and it's always some Elvis impersonator. Do you know how many full-time professional Elvis Presley impersonators there are in America today?"

"No."

"Neither do I, but I have a feeling that Holly Danahy could probably supply a figure, and that it would be an impressive one. Anyway, the third-best possible picture, and the one she seems to want almost more than life itself, is a shot of The King's bedroom."

"At Graceland?"

"That's the one. Six thousand people visit Graceland every day. Two million of them walked through it last year."

"And none of them brought a camera?"

"Don't ask me how many cameras they brought, or how many rolls of film they shot. Or how many souvenir ashtrays and paintings on black velvet they bought and took home with them. But how many of them got above the first floor?"

"How many?"

"None. Nobody gets to go upstairs at Graceland. The staff isn't allowed up there, and people who've worked there for years have never set foot above the ground floor. And you can't bribe your way up there, either, according to Holly, and she knows because she tried, and she had all the *Galaxy*'s resources to play with. Two million people a year go to Graceland, and they'd all love to know what it looks like upstairs, and the *Weekly Galaxy* would just love to show them."

"Enter a burglar."

"That's it. That's Holly's master stroke, the one designed to win her a bonus and a promotion. Enter an expert at illegal entry; i.e., a burglar. *Le burglar, c'est moi.* Name your price, she told me."

"And what did you tell her?"

"Twenty-five thousand dollars. You know why? All I could think of was that it sounded like a job for Nick Velvet. You remember him, the thief in the Ed Hoch stories who'll steal only worthless objects." I sighed. "When I think of all the worthless objects I've stolen over the years, and never once has anyone offered to pay me a fee of twenty-five grand for my troubles. Anyway, that was the price that popped into my head, so I tried it out on her. And she didn't even try to haggle."

"I think Nick Velvet raised his rates," Carolyn said. "I think his price went up in the last story or two."

I shook my head. "You see what happens? You fall behind on your reading and it costs you money."

Holly and I flew first class from JFK to Memphis. The meal was still airline food, but the seats were so comfortable and the stewardess so attentive that I kept forgetting that.

"At the *Weekly Galaxy*," Holly said, sipping an after-dinner something or other, "everything's first class. Except the paper itself, of course."

We got our luggage, and a hotel courtesy car whisked us to the Howard Johnson's on Elvis Presley Boulevard, where we had adjoining rooms reserved. I was just about unpacked when Holly knocked on the door separating the two rooms. I unlocked it for her and she came in carrying a bottle of Scotch and a full ice bucket.

"I wanted to stay at the Peabody," she said. "That's the great old downtown hotel and it's supposed to be wonderful, but here we're only a couple of blocks from Graceland, and I thought it would be more convenient."

"Makes sense," I agreed.

"But I wanted to see the ducks," she said. She explained that ducks were the symbol of the Peabody, or the mascots, or something. Every day, the hotel's guests could watch the hotel's ducks waddle across the red carpet to the fountain in the middle of the lobby.

"Tell me something," she said. "How does a guy like you get into a business like this?"

"Bookselling?"

"Get real, honey. How'd you get to be a burglar? Not for the edification of our readers, because they couldn't care less. But to satisfy my own curiosity."

I sipped a drink while I told her the story of my misspent life, or as much of it as I felt like telling. She heard me out and put away four stiff Scotches in the process, but if they had any effect on her, I couldn't see it.

"And how about you?" I said after a while. "How did a nice girl like you—"

"Oh, Gawd," she said. "We'll save that for another evening, okay?"

And then she was in my arms, smelling and feeling better than a body had a right to, and just as quickly, she was out of them and on her way to the door.

"You don't have to go," I said.

"Ah, but I do, Bernie. We've got a big day tomorrow. We're going to see Elvis, remember?"

She took the Scotch with her. I poured out what remained of my own drink, finished unpacking, took a shower. I got into bed, and after fifteen or twenty minutes, I got up and tried the door between our two rooms, but she had locked it on her side. I went back to bed.

Our tour guide's name was Stacy. She wore the standard Graceland uniform—a blue-and-white-striped shirt over navy chinos—and she looked like someone who'd been unable to decide whether to become a stewardess or a cheerleader. Cleverly, she'd chosen a job that combined both professions.

"There were generally a dozen guests crowded around this dining table," she told us. "Dinner was served nightly between 9 and 10 P.M., and Elvis always sat right there at the head of the table. Not because he was head of the family but because it gave him the best view of the big color TV. Now, that's one of fourteen TV sets here at Graceland, so you know how much Elvis liked to watch TV."

"Was that the regular china?" someone wanted to know.

"Yes, ma'am, and the name of the pattern is Buckingham. Isn't it pretty?"

I could run down the whole tour for you, but what's the point? Either you've been there yourself or you're planning to go or you don't care, and at the rate people are signing up for the tours, I don't think there are many of you in the last group. Elvis was a good pool player, and his favorite game was rotation. Elvis ate his breakfast in the Jungle Room, off a cypress coffee table. Elvis's own favorite singer was Dean Martin. Elvis liked peacocks, and at one time, more than a dozen of them roamed the grounds of Graceland. Then they started eating the paint off the cars, which Elvis liked even more than peacocks, so he donated them to the Memphis zoo. The peacocks, not the cars.

There was a gold rope across the mirrored staircase and what looked like an electric eye a couple of stairs up. "We don't allow tourists into the upstairs," our guide chirped. "Remember, Graceland is a private home and Elvis's aunt Mrs. Delta Biggs still lives here. Now, I can *tell* you what's upstairs. Elvis's bedroom is located directly above the living room and music room. His office is also upstairs, and there's Lisa Marie's bedroom, and dressing rooms and bathrooms, as well."

"And does his aunt live up there?" someone asked.

"No, sir. She lives downstairs, through that door over to your left. None of us have ever been upstairs. Nobody goes there anymore."

"I bet he's up there now," Holly said. "In a La-Z-Boy, with his feet up, eating one of his famous peanut-butter-and-banana sandwiches and watching three television sets at once."

"And listening to Dean Martin," I said. "What do you really think?"

"What do I really think? I think he's down in Paraguay playing three-handed pinochle with James Dean and Adolf Hitler. Did you know that Hitler masterminded Argentina's invasion of the Falkland Islands? We ran that story, but it didn't do as well as we'd hoped."

"Your readers didn't remember Hitler?"

"Hitler was no problem for them. But they didn't know what the Falklands were. Seriously, where do I think Elvis is? I think he's in the grave we just looked at, surrounded by his nearest and dearest. Unfortunately, 'ELVIS STILL DEAD' is not a headline that sells papers."

"I guess not."

We were back in my room at the HoJo, eating a lunch Holly had ordered from room service. It reminded me of our in-flight meal the day before—luxurious but not terribly good.

"Well," she said brightly, "have you figured out how we're going to get in?"

"You saw the place," I said. "They've got gates and guards and alarm systems everywhere. I don't know what's upstairs, but it's a more closely guarded secret than Zsa Zsa Gabor's true age."

"That'd be easy to find out," Holly said. "We could just hire somebody to marry her."

"Graceland is impregnable," I went on, hoping we could drop the analogy right there. "It's almost as bad as Fort Knox."

Her face fell. "I was sure you could find a way in."

"Maybe I can."

"But—"

"For one. Not for two. It'd be too risky for you, and you don't have the skills for it. Could you shinny down a gutterspout?"

"If I had to."

"Well, you won't have to, because you won't be going in." I paused for thought. "You'd have a lot of work to do," I said. "On the outside, coordinating things."

"I can handle it."

"And there would be expenses, plenty of them."

"No problem."

"I'd need a camera that can take pictures in full dark. I can't risk a flash."

"That's easy. We can handle that."

"I'll need to rent a helicopter, and I'll have to pay the pilot enough to guarantee his silence."

"A cinch."

"I'll need a diversion. Something fairly dramatic."

"I can create a diversion. With all the resources of the *Galaxy* at my disposal, I could divert a river."

"That shouldn't be necessary. But all of this is going to cost money."

"Money," she said, "is no object."

"So you're a friend of Carolyn's," Lucian Leeds said. "She's wonderful, isn't she? You know, she and I are the next closest thing to blood kin."

"Oh?"

"A former lover of hers and a former lover of mine were brother and sister. Well, sister and brother, actually. So that makes Carolyn my something-in-law, doesn't it?"

"I guess it must."

"Of course," he said, "by the same token, I must be related to half the known world. Still, I'm real fond of our Carolyn. And if I can help you . . ."

I told him what I needed. Lucian Leeds was an interior decorator and a dealer in art and antiques. "Of course, I've been to Graceland," he said. "Probably a dozen times, because whenever a friend or a relative visits, that's where one has to take them. It's an experience that somehow never palls."

"I don't suppose you've ever been on the second floor."

"No, nor have I been presented at court. Of the two, I suppose I'd prefer the second floor at Graceland. One can't help wondering, can one?" He closed his eyes, concentrating. "My imagination is beginning to work," he announced.

"Give it free rein."

"I know just the house, too. It's off Route 51 across the state line, just this side of Hernando, Mississippi. Oh, and I know someone with an Egyptian piece that would be perfect. How soon would everything have to be ready?"

"Tomorrow night?"

"Impossible. The day after tomorrow is barely possible. Just barely. I really ought to have a week to do it right."

"Well, do it as right as you can."

"I'll need trucks and *schleppers,* of course. I'll have rental charges to pay, of course, and I'll have to give something to the old girl who owns the house. First I'll have to sweet-talk her, but there'll have to be something tangible in it for her, as well, I'm afraid. But all of this is going to cost you money."

That had a familiar ring to it. I almost got caught up in the rhythm of it and told him money was no object, but I managed to restrain myself. If money weren't the object, what was I doing in Memphis?

"Here's the camera," Holly said. "It's all loaded with infrared film. No flash, and you can take pictures with it at the bottom of a coal mine."

"That's good," I said, "because that's probably where I'll wind up if they catch me. We'll do it the day after tomorrow. Today's what— Wednesday? I'll go in Friday."

"I should be able to give you a terrific diversion."

"I hope so," I said. "I'll probably need it."

Thursday morning, I found my helicopter pilot. "Yeah, I could do it," he said. "Cost you two hundred dollars, though."

"I'll give you five hundred."

He shook his head. "One thing I never do," he said, "is get to haggling over prices. I said two hundred, and— Wait a darn minute."

"Take all the time you need."

"You weren't haggling me down," he said. "You were haggling me up. I never heard tell of such a thing."

"I'm willing to pay extra," I said, "so that you'll tell people the right story afterward. If anybody asks."

"What do you want me to tell 'em?"

"That somebody you never met before in your life paid you to fly over Graceland, hover over the mansion, lower your rope ladder, raise the ladder, and then fly away."

He thought about this for a full minute. "But that's what you said you wanted me to do," he said.

"I know."

"So you're fixing to pay me an extra three hundred dollars just to tell people the truth."

"If anybody should ask."

"You figure they will?"

"They might," I said. "It would be best if you said it in such a way that they thought you were lying."

"Nothing to it," he said. "Nobody ever believes a word I say. I'm a pretty honest guy, but I guess I don't look it."

"You don't," I said. "That's why I picked you."

That night, Holly and I dressed up and took a cab downtown to the Peabody. The restaurant there was named Dux, and they had *canard aux cerises* on the menu, but it seemed curiously sacrilegious to have it there. We both ordered the blackened redfish. She had two rob roys first, most of the dinner wine and a stinger. I had a bloody mary for openers, and my after-dinner drink was coffee. I felt like a cheap date.

Afterward, we went back to my room and she worked on the Scotch while we discussed strategy. From time to time, she would put her drink down and kiss me, but as soon as things threatened to get interesting, she'd draw away and cross her legs and pick up her pencil and note pad and reach for her drink.

"You're a tease," I said.

"I am not," she insisted. "But I want to, you know, save it."

"For the wedding?"

"For the celebration. After we get the pictures, after we carry the day. You'll be the conquering hero and I'll throw roses at your feet."

"Roses?"

"And myself. I figured we could take a suite at the Peabody and never leave the room except to see the ducks. You know, we never did see the ducks do their famous walk. Can't you just picture them waddling across the red carpet and quacking their heads off?"

"Can't you just picture what they go through cleaning that carpet?"

She pretended not to have heard me. "I'm glad we didn't have duckling," she said. "It would have seemed cannibalistic." She fixed her eyes on me. She'd had enough booze to induce a coma in a six-hundred-pound gorilla, but her eyes looked as clear as ever. "Actually," she said, "I'm very strongly attracted to you, Bernie. But I want to wait. You can understand that, can't you?"

"I could," I said gravely, "if I knew I was coming back."

"What do you mean?"

"It would be great to be the conquering hero," I said, "and find you and the roses at my feet, but suppose I come home on my shield instead? I could get killed out there."

"Are you serious?"

"Think of me as a kid who enlisted the day after Pearl Harbor, Holly. And you're his girlfriend, asking him to wait until the war's over. Holly, what if that kid doesn't come home? What if he leaves his bones bleaching on some little hell hole in the South Pacific?"

"Oh, my God," she said. "I never thought of that." She put down her pencil and note pad. "You're right, damn it. I *am* a tease. I'm worse than that." She uncrossed her legs. "I'm thoughtless and heartless. Oh, Bernie!"

"There, there," I said.

Graceland closes every evening at six. At precisely five-thirty Friday afternoon, a girl named Moira Beth Calloway detached herself from her tour group. "I'm coming, Elvis!" she cried, and she lowered her head and ran full speed for the staircase. She was over the gold rope and on the sixth step before the first guard laid a hand on her.

Bells rang, sirens squealed, and all hell broke loose. "Elvis is calling me," Moira Beth insisted, her eyes rolling wildly. "He needs me, he wants me, he loves me tender. Get your hands off me. Elvis! I'm coming, Elvis!"

ID in Moira Beth's purse supplied her name and indicated that she was seventeen years old and a student at Mount St. Joseph Academy in

Millington, Tennessee. That was not strictly true, in that she was actually twenty-two years old, a member of Actors' Equity, and a resident of Brooklyn Heights. Her name was not Moira Beth Calloway, either. It was (and still is) Rona Jellicoe. I think it may have been something else in the dim dark past before it became Rona Jellicoe, but who cares?

While a variety of people, many of them wearing navy chinos and blue-and-white-striped shirts, did what they could to calm Moira Beth, a middle-aged couple in the Pool Room went into their act. "Air!" the man cried, clutching at his throat. "Air! I can't breathe!" And he fell down, flailing at the wall, where Stacy had told us some 750 yards of pleated fabric had been installed.

"Help him," cried his wife. "He can't breathe! He's dying! He needs air!" And she ran to the nearest window and heaved it open, setting off whatever alarms hadn't already been shrieking over Moira Beth's assault on the staircase.

Meanwhile, in the TV Room, done in the exact shades of yellow and blue used in Cub Scout uniforms, a gray squirrel had raced across the rug and was now perched on the jukebox. "Look at that awful squirrel!" a woman was screaming. "Somebody get that squirrel! He's gonna kill us all!"

Her fear would have been harder to credit if people had known that the poor rodent had entered Graceland in her handbag and that she'd been able to release it without being seen because of the commotion in the other room. Her fear was contagious, though, and the people who caught it weren't putting on an act.

In the Jungle Room, where Elvis's *Moody Blue* album had been recorded, a woman fainted. She'd been hired to do just that, but other unpaid fainters were dropping like flies all over the mansion. And while all of this activity was hitting its absolute peak, a helicopter made its noisy way through the sky over Graceland, hovering for several long minutes over the roof.

The security staff at Graceland couldn't have been better. Almost immediately, two men emerged from a shed carrying an extension ladder, and in no time at all, they had it propped against the side of the building. One of them held it while the other scrambled up it to the roof.

By the time the security man got there, the helicopter was going *pocketa-pocketa-pocketa* and disappearing off to the west. The man raced around the roof but didn't see anyone. Within the next ten minutes, two others joined him on the roof and searched it thoroughly. They found a sneaker, but that was all they found.

At a quarter to five the next morning, I let myself into my room at Howard Johnson's and knocked on the door to Holly's room. There was no response. I knocked again, louder, then gave up and used the phone. I could hear it ringing in her room, but evidently she couldn't.

So I used the skills God gave me and opened her door. She was sprawled out on the bed, with her clothes scattered where she had flung them. The TV was on and some guy with a sports jacket and an Ipana smile was explaining how you could get cash advances on your credit cards and buy penny stocks, an enterprise that struck me as a lot riskier than burglarizing mansions by helicopter.

Holly didn't want to wake up, but when I got past the veil of sleep, she came to as if transistorized. One moment she was comatose and the next she was sitting up, eyes bright, an expectant look on her face. "Well?" she demanded.

"I shot the whole roll."

"You got in."

"Uh-huh."

"And you got out."

"Right again."

"And you got the pictures!" She clapped her hands, giddy with glee. "I knew it," she said. "I was a positive genius to think of you. Oh, they ought to give me a bonus, a raise, a promotion. Oh, I bet I get a company Cadillac next year instead of a lousy Chevy. Oh, I'm on a roll, Bernie, I swear I'm on a roll!"

"That's great."

"You're limping," she said. "Why are you limping? Because you've got only one shoe on, that's why. What happened to your other shoe?"

"I lost it on the roof."

"God," she said. She got off the bed and began picking up her clothes from the floor and putting them on. "You know, when I saw them race up the ladder, I thought you were finished. How did you get away from them?"

"It wasn't easy."

"I bet. And you managed to get down onto the second floor? And into his bedroom? What's it like?"

"I don't know."

"You don't *know*? Weren't you in there?"

"Not until it was pitch-dark. I hid in a hall closet and locked myself in. They gave the place a pretty thorough search, but nobody had a key to the closet. I don't think there is one; I locked it by picking it. I let myself out somewhere around two in the morning and found my way into the bedroom. There was enough light to keep from bumping into things but not enough to tell what it was I wasn't bumping into. I just walked around pointing the camera and shooting."

She wanted more details, but I don't think she paid very much attention to them. I was in the middle of a sentence when she picked up the phone and made a plane reservation to Miami.

"They've got me on a ten-twenty flight," she said. "I'll get these right into the office and we'll get a check out to you as soon as they're developed. What's the matter?"

"I don't think I want a check," I said. "And I don't want to give you the film without getting paid."

"Oh, come on," she said. "You can trust us, for God's sake."

"Why don't you trust me, instead?"

"You mean pay you without seeing what we're paying for? Bernie, you're a burglar. How can I trust you?"

"You're the *Weekly Galaxy*," I said. "*Nobody* can trust you."

"You've got a point," she said.

"We'll get the film developed here," I said. "I'm sure there are some good commercial photo labs in Memphis that can handle infrared film. First you'll call your office and have them wire cash here or set up an interbank transfer, and as soon as you see what's on the film, you can hand over the money. You can even fax them one of the prints first to get approval, if you think that'll make a difference."

"Oh, they'll love that," she said. "My boss loves it when I fax him stuff."

"And that's what happened," I told Carolyn. "The pictures came out really beautifully. I don't know how Lucian Leeds turned up all those Egyptian pieces, but they looked great next to the forties Wurlitzer jukebox and the seven-foot statue of Mickey Mouse. I thought Holly was going to die of happiness when she realized the thing next to Mickey was a sarcophagus. She couldn't decide which tack to take—that he's mummified and they're keeping him in it or that he's alive and really weird and uses it for a bed."

"Maybe they can have a reader poll. Call a nine-hundred number and vote."

"You wouldn't believe how loud helicopters are when you're inside them. I just dropped the ladder and pulled it back in again. And tossed an extra sneaker onto the roof."

"And wore its mate when you saw Holly."

"Yeah, I thought a little verisimilitude wouldn't hurt. The chopper pilot dropped me back at the hangar and I caught a ride down to the Burrell house in Mississippi. I walked around the room Lucian had decorated for the occasion, admired everything, then turned out all the lights and took my pictures. They'll be running the best ones in the *Galaxy*."

"And you got paid."

"Twenty-five grand, and everybody's happy, and I didn't steal anything. The *Galaxy* got some great pictures that'll sell a lot of copies of their horrible paper. The readers get a peek at a room no one has ever seen before."

"And the folks at Graceland?"

"They got a good security drill," I said. "Holly created a peach of a diversion to hide my entering the building, and that fact should stay hidden forever. Most of the Graceland people have never seen Elvis's bedroom, so they'll think the photos are legit. The few who know better will just figure my pictures didn't come out, or that they weren't exciting enough, so the *Galaxy* decided to run fakes instead. Anybody with any sense figures the whole paper's a fake, anyway, so what difference does it make?"

"Was Holly a fake?"

"Not really. I'd say she's an authentic specimen of what she is. Of course, her little fantasy about a hot weekend watching the ducks blew away with the morning mist. All she wanted to do was get back to Florida and collect her bonus."

"So it's just as well you got your bonus ahead of time. You'll hear from her again the next time the *Galaxy* needs a burglar."

"Well, I'd do it again," I said. "My mother was always hoping I'd go into journalism. I wouldn't have waited so long if I'd known it would be so much fun."

"Yeah," she said.

"What's the matter?"

"Nothing, Bern."

"Come on. What is it?"

"Oh, I don't know. I just wish, you know, that you'd gone in there and got the real pictures. He could be in there, Bern. I mean, why else would they make such a big thing out of keeping people out of there? Did you ever stop to ask yourself that?"

"Carolyn—"

"I know," she said. "You think I'm nuts. But there are a lot of people like me, Bern."

"It's a good thing," I told her. "Where would American journalism be without you?"

JOYCE CAROL OATES is one of America's most respected novelists and short-story writers. Since the early sixties she's produced a steady, impressive stream of work; short-story collections (By the North Gate), *novels* (Son of the Morning), *trilogies* (A Garden of Earthly Delights, Expensive People, them), *mysteries* (Mysteries of Winterthurn), *and films* (Smooth Talk *was based on an Oates short story*). *Oates also is a poet and critic—1982 saw the publication of* Invisible Woman; New and Selected Poems, *while her critical works include 1972's* The Edge of Impossibility *and 1983's* The Profane Art.

Oates's prolific output is matched only by its variegation. She's an unpredictable artist; her formidable talents easily slide across the literary spectrum. One year Oates might do a naturalistic observation of urban life, the next will see a full-blown Gothic melodrama.

Yet certain themes consistently appear in Oates's fiction.

Three of them are frustration, violence, and the search for identity.

Qualities that resurface once again in the wittily titled "Elvis Is Dead: Why Are You Alive?" This hallucinatory effort signals Oates's awareness of the ongoing Presley phenomenon, one that's become so unavoidable—Joyce seems to be warning us—that Dead Elvis is capable of taking over our dreams.

And nightmares . . .

Elvis Is Dead: Why Are *You* Alive?

by Joyce Carol Oates

The first wrong thing about the funeral, which registered upon Meredith's consciousness as not simply wrong but disconcerting, frightening, was that the casket was on an elevated, spotlighted platform at the front of the church, nearly up on the altar; and that the casket was open, as at a ceremonial wake. But this *was* wrong, surely?—this should not have been? Meredith glanced about nervously, seeing that his fellow mourners—for it seemed that he was a mourner, stricken and angry with grief —took no notice of anything inappropriate or out of place. They were crying, sobbing, their faces shining with tears and distended with emotion, the grief of stunned children, but anger, even rage, too. Meredith felt a wave of dizziness rise in him—he was revulsed by these people, packed so solidly into the rows of pews, crowding him, who disliked crowds on principle, and often felt that he could not breathe even at a concert or a play in elegant surroundings, with cushioned seats and faultless ventilation, and had to excuse himself to hurry out into the lobby or outside into the night for fresh air. But *these* people!—coarse-faced, squat, many of the women conspicuously overweight, and many of the men bloated in the belly as if carrying a watermelon inside their ill-fitting suits!—who were they? And why was *he*, an executive at Trans-Continental Insurance, among them?

Mourning our dead King.

Our beloved Elvis who has passed over, God have mercy on his soul.

Yes but is The King really dead?—I can't believe he is really truly dead, God would not be so cruel would He?

But yes: the Lord thy God moves in ways that passeth mortal comprehension, praise to Him.

And Elvis our dead King is with Him, his soul in glory, and at peace, after

88

the sorrows of this Vale of Tears, where so many jeered and mocked him, The King now in the bosom of the Lord in the rapture of glory, Alleluia!

Gathered in His bosom as His Only Begotten Son has been gathered in His bosom after the agony in the garden, the crown of thorns, the sorrow and the sacrifice and the outrage of Golgotha.

Alleluia!

All this Meredith knew, without needing to be told.

Knowing too, though, jammed into a pew of perspiring mourners at the rear of the church, he could not see the casket clearly, that it was Elvis himself who lay in state, beneath brilliant white lights like those of an operating room; propped at a slant before the altar amid hundreds of floral displays of all varieties (including giant gladioli in Day-Glo hues of orange and crimson, and immense sprays of purple bougainvillea, and those shiny-red plastic-looking phallic-shaped flowers found primarily in mobile home parks); and that the funeral was both immediately after Elvis's death and at the same time in the present. So many years later!

Meredith was to recall afterward that he knew these things without knowing how he knew. Except: why was *he* here? And why alone, amid such inhospitable strangers?

And why afterward, waking, and through much of the day that followed, did he continue to feel choked with grief, and that deeper, inchoate anger?—staring at others, his colleagues at TransContinental and friendly acquaintances, even his wife, thinking *Elvis is dead: why are* you *alive?*

The next time, Meredith managed to crowd into a pew nearer the front of the little church, where, though his eyes misted over with tears, he could more clearly make out the black-leather-clad figure of the dead Elvis (a young Elvis, apparently?) lying in state in a splendid gleaming mother-of-pearl casket beneath the blazing-white lights and surrounded by the luridly bright flowers; he could hear the minister's impassioned eulogy, which went on for some time, delivered in a high-pitched, mournful, ranting-angry voice, though he could not distinguish most of the words, nor could he see the minister clearly—except to know that the man was big-bellied like so many of the congregation, with a flushed, contorted face, wide jaws, and gleaming white dentures that flashed with spittle as he spoke. And he was white, of course: all the men and women packed into the church appeared to be white.

Caucasian, the superior race. Master race?
Yes! But you must not say so.

Meredith had no idea if Elvis himself had been a believer, probably not, though certainly he must have been born of Protestant-Christian folks, possibly Baptists. The interior of this church was not familiar to Meredith, who knew little about religion, and who had been brought up in a free-thinking, informally Unitarian household, but he understood from the minister's dress (a black mourner's suit with white shirt, black string necktie) and the absence of statues and stained glass windows that it was a Protestant church; he seemed to know too that it was one of those cheaply "modern" churches that resemble discount stores from the outside, often built in starkly treeless lots adjacent to shopping malls or rural-suburban housing developments. Driving past, Meredith would scarcely glance at such a place, not out of a sense of class superiority (though of course he *did* feel, he *was,* superior to such Americans, wasn't he?) so much as indifference. He had his life, and it was not a life that touched upon such folk in the slightest. The odd, mildly comic names of such churches—Calvary Assembly of God, Friendship Baptist, Calvary Gospel, Bible Fellowship Evangelical Church—passed before his gaze without making the slightest impression upon him.

Except, perhaps, something about these churches *had* made an impression upon him?

Meredith found himself suddenly on his feet. He was weak-kneed, frightened. What was expected of him?—why was the air in the little church so heated, like the interior of a great mouth, and so highly charged? He wanted only to push his way out and escape (he seemed to know that his car was outside, but he could not recall which car it was, or whether it was any car he would recognize: nor did he know how far he'd driven to get to this place) but at the same time a terrible yearning, powerful as physical hunger or thirst, or sexual desire, was drawing him forward toward the front of the church and the mannequin-like figure of Elvis in the mother-of-pearl casket. *All rise! all pray! All come forward to honor The King!*

Clumsy on his feet, feeling like a stork towering half a head over the tallest of the other mourners, Meredith was being rather rudely jostled, nudged along. How impatient these men and women were! How fierce their grief, how they not only wept, but sweated with it! Meredith shrank from them, disdaining them, yet, unashamed and open as they were with their emotion, not seeming to know, nor certainly to care, how ugly, how red-faced and absurd they were, Meredith could not help but admire them. Yes and perhaps he wanted to be accepted as one of them. *Mourning our dead King. He who will never come again. He who is with the Lord Our God, sitting on His right hand, amid all His high host. Alleluia!*

Meredith wondered if the other mourners, or the minister at his pulpit, noticed him: his expensive charcoal-gray pinstripe suit, his off-white silk shirt, his striped silk necktie? his black leather Florsheim shoes? his hair which was silvery-blond, and cut in a way very different from their own? Did they notice his height? The expression of wonderment and revulsion in his face, as if he were a dreamer who had wandered into a dream of strangers, and could not comprehend where he was? *Are ye washed in the Blood of the Lamb? Do ye take upon yourself the holy wrath of the King?* Close behind Meredith, pressing against him with pendulous breasts, was an obese woman of young middle-age, in a black polyester pants suit, with a wet, flushed, jowly face and small beady eyes all but lost in the fatty recesses of her cheeks—she did take notice of Meredith, when he glanced nervously back at her, and nodded, and smiled, a small tight reproachful grimace of a smile, *Elvis is dead: why are* you *alive?* It was a question so mysterious and so profound, so terrible, that it pierced Meredith's heart like a sliver of glass.

Meredith was being pushed along, Meredith had no choice but to go forward, filing up the aisle to the immense opalescent casket that, up-ended, looked like a candy box (cushioned in puckered white satin! gleaming with gold ornamentation!) about to spill its contents. And there was Elvis the King: dead, yet looking as if he were but playing at death, a sassy young Elvis with oily black pompadour rising like a rooster's comb over his forehead, and hooded, thick-lashed eyes that seemed about to spring open at any moment, and those full, sulky lips shaped to the faintest suggestion of a smile—or was it a sneer? Elvis still in his twenties, as his mourners wished to remember him, clad in his biker's regalia of black leather jacket with silver stud ornamentation and numerous zippers, tight-fitting black trousers and high-heeled leather boots. This was the Elvis Meredith remembered most distinctly, the Elvis of Meredith's young adolescence, how many years, in fact decades ago, a dizzying amount of time ago, could it be—nearly forty years? *Forty years since Meredith had been young? He who felt he'd never begun to live his life, or had, unaccountably, led the wrong life, the life of a stranger?* As

Meredith approached the casket, hesitantly, his heart beating hard, he saw Elvis's long eyelashes quiver—it was obvious, the man was still alive. From the four corners of the church, out of speakers that amplified words, music, and thrusting percussive rhythm, there came, suddenly, the song of Elvis's Meredith had both loved and detested the summer of his fourteenth birthday, "Don't Be Cruel"—Meredith had been unable to get the infantile tune out of his head. And now it was being played, rippling and pulsing in the warm, close air surrounding him, unless it was sounding inside his very skull, *don't be cruel, don't be cruel, don't be cruel, a heart that's true, a heart that's true, a heart that's true,* unbearable drivel, brain-rot, nursery rhymes in the guise of pop trash. And yet, Meredith found himself weeping like a child, bending over the opened casket and the living-dead figure of the King, a violent paroxysm of grief and desire overcoming him as, nudged by the obese woman behind him, and urged, it seemed, by the other mourners, his brothers and sisters in sorrow, and in the singular exhilaration of such sorrow, Meredith bowed his head, stooped, clumsily but warmly, and damply, and with some pressure, kissed Elvis on the lips—those lips that had so long ago fascinated him, fleshy and crude, mocking, unpredictable in what they might part to utter, that he, Meredith, would never dare utter, through a lifetime. *Mourning our dead King. Praise to the Lord. Praise to The King. Alleluia!*

Meredith whispered, his lips puffy and cracked, *Alleluia.*

Meredith was weeping as if his heart was broken. For joy. Or was it shame.

The obese perspiring woman in the black polyester pants suit hugged him and patted his back and wept with him in sisterly commiseration, *I can't believe that he is really truly dead, oh but he is with God in Heaven and will live forever, free of this Vale of Tears,* and another mourner, a man, in fact it was the big-bellied minister himself, a short, squat, but forceful man of vigorous middle age, gripped Meredith by the upper arm and urged him back into the aisle and on his way, *Walk tall, son! tall like a man! let the others pay their final respects too, son!* clamping a hand on Meredith's shoulder in parting: *the King is beyond mere mortal comprehension seated at the right hand of the Father, gathered in His Bosom as His Only Begotten Son has been gathered in His Bosom, it is not for mere humankind to question such* and humbly Meredith whispered, *Yes, yes I know. Amen.*

And then he was outside the church in the parking lot (which was far larger than one would have expected, judging by the interior of the church: acres of shining American cars extending to the hazy horizon) being issued a *scourge,* the fattish baby-faced middle-aged man who pressed it into his hand spoke of it as a *scourge,* and the word did not baffle Meredith but seemed entirely appropriate: the thing was a weapon of a kind Meredith had never seen before, let alone held in his hand, he who was the gentlest of men and abhorred violence, a man of the highest integrity among his professional colleagues as among his family, friends, neighbors, still it was with a stab of excitement he gripped the *scourge,* examining it in wonder: a kind of machete, yet with numerous blades, and shaped like an old-fashioned wire rug beater, with a solid rubberized handle, *a scourge! a scourge! at last, a scourge!* which Meredith realized he had been missing these many years, all the years of his lost life.

With a pack of other mourners, all of them save Meredith short, stocky, squat, but surprisingly energetic, even agile, he found himself in a shopping mall, not one of the new, gigantic malls in the vicinity of his suburban home but an older, less luxurious mall, not one Meredith recognized, yet he seemed to know it was somewhere near his home, or where he'd once lived, and with the others he was accosting men and women to put to them the angry proclamation *Elvis is dead: why are* you *alive?* and as they stared in alarm, or shrank away, or tried to flee in terror, Meredith and the other mourners hacked away with their *scourges,* slicing their victims in the faces, in the necks, bringing the razor-sharp blades of the *scourge* down as solidly on a fleeing back as if indeed it were a rug beater, and the victim a rug so imbued with filth it required the most vigorous beating one could administer to be cleaned.

In his waking hours, in his daylight self, Meredith was a man of strong convictions, but rarely passions: he was not susceptible to swings of emotion, and did not value such behavior in others. If he were to contemplate his mind, his very brain, he would have envisioned it as a medical school model of some lightweight synthetic material, the brain tissue with a suggestion of veined and imbricated porousness yet smooth to the touch, and shadowless—a matter of anatomical surfaces. Mystery? —maybe. But so long as the mechanism functions, why ponder its depths?

Yet now that he was besieged almost nightly by this strange, ugly, obsessive dream, so unlike any dream he'd ever had before in his life, Meredith found himself lapsing into long minutes of contemplation, anxiety. He feared sleep, yet longed for sleep. He slept deeply, yet woke feeling exhausted, as if he'd scarcely slept at all. He was sickened with disgust but he was also curious. He felt repugnance, but also intrigue. How bizarre, yet how vividly real: the interior of the little church, the mother-of-pearl casket beneath the intense lights, Elvis who was dead yet not-dead, his amplified voice hammering from all sides *don't be cruel, cruel, cruel, a heart that's true, true, true,* until Meredith ground his teeth in misery, and laughed—"Christ, is it possible? But what *is* it?" With revulsion he recalled the pack of flush-faced, dwarfish mourners streaming out of the church as out of a hive, his fellow Americans, whom life since Elvis had cheated, furious and deadly as maddened bees. And the peculiar weapon each wielded, part machete and part rug beater!— comical in theory, but murderous in execution. Empowered with its latticework of razor-sharp blades to lacerate human flesh. To punish.

Elvis is dead: why are you *alive?*

Driving on the Turnpike twice daily, to and from TransContinental's corporate headquarters eleven miles from his home, seeing the faces of drivers in other vehicles, Meredith heard the percussive notes sounding in his head, the unanswerable riddle—*Elvis is dead: why are* you *alive?* He was increasingly susceptible, through much of the day, to lapsing into long minutes of abstraction, gazing at office workers, strangers on the street, or, in fact, and this was especially disturbing to him, his colleagues at TransContinental, his neighbors, friends, even his wife Sarah, unconsciously grinding his teeth, narrowing his eyes that were bright with baffled, resentful tears—*Elvis is dead: why are* you *alive?*

And why was he, Meredith, compelled to ask such a riddle?—why, virtually every night of his life now, was he compelled to punish, to kill, in the name of The King?

He did not want to know, for he understood it would be better for him not to know. *For then I would no longer be Meredith, but another.*

And the injustice of it! So many years of it!

Die! die! die! die! unbeliever! Meredith, panting and sobbing with emotion, was one of a furious group of Elvis's mourners who swarmed upon a man as he was unlocking his car in a suburban parking lot, the setting was nowhere Meredith knew, yet somehow familiar to him, the backs of commercial buildings, a stained-red translucent Western sky of a kind depicted on scenic calendars, the mob was led by a frantic bull-necked little man who wore a tiny American flag in his lapel, all were wielding their *scourges,* hacking violently away until, bloodied, on his knees, trying vainly to shield his head, the victim looked up screaming in pain and terror—and Meredith saw, to his horror, that he was a business acquaintance of Meredith's, a corporate lawyer who did consulting work for TransContinental, and for an instant their eyes locked, even as, swept up by the passion of his brothers and sisters, Meredith raised his *scourge,* already glistening with blood, and brought it down again, and again.

Elvis is dead: why are you *alive?*

Cruelest, most unanswerable of riddles!

Meredith woke in his bed agitated, sweating—heart beating dangerously hard—nausea deep in his bowels—yet suffused, like that stained-red translucent sky, with the conviction that some secret, some revelation, was close at hand. So close! But someone was shaking his shoulder, Sarah was shaking his shoulder, asking what was wrong, was it another of his nightmares, begging him please, please wake up, Meredith, at such times she was wary of him, and annoyed, for he might flail out and hit her like a terrified child, eyes rolling wildly in his head. Where was he? —who was this woman beside him?—what was this unfamiliar darkness? Meredith wrenched himself away from his wife swinging his legs around off the bed so that he could sit up, he could not bear the weight of her hand, he could not at such a time bear the weight of her hand, she whom he loved and had loved for thirty-three years *a lifetime! but not his,* wiping his heated face on a sheet, rubbing his eyes that were dazed and stunned as if they had beheld wonders, no not a nightmare he murmured, it had been a good dream actually—"A happy dream."

"A happy dream!" Sarah's voice was flat with disbelief. She must have stared at the back of his head in the dark, he could imagine her frowning, creased face, yet that look in her eyes of incredulity, bemusement, she knew him or believed she knew him, for thirty-three years is a long time, indeed a lifetime. "Well. You can tell me about it in the morning, Meredith."

Yes. Of course. Never.

The riddle was, by daylight, what *was* Elvis Presley to Meredith Bernhardt, and to this riddle too there was no answer, or none that Meredith Bernhardt could comprehend.

He'd been an adopted child. Or was he still an adopted child?—you did not lose such a designation, simply by growing into an adult.

Simply by becoming, as he had, in time, become, a father himself.

(In his dreams, he had no children, nor any memory of them, who were now grown and living elsewhere, fully autonomous and self-absorbed adults. Nor had he any wife, Sarah or otherwise. Nor any name, in fact: "Meredith" was unknown in that other, so rich and so intriguing world.)

Meredith had graduated from high school in Shaker Heights, Ohio, in 1958. He could recall those years only in patchy fragments, as if another person had experienced them: a tall, skinny, soft-spoken, and obsessively hard-working boy with horn-rimmed glasses and a perpetually blemished skin and an air, secret beneath his congenial, low-keyed manner, of knowing himself superior to most of his classmates, for his grades bore this conviction out, and his teachers' praise for him, and his adoptive parents'—the Bernhardts were both professional people, educated people, Meredith's father a doctor and his mother a public health administrator for the state of Ohio. They were childless and liberal and cultivated and had an association with the Unitarian Church that was rather more sociable than religious or indeed passionate and Meredith had no vivid memories of attending that church or of any other church through his childhood and adolescence. Nor had he any vivid memories of Elvis Presley in that era, the only era in which Meredith might plausibly have been involved in rock and roll music, of course his classmates were caught up in the Presley craze, and there was the exasperating summer he'd been infected with one of the ridiculous Presley songs, but, in truth, Meredith remembered little of such things for he was, for some years, a serious music student, he took piano lessons each Saturday morning given by a locally renowned performing woman pianist, and his impression of his high school years was, in retrospect, that of having walked blindfolded through the 1950s as if quite literally blindfolded making his way through the corridors of the high school, past the rows of green metal lockers stretching to the very horizon, dim as dream-memory. He remembered little, and he regretted remembering little, he *was* superior, if sometimes a bit lonely.

As an adopted child, Meredith knew himself lucky, so lucky he dared not think of what might have been, what his other life might have been, what brothers and sisters he might have, living unknown to him, as he to them. His biological mother (which, even as a boy, he knew not to call his "real" or "actual" mother—that would have been stupidly cruel to his adoptive mother) had been only fifteen years old when she'd given birth to him and given him away, first to relatives, then to an adoption agency, she'd allegedly "disappeared" with a man and there was no trace of her and Meredith had never thought of her for there was no one of whom to think and the mind cannot comprehend nothingness though he knew she'd been very poor, her people very poor, West Virginia background, they'd moved to Youngstown, Ohio, at the start of the war and Meredith was born in 1941 and that was all he knew except to know himself blessed for had his young mother been more loving and true as a mother, had she loved him, and not given him him away, how different, how meager and impoverished his life would have been and knowing this he shuddered and wept for very gratitude for *God's ways are not our ways, praise to Him.*

"You sleep so well now, so deeply," Sarah observed, some weeks after the onset of the dreams. "You look forward to sleep, I think, Meredith, don't you?" not precisely accusatory but probing, assessing him with her eyes, watchful eyes for the Bernhardts lived alone now in the large handsome house of pale yellow stone, their children grown and gone and the house echoing with quiet, the peace of a prosperous middle age, a marriage of thirty-three years for which Meredith was grateful, such stability, such companionship, it was perhaps true that he might not have married Sarah had she not been the daughter of parents as prosperous as Meredith's own, not that he had not loved her for of course he had, we love those we love for all that is theirs, and why not a father's income as well as a pretty face, a winning smile, a pleasing voice, why not. Meredith reasoned that Sarah, for her part, would not have married *him* had he been, not Meredith Bernhardt, but someone else. Who?

Meredith laughed. Though it was not a laughing matter—this woman's probing, interrogation.

Meredith laughed, and said, "I look forward to every hour of my life, waking and sleeping, Sarah, don't you?"

Sarah regarded him for a moment in silence. Her eyes, which were no longer young eyes, seemed to have grown doubtful, opaque. She was a handsome woman with an erect way of holding herself, a squarish set to the shoulders as to the jaws, and the unbidden thought flashed to Meredith in that instant *Elvis is dead: why are you alive?*

As if reading his mind, Sarah said, ironically, "Yes, of course, darling. Have we any choice?"

Late that evening, which was a blowy Sunday evening in November, Meredith found himself on the cellar steps, descending the steps into the earthy-smelling darkness. *Why? where? cruel? true?* The house was a century old, an expensive property, yes but the mortgage was completely paid off, Meredith had done well through his business career, he'd been an excellent provider, and had reason to take pride. Didn't he. Not like his biological father who did not in fact exist. Not like any of them who did not in fact exist.

Most of the cellar had long since been renovated and made comfortably modern, but there was, at the rear, beyond a door, an old unused fruit cellar, and an old coal bin unused for decades, and for some reason Meredith found himself there, groping in the semidark, on a top shelf of the fruit cellar, amid dust and the desiccated remains of insects, something with a rubberized handle, it *was* here!—Meredith's instinct had not failed him.

Metal, glittering blades, rubberized handle.

Yet, by day, how disappointing it was: smaller than the remarkable *scourge* of his dreams, measuring perhaps fifteen inches in diameter, sickle-sized, made of an actual rug beater, razor blades and shards of wicked-looking glass clamped onto the heavy metal in a bizarre fan-shaped display. Meredith gripped it, held it, weighed it in his trembling hand.

From the stairs, a very long distance away, so that her voice, though raised, sounded faint, Meredith's wife called, "Meredith? Where *are* you?"

At just under three hundred words, "The Shoemaker's Tale" is the shortest short story in this rather large anthology.

Isn't it fitting, then, that its author get one of the shortest introductions?

LEWIS SHINER is a member of the same Texas mafia that's produced such locoweed talents as Joe R. Lansdale and Neal Barrett, Jr. Like those other mavericks, Lew takes the best elements of Texas's barband/cowboy mentality—its rowdy energy and fierce individuality—and redirects them through brisk, singular prose.

Lew's books include Slam and Deserted Cities of the Heart; forthcoming is Glimpses, a novel of imagined rock 'n' roll history. His short pieces have appeared in the New York Times, Spin, and the anthology In the Field of Fire.

"The Shoemaker's Tale" is something different. Even for Lew. A prime example of how far Dead Elvis has thrown his cape beyond simple rock 'n' roll.

This is also, you should know, a fractured fairy tale.

Straight from the Brothers Grin.

THE SHOEMAKER'S TALE
by Lewis Shiner

Okay, so once upon a time there was this shoemaker, this was back when people made shoes by hand, okay? He was really poor and the IRS was shafting him and the SBA was trying to call in his loan and he'd had to lay off all his employees who then sued him and called for federal arbitration. So he's in really bad shape. Besides he's old and his eyes are going bad and he can barely manage to get any shoes made at all.

But in spite of all that he's a pretty nice guy and he's got a good heart and everything. And every night before he goes to sleep he kneels down by his bed and prays to the King for help.

So one night he wakes up and there's all kinds of loud music and bright lights coming from his workshop. At first he's terrified, then he recognizes the music: "Now or Never." He creeps out of bed and looks through a knothole in the wall and sees them.

There's about a hundred of them, no more than three feet tall, pudgy little guys running around his workshop, making shoes like crazy. All of them with their jet black hair and sideburns and their jewel-studded white leather jumpsuits.

"It's true," the old shoemaker whispers. "The elvises have come to save me."

He goes back to bed, but he's so excited he can't really sleep. He lies there till dawn when he hears, faintly, a voice say, "Ladies and gentlemen, the elvises have left the building."

Then he gets back out of bed and goes into the workshop, and when he sees what they've done he clutches his chest and sits down on his workbench. "This is really cool and all," he says. "But what am I going to do with five hundred pairs of blue suede shoes?"

Ever thought how easy it would be to bring Elvis back?

Not through impersonators, records, or movies, you understand. I mean a real Elvis. One you could talk to, and touch.

CHRISTOPHER FAHY has.

Fahy lives in Thomaston, Maine, in the shadow of the state penitentiary. His most recent works of fiction are the suspense novels Eternal Bliss *and* The Lyssa Syndrome; *his recently completed mainstream novel,* Fever 42, *has been optioned as a motion picture by the Matthau Company.*

"Want" is a melancholy lament, Fahy's poignant dirge to the emptiness the living Presley left behind. An aching void the cult of Dead Elvis will never, ever fill.

And for those who think this story science fiction, I leave you with a thought—Remember your last trip to Disneyland?

WANT

by Christopher Fahy

"I shoulda just kept my mouth shut about it," said Linda Sue.

"All I asked's who you chose," said Arlene in her high-pitched whine.

"Huh. *All* you asked?"

"Well I just wanna know. Jesus, who wouldn't wanna know, what's wrong with that?"

Linda Sue tossed her head. "Well first of all, I ain't really sure who they got. I can't do much choosin' till I see who they got."

"I thought they made you pick aheada time," Arlene said, frowning skeptically and pouting her purple lips.

"Well they don't," said Linda Sue. "You're wrong."

A lie. Of course you had to pick ahead of time, and she'd known from the very first moment she'd ever considered this who it was going to be.

"Well then, if you don't know who it is, I ain't goin' with you," Arlene said, smacking her gum.

"Well that's just fine," said Linda Sue. "I don't know why I asked you anyway, I'm sorry I did."

As she locked her car, she knew very well why she'd asked Arlene to come: she was scared to death. The parking garage was bleak and damp, with feeble orange-colored lights that looked like evil, dying suns, and her stomach plunged. *Oh for God's sake, stop,* she told herself, *it's gonna be fine, it's gonna be great, that's why it costs so much.*

Alone in the elevator, she took out her compact and checked herself. Her hair had been done just yesterday and looked real nice—high piles of brassy curls—and her makeup was also fine: green shadow on upper eyelids, black false lashes, glittery silver-pink lips. On the negative side, a chin pimple poked its sharp tip through her base, and her cheeks—

Were fat. Goddamn it, she still looked fat. She had damn near starved herself for almost a month, lost twenty-six pounds, and . . . damn. "Who *cares* how you look?" Arlene had said. "It won't matter a bit to *him.*" "Well it matters to *me,*" Linda Sue had replied, "it matters a *lot* to *me.*" Arlene had given that shrug of hers that Linda Sue hated so much. *Pain in the butt,* she thought as she snapped her compact shut and shoved it away—*but I wish she was here.*

The motion as the elevator stopped made her stomach feel worse. The doors slid open, revealing a small green room. The stern-looking middle-aged woman behind the lone desk said, "Hello. May I help you?"

"I'm here for a two o'clock appointment," said Linda Sue, and her voice sounded thin in her ears. "Here's my card."

The woman took it and said, "Be seated, please."

A single picture hung on the wall; stark trees and a setting sun. A couple of vinyl chairs, and Linda Sue sat. Some old magazines on a brown plastic table. You'd think with all the money they made, the place would look nicer than this. She'd been paying installments for six months now, and she suddenly feared it had been a mistake. If she backed out, though, she'd lose half the money, that was the way it worked.

It's going to be just fine, she told herself, calm down. Too nervous to look at a magazine, she picked at a stray piece of cuticle on her thumb. She hoped he liked silver nails—

"Linda Sue?"

The man was short and thin and tanned, with black slick wiry hair. His black pinstriped suit was impeccable, his smile precise and empty.

She nodded. The man shook her hand. "Dick Harris. Follow me, please."

He turned and walked briskly down a long hallway, his sparkling shoes clicking against the fake marble floor. The walls were lined with photographs of dead celebrities, a thousand of them at least. No time for Linda Sue to examine them, Harris was moving too fast.

Stopping abruptly, he opened a door. With a brusque little bow, he held his hand out toward the room.

Now this is more like it! Linda Sue thought as she stepped inside. Her eyes widened. *Why, this is—fantastic!*

The room was huge and round, with a huge round bed in its center. Its windows were hung with gold velvet drapes, its snow-white carpet was half an inch thick, its walls were a white and gold brocade with incredible velvet paintings in ornate gold frames: heads of tigers and horses, a shiny blue fish, and a fruit bowl so bright that it practically hurt your eyes. There were vases and vases of lush golden flowers, a bucket of champagne on ice on a white wooden cart, a credenza heaped high with all kinds of goodies: cold cuts and cupcakes and bowls full of candy, and frozen concoctions on ice. Also a jar of peanut butter. Gleaming gold and platinum records covered an entire wall.

"You approve?" Harris asked.

"Oh yes," Linda Sue said, her eyes still wide.

"We're so glad. Please be seated."

She sat on a white plush couch, knees together, her hands on the purse in her lap. Across from her, in a golden chair, Harris said, "Now before you begin, I'd like to run through the procedures again."

"Okay."

"Would you care for a drink?"

"Oh no, no thanks."

The crisp little man leaned forward. "The main thing you have to remember is, whatever you see, whatever you do, you're dealing with an illusion."

"I realize that."

"Of course you do. I just want you to be aware that it's all going to seem very real. Unbelievably real."

"Yeah, that's what they say."

"And it's true. We've used the information you gave us to fashion a drama that perfectly meets your needs. It's going to be as real—perhaps more real—than anything you've ever known before. But you have to remember—it *is* a performance."

"Okay," Linda Sue said, thinking: *Come on, let's just do it!*

"I'm so glad you understand," said Harris, reaching inside his jacket. "And here's the release for you to sign. It's our standard form."

He handed it to her. She tried to read it. "Will not be responsible . . . In case of . . . Under no circumstances . . . Liability limited . . ." Garbage, far as she could see.

"Okay?" asked Harris. He whipped out a pen.

"Sure," Linda Sue said.

"Good," Harris said, and watched her sign. He took the pen back, took the paper, put it away, and stood. "Your drama will start in a couple of minutes," he said. "We hope it is totally satisfying."

"Thanks," said Linda Sue, nodding.

Harris bowed once again, then left the room, closing the door.

She was suddenly very excited—and very afraid. Her heart made a squooshy loud sound in her ears. She reached in her purse for some gum; unwrapped it, popped it in her mouth; began to chew. Sat chewing on the edge of the couch, the excited feeling thick in her stomach and chest. Soon, any minute now. She wondered where—?

A door to the left of the bed flew open—she'd never even seen it before—and—oh my God, there he *was*.

He tossed his head back, smiling, his smile a sneer. His teeth were huge and shiny white. He jerked his guitar and nodded coolly and said, "Hello there, Linda Sue."

She was going to die. She could feel her heart swelling and straining, preparing to burst. She opened her mouth and no words would come out. Her gum was stuck to her teeth.

"What'sa matter?" he said in his mellow deep voice. "Cat gotcha tongue?"

"Oh," she squeaked. "Oh." She stared.

He looked marvelous, marvelous, better than ever. His blue-black hair was shiny and full, his complexion was bright, his eyes gleamed. His white silk shirt was open to the waist, and his waist was firm and slim. He wore gold lamé skin-tight pants, black pointy suede shoes, and a golden chain that dipped down into the cleft of his hairless chest. "Oh my God," whispered Linda Sue.

"Love me, love me, love me, love me, love me," he bubbled, and strummed a soft mournful chord. He stared with his gray-brown eyes. She could feel herself melting, her mind disappearing.

"Love me lovely, love me deep," he sang, and she thought she might swoon. She bit her lip and covered her mouth with her hands. He thrust his hips; the bulge in his gold lamé grew prominent; she gasped. "And who's the gal I love?" he crooned, staring down with his burning eyes.

"Why it's you,
Yes it's you,
Linda Sue."

Her mind was reeling. She didn't know whether to shout or clap or jump up and hug him or what, so she just stayed sitting.

"You like it?" he asked with another snide smile. Sweat shone on his wide tanned forehead.

She nodded.

"I'm so, so glad," he said, and strummed again, and this time sang "I Need You Like the Ocean Needs the Stream," one of his all-time greatest. In his spell, she flowed over the ripples of song like a leaf in the stream he was singing about. *Oh my God, oh my God,* she kept telling herself, *this is just so* real.

He finished with a soft sweet chord, laid his instrument down, took a bright silver cloth from his pocket and wiped his flushed face. "Did it please you?" he asked, head cocked, his smile coy. "Now, tell the truth."

"I . . . adored it," Linda Sue replied, her chewing gum lost in the gap between cheek and teeth.

"I'm so happy to hear that," he said. " 'Cause I want to please you so very much—in any way I can. Mind if I take a load off my feet?"

"Oh—of course not," she said.

He nodded and sat in the chair where Harris had been. "We got all kindsa goodies," he said, "if you feel like eatin'."

"Oh no. No thanks," she said.

"Well you got any more of that gum?"

She felt paralyzed; then, "Oh, sure," she said, and reached in her purse and came out with a stick. He got up and took it, and as he did, his fingers grazed her hand. An electric thrill shot into her arms and chest. "I 'preciate it, thanks," he said, and sat again.

He tossed the gum wrappings aside—right onto the thick white rug—and shoved the stick into his mouth. "Now, what would you like to hear next?" he asked. "Or you wanna just talk for a while?"

"Yes. Let's just talk," she said.

"Good, that's what I want, too," he said, "an' you wanna know why? 'Cause you're somethin' special, you really are. I knew it the minute I walked through that door. As soon as I looked at your sweet angel face, I said to myself, "This gal's somethin' special. This gal is the one you been waitin' for.""

"That's . . . nice of you to say," said Linda Sue. Her heart was beating so fast she could scarcely stand it.

Leaning back, his shirt spreading wider and showing more skin, he said, "You think it's just part of the show, I guess. You think it's just part of the act. You think I say that to all the girls, but it just ain't true. You're special. Real special. You're the one I been waitin' for—the one I want."

Linda Sue couldn't swallow. She shook her head. "I don't think you oughtta say this stuff," she said. "It's nice to hear, real nice, but it's not what I had in mind."

His eyebrows went up. "Oh? But I think it *is* what you had in mind. And if I'm wrong? Can you blame a man for sayin' how he really feels?" Suddenly he was on his feet, and then he was sitting beside her.

He pulsed with heat; she bathed in his glow, and she suddenly felt so *alive*. "No," she said. "This ain't right. I mean, I was ready for—well, you know—an' I still am ready, but this . . . ." She shook her head again. "It's just too much."

"Not at all," he said. "It's perfect. Touch my arm."

"What?"

"Go ahead, touch my arm."

She did, at the elbow; felt silken warmth—and she loved him with all her heart.

"Come away with me, li'l lady," he said, looking into her eyes, chewing gum.

She frowned and said, "I didn't think . . . I mean . . . I thought they didn't let . . ." She looked in those eyes, her heart swollen and hot, and said, "See, what I mean is, I'm only a factory girl. I put this tiny transistor thing, a component they call it, onto these what they call memory boards? I been doin' it four years now, and I'll probably do it the rest of my life. I don't have a boyfriend, the guys that I meet are so . . . plain, and all I wanted was just to . . . just . . . ."

"I know, I know," he said, and he put his arm over her shoulder. Heat raged in her brain. "Years back, I used to drive a truck, an' I know how it is. I know what it's like to be you, 'cause I *was* you. And that's why I like you so very much. That's why—I *love* you."

His minty hot breath made her weak all through. "I wanta get outta there terrible bad," she said. "The work hurts my hands, it hurts my eyes, and sometimes I think . . . it's like already being *dead*. I'd love to go away with you, but the problem is, you ain't . . . you ain't—"

Sealing her lips with a blazing finger, he said, "Does this feel like I ain't? Just shush now, gal, I'm tellin' you, dreams can come true."

He took his hand down. Its imprint had branded her mouth; she was shaking all over. "But how does it work?" she asked. "I don't understand. Do I . . . buy you, or what?"

Tossing his head with a haughty sniff, he said, "Nobody buys *me,* ma'am. *N*obody."

"But the thing is, outside of this room—"

Leaning forward, he said in a soft voice, "Well doancha see? They never gimme a chance. And to tell you the truth, I never wanted a chance—till now, till you came along."

Her pulse fluttered into her throat. "But . . ." She thought she might cry.

"Come on, darlin', doan be a hound dog. You really gonna break my heart?"

She swallowed hard, dazed and confused. "I want you, I need you," she said. "Oh I need you so bad. But tell me somethin'—an' tell me true."

"What's that, sweet thing?" Spreading his arms he leaned back again, and one of his huge hands settled beside her hair. Its nearness gave her a neck full of goosebumps.

"Tell me true, now," she said. "Did you beat your wife?"

A snort. "Beat my wife, what a crock. Course not, li'l lover. I wouldn't lay a hand on a lady, you oughta know that."

"An' what about that story I read about those little girls? That you paid them to rassle in their underwear?"

"You know the papers, you know how they are. Anything to make money."

"Yeah."

She chewed on her tasteless stiff gum and believed him—with all of her loving heart. She squeezed her legs together, folded her hands, and said with a little grin, "Did you really fly to Denver to pick up your favorite peanut butter?"

Laughing, he said, "Now that, I confess to, I *did* do that. An' a jar of it's sittin' right there, if you want a taste." He jerked his head backward.

"Oh no," she said. "I can't eat a thing. Not now. Not the way I feel."

He touched her arm; a thrill hummed in her veins. "I'll play you another song," he said, and reached for his shining guitar.

He strummed a chord, then sang:

"You're the gal
I got in mind.
The gal I looked
All my life to find . . ."

His oily baritone oozed its way into her open, defenseless soul. She squeezed her eyes shut; opened them carefully. Yes, it was real. *He* was real. This was actually *happening* to her.

He sang. She hung on his every word, intermittently chewing her gum.

"You're the one
You're the one . . ."

He blinked with heavy lids. "You *are* the one, li'l gal. I want you, I want you."

"And I want *you*," said Linda Sue, her whole body congested with love. "I want you so very much."

"I want you. I want you. I want you."

"I know you do. Oh I know it."

"I want . . . you."

"Yes, yes."

"I want . . . want . . . want . . ."

His fingers struck a chord that sounded wrong, and his smile this time was—geez, it was really *weird*. And now as she watched his mouth as he sang, she saw that thing that happens in movies sometimes, when the lips and the voice are a little bit off, a little bit out of synch. Was she losing her mind? Was she starting to faint? Was this happening in a dream?

She took a deep breath and pinched herself, and it *wasn't* anything wrong with her, it was him, she was sure it was. His words were sluggish, gooey, slow; his fingers stumbled on the strings.

"You all right?" she asked, sitting straighter. "You feelin' okay?"

His shoulders heaved. His head weaved back and forth. His voice was droopy, an octave too deep, a forty-five record on thirty-three and a third.

"I . . . want . . . you . . ." he said, so slowly, so slowly, his wide jaw sloppy and slack. His fingers stopped strumming. His eyes had a blank, milky look.

"No!" Linda Sue cried. "You're doin' drugs! You're doin' drugs again! It ain't right, it ain't fair, I put that in the agreement—"

"I . . . I . . ." he said.

"Don't lie to me! You're doin' drugs!"

The guitar slid out of his sleepy hands; it dangled around his neck on its golden strap. "I . . ."

"It's the one thing I insisted on," she said. "No drugs. For God's sake, that's why you *died*."

His jaw hung open. His tongue hung out.

She grabbed his shoulders. "Stop!" she cried. "Get aholda yourself! Don't do this to me! It ain't fair!"

"I want . . . I want . . ."

"Please. *Please*."

His eyes struggled to focus. "It ain't . . . it ain't drugs . . ." He spoke with great effort, his breath coming hard. Her hands were glued to his shoulders. "It's . . . jus' that . . . we doan last . . . forever . . ."

His tongue made a whirring, clicking sound; his crooked eyes rolled back. "Love . . . me . . . cruel . . ." he said in a cracked, dull drawl. Then his breathing stopped.

"No, no!" screamed Linda Sue.

Then he started to tilt, his weight was too much for her quivering hands, and he fell with a terrible crash, the guitar sounding one harsh chord.

She sprang to the floor and shook him hard. "No! No!" she cried. "Get up! Wake up! Please! *No*!" And then she wept.

She was down on her knees, her face in her hands, and Harris was there beside her. "Linda Sue," he said. "Linda Sue, please, listen to me."

"No, no," she wailed. "He's dead. He's dead."

"He isn't dead," Harris said. "He's just—expired. It happens—rarely, our maintenance program is truly superb, but it happens. We can start all over again, some other day. As a matter of fact, you'll get two dramas next time, with a brand-new Elvis."

"I don't *want* a brand-new Elvis," Linda Sue moaned. "I want *this* Elvis. But he's broke. He's goddamn broke."

"We can program another Elvis to be just the same."

"No you *can't*," Linda Sue said hotly. "This Elvis was special. This was *my* Elvis. There'll never be another one like him."

Harris sighed. "I believe I have heard this before somewhere."

"You just shut up!" snapped Linda Sue. "He was goin' to take me away. He was goin' to take me outta the factory, take me away to Graceland."

"We programmed that in. You requested that."

"I never did."

"Oh yes, it's right in the contract. You get double your money back or two dramas, it's up to you, it's our standard guarantee."

"And what about my *life*?" wailed Linda Sue, wiping her tear-filled eyes with her fingertips. "What about *that*? You killed my Elvis and left me alone and broke my heart forever, what about *that*?"

"*That* we cannot adjust," Harris said, reaching into his jacket pocket. " 'Not responsible for broken hearts,' it says it right here. You signed the release."

"I know, I know, but—"

"Double your money back or two dramas, it's the best we can do."

Linda Sue closed her eyes: and she saw him again, saw him singing— to *her*. She choked on a sob and shook her head and rubbed the tears away; then opened her eyes again, sighing, and slowly leaned forward, touching her lips to the cheek of the fallen star. "Good-bye," she said, her voice broken and hoarse. "I'll love you forever and ever."

His marble eyes stared up at nothing. His skin was as cold as glass.

At the work station, Arlene said, "Was it worth it?"

"It was," replied Linda Sue. She stuck the component onto the board. Her wrists and fingers ached. Her temples throbbed.

"Would you do it again? Spend all that much money again?"

"Maybe someday. But not for a while."

"So who did you pick, anyway?"

"That's still nunna your goddamn business."

"I bet it was Elvis," Arlene said.

"It wasn't George Washington," Linda Sue said.

"I bet it was Elvis."

Linda Sue looked at the parts on the line. Through the mist that had suddenly filled her eyes they kept coming and coming, steadily, endlessly, thousands of them, like days.

J. S. RUSSELL is the pseudonym for a mysterious Southern California writer.

He was newly arrived to the fiction field, and little is known about Russell beyond the fact that he once worked for a detective agency. However, Russell's handful of distinctive short stories have appeared in such publications as Midnight Graffiti, Science Fiction Review, and Iniquities, which may give some indication of the man's personal tastes.

Another tip-off to Russell's character could be "City of Angels," his first published work. "Angels" was Russell's short contribution to Splatterpunks, my 1990 anthology of "extreme" horror stories. This gut-wrenching tale of decomposing postholocaust survivors packed one hell of a punch; it also became the most talked-about effort in the book.

Now comes "Limited Additions." While it may lack the Technicolor gore splashed throughout "City of Angels," "Additions" could arouse controversy, too. For this bleak observation on the World of Dead Elvis takes your basic Presley collectors—the ones who hoard those old concert tickets or order the Franklin Mint's newest Elvis medallion—and dropkicks them straight into the Twilight Zone.

A cautionary tale, then.

Especially for those who can't live without that copy of Elvis's first commercial recording session. ★

★ A 45 rpm 1954 Sun Records pressing of "That's All Right (Mama)."

LIMITED ADDITIONS

by J. S. Russell

I Am a Fugitive from a Chain Gang plays on TV in the background. I've always loved Paul Muni. As an actor, I mean. From a business point of view, he's no damn good at all.

I sit with my back to the wall, stealing glances through the curtain at every set of headlights that flashes by.

Waiting.

I've tried three times to get to sleep, but my brain won't let me. Overtired, I think they call it. It's usually kids who are overtired. Babies. Isn't that what people say when a baby's cranky? Am I cranky? I'm not sure. I'm all alone, here, so there's no one to be cranky at but myself.

The negatives sit in their little metal box on top of the television. I really should do something about them, but I haven't the slightest idea what.

Next to the box is the white envelope. With her pictures. They make an interesting pair in their way. Him in the negatives, her in the positives. That sounds like it should have some deep meaning. Too bad it doesn't.

Another set of headlights, another glance. It passes by.

On TV, Paul Muni's in trouble. In real life, so am I.

Kimodo had a friend who had a friend. You know how it goes.

The mansion was built on the palisade above Malibu, at the end of one of those winding canyon roads with a seemingly impossible slope. I braced myself against the dash, certain that the angle was too steep and the Porsche would go tumbling end over end all the way back down to Pacific Coast Highway. Kimodo just laughed and inched the tach closer to the red. I swore I could feel the front end start to lift off the ground just as the road finally leveled out and a bald valet in a kilt came running up on the driver's side.

Kimodo gave the engine a final, noisy rev and hopped out. A second valet, also bald but wearing a different tartan, opened the passenger door. I grabbed my briefcase from behind the seat and trotted to catch up with Kimodo, who was already walking toward the house. It was one of those postmodern monstrosities with jutting angles and contrasting facets that looked like it had been put together by three blind guys speaking different languages. It couldn't have been worth more than four or five million.

"Remember," Kimodo said again as we approached the door, "no names."

"Hey, what'd I? Fall off a lettuce truck? Chill, Sunshine."

Kimodo nodded and reached for the bell, but it opened before he could press the buzzer. We were greeted by a small Asian man in a French maid's skirt. Death's-head nipple rings dangled from his naked, golden chest and a brilliant tattoo of Curly from the Three Stooges was etched on his belly. His navel formed the Stooge's lips. It was an "outie," lending the curious impression that Curly was wagging his tongue in a quasi-obscene manner. "Nyuk-nyuk-nyuk" was tattooed up the man's rib cage.

"Kiss-kiss," he said, and wandered back into the mansion, wiggling his butt as he walked.

"Welcome to Wonderland," Kimodo said. He licked his lips, rubbed his hands, and set off after the Asian. I felt a tug at my pant leg and looked down. A toothless dwarf of indeterminate gender was rubbing against my leg like a cat in heat.

"Blow job?" s/he gummed.

"Giving or getting?" I asked.

It shrugged and smiled.

Wonderland indeed.

Hollywood is everything you imagine it be.
And less.
And more.

I could name names—I mean, how much more trouble could I be in? —but I won't.

You'd know them, though. Some were the faces behind the faces, the powers behind the throne, but most of the guests that night would be all too familiar to you. Like the beloved and avuncular network anchor with a penchant for prepubescent girls and concentration camp footage. Or "The Sexiest Man Alive" from a few years back, who tithes a third of his earnings to a black coven and shells out another quarter to strange fat men for the privilege of giving them enemas. Or the teenaged sitcom starlet who can't have sex without a live audience *and* a laugh track.

I mingled for a while, exchanging small talk and nods and smiles. I spotted two of my competitors hovering at the fringes, also clutching briefcases and looking as uncomfortable as I felt. I imagined that breeders of Thoroughbreds must often feel this way: the fact that you had a professional interest in the business didn't mean you wanted to actually watch the horses fuck.

I ran into an old acquaintance I hadn't seen since the Cincinnati convention back in '89. He was a mountain of a man, but his head was too small for his massive frame, like a lime set atop a watermelon, and he lisped like Daffy Duck. He was known as the Zookeeper because he specialized in animal shots; mostly dog and pony shows, but you'd be surprised.

"Hey, what it is Keep?"

"I don't know about thith group, I gotta tell ya," he said. "It'th crowdth like thith maketh me wonder thometimeth."

"How do you mean?"

"Don't it ever make you a little nervouth?"

" 'A place for every fetish, and every fetish in its place,' my mother always said. She wore fur underpants, you know."

"Live and let live. I know. But . . . all thoth bodily fluidth being exthchanged. Ithn't it dangerouth? Doeth'nt anybody read the paperth?"

This struck me as perhaps overly judgmental coming from a man spraying saliva filaments about his immediate vicinity, one who made a living selling photographs of women and dogs having sex. But I let it go.

"Well, there's a heaping bowl of condoms on the table there for what it's worth. And I *have* seen less discreet crowds than this. Christ, Keep, they're just customers and besides," I said, lowering my voice to a whisper, "they're mostly actors."

He shuddered slightly and nodded, then walked off shaking his little head.

I don't know what it is exactly that pushes people out over that edge, or why show-biz types seem to go so far over the top, but I know it's something that those of us who don't lead our lives in the spotlight can never entirely understand. For me it was just a hobby and then a business, but for them it seems to be something more. It's not so much that polymorphous perversity is reserved as a lifestyle for the rich and famous —I have clients who are plumbers and stockbrokers and college professors—only that they seem to be so damn good at it.

Truth be known, the bodily fluids thing bothered me, too, but from the stories I've heard, these parties aren't anything close to what they used to be. Maybe it's all a part of the same syndrome; a sense of superiority and invulnerability that goes hand in hand with an elevation in stature above and beyond us lumpy proletariat. How else to explain it? I mean, these days I don't even like flushing the toilets in public rest rooms.

"Hey! Mr. Fantastic!"

I was approached by a young man wearing pretorn jeans and a pink T-shirt emblazoned with a likeness of Angelyne, a local legend. I didn't recognize him at first until he turned his head and I saw the gold hammer-and-sickle earring.

"Oh, hi," I said.

"What the fuck are you doing here, my man? You're not here for the fucking auction?"

"Yes, as a matter of fact I am."

"I ain't seen you here before."

"Well, I'm branching out. Going where no man has collected before."

"No shit! Man, wish I had known. I'm here for the auction, too. Not that I mind the other action, you understand. Heh-heh."

The kid had once been a regular customer at my old store, Fantastic Comix. None too bright as I recalled, but his father was a big mucky-muck at one of the talent agencies and the kid was spoiled rotten. I'd sold him a complete run of *Wolverine* comics at better than double the guide price and the kid never batted an eye. I didn't know his collecting habits ran in other directions.

"So, uh, what'dya got tonight?"

"Well, a variety of items actually." This really wasn't the place to discuss it. I had photos of several of the people in the room.

"Yeah, like what?"

I glanced around cautiously. "I specialize in fifties materials."

The kid grabbed me by the arm, nearly pulling me off-balance.

"Betty Page?" he whispered.

Lord spare me, I thought, from the Betty Page freaks. She had a hell of a rack, sure, but I could never figure out all the fuss over her. *Page-ination*, Kimodo calls it.

The kid's eyes had gone all wide and his hammer-and-sickle earring suddenly looked more like a dollar sign to me. Maybe I didn't much care for Betty Page, but I recognized a cash machine when I saw one.

"Nothing tonight," I said, and I saw the dollar signs taking wing and quickly added: "But I may have a line on something coming up."

I didn't really, but wasn't about to let the flounder slip off the hook. He patted me on the back and handed me a business card: no name, just a Valley phone number and a tiny Betty-in-bondage picture.

"You call me first," he said, "and we'll do us some business. She's still alive, you know."

"I've heard the stories."

"Yeah, I got fucking detectives looking for her."

I nodded appreciatively. I didn't really care.

"We're getting a line on her. Gonna do some things when we find her, too. You bet."

I didn't much like the sound of that and feared he was about to expound when Kimodo caught my eye from across the room and waved me over.

"You call *me* first," the kid said as I pried his fingers off my arm. I nodded again and pardoned and excused my way through the guests to Kimodo. He was still eyeing the kid when I came up beside him.

"You know him?" he said.

I shrugged. "Old customer from comic book days. He recognized me."

Kimodo was squinting. "Stay away from him. He's a major freak."

"In this crowd? How can you tell?"

"I hear things. Anyway, it's show time."

I followed Kimodo up the hall to a small elevator which led to a screening room downstairs where the auction would take place.

"I still haven't met our host," I said as we rode down.

"Sure you have. In the playroom. The dude in the gravity boots with the hooter twins."

"With the bratwurst?"

"Uh-huh."

"In the Reagan mask?"

"No. Quayle."

"Ohhhh," I said. "Will he be joining us?"

"He doesn't attend the auctions. He just provides the facility in exchange for a small . . . consideration."

"The twins," I said.

"The bratwurst," Kimodo corrected.

I did okay at the auction, not great. Sold a nice Sal Mineo fellatio and a Mama Cass autopsy series. The Martin Luther King stuff didn't fly at all—old-fashioned racism, if you ask me—but I hit pay dirt with a Jayne Mansfield nut who overbid for a rare, color beaver shot, and a Garland queen who went apeshit over a Dorothy/Cowardly Lion doggy-style candid. So go figure. I almost bid myself on a stunning Erroll Flynn wet shot (Nazi or not, that boy was *hung),* but the price went stratospheric because you could sort of make out Clark Gable and George Cukor in the background.

The phone call came the following week.

"Mr. Fan-fucking-tastic!" The kid again.

"Yeah, hi," I said.

"Any skinny on the goddess?"

"Come again?"

"Three times a night, babe. Once in each hole. Heh-heh. I mean Betty. The pictures."

Actually, I *had* reached a contact in the Betty trade, but the pipeline was dry and the prices were inflated.

"Ummm, still working on it. I've got your card so I'll let you know if anything turns up."

"Whoa! Listen up. Are you doing the Vegas thing?" Vegas thing? I hadn't heard about any Vegas shows.

"Err, which Vegas thing would that be, exactly?"

"Shit, Mr. F, are you a player or what? Elvis. Vegas. Saturday. The birthday thing."

"Oh, *that.*" I didn't have a clue. "I hadn't decided yet, to tell you the truth. There's that *other* Vegas show coming up and I don't know if I want to do them both." When in doubt, vamp.

"Jesus Jerk-off Christ! Listen, dude: I need you to be there. I need a—whatyacallit—an in-between."

"You mean a go-between?" I asked.

"Yeah! A go-between. There's gonna be some people at the show. Connected people, if you know what I'm saying. People who can help me with this Betty situation."

"Sounds like a done deal. What do you need me for?"

"Ahhhh, these people. They say that I irritate them the wrong way. They want to do business, you understand, 'cause I got something to offer. But they're what you might call on the hinky side. Yeah, definitely hinkitudinous."

"Ummm, listen, kid. This really doesn't sound like my kind of deal. I just sell to collectors, you know? Not a lot of haggling in this trade. I want to do business as much as the next guy, but this doesn't smell so good to me."

"Hey, Mr. F! This is me you're talking to here. And I understand what you're saying. You got every right to see some profit margin on this action. You still got that I-Have-a-Wet-Dream crap from the other day?"

"Ummm, yes, I believe the King material is still available."

"Still available like my grandma's cunt. You can't give that shit away. Name a price."

I thought for a moment and said triple what they were worth.

"Fine," he snapped. "I'll *double* that if you come to Vegas with me. Not to mention the connections you make at the show."

It was an awesome amount of money and he was right about the possible extra action, but I was still dubious. "What exactly is this deal all about?"

"I'll fill you in on the way. I got a plane chartered for early Saturday. Out of Burbank. You're in, right?"

"I . . . I'd like to think about it."

"Shit. What's to think? It's *eeeasy* money."

The duck should always come down at the mention of those two words, but what can you do? I'm as greedy as the next guy.

"Can I call you back?" I asked.

"Listen. I'm just gonna assume you're coming. It's private hangar 23-L. Saturday morning, 7 A.M. I'll be the man with the cash."

He hung up.

I spent the rest of the day making calls and finally managed to confirm that there was indeed an event in Vegas on Saturday—Elvis's birthday—but that it was very selective. Invitation only. Big money. I was suddenly very interested.

I tried to get in touch with Kimodo, remembering his warning about the kid, but was told he was "in retreat," which meant he was off with a gaggle of boys and a couple grams of coke. I called the agency where the kid's father had been head honcho to make sure he was still there. He was, so I figured the kid had insurance against serious trouble.

Finally, I found the card the kid gave me and dialed the number. His phone message was a recording of flesh being whipped and orgasmic female grunts. Just before the beep a voice—the kid's—said: "Betty. Then. Now. Forever."

"I'm in," I said, sealing my fate.

ELVIS DIED FOR YOUR SINS was stenciled in red on the receptionist's T-shirt. Below the words was a photo of the dead king on his porcelain throne. I'd once sold a not dissimilar shot for ten thousand dollars.

The kid was puffing on a Tiparillo and wearing one of those gaudy Hawaiian shirts with little neon-pink pineapples and topless Hula girls. The essence of Vegas-wear. He bragged about the fact that he had paid only two hundred dollars for it at a vintage clothing store on Melrose. I smiled and nodded and realized I should have hit him up for more for the King pictures.

"Name?" the Dead Elvis guy asked.

"Buchmeister," the kid said, and winked at me. On the plane, the kid had told me it was German for "Page Master," and that it was the name he always used. I started to ask him why German, but caught myself and did another smile and nod. "And associate," the kid added.

Dead Elvis flipped through a sheaf of fanfold paper until he found the name and drew a line through it. He handed over a couple of badges which ostensibly identified us as participants in a shareholder's meeting for American Marmite. I was embarrassed to note that my badge was also made out in the name Buchmeister, but with "Guest" in parentheses.

"All business will be conducted in the penthouse suite," Dead Elvis recited. "Please display your badges to the penthouse elevator operator and wear them at all times in convention areas. Viva Las Vegas. Next!"

The kid's big deal wasn't supposed to go down until late afternoon, so I had all day to wander the show while he was off doing God knows what. The penthouse suite was no bigger than your average concert hall, but there were only about a hundred attendees. Except for the fact that the crowd was about three-quarters male, it couldn't have been more different from the Malibu scene. This group was all Italian suits and silk ties, with nary a nipple ring or tattoo in sight. The obligatory sex rooms were set up for all preferences, but they were discreetly set off from the dealers' area. This was a genuinely professional gathering and I was impressed.

The first panel, "Autopsies and Airbrushes: Ethics or Aesthetics," was quite interesting. I missed the "Elvis: Friend of the Animals" slide show, but it was worth it to swing a deal for some exceptional Natalie Wood nudes from her *Searchers* period. The "Kids Suck the Darnedest Things" exhibit was a bit of a disappointment—although the Buffy and Mr. French shots were sort of cute—and I'm so sick of Jim Morrison ephemera that I just skipped down to the casino for a few hands of Red Dog.

I was just settling in for the showstopper, an Elvis passion play, when the kid tapped me on the shoulder.

"Pssst. Mr. F! Let's do it."

The kid was about as discreet as a tractor pull, so I hustled us out of the suite just as, on the stage, Colonel Parker was denying Elvis for the third time.

The kid had been pretty vague so far regarding the details of this deal. He told me it was a simple exchange, but kept changing the subject when I tried to pin him down. All he would say for sure was that he had once had some action go sour with these contacts and needed a beard to make the new deal work.

"Do they know *you're* involved in this?" I asked, suddenly nervous.

"Ahhhh . . . not exactly," he said, looking everywhere but at me. "As far as they know, my name—which is to say *your* name—is Mr. Piaget. That's French for Page, you know."

I didn't have the heart or stomach to break it to him. "And these pictures are of what exactly?" I asked.

"Not to worry," he said, "just some unusual Elvis material. Something I lucked into." He wouldn't tell me any more about the merchandise, either what he was giving or what I was supposed to be getting.

"You mean you want me to accept the stuff blind?"

"It'll be all right," he nodded. "I trust these guys."

I had a queasy gizzard about this transaction, but accepted that it was too late to back out now. It wasn't until the kid pulled up in front of Circus, Circus that he handed me the manila envelope.

"Remember," he said, "sit at the revolving bar on the arcade level."

"How will I know them?"

"Not to worry. *They'll* know *you*. I'll meet you back at the hotel."

And he was gone. I looked over the envelope, hefted it. It felt like there were maybe half a dozen 8-by-10 photos. I flipped the envelope over, but the flap was sealed with wax, embossed with a likeness of Betty Page. No way to open and reseal it. I thought for a moment that the contacts probably wouldn't know if I looked at the photos and then resealed them in a regular envelope, but decided I was getting good money for the job, so I might as well just do it right.

If Vegas is America's glowing neon monument to the grotesque, then surely Circus, Circus is the zircon in its navel. I know that Caesar's is tackier, and Mirage and Excalibur are gaudier and goofier, but there may be no place in the world which better lives up to its name than Circus, Circus. On the one hand you've got throngs of little kids milling around the games and arcades, while just below, hordes of greed-crazed "adults" pull onanistically on the one-armed bandits. What kind of parent would bring his kids to Vegas to begin with, I don't know; but to drop the kids amid the tawdry plasticity of this would-be carnival and then run downstairs to lose their college money at the craps tables qualifies in this bad boy's book as felony child endangerment.

I elbowed my way through the munchkins toward the revolving lounge, which was itself somewhat out of place amid the clowns and calliopes, and sat down at the only empty stool at the bar. I ordered a beer and was given some amber-colored water that only cost me four bucks. This was another of the many wonderful Vegas perversities: sit at the tables and they'd comp you Heinekens till Bugsy Siegel came back from the grave; sit at a bar and they charged you like it was a Paris disco. They don't like people sitting at the bars.

A fat guy to my left was hitting on a good-looking hooker and laughing uproariously. He would alternately jostle me with his bony elbow and then apologize for the pokes. I just nodded and repeatedly said it was all right. The easiest way to deal with a drunk. I was a little surprised the bartender didn't have him tossed.

I was on my second watery brew, when the guy to my right got up and his seat was immediately taken by a tall, thin man in a navy blue suit. He had on a white shirt with a plain tie and wore dark Ray-Bans. His wavy, dirty blond hair was neatly parted on the left and he was immaculately shaved. I caught a whiff of talc and thought that he must have just come from the barber. He held a small white envelope.

"Mr. Piaget," he said.

I nodded. He didn't say anything else, nor did he look at me. I wasn't sure what to do. Exchanging envelopes with a man in dark glasses in a casino bar struck me as a not entirely inconspicuous thing to do. The fat guy poked me again, laughed some more and apologized again.

The Ray-Ban man reached over and plucked my envelope from the bar. He slid his packet over in its place. It, too, was sealed and I quickly thrust it into my jacket pocket. He half-turned away from me and popped open the seal on the kid's envelope, slitting Betty's waxen throat. He didn't take the photos out, but peered down into the envelope and thumbed the pictures the way you'd leaf through a stuffed file drawer. I tried to look over his shoulder, but I couldn't make out any of the images.

"S'all right?" I said, trying a smile.

He resealed the envelope as best he could and turned back around, but still didn't look at me. He nodded, it seemed, to his own face in the mirror above the bar. Just then, the fat guy poked me again, very sharply. He didn't laugh this time, or apologize. And his elbow stayed wedged in my side.

It took a few moments before I realized that it wasn't his elbow, nor was he just happy to see me. I glanced down at the dull barrel of a silencer. It was attached to a .45 that was hidden from prying eyes by the thick folds of the man's bulging gut.

"Uh-oh," I actually said.

I looked up for the bartender, but he was crouched by a freezer at the far end of the bar. I started to get up, but Fat Boy nudged the barrel a little deeper into my ribs, laughing and throwing his right arm around my shoulders to disguise his actions.

"Easy, pilgrim," Ray-Ban said. "We're about to take a walk."

The entire lounge jutted out from the arcade level and was suspended over the casino several floors below, spinning in slow, graceful circles. They could have just walked me across the diameter of the lounge and exited back on to the arcade, but I got the feeling they were waiting until our spot on the circle came back around by the entrance, to minimize visibility.

I looked for a security guard, but they were all down on the floor below. The bartender was still busy restocking beer and as I scanned the faces in the bar for someone who might be able to help me, I suddenly realized there were at least three other men strategically positioned around the room, all wearing sunglasses and plain blue suits, with their hands conspicuously nestled inside their jackets.

The lounge had turned another quarter revolution and Ray-Ban slid off his stool and nodded at Fat Boy. Just at that moment the houselights dimmed and a thundering, musical "TAAAA-DAAAA" burst from hidden loudspeakers. A spotlight flared on, illuminating a sequined acrobat several levels above us. He was about to ride a tiny bicycle down a thin cable strung from the high ceiling, past the spinning lounge and down to the casino floor.

Show time.

Both Ray-Ban and Fat Boy were distracted by the blare of lights and music. It was only for a moment, but it was long enough. I went limp and collapsed to the floor while their attention was focused on the performer. A second after I dropped I heard the muffled whump! of Fat Boy's .45. I started to roll as soon as I was down, but glanced up in time to see a bright red flower blossom across Ray-Ban's white shirt. Fat-boy was already lowering his sights toward me, but I scurried off on hands and knees between the muumuued legs of a blue-haired lady clutching a paper cup full of quarters.

I saw Ray-Ban collapse onto the bar and heard Muumuu shriek behind me. The other blue suits were edging toward me with guns drawn. Fat Boy waved at one of them to cut off the exit to the arcade. Security guards from below were pointing up toward the lounge. It would only be a matter of seconds before they were all on me. Just then I saw the cyclist start his ride down the cable.

There was really no other choice.

I took a running jump across the revolving floor and hopped the low rail just as the cyclist was zooming by on his downward trajectory. With a breathless leap, I was airborne, and a moment later I found myself dangling from the handlebars of the tiny cycle. The cycle was actually attached to the cable—everything in Vegas is fake—and my weight flipped the bicycle upside down, sending the surprised rider crashing to the gambling tables below.

The floor was coming up fast now. I let myself drop at the last minute and landed with a painful thud. I risked a glance up and saw Fat Boy standing at the rail of the lounge, slack-jawed. A team of hotel security guards came up behind him and knocked the gun out of his hand.

Smiling gamblers helped me up and patted me on the back for a job well done, and the crowd was whistling and clapping at what they assumed was another great Circus, Circus show. I spotted more guards coming my way and, without stopping to bow, wound my way through the dense crowd and out a side door.

I could hear the lingering applause as I jumped into a cab.

I kept glancing out the rear windshield as the cab proceeded up the Strip. My heart was still pounding when I got out at our hotel, but I felt a crazy kind of elation, too, and thought that maybe I now understood the thrill of sports like skydiving and mountain climbing.

The thrill dissipated as soon as I entered the lobby and saw a crowd gathering around the immense fountain that stood in the middle of the atrium. It was one of those hotels with the rooms set in cantilevered walls around an empty, central cylinder. From the lobby, you could look up and see the cascading levels of rooms all the way up to the great skylights in the roof.

I elbowed my way through the rubberneckers until I saw the body that floated in the now-reddish water. I instantly recognized the pink pineapples on his Hawaiian shirt. I looked up and spotted a couple of blue suits scanning the crowd, pressing earpieces into place and talking into their collars. Cautiously, I made my way back toward an exit.

I didn't need a closer look at the kid; our room had been on the eighteenth floor.

I sauntered slowly through the parking lot, head down but eyes peeled for signs of blue. I had to get out of there, but didn't know where to go. My stash of buy-money was back in the hotel safe and my belongings were still up in the room. I thought it best to walk away from the Strip and call a cab from some secluded pay phone.

I was nearly out of the lot when I spotted the kid's Mustang. I worked my way over to it, but didn't have the keys. I took a shot and felt around under the fenders for a hide-a-key and nearly whooped with joy when I found a little metal box attached near the rear wheel-well. The joy quickly faded, though, as I flicked open the latch and saw there was no key inside.

Instead, it was filled with photographic negatives.

A convoy of dark, late model sedans was pulling up in front of the hotel and I dropped to my knees. More blue suits got out and quickly spread across the area. At a furious crawl, I worked my way off the lot and jumped down into a drainage ravine that was concealed behind some brush. Thankfully, the ravine was dry and out of sight of the parking lot.

I got to my feet and ran like hell.

I've collected so many things in my life, it's sometimes hard to keep track. A strange compulsion, collecting. Coins and stamps. Comic books and baseball cards. Rare books and prints and lithographs. Signed and numbered with certificates of authenticity and always—especially—in limited editions.

The motel is well off the Strip. It's pretty run-down, but nothing is *too* grungy in Vegas. It's simply not allowed. On TV, Paul Muni's on the lam, nearing the end of his rope.

I didn't have time to examine the merchandise until I checked in. I registered as Mr. Verso. For the kid. My little joke.

I can't for the life of me—you should pardon the expression—figure out why Ray-Ban handed the white envelope over to me or why he even brought it along. He obviously had no intention of letting Mr. Piaget get away.

I've been staring at the pictures for hours. I know I said that I never much liked her, but she does sort of grow on you. It's something in the eyes; a visible weakness, a tender fragility that's hard to resist. The kid would have died for these shots.

Oh.

Anyway, from what I know, she must be about seventy now, but she looks younger. Not young, but attractive middle-aged. There are wrinkles and spots on her face and sags and stretch marks in her once taut flesh. Her tits look surprisingly good, though, and her hair is still dark. She wears it short, now. Befitting a woman of her years.

They're classic bondage shots. She's sitting on the floor in front of a nondescript backdrop. Her manacled arms are thrown back over her head, the chain draped across her shoulder and secured again at her ankles. Her legs are spread and you see all the things that you couldn't back in the fifties. The things that you so wanted to see, that were all the more exciting for being only suggested. Her head is tilted back and that beguiling Betty pout is strained, but it's there. As is the fragility.

Did they already have the pictures, or did they get them—get her—just for the kid? I'm sure they could have found her if they wanted to. No problem.

Maybe they let her go after. She's just an old lady now. Maybe one of them was a fan.

Yeah. Right.

As for what I found in the kid's metal box, it's quite an interesting little package he was trading for his goddess. The negatives look authentic to me, but then you can't really tell with the naked eye. I can't imagine where the kid got them. But he must have known or believed that they were fake. He was a pretty good salesman, though. He sold me and more importantly, he sold *them*.

I'm not entirely sure who *they* are, but I can guess. The negatives pretty much give it away.

There's only five of them and they're near-identical shots. Poorly taken with an obviously cheap camera. Russian, probably. Slightly overexposed, but in focus.

Elvis always looked good, at least he still did at that point in his life—1960 or 1961, I make it. Lean and hard, he was, with the haughtiness of a sovereign in his prime. The curled lip was still a dare and not just a parody.

Lee Harvey, on the other hand, always photographed as the weasel he was. Even with his arm around the King, posed and posing before the exquisite, bulbous minarets of the Kremlin, Oswald still looks like a creep.

Cameras don't lie.

Were the negatives worth killing for? I don't know. I don't know what they really mean or who would even believe them. I've tried thinking about the possibilities, but it just makes my head hurt.

I've collected so many objects and images. I've collected what I've dreamed about and what I've feared, living vicariously through my treasured things. And when I finished a collection, I always found a new one to begin. Limitless, like desire. Sealed in mylar and under glass, stored in acid-free boxes in vaults and cool, dry places.

Always owning, but never owning up.

"I steal," Paul Muni hisses, and the movie is over. I turn off the TV. I look again at the negatives and positives, and sigh.

And wait to be collected.

According to Neal and Janice Gregory's When Elvis Died, *the first recorded Elvis Sighting took place in 1988.*

The site of this historic occasion was Felpausch's Supermarket in Vicksburg, Michigan; a certain Louise Willing was "absolutely certain" she saw Elvis waiting in line at checkout counter Number 2.

Since then, Elvis Sightings have become as common as albino alligators slithering through the sewers of New York. And just as authentic. For what we're actually witnessing is a new wrinkle in the fabric of oral folklore, as Elvis Sightings shoulder aside other urban myths like the one about the harried babysitter who dried off a toddler by sticking it in a microwave oven.

That's almost as good as one about Old Man Elvis meeting up with the black JFK in this Texas retirement home . . .

JOE R. LANSDALE lives in the town of Nacogdoches, Texas. He's prolific and multigeneric; Joe's written many unique novels and short stories, including westerns (The Magic Wagon), *mysteries* (Cold in July), *and black comedies* (The Drive-In).

Critics like to cite Lansdale's ongoing fascination with the voices, geography, and culture of his Lone Star State. Me, I think Joe's fiction is funny. And macabre.

And, doggone it, a master of a venerable American tradition.

The Texas Tall Tale.

Well, Lansdale's outdone himself this time.

How many other Elvis stories do you know that come equipped with genuine Egyptian hieroglyphics?★

★ Hieroglyphics especially prepared for *The King Is Dead* by Mark A. Nelson.

Best hang onto your Stetsons, folks.
This one's a real humdinger.
The zaniest, craziest, full-tilt-over-the-top Dead Elvis yarn you're likely to encounter for a very long time.

(BUBBA HO-TEP)

(by Joe R. Lansdale)

(For Chet Williamson)

Elvis dreamed he had his dick out, checking to see if the bump on the head of it had filled with pus again. If it had, he was going to name the bump Priscilla, after his ex-wife, and bust it by jacking off. Or he liked to think that's what he'd do. Dreams let you think like that. The truth was, he hadn't had a hard-on in years.

That bitch, Priscilla. Gets a new hairdo and she's gone, just because she caught him fucking a big-tittied gospel singer. It wasn't like the singer had mattered. Priscilla ought to have understood that, so what was with her making a big deal out of it?

Was it because she couldn't hit a high note same and as good as the singer when she came?

When had that happened anyway, Priscilla leaving?

Yesterday? Last year? Ten years ago?

Oh God, it came to him instantly as he slipped out of sleep like a soft turd squeezed free of a loose asshole—for he could hardly think of himself or life in any context other than sewage, since so often he was too tired to do any thing other than let it all fly in his sleep, wake up in an ocean of piss or shit, waiting for the nurses or the aides to come in and wipe his ass. But now it came to him. Suddenly he realized it had been years ago that he had supposedly died, and longer years than that since Priscilla left, and how old was she anyway? Sixty-five? Seventy?

And how old was he?

Christ! He was almost convinced he was too old to be alive, and had to be dead, but he wasn't convinced enough, unfortunately. He knew where he was now, and in that moment of realization, he sincerely wished he were dead. This was worse than death.

From across the room, his roommate, Bull Thomas, bellowed and coughed and moaned and fell back into painful sleep, the cancer gnawing at his insides like a rat plugged up inside a watermelon.

Bull's bellow of pain and anger and indignation at growing old and diseased was the only thing bullish about him now, though Elvis had seen photographs of him when he was younger, and Bill had been very bullish indeed. Thick-chested, slab-faced, and tall. Probably thought he'd live forever, and happily. A boozing, pill-popping, swinging dick until the end of time.

Now Bill was shrunk down, was little more than a wrinkled sheet-white husk that throbbed with occasional pulses of blood while the carcinoma fed.

Elvis took hold of the bed's lift button, eased himself upright. He glanced at Bull. Bull was breathing heavily and his bony knees rose up and down like he was peddling a bicycle; his kneecaps punched feebly at the sheet, making puptents that rose up and collapsed, rose up and collapsed.

Elvis looked down at the sheet stretched over his own bony knees. He thought: *My God, how long have I been here? Am I really awake now, or am I dreaming I'm awake? How could my plans have gone so wrong? When are they going to serve lunch, and considering what they serve, why do I care? And if Priscilla discovered I was alive, would she come see me, would she want to see me, and would we still want to fuck, or would we have to merely talk about it? Is there finally, and really, anything to life other than food and shit and sex?*

Elvis pushed the sheet down to do what he had done in the dream. He pulled up his gown, leaned forward, and examined his dick. It was wrinkled and small. It didn't look like something that had dive-bombed movie starlet pussies or filled their mouths like a big zucchini or pumped forth a load of sperm frothy as cake icing. The healthiest thing about his pecker was the big red bump with the black ring around it and the pus-filled white center. Fact was, that bump kept growing, he was going to have to pull a chair up beside his bed and put a pillow in it so the bump would have some place to sleep at night. There was more pus in that damn bump than there was cum in his loins. Yep. The old diddlebopper was no longer a flesh cannon loaded for bare ass. It was a peanut too small to harvest; wasting away on the vine. His nuts were a couple of darkening, about-to-rot grapes, too limp to produce juice for life's wine. His legs were stick and paper things with overlarge, vein-swollen feet on the ends. His belly was such a bloat, it was a pain for him to lean forward and scrutinize his dick and balls.

Pulling his gown down and the sheet back over himself, Elvis leaned back and wished he had a peanut butter and banana sandwich fried in butter. There had been a time when he and his crew would board his private jet and fly clean across country just to have a special made fried peanut butter and nanner sandwich. He could still taste the damn things.

Elvis closed his eyes and thought he would awake from a bad dream, but didn't. He opened his eyes again, slowly, and saw that he was still where he had been, and things were no better. He reached over and opened his dresser drawer and got out a little round mirror and looked at himself.

He was horrified. His hair was white as salt and had receded dramatically. He had wrinkles deep enough to conceal outstretched earthworms, the big ones, the night crawlers. His pouty mouth no longer appeared pouty. It looked like the dropping wattles of a bulldog, seeming more that way because he was slobbering a mite. He dragged his tired tongue across his lips to daub the slobber, revealed to himself in the mirror that he was missing a lot of teeth.

Goddamn it! How had he gone from King of Rock and Roll to this? Old guy in a rest home in East Texas with a growth on his dick?

And what was that growth? Cancer? No one was talking. No one seemed to know. Perhaps the bump was a manifestation of the mistakes of his life, so many of them made with his dick.

He considered on that. Did he ask himself this question everyday, or just now and then? Time sort of ran together when the last moment and the immediate moment and the moment forthcoming were all alike.

Shit, when was lunchtime? Had he slept through it?

Was it about time for his main nurse again? The good-looking one with the smooth chocolate skin and tits like grapefruits. The one who came in and sponge-bathed him and held his pitiful little pecker in her gloved hands and put salve on his canker with all the enthusiasm of a mechanic oiling a defective part?

He hoped not. That was the worst of it. A doll like that handling him without warmth or emotion. Twenty years ago, just twenty, he could have made with the curled lip smile and had her eating out of his asshole. Where had his youth gone? Why hadn't fame sustained old age and death, and why had he left his fame in the first place, and did he want it back, and could he have it back, and if he could, would it make any difference?

And finally, when he was evacuated from the bowels of life into the toilet bowl of the beyond and was flushed, would the great sewer pipe flow him to the other side where God would—in the guise of a great all-seeing turd with corn kernel eyes—be waiting with open turd arms, and would there be among the sewage his mother (bless her fat little heart) and father and friends, waiting with fried peanut butter and nanner sandwiches and ice cream cones, predigested, of course?

He was reflecting on this, pondering the afterlife, when Bull gave out with a hell of a scream, pouched his eyes damn near out of his head, arched his back, grease-farted like a blast from Gabriel's trumpet, and checked his tired old soul out of the Mud Creek Shady Rest Convalescent Home; flushed it on out and across the great shitty beyond.

Later that day, Elvis lay sleeping, his lips fluttering the bad taste of lunch—steamed zucchini and boiled peas—out of his belly. He awoke to a noise, rolled over to see a young attractive woman cleaning out Bull's dresser drawer. The curtains over the window next to Bull's bed were pulled wide open, and the sunlight was cutting through it and showing her to great advantage. She was blond and Nordic-featured and her long hair was tied back with a big red bow and she wore big gold hoop earrings that shimmered in the sunlight. She was dressed in a white blouse and a short black skirt and dark hose and high heels. The heels made her ass ride up beneath her skirt like soft bald baby heads under a thin blanket.

She had a big yellow plastic trash can and she had one of Bull's dresser drawers pulled out, and she was picking through it, like a magpie looking for bright things. She found a few—coins, a pocketknife, a cheap watch. These were plucked free and laid on the dresser top, then the remaining contents of the drawer—Bull's photographs of himself when young, a rotten pack of rubbers (wishful thinking never deserted Bull), a Bronze Star and a Purple Heart from his performance in the Vietnam War—were dumped into the trash can with a bang and a flutter.

Elvis got hold of his bed lift button and raised himself for a better look. The woman had her back to him now, and didn't notice. She was replacing the dresser drawer and pulling out another. It was full of clothes. She took out the few shirts and pants and socks and underwear, and laid them on Bull's bed—remade now, and minus Bull, who had been toted off to be taxidermied, embalmed, burned up, whatever.

"You're gonna toss that stuff," Elvis said. "Could I have one of them pictures of Bull? Maybe that Purple Heart? He was proud of it."

The young woman turned and looked at him. "I suppose," she said. She went to the trash can and bent over it and showed her black panties to Elvis as she rummaged. He knew the revealing of her panties was neither intentional or unintentional. She just didn't give a damn. She saw him as so physically and sexually nonthreatening, she didn't mind if he got a bird's eye view of her; it was the same to her as a house cat sneaking a peek.

Elvis observed the thin panties straining and slipping into the caverns of her ass cheeks and felt his pecker flutter once, like a bird having a heart attack, then it lay down and remained limp and still.

Well, these days, even a flutter was kind of reassuring.

The woman surfaced from the trash can with a photo and the Purple Heart, went over to Elvis's bed, and handed them to him.

Elvis dangled the ribbon that held the Purple Heart between his fingers, said, "Bull your kin?"

"My daddy," she said.

"I haven't seen you here before."

"Only been here once before," she said. "When I checked him in."

"Oh," Elvis said. "That was three years ago, wasn't it?"

"Yeah. Were you and him friends?"

Elvis considered the question. He didn't know the real answer. All he knew was Bull listened to him when he said he was Elvis Presley and seemed to believe him. If he didn't believe him, he at least had the courtesy not to patronize. Bull always called him Elvis, and before Bull grew too ill, he always played cards and checkers with him.

"Just roommates," Elvis said. "He didn't feel good enough to say much. I just sort of hated to see what was left of him go away so easy. He was an all right guy. He mentioned you a lot. You're Callie, right?"

"Yeah," she said. "Well, he was all right."

"Not enough you came and saw him though."

"Don't try to put some guilt trip on me, mister. I did what I could. Hadn't been for Medicaid, Medicare, whatever that stuff was, he'd have been in a ditch somewhere. I didn't have the money to take care of him."

Elvis thought of his own daughter, lost long ago to him. If she knew he lived, would she come to see him? Would she care? He feared knowing the answer.

"You could have come and seen him," Elvis said.

"I was busy. Mind your own business. Hear?"

The chocolate-skin nurse with the grapefruit tits came in. Her white uniform crackled like cards being shuffled. Her little white nurse-hat was tilted on her head in a way that said she loved mankind and made good money and was getting regular dick. She smiled at Callie and then at Elvis. "How are you this morning, Mr. Haff?"

"All right," Elvis said. "But I prefer Mr. Presley. Or Elvis. I keep telling you that. I don't go by Sebastian Haff anymore. I don't try to hide anymore."

"Why, of course," said the pretty nurse. "I knew that. I forgot. Good morning, Elvis."

Her voice dripped with sorghum syrup. Elvis wanted to hit her with his bedpan.

The nurse said to Callie: "Did you know we have a celebrity here, Miss Jones? Elvis Presley. You know, the rock and roll singer?"

"I've heard of him," Callie said. "I thought he was dead."

Callie went back to the dresser and squatted and set to work on the bottom drawer. The nurse looked at Elvis and smiled again, only she spoke to Callie. "Well, actually, Elvis is dead, and Mr. Haff knows that, don't you, Mr. Haff?"

"Hell no," said Elvis. "I'm right here. I ain't dead, yet."

"Now, Mr. Haff, I don't mind calling you Elvis, but you're a little confused, or like to play sometimes. You were an Elvis impersonator. Remember? You fell off a stage and broke your hip. What was it . . .

Twenty years ago? It got infected and you went into a coma for a few years. You came out with a few problems."

"I was impersonating myself," Elvis said. "I couldn't do nothing else. I haven't got any problems. You're trying to say my brain is messed up, aren't you?"

Callie quit cleaning out the bottom drawer of the dresser. She was interested now, and though it was no use, Elvis couldn't help but try and explain who he was, just one more time. The explaining had become a habit, like wanting to smoke a cigar long after the enjoyment of it was gone.

"I got tired of it all," he said. "I got on drugs, you know. I wanted out. Fella named Sebastian Haff, an Elvis imitator, the best of them. He took my place. He had a bad heart and he liked drugs too. It was him died, not me. I took his place."

"Why would you want to leave all that fame," Callie said, "all that money?" and she looked at the nurse, like, "Let's humor the old fart for a lark."

" 'Cause it got old. Woman I loved, Priscilla, she was gone. Rest of the women . . . were just women. The music wasn't mine anymore. *I* wasn't even me anymore. I was this thing they made up. Friends were sucking me dry. I got away and liked it, left all the money with Sebastian, except for enough to sustain me if things got bad. We had a deal, me and Sebastian. When I wanted to come back, he'd let me. It was all written up in a contract in case he wanted to give me a hard time, got to liking my life too good. Thing was, copy of the contract I had got lost in a trailer fire. . . . I was living simple. Way Haff had been. Going from town to town doing the Elvis act. Only I felt like I was really me again. Can you dig that?"

"We're digging it, Mr. Haff . . . Mr. Presley," said the pretty nurse.

"I was singing the old way. Doing some new songs. Stuff I wrote. I was getting attention on a small but good scale. Women throwing themselves at me, 'cause they could imagine I was Elvis, only I was Elvis, playing Sebastian Haff playing Elvis . . . It was all pretty good. I didn't mind the contract being burned up. I didn't even try to go back and convince anybody. Then I had the accident. Like I was saying, I'd laid up a little money in case of illness, stuff like that. That's what's paying for here. These nice facilities. Ha!"

"Now, Elvis," the nurse said. "Don't carry it too far. You may just get way out there and not come back."

"Oh fuck you," Elvis said.

The nurse giggled.

Shit, Elvis thought. *Get old, you can't even cuss somebody and have it bother them. Everything you do is either worthless or sadly amusing.*

"You know, Elvis," said the pretty nurse, "we have a Mr. Dillinger here too. And a President Kennedy. He says the bullet only wounded him and his brain is in a fruit jar at the White House, hooked up to some wires and a battery, and as long as the battery works, he can walk around without it. His brain, that is. You know, he says everyone was in on trying to assassinate him. Even Elvis Presley."

"You're an asshole," Elvis said.

"I'm not trying to hurt your feelings, Mr. Haff," the nurse said. "I'm merely trying to give you a reality check."

"You can shove that reality check right up your pretty black ass," Elvis said.

The nurse made a sad little snicking sound. "Mr. Haff, Mr. Haff. Such language."

"What happened to get you here?" said Callie. "Say you fell off a stage?"

"I was gyrating," Elvis said. "Doing 'Blue Moon,' but my hip went out. I'd been having trouble with it." Which was quite true. He'd sprained it making love to a blue-haired old lady who had ELVIS tattooed in a heart on her fat ass. He couldn't help himself from wanting to fuck her. She'd looked like his mother, Gladys.

"You swiveled right off the stage?" Callie said. "Now that's sexy."

Elvis looked at her. She was smiling. This was great fun for her, listening to some nut tell a tale. She hadn't had this much fun since she put her old man in the rest home.

"Oh, leave me the hell alone," Elvis said.

The women smiled at one another, passing a private joke. Callie said to the nurse: "I've got what I want." She scraped the bright things off the top of Bull's dresser into her purse. "The clothes can go to Goodwill or the Salvation Army."

The pretty nurse nodded to Callie. "Very well. And I'm very sorry about your father. He was a nice man."

"Yeah," said Callie, and she started out of there. She paused at the foot of Elvis's bed. "Nice to meet you, Mr. Presley."

"Get the hell on," Elvis said.

"Now, now," said the pretty nurse, patting his foot through the covers, as if it were a little cantankerous dog. "I'll be back later to do that . . . little thing that has to be done. You know?"

"I know," Elvis said, not liking the words "little thing."

Callie and the nurse started away then, punishing him with the clean lines of their faces and the sheen of their hair, the jiggle of their asses and tits. When they were out of sight, Elvis heard them laugh about something in the hall, then they were gone, and Elvis felt as if he were on the far side of Pluto without a jacket. He picked up the ribbon with the Purple Heart and looked at it.

Poor Bull. In the end, did anything really matter?

Meanwhile . . .

The earth swirled around the sun like a spinning turd in a toilet bowl (to keep up with Elvis's metaphors) and the good old abused earth clicked about on its axis and the hole in the ozone spread slightly wider, like a shy lady fingering open her vagina, and the South American trees that had stood for centuries were visited by the dozer the chainsaw and the match, and they rose up in burned black puffs that expanded and dissipated into minuscule wisps, and while the puffs of smoke dissolved, there were IRA bombings in London, and there was more war in the Mideast. Blacks died in Africa of famine, the HIV virus infected a million more, the Dallas Cowboys lost again, and that Ole Blue Moon that Elvis and Patsy Cline sang so well about, swung around the earth and came in close and rose over the Shady Rest Convalescent Home, shone its bittersweet silver-blue rays down on the joint like a flashlight beam shining through a blue-haired lady's do, and inside the rest home, evil waddled about like a duck looking for a spot to squat, and Elvis rolled over in his sleep and awoke with the intense desire to pee.

All right, thought Elvis. *This time I make it.* No more piss or crap in the bed. (Famous last words.)

Elvis sat up and hung his feet over the side of the bed and the bed swung far to the left and around the ceiling and back, and then it wasn't moving at all. The dizziness passed.

Elvis looked at his walker and sighed, leaned forward, took hold of the grips and eased himself off the bed and clumped the rubber padded tips forward, made for the toilet.

He was in the process of milking his bump-swollen weasel, when he heard something in the hallway. A kind of scrambling, like a big spider scuttling about in a box of gravel.

There was always some sound in the hallway, people coming and going, yelling in pain or confusion, but this time of night, 3 A.M. was normally quite dead.

It shouldn't have concerned him, but the truth of the matter was, now that he was up and had successfully pissed in the pot, he was no longer sleepy; he was still thinking about that bimbo, Callie, and the nurse (what the hell was her name?) with the tits like grapefruits, and all they had said.

Elvis stumped his walker backward out of the bathroom, turned it, made his way forward into the hall. The hall was semidark, with every other light cut, and the lights that were on were dimmed to a watery egg yoke yellow. The black and white tile floor looked like a great chessboard, waxed and buffed for the next game of life, and here he was, a semicrippled pawn, ready to go.

Off in the far wing of the home, Old Lady McGee, better known in the home as The Blue Yodeler, broke into one of her famous yodels (she claimed to have sung with a country and western band in her youth) then ceased abruptly. Elvis swung the walker forward and moved on. He hadn't been out of his room in ages, and he hadn't been out of his bed much either. Tonight, he felt invigorated because he hadn't pissed his bed, and he'd heard the sound again, the spider in the box of gravel. (Big spider. Big box. Lots of gravel.) And following the sound gave him something to do.

Elvis rounded the corner, beads of sweat popping out on his forehead like heat blisters. Jesus. He wasn't invigorated now. Thinking about how invigorated he was had bushed him. Still, going back to his room to lie on his bed and wait for morning so he could wait for noon, then afternoon and night, didn't appeal to him.

He went by Jack McLaughlin's room, the fellow who was convinced he was John F. Kennedy, and that his brain was in the White House running on batteries. The door to Jack's room was open. Elvis peeked in as he moved by, knowing full well that Jack might not want to see him.

Sometimes he accepted Elvis as the real Elvis, and when he did, he got scared, saying it was Elvis who had been behind the assassination.

Actually, Elvis hoped he felt that way tonight. It would at least be some acknowledgment that he was who he was, even if the acknowledgment was a fearful shriek from a nut.

Course, Elvis thought, *maybe I'm nuts too. Maybe I am Sebastian Haff and I fell off the stage and broke more than my hip, cracked some part of my brain that lost my old self and made me think I'm Elvis.*

No. He couldn't believe that. That's the way they wanted him to think. They wanted him to believe he was nuts and he wasn't Elvis, just some sad old fart who had once lived out part of another man's life because he had none of his own.

He wouldn't accept that. He wasn't Sebastian Haff. He was Elvis Goddamn Aaron Fucking Presley with a boil on his dick.

Course, he believed that, maybe he ought to believe Jack was John F. Kennedy, and Mums Delay, another patient here at Shady Rest, was Dillinger. Then again, maybe not. They were kind of scanty on evidence. He at least looked like Elvis gone old and sick. Jack was black— he claimed The Powers That Be had dyed him that color to keep him hidden—and Mums was a woman who claimed she'd had a sex change operation.

Jesus, was this a rest home or a nut house?

Jack's room was one of the special kind. He didn't have to share. He had money from somewhere. The room was packed with books and little luxuries. And though Jack could walk well, he even had a fancy electric wheelchair that he rode about in sometimes. Once, Elvis had seen him riding it around the outside circular drive, popping wheelies and spinning doughnuts.

When Elvis looked into Jack's room, he saw him lying on the floor. Jack's gown was pulled up around his neck, and his bony black ass appeared to be made of licorice in the dim light. Elvis figured Jack had been on his way to the shitter, or was coming back from it, and had collapsed. His heart, maybe.

"Jack," Elvis said.

Elvis clumped into the room, positioned his walker next to Jack, took a deep breath and stepped out of it, supporting himself with one side of it. He got down on his knees beside Jack, hoping he'd be able to get up again. God, but his knees and back hurt.

Jack was breathing hard. Elvis noted the scar at Jack's hairline, a long scar that made Jack's skin lighter there, almost gray. ("That's where they took the brain out," Jack always explained, "put it in that fucking jar. I got a little bag of sand up there now.")

Elvis touched the old man's shoulder. "Jack. Man, you okay?"

No response.

Elvis tried again. "Mr. Kennedy."

"Uh," said Jack (Mr. Kennedy).

"Hey, man. You're on the floor," Elvis said.

"No shit? Who are you?"

Elvis hesitated. This wasn't the time to get Jack worked up.

"Sebastian," he said. "Sebastian Haff."

Elvis took hold of Jack's shoulder and rolled him over. It was about as difficult as rolling a jelly roll. Jack lay on his back now. He strayed an eyeball at Elvis. He started to speak, hesitated. Elvis took hold of Jack's nightgown and managed to work it down around Jack's knees, trying to give the old fart some dignity.

Jack finally got his breath. "Did you see him go by in the hall? He scuttled like."

"Who?"

"Someone they sent."

"Whose they?"

"You know. Lyndon Johnson. Castro. They've sent someone to finish me. I think maybe it was Johnson himself. Real ugly. Real goddamn ugly."

"Johnson's dead," Elvis said.

"That won't stop him," Jack said.

Later that morning, sunlight shooting into Elvis's room through venetian blinds, Elvis put his hands behind his head and considered the night before while the pretty black nurse with the grapefruit tits salved his dick. He had reported Jack's fall and the aides had come to help Jack back in bed, and him back on his walker. He had clumped back to his room (after being scolded for being out there that time of night) feeling that an air of strangeness had blown into the rest home, an air that wasn't there as short as the day before. It was at low ebb now, but certainly still present, humming in the background like some kind of generator ready to buzz up to a higher notch at a moment's notice.

And he was certain it wasn't just his imagination. The scuttling sound he'd heard last night, Jack had heard it too. What was that all about? It wasn't the sound of a walker or a crip dragging his foot or a wheelchair creeping along, it was something else, and now that he thought about it, it wasn't exactly spider legs in gravel, more like a roll of barbed wire tumbling across tile.

Elvis was so wrapped up in these considerations, he lost awareness of the nurse until she said, "Mr. Haff!"

"What . . ." and he saw that she was smiling and looking down at her hands. He looked too. There, nestled in one of her gloved palms was a massive, blue-veined hooter with a pus-filled bump on it the size of a pecan. It was his hooter and his pus-filled bump.

"You ole rascal," she said, and gently lowered his dick between his legs. "I think you better take a cold shower, Mr. Haff."

Elvis was amazed. That was the first time in years he'd had a boner like that. What gave here?

Then he realized what gave. He wasn't thinking about not being able to do it. He was thinking about something that interested him, and now, with something clicking around inside his head besides old memories and confusions, concerns about his next meal and going to the crapper, he had been given a dose of life again. He grinned his gums and what teeth were in them at the nurse.

"You get in there with me," he said, "and I'll take that shower."

"You silly thing," she said, and pulled his nightgown down and stood and removed her plastic gloves and dropped them in the trash can beside his bed.

"Why don't you pull on it a little," Elvis said.

"You ought to be ashamed," the nurse said, but she smiled when she said it.

She left the room door open after she left. This concerned Elvis a little, but he felt his bed was at such an angle no one could look in, and if they did, tough luck. He wasn't going to look a gift hard-on in the pee-hole. He pulled the sheet over him and pushed his hands beneath the sheets and got his gown pulled up over his belly. He took hold of his snake and began to choke it with one hand, running his thumb over the pus-filled bump. With his other hand, he fondled his balls. He thought of Priscilla and the pretty black nurse and Bull's daughter and even the blue-haired fat lady with ELVIS tattooed on her butt, and he stroked harder and faster, and goddamn but he got stiffer and stiffer, and the bump on his cock gave up its load first, exploded hot pus down his thighs, and then his balls, which he thought forever empty, filled up with juice and electricity, and finally he threw the switch. The dam broke and the juice flew. He heard himself scream happily and felt hot wetness jetting down his legs, splattering as far as his big toes.

"Oh God," he said softly. "I like that. I like that."

He closed his eyes and slept. And for the first time in a long time, not fitfully.

Lunchtime. The Shady Rest lunch room.

Elvis sat with a plate of steamed carrots and broccoli and flaky roast beef in front of him. A dry roll, a pat of butter, and a short glass of milk soldiered on the side. It was not inspiring.

Next to him, The Blue Yodeler was stuffing a carrot up her nose while she expounded on the sins of God, the Heavenly Father, for knocking up that nice Mary in her sleep, slipping up her ungreased poontang while she snored, and—bless her little heart—not even knowing it, or getting a clit throb from it, but waking up with a belly full of a baby and no memory of action.

Elvis had heard it all before. It used to offend him, this talk of God as rapist, but he'd heard it so much now he didn't care. She rattled on.

Across the way, an old man who wore a black mask and sometimes a white Stetson, known to residents and staff alike as Kemosabe, snapped one of his two capless cap pistols at the floor and called for an invisible Tonto to bend over so he could drive him home.

At the far end of the table, Dillinger was talking about how much whiskey he used to drink, and how many cigars he used to smoke before he got his dick cut off at the stump and split so he could become a she and hide out as a woman. Now she said she no longer thought of banks and machine guns, women and fine cigars. She now thought about spots on dishes, the colors of curtains and drapes as coordinated with carpets and walls.

Even as the depression of his surroundings settled over him again, Elvis deliberated last night, and glanced down the length of the table at Jack (Mr. Kennedy), who headed its far end. He saw the old man was looking at him, as if they shared a secret. Elvis's ill mood dropped a notch; a real mystery was at work here, and come nightfall, he was going to investigate.

Swing the Shady Rest Convalescent Home's side of the earth away from the sun again, and swing the moon in close and blue again. Blow some gauzy clouds across the nasty black sky. Now ease on into 3 A.M.

Elvis awoke with a start and turned his head toward the intrusion. Jack stood next to the bed looking down at him. Jack was wearing a suit coat over his nightgown and he had on thick glasses. He said, "Sebastian. It's loose."

Elvis collected his thoughts, pasted them together into a not too scattered collage. "What's loose?"

"It," said Sebastian. "Listen."

Elvis listened. Out in the hall he heard the scuttling sound of the night before. Tonight, it reminded him of great locusts' wings beating frantically inside a small cardboard box, the tips of them scratching at the cardboard, cutting it, ripping it apart.

"Jesus Christ, what is it?" Elvis said.

"I thought it was Lyndon Johnson, but it isn't. I've come across new evidence that suggests another assassin."

"Assassin?"

Jack cocked an ear. The sound had gone away, moved distant, then ceased.

"It's got another target tonight," said Jack. "Come on. I want to show you something. I don't think it's safe if you go back to sleep."

"For Christ sake," Elvis said. "Tell the administrators."

"The suits and the white starches," Jack said. "No thanks. I trusted them back when I was in Dallas, and look where that got my brain and me. I'm thinking with sand here, maybe picking up a few waves from my brain. Someday, who's to say they won't just disconnect the battery at the White House?"

"That's something to worry about, all right," Elvis said.

"Listen here," Jack said. "I know you're Elvis, and there were rumors, you know . . . about how you hated me, but I've thought it over. You hated me, you could have finished me the other night. All I want from you is to look me in the eye and assure me you had nothing to do with that day in Dallas, and that you never knew Lee Harvey Oswald or Jack Ruby."

Elvis stared at him as sincerely as possible. "I had nothing to do with Dallas, and I knew neither Lee Harvey Oswald or Jack Ruby."

"Good," said Jack. "May I call you Elvis instead of Sebastian?"

"You may."

"Excellent. You wear glasses to read?"

"I wear glasses when I really want to see," Elvis said.

"Get 'em and come on."

Elvis swung his walker along easily, not feeling as if he needed it too much tonight. He was excited. Jack was a nut, and maybe he himself was nuts, but there was an adventure going on.

They came to the hall rest room. The one reserved for male visitors. "In here," Jack said.

"Now, wait a minute," Elvis said. "You're not going to get me in there and try and play with my pecker, are you?"

Jack stared at him. "Man, I made love to Jackie and Marilyn and a ton of others, and you think I want to play with your nasty ole dick?"

"Good point," said Elvis.

They went into the rest room. It was large, with several stalls and urinals.

"Over here," said Jack. He went over to one of the stalls and pushed open the door and stood back by the commode to make room for Elvis's walker. Elvis eased inside and looked at what Jack was now pointing to.

Graffiti.

"That's it?" Elvis said. "We're investigating a scuttling in the hall, trying to discover who attacked you last night, and you bring me in here to show me stick pictures on the shit house wall?"

"Look close," Jack said.

Elvis leaned forward. His eyes weren't what they used to be, and his glasses probably needed to be upgraded, but he could see that instead of writing, the graffiti was a series of simple pictorials.

A thrill, like a shot of good booze, ran through Elvis. He had once been a fanatic reader of ancient and esoteric lore, like *The Egyptian Book of the Dead* and *The Complete Works of H. P. Lovecraft,* and straight away he recognized what he was staring at. "Egyptian hieroglyphics," he said.

"Right-a-reen-O," Jack said. "Hey, you're not as stupid as some folks made you out."

"Thanks," Elvis said.

Jack reached into his suit coat pocket and took out a folded piece of paper and unfolded it. He pressed it to the wall. Elvis saw that it was covered with the same sort of figures that were on the wall of the stall.

"I copied this down yesterday. I came in here to shit because they hadn't cleaned up my bathroom. I saw this on the wall, went back to my room, and looked it up in my books and wrote it all down. The top line translates something like: *Pharaoh gobbles donkey goober.* And the bottom line is: *Cleopatra does the dirty.*"

"What?"

"Well, pretty much," Jack said.

Elvis was mystified. "All right," he said. "There's scuttling in the hall and one of the nuts here, present company excluded, thinks he's Tutankhamen or something, and he writes on the wall in hieroglyphics. So what? I mean, what's the connection? Why are we hanging out in a toilet?"

"I don't know how they connect exactly," Jack said. "Not yet. But this . . . thing, it caught me asleep last night, and I came awake just in time to . . . well, he had me on the floor and had his mouth over my asshole."

"A shit eater?" Elvis said.

"I don't think so," Jack said. "He was after my soul. You can get that out of any of the major orifices in a person's body. I've read about it."

"Where?" Elvis asked. *"Hustler?"*

"The Everyday Man or Woman's Book of the Soul" by David Webb. It has some pretty good movie reviews about stolen soul movies in the back too."

"Oh, that sounds trustworthy," Elvis said.

They went back to Jack's room and sat on his bed and looked through his many books on astrology, the Kennedy assassination, and a number of esoteric tomes, including the philosophy book *The Everyday Man or Woman's Book of the Soul.*

Elvis found that book fascinating in particular; it indicated that not only did humans have a soul, but that the soul could be stolen, and there was a section concerning vampires and ghouls and incubi and succubi, as well as related soul suckers. Bottom line was, one of those dudes was around, you had to watch your holes. Mouth hole. Nose hole. Asshole. If you were a woman, you needed to watch a different hole. Dick pee holes and ear holes—male or female—didn't matter. The soul didn't hang out there. They weren't considered major orifices for some reason.

In the back of the book was a list of items, related and not related to the book, that you could buy. Little plastic pyramids. Hats you could wear while channeling. Subliminal tapes that would help you learn Arabic. Postage was paid.

"Every kind of soul eater is in that book except politicians and science fiction fans," Jack said. "And I think that's what we got here in Shady Rest. A soul eater. Turn to the Egyptian section."

Elvis did. The chapter was prefaced by a movie still from the *Ten Commandments* with Yul Brynner playing Pharaoh. He was standing up in his chariot looking serious, which seemed a fair enough expression, considering the Red Sea, which had been parted by Moses, was about to come back together and drown him and his army.

Elvis read the article slowly while Jack heated hot water with his plug-in heater and made cups of instant coffee. "I get my niece to smuggle this stuff in," said Jack. "Or she claims to be my niece. She's a black woman. I never saw her before I was shot that day in Dallas and they took my brain out. She's part of the new identity they've given me. She's got a great ass."

"Damn," said Elvis. "What it says here, is that you can bury some dude, and if he gets the right tanna leaves and spells said over him and such bullshit, he can come back to life some thousands of years later, and to stay alive, he has to suck on the souls of the living, and that if the souls are small, his life force doesn't last long. Small. What's that mean?"

"Read on . . . No, never mind, I'll tell you." Jack handed Elvis his cup of coffee and sat down on the bed next to him. "Before I do, want a

Ding Dong? Not mine. The chocolate kind. Well, I guess mine is chocolate, now that I've been dyed."

"You got Ding Dongs?" Elvis asked.

"Couple of Pay Day's and Baby Ruth too," Jack said. "Which will it
be? Let's get decadent."

Elvis licked his lips. "I'll have a Ding Dong."

While Elvis savored the Ding Dong, gumming it sloppily, sipping his
coffee between bites, Jack, coffee cup balanced on his knee, a Baby Ruth
in one mitt, expounded.

"Small souls means those without much fire for life," Jack said. "You
know, a place like that?"

"If souls were fires," Elvis said, "they couldn't burn much lower
without being out than here. Only thing we got going in this joint is the
pilot light."

"Exactamundo," Jack said. "What we got here in Shady Rest is an
Egyptian soul sucker of some sort. A mummy hiding out, coming in
here to feed on the sleeping. It's perfect, you see. The souls are little, and
don't provide him with much. If this thing comes back two or three
times in a row to wrap his lips around some elder's asshole, that elder is
going to die pretty soon, and who's the wiser? Our mummy may not be
getting much energy out of this, way he would with big souls, but the
prey is easy. A mummy couldn't be too strong, really. Mostly just husk.
But we're pretty much that way ourselves. We're not too far off being
mummies."

"And with new people coming in all the time," Elvis said, "he can
keep this up forever, this soul robbing."

"That's right. Because that's what we're brought here for. To get us
out of the way until we die. And the ones don't die first of disease, or
just plain old age, he gets."

Elvis considered all that. "That's why he doesn't bother the nurses and
aides and administrators? He can go unsuspected."

"That, and they're not asleep. He has to get you when you're sleeping
or unconscious."

"All right, but the thing throws me, Jack, is how does an ancient
Egyptian end up in an East Texas rest home, and why is he writing on
shit house walls?"

"He went to take a crap, got bored, and wrote on the wall. He
probably wrote on pyramid walls, centuries ago."

"What would he crap?" Elvis said. "It's not like he'd eat, is it?"

"He eats souls," Jack said, "so I assume, he craps soul residue. And what that means to me is you die by his mouth, you don't go to the other side, or wherever souls go. He digests the souls till they don't exist anymore—"

"And you're just so much toilet water decoration," Elvis said.

"That's the way I've got it worked out," Jack said. "He's just like anyone else when he wants to take a dump. He likes a nice clean place with a flush. They didn't have that in his time, and I'm sure he finds it handy. The writing on the walls is just habit. Maybe, to him, Pharaoh and Cleopatra were just yesterday."

Elvis finished off the Ding Dong and sipped his coffee. He felt a rush from the sugar and he loved it. He wanted to ask Jack for the Pay Day he had mentioned, but restrained himself. Sweets, fried foods, late nights, and drugs, had been the beginning of his original downhill spiral. He had to keep himself collected this time. He had to be ready to battle the Egyptian soul-sucking menace.

Soul-sucking menace?

God. He *was* really bored. It was time for him to go back to his room and to bed so he could shit on himself, get back to normal.

But Jesus and Ra, this was different from what had been going on up until now! It might all be bullshit, but considering what was going on in his life right now, it was absorbing bullshit. It might be worth playing the game to the hilt, even if he was playing it with a black guy who thought he was John F. Kennedy and believed an Egyptian mummy was stalking the corridors of Shady Rest Convalescent Home, writing graffiti on toilet stalls, and sucking people's souls out through their assholes, digesting them, crapping them down the visitors' toilet.

Suddenly Elvis was pulled out of his considerations. There came from the hall the noise again. The sound that each time he heard it reminded him of something different. This time it was dried corn husks being rattled in a high wind. He felt goose bumps travel up his spine and the hairs on the back of his neck and arms stood up. He leaned forward and put his hands on his walker and pulled himself upright.

"Don't go in the hall," Jack said.

"I'm not asleep."

"That doesn't mean *it* won't hurt you."

"*It,* my ass. There isn't any mummy from Egypt."

"Nice knowing you, Elvis."

Elvis inched the walker forward. He was halfway to the open door when he spied the figure in the hallway.

As the thing came even with the doorway, the hall lights went dim and sputtered. Twisting about the apparition, like pet crows, were flutters of shadows. The thing walked and stumbled, shuffled and flowed. Its legs moved like Elvis's own, meaning not too good, and yet, there was something about its locomotion that was impossible to identify. Stiff, but ghostly smooth. It was dressed in nasty-looking jeans, a black shirt, a black cowboy hat that came down so low it covered where the thing's eyebrows should be. It wore cowboy boots, and they were large with the toes curled up, and there came from the thing a kind of mixed-stench: a compost pile of mud, rotting leaves, resin, spoiled fruit, dry dust, and gassy sewage.

Elvis found that he couldn't scoot ahead another inch. He froze. The thing stopped and cautiously turned its head on its apple stem neck and looked at Elvis with empty eye sockets, revealing that it was, in fact, uglier than Lyndon Johnson.

Surprisingly, Elvis found he was surging forward as if on a zooming camera dolly, and that he was plunging into the thing's right eye socket, which swelled speedily to the dimensions of a vast canyon bottomed by blackness.

Down Elvis went, spinning and spinning, and out of the emptiness rushed resin-scented memories of pyramids and boats on a river, hot blue skies, and a great silver bus lashed hard by black rain, a crumbling bridge and a charge of dusky water and a gleam of silver. Then there was a darkness so caliginous it was beyond being called dark, and Elvis could feel and taste mud in his mouth and a sensation of claustrophobia beyond expression. And he could perceive the thing's hunger, a hunger that prodded him like hot pins, and then—

—there came a *popping sound* in rapid succession, and Elvis felt himself whirling even faster, spinning backward out of that deep memory canyon of the dusty head, and now he stood once again within the framework of his walker, and the mummy—for Elvis no longer denied to himself that it was such—turned its head away and began to move again, to shuffle, to flow, to stumble, to glide, down the hall, its pet shadows screeching with rusty throats around its head. *Pop! Pop! Pop!*

As the thing moved on Elvis compelled himself to lift his walker and advance into the hall. Jack slipped up beside him, and they saw the mummy in cowboy clothes traveling toward the exit door at the back of the home. When it came to the locked door, it leaned against where the door met the jam and twisted and writhed, squeezed through the invisible crack where the two connected. Its shadows pursued it, as if sucked through by a vacuum cleaner.

The popping sound went on, and Elvis turned his head in that direction, and there, in his mask, his double concho-studded holster belted around his waist, was Kemosabe, a silver Fanner Fifty in either hand. He was popping caps rapidly at where the mummy had departed, the black spotted red rolls flowing out from behind the hammers of his revolvers in smoky relay.

"Asshole!" Kemosabe said. "Asshole!"

And then Kemosabe quivered, dropped both hands, and popped a cap from each gun toward the ground, stiffened, collapsed.

Elvis knew he was dead of a ruptured heart before he hit the black and white tile; gone down and out with both guns blazing, soul intact.

The hall lights trembled back to normal.

The administrators, the nurses, and the aides came then. They rolled Kemosabe over and drove their palms against his chest, but he didn't breathe again. No more Hi-yo Silver. They sighed over him and clucked their tongues, and finally an aide reached over and lifted Kemosabe's mask, pulled it off his head and dropped it on the floor, nonchalantly, and without respect, revealed his identity.

It was no one anyone really knew.

Once again, Elvis got scolded, and this time he got quizzed about what had happened to Kemosabe, and so did Jack, but neither told the truth. Who was going to believe a couple of nuts? Elvis and Jack Kennedy explaining that Kemosabe was gunning for a mummy in cowboy duds, a Bubba Ho-Tep with a flock of shadows roiling about his cowboy-hatted head?

So, what they did was lie.

"He came snapping caps and then he fell," Elvis said, and Jack corroborated his story, and when Kemosabe had been carried off, Elvis, with some difficulty, using his walker for support, got down on his knee and

picked up the discarded mask and carried it away with him. He had
wanted the guns, but an aide had taken those for her four-year-old son.

Later, he and Jack learned through the grapevine that Kemosabe's
roommate, an eighty-year-old man who had been in a semicomatose
condition for several years, had been found dead on the floor of his
room. It was assumed Kemosabe had lost it and dragged him off his bed
and onto the floor and the eighty-year-old man had kicked the bucket
during the fall. As for Kemosabe, they figured he had then gone nuts
when he realized what he had done, and had wandered out in the hall
firing, and had a heart attack.

Elvis knew different. The mummy had come and Kemosabe had tried
to protect his roommate in the only way he knew how. But instead of
silver bullets, his gun smoked sulphur. Elvis felt a rush of pride in the old
fart.

He and Jack got together later, talked about what they had seen, and
then there was nothing left to say.

Night went away and the sun came up, and Elvis who had slept not a
wink, came up with it and put on khaki pants and a khaki shirt and used
his walker to go outside. It had been ages since he had been out, and it
seemed strange out there, all that sunlight and the smells of flowers and
the Texas sky so high and the clouds so white.

It was hard to believe he had spent so much time in his bed. Just the
use of his legs with the walker these last few days had tightened the
muscles, and he found he could get around better.

The pretty nurse with the grapefruit tits came outside and said: "Mr.
Presley, you look so much stronger. But you shouldn't stay out too long.
It's almost time for a nap and for us, to, you know . . ."

"Fuck off, you patronizing bitch," said Elvis. "I'm tired of your shit.
I'll lube my own transmission. You treat me like a baby again, I'll wrap
this goddamn walker around your head."

The pretty nurse stood stunned, then went away quietly.

Elvis inched his way with the walker around the great circular drive
that surrounded the home. It was a half-hour later when he reached the
back of the home and the door through which the mummy had departed. It was still locked, and he stood and looked at it amazed. How in
hell had the mummy done that, slipping through an indiscernible chink
between door and frame?

Elvis looked down at the concrete that lay at the back of the door. No clues there. He used the walker to travel toward the growth of trees out back, a growth of pin oaks and sweet gums and hickory nut trees that shouldered on either side of the large creek that flowed behind the home.

The ground tipped sharply there, and for a moment he hesitated, then reconsidered. *Well, what the fuck?* he thought.

He planted the walker and started going forward, the ground sloping ever more dramatically. By the time he reached the bank of the creek and came to a gap in the trees, he was exhausted. He had the urge to start yelling for help, but didn't want to belittle himself, not after his performance with the nurse. He knew that he had regained some of his former confidence. His cursing and abuse had not seemed cute to her that time. The words had bitten her, if only slightly. Truth was, he was going to miss her greasing his pecker.

He looked over the bank of the creek. It was quite a drop there. The creek itself was narrow, and on either side of it was a gravel-littered six feet of shore. To his left, where the creek ran beneath a bridge, he could see where a mass of weeds and mud had gathered over time, and he could see something shiny in their midst.

Elvis eased to the ground inside his walker and sat there and looked at the water churning along. A huge woodpecker laughed in a tree nearby and a jay yelled at a smaller bird to leave his territory.

Where had ole Bubba Ho-Tep gone? Where did he come from? How in hell did he get here?

He recalled what he had seen inside the mummy's mind. The silver bus, the rain, the shattered bridge, the wash of water and mud.

Well, now wait a minute, he thought. Here we have water and mud and a bridge, though it's not broken, and there's something shiny in the midst of all those leaves and limbs and collected debris. All these items were elements of what he had seen in Bubba Ho-Tep's head. Obviously there was a connection.

But what was it?

When he got his strength back, Elvis pulled himself up and got the walker turned, and worked his way back to the home. He was covered in sweat and stiff as wire by the time he reached his room and tugged himself into bed. The blister on his dick throbbed and he unfastened his pants and eased down his underwear. The blister had refilled with pus, and it looked nastier than usual.

It's a cancer, he determined. He made the conclusion in a certain final rush. They're keeping it from me because I'm old and to them it doesn't matter. They think age will kill me first, and they are probably right.

Well, fuck them. I know what it is, and if it isn't, it might as well be.

He got the salve and doctored the pus–filled lesion, put the salve away, pulled up his underwear and pants, and fastened his belt.

Elvis got his TV remote off the dresser and clicked it on while he waited for lunch. As he ran the channels, he hit upon an advertisement for Elvis Presley week. It startled him. It wasn't the first time it had happened, but at the moment it struck him hard. It showed clips from his movies, *Clambake, Roustabout,* several others. All shit movies. Here he was complaining about loss of pride and how life had treated him, and now he realized he'd never had any pride and much of how life had treated him had been quite good, and the bulk of the bad had been his own fault. He wished now he'd fired his manager, Colonel Parker, about the time he got into films. The old fart had been a fool, and he had been a bigger fool for following him. He wished too he had treated Priscilla right. He wished he could tell his daughter he loved her.

Always the questions. Never the answers. Always the hopes. Never the fulfillments.

Elvis clicked off the set and dropped the remote on the dresser just as Jack came into the room. He had a folder under his arm. He looked like he was ready for a briefing at the White House.

"I had the woman who calls herself my niece come get me," he said. "She took me downtown to the newspaper morgue. She's been helping me do some research."

"On what?" Elvis said.

"On our mummy."

"You know something about him?" Elvis asked.

"I know plenty."

Jack pulled a chair up next to the bed, and Elvis used the bed's lift button to raise his back and head so he could see what was in Jack's folder.

Jack opened the folder, took out some clippings, and laid them on the bed. Elvis looked at them as Jack talked.

"One of the lesser mummies, on loan from the Egyptian government, was being circulated across the United States. You know, museums, that kind of stuff. It wasn't a major exhibit, like the King Tut exhibit some years back, but it was of interest. The mummy was flown or carried by train from state to state. When it got to Texas, it was stolen.

"Evidence points to the fact that it was stolen at night by a couple of guys in a silver bus. There was a witness. Some guy walking his dog or something. Anyway, the thieves broke in the museum and stole it, hoping to get a ransom probably. But in came the worst storm in East Texas history. Tornadoes. Rain. Hail. You name it. Creeks and rivers overflowed. Mobile homes were washed away. Livestock drowned. Maybe you remember it . . . No matter. It was one hell of a flood.

"These guys got away, and nothing was ever heard from them. After you told me what you saw inside the mummy's head—the silver bus, the storm, the bridge, all that—I came up with a more interesting, and I believe, considerably more accurate, scenario."

"Let me guess. The bus got washed away. I think I saw it today. Right out back in the creek. It must have washed up there years ago."

"That confirms it. The bridge you saw breaking, that's how the bus got in the water, which would have been as deep then as a raging river. The bus was carried downstream. It lodged somewhere nearby, and the mummy was imprisoned by debris, and recently it worked its way loose."

"But how did it come alive?" Elvis asked. "And how did I end up inside its memories?"

"The speculation is broader here, but from what I've read, sometimes mummies were buried without their names, a curse put on their sarcophagus, or coffin, if you will. My guess is our guy was one of those. While he was in the coffin, he was a drying corpse. But when the bus was washed off the road, the coffin was overturned, or broken open, and our boy was freed of coffin and curse. Or more likely, it rotted open in time, and the holding spell was broken. And think about him down there all that time, waiting for freedom, alive, but not alive. Hungry, and no way to feed. I said he was free of his curse, but that's not entirely true. He's free of his imprisonment, but he still needs souls.

"And now, he's free to have them, and he'll keep feeding unless he's finally destroyed . . . You know, I think there's a part of him, oddly enough, that wants to fit in. To be human again. He doesn't entirely know what he's become. He responds to some old desires and the new desires of his condition. That's why he's taken on the illusion of clothes, probably copying the dress of one of his victims.

"The souls give him strength. Increase his spectral powers. One of which was to hypnotize you, kinda, draw you inside his head. He couldn't steal your soul that way, you have to be unconscious to have that done to you, but he could weaken you, distract you."

"And those shadows around him?"

"His guardians. They warn him. They have some limited powers of their own. I've read about them in the *Everyday Man or Woman's Book of the Soul*."

"What do we do?" Elvis said.

"I think changing rest homes would be a good idea," Jack said. "I can't think of much else. I will say this. Our mummy is a nighttime kind of guy—3 A.M. actually. So, I'm going to sleep now, and again after lunch. Set my alarm for before dark so I can fix myself a couple cups of coffee. He comes tonight, I don't want him slapping his lips over my asshole again. I think he heard you coming down the hall about the time he got started on me the other night, and he ran. Not because he was scared, but because he didn't want anyone to find out he's around. Consider it. He has the proverbial bird's nest on the ground here."

After Jack left, Elvis decided he should follow Jack's lead and nap. Of course, at his age, he napped a lot anyway, and could fall asleep at anytime, or toss restlessly for hours. There was no rhyme or reason to it.

He nestled his head into his pillow and tried to sleep, but sleep wouldn't come. Instead, he thought about things. Like, what did he really have left in life but this place? It wasn't much of a home, but it was all he had, and he'd be damned if he'd let a foreign, graffiti-writing, soul-sucking sonofabitch in an oversized hat and cowboy boots (with elf toes) take away his family member's souls and shit them down the visitors' toilet.

In the movies he had always played heroic types. But when the stage lights went out, it was time for drugs and stupidity and the coveting of women. Now it was time to be a little of what he had always fantasized being.

A hero.

Elvis leaned over and got hold of his telephone and dialed Jack's room. "Mr. Kennedy," Elvis said when Jack answered. "Ask not what your rest home can do for you. Ask what you can do for your rest home."

"Hey, you're copping my best lines," Jack said.

"Well then, to paraphrase one of my own, 'Let's take care of business.'"

"What are you getting at?"

"You know what I'm getting at. We're gonna kill a mummy."

The sun, like a boil on the bright blue ass of day, rolled gradually forward and spread its legs wide to reveal the pubic thatch of night, a hairy darkness in which stars crawled like lice, and the moon crabbed slowly upward like an albino dog tick thriving for the anal gulch.

During this slow rolling transition, Elvis and Jack discussed their plans, then they slept a little, ate their lunch of boiled cabbage and meat loaf, slept some more, ate a supper of white bread and asparagus and a helping of shit on a shingle without the shingle; then they slept again, awoke about the time the pubic thatch appeared and those starry lice began to crawl.

And even then, with night about them, they had to wait until midnight to do what they had to do.

Jack squinted through his glasses and examined his list. "Two bottles of rubbing alcohol?" Jack said.

"Check," said Elvis. "And we won't have to toss it. Look here." Elvis held up a paint sprayer. "I found this in the storage room."

"I thought they kept it locked," Jack said.

"They do. But I stole a hair pin from Dillinger and picked the lock."

"Great!" Jack said. "Matches?"

"Check. I also scrounged a cigarette lighter."

"Good. Uniforms?"

Elvis held up his white suit, slightly grayed in spots with a chili stain on the front. A white silk scarf and the big gold and silver and ruby-studded belt that went with the outfit lay on the bed. There were zippered boots from Kmart. "Check."

Jack held up a gray business suit on a hanger. "I've got some nice shoes and a tie to go with it in my room."

"Check," Elvis said.

"Scissors?"

"Check."

"I've got my motorized wheelchair oiled and ready to roll," Jack said, "and I've looked up a few words of power in one of my magic books. I don't know if they'll stop a mummy, but they're supposed to ward off evil. I wrote them down on a piece of paper."

"We use what we got," Elvis said. "Well then. Two forty-five out back of the place."

"Considering our rate of travel, better start moving about two-thirty," Jack said.

"Jack," Elvis asked. "Do we know what we're doing?"

"No, but they say fire cleanses evil. Let's hope they, whoever they are, is right."

"Check on that too," said Elvis. "Synchronize watches."

They did, and Elvis added: "Remember. The key words for tonight are Caution and Flammable. And Watch Your Ass."

The front door had an alarm system, but it was easily manipulated from the inside. Once Elvis had the wires cut with the scissors, they pushed the compression lever on the door, and Jack pushed his wheelchair outside, and held the door while Elvis worked his walker through. Elvis tossed the scissors into the shrubbery, and Jack jammed a paperback book between the doors to allow them reentry, should reentry be an option at a later date.

Elvis was wearing a large pair of glasses with multicolored gem-studded chocolate frames and his stained white jumpsuit with scarf and belt and zippered boots. The suit was open at the front and hung loose on him, except at the belly. To make it even tighter there, Elvis had made up a medicine bag of sorts, and stuffed it inside his jumpsuit. The bag contained Kemosabe's mask, Bull's Purple Heart, and the newspaper clipping where he had first read of his alleged death.

Jack had on his gray business suit with a black-and-red-striped tie knotted carefully at the throat, sensible black shoes, and black nylon socks. The suit fit him well. He looked like a former president.

In the seat of the wheelchair was the paint sprayer, filled with rubbing alcohol, and beside it, a cigarette lighter and a paper folder of matches. Jack handed Elvis the paint sprayer. A strap made of a strip of torn sheet had been added to the device. Elvis swung the sprayer over his shoulder, reached inside his belt, and got out a flattened, half-smoked stogie he had been saving for a special occasion. An occasion he had begun to think would never arrive. He clenched the cigar between his teeth, picked the matches from the seat of the wheelchair, and lit his cigar. It tasted like a dog turd, but he puffed it anyway. He tossed the folder of matches back on the chair and looked at Jack, said, "Let's do it, *amigo*."

Jack put the matches and the lighter in his suit pocket. He sat down in the wheelchair, kicked the foot stanchions into place, and rested his feet on them. He leaned back slightly and flicked a switch on the arm rest. The electric motor hummed, the chair eased forward.

"Meet you there," said Jack. He rolled down the concrete ramp, on out to the circular drive, and disappeared around the edge of the building.

Elvis looked at his watch. It was nearly two forty-five. He had to hump it. He clenched both hands on the walker and started truckin'.

Fifteen exhaustive minutes later, out back, Elvis settled in against the door, the place where Bubba Ho-Tep had been entering and exiting. The shadows fell over him like an umbrella. He propped the paint gun across the walker and used his scarf to wipe the sweat off his forehead.

In the old days, after a performance, he'd wipe his face with it and toss it to some woman in the crowd, watch as she creamed on herself. Panties and hotel keys would fly onto the stage at that point, bouquets of roses.

Tonight, he hoped Bubba Ho-Tep didn't use the scarf to wipe his ass after shitting him down the crapper.

Elvis looked where the circular concrete drive rose up slightly to the right, and there, seated in the wheelchair, very patient and still, was Jack. The moonlight spread over Jack and made him look like a concrete yard gnome.

Apprehension spread over Elvis like a dose of the measles. He thought: *Bubba Ho-Tep comes out of that creek bed, he's going to come out hungry and pissed, and when I try to stop him, he's going to jam this paint gun up my ass, then jam me and that wheelchair up Jack's ass.*

He puffed his cigar so fast it made him dizzy. He looked out at the creek bank, and where the trees gaped wide, a figure rose up like a cloud of termites, scrabbled like a crab, flowed like water, chunked and chinked like a mass of oil field tools tumbling downhill.

Its eyeless sockets trapped the moonlight and held it momentarily before permitting it to pass through and out the back of its head in irregular gold beams. The figure that simultaneously gave the impression of shambling and gliding appeared one moment as nothing more than a shadow surrounded by more active shadows, then it was a heap of twisted brown sticks and dried mud molded into the shape of a human being, and in another moment, it was a cowboy-hatted, booted thing taking each step as if it were its last.

Halfway to the rest home it spotted Elvis, standing in the dark framework of the door. Elvis felt his bowels go loose, but he determined not to shit his only good stage suit. His knees clacked together like stalks of ribbon cane rattling in a high wind. The dog turd cigar fell from his lips.

He picked up the paint gun and made sure it was ready to spray. He pushed the butt of it into his hip and waited.

Bubba Ho-Tep didn't move. He had ceased to come forward. Elvis began to sweat more than before. His face and chest and balls were soaked. If Bubba Ho-Tep didn't come forward, their plan was fucked. They had to get him in range of the paint sprayer. The idea was he'd soak him with the alcohol, and Jack would come wheeling down from behind flipping matches or the lighter at Bubba, catching him on fire.

Elvis said softly, "Come and get it, you dead piece of shit."

Jack had nodded off for a moment, but now he came awake. His flesh was tingling. It felt as if tiny ball bearings were being rolled beneath his skin. He looked up and saw Bubba Ho-Tep paused between the creek bank, himself, and Elvis at the door.

Jack took a deep breath. This was not the way they had planned it. The mummy was supposed to go for Elvis because he was blocking the door. But, no soap.

Jack got the matches and the cigarette lighter out of his coat pocket and put them between his legs on the seat of the chair. He put his hand on the gear box of the wheelchair, gunned it forward. He had to make things happen; had to get Bubba Ho-Tep to follow him, come within range of Elvis's spray gun.

Bubba Ho-Tep stuck out his arm and clotheslined Jack Kennedy. There was a sound like a rifle crack (no question Warren Commission, this blow was from the front), and over went the chair, and out went Jack, flipping and sliding across the driveway, the cement tearing his suit knees open, gnawing into his hide. Around and around Jack whirled, like a bottle being rapidly turned in a game of Spin the Bottle, and the chair, minus its rider, tumbled over and came upright, and still rolling, veered downhill toward Elvis in the doorway, leaning on his walker, spray gun in hand.

The wheelchair hit Elvis's walker, and Elvis bounced against the door, popped forward, grabbed the walker just in time, but dropped his spray gun.

He glanced up to see Bubba Ho-Tep leaning over the unconscious Jack. Bubba Ho-Tep's mouth went wide, and wider yet, and became a black toothless vacuum that throbbed pink as a raw wound in the moonlight; then Bubba Ho-Tep turned his head and the pink was not visible. Bubba Ho-Tep's mouth went down over Jack's face, and as Bubba Ho-Tep sucked, the shadows about it thrashed and gobbled like turkeys.

Elvis used the walker to allow him to bend down and get hold of the paint gun. When he came up with it, he tossed the walker aside, eased himself around, and into the wheelchair. He found the matches and the lighter there. Jack had done what he had done to distract Bubba Ho-Tep, to try and bring him down closer to the door. But he had failed. Yet by accident, he had provided Elvis with the instruments of mummy destruction, and now it was up to him to do what he and Jack had hoped to do together. Elvis put the matches inside his open-chested outfit, pushed the lighter tight under his ass.

Elvis let his hand play over the wheelchair switches, as nimbly as he had once played with studio keyboards. He roared the wheelchair up the incline toward Bubba Ho-Tep, terrified, but determined, and as he rolled, in a voice cracking, but certainly reminiscent of him at his best, he began to sing "Don't Be Cruel," and within instants, he was on Bubba Ho-Tep and his busy shadows.

Bubba Ho-Tep looked up as Elvis roared into range, singing. Bubba Ho-Tep's open mouth irised to normal size, and teeth, formerly nonexistent, rose up in his gums like little black stumps. Electric locusts crackled and hopped in his empty sockets. He yelled something in Egyptian. Elvis saw the words jump out of Bubba Ho-Tep's mouth in visible hieroglyphics, like dark beetles and sticks.

6★

★ "By the unwinking red eye of Ra!"

Elvis bore down on Bubba Ho-Tep. When he was in range, he ceased singing, and gave the paint sprayer trigger a squeeze. Rubbing alcohol squirted from the sprayer and struck Bubba Ho-Tep in the face.

Elvis swerved, screeched around Bubba Ho-Tep in a sweeping circle, came back, the lighter in his hand. As he neared Bubba, the shadows swarming around the mummy's head separated and flew high up above him like startled bats.

The black hat Bubba wore wobbled and sprouted wings and flapped away from his head, becoming what it had always been, a living shadow. The shadows came down in a rush, screeching like harpies. They swarmed over Elvis's face, giving him the sensation of skinned animal pelts—blood-side in—being dragged over his flesh.

Bubba bent forward at the waist like a collapsed puppet, bopped his head against the cement drive. His black bat hat came down out of the dark in a swoop, expanding rapidly and falling over Bubba's body, splattering it like spilled ink. Bubba blob-flowed rapidly under the wheels of Elvis's mount and rose up in a dark swell beneath the chair and through the spokes of the wheels and billowed over the front of the chair and loomed upward, jabbing his ravaged, ever-changing face through the flittering shadows, poking it right at Elvis.

Elvis, through gaps in the shadows, saw a face like an old jack-o'-lantern gone black and to rot, with jagged eyes, nose, and mouth. And that mouth spread tunnel wide, and down that tunnel-mouth Elvis could see the dark and awful forever that was Bubba's lot, and Elvis clicked the lighter to flame, and the flame jumped, and the alcohol lit Bubba's face, and Bubba's head turned baby-eye blue, flowed jet-quick away, splashed upward like a black wave carrying a blazing oil slick. Then Bubba came down in a shuffle of blazing sticks and dark mud, a tar baby on fire, fleeing across the concrete drive toward the creek. The guardian shadows flapped after it, fearful of being abandoned.

Elvis wheeled over to Jack, leaned forward and whispered: "Mr. Kennedy."

Jack's eyelids fluttered. He could barely move his head, and something grated in his neck when he did. "The President is soon dead," he said, and his clenched fist throbbed and opened, and out fell a wad of paper. "You got to get him."

Jack's body went loose and his head rolled back on his damaged neck and the moon showed double in his eyes. Elvis swallowed and saluted Jack. "Mr. President," he said.

Well, at least he had kept Bubba Ho-Tep from taking Jack's soul. Elvis leaned forward, picked up the paper Jack had dropped. He read it aloud to himself in the moonlight: "You nasty thing from beyond the dead. No matter what you think and do, good things will never come to you. If evil is your black design, you can bet the goodness of the Light Ones will kick your bad behind."

That's it? thought Elvis. That's the chant against evil from the *Book of the Soul*? Yeah, right, boss. And what kind of decoder ring does that come with? Shit, it doesn't even rhyme well.

Elvis looked up. Bubba Ho-Tep had fallen down in a blue blaze, but he was rising up again, preparing to go over the lip of the creek, down to wherever his sanctuary was.

Elvis pulled around Jack and gave the wheelchair full throttle. He gave out with a rebel cry. His white scarf fluttered in the wind as he thundered forward.

Bubba Ho-Tep's flames had gone out. He was on his feet. His head was hissing gray smoke into the crisp night air. He turned completely to face Elvis, stood defiant, raised an arm and shook a fist. He yelled, and once again Elvis saw the hieroglyphics leap out of his mouth. The characters danced in a row, briefly—

⁷†

—and vanished.

Elvis let go of the protective paper. It was dog shit. What was needed here was action.

When Bubba Ho-Tep saw Elvis was coming, chair geared to high,

---

† "Eat the dog dick of Anubis, you asswipe!"

holding the paint sprayer in one hand, he turned to bolt, but Elvis was on him.

Elvis stuck out a foot and hit Bubba Ho-Tep in the back, and his foot went right through Bubba. The mummy squirmed, spit on Elvis's leg. Elvis fired the paint sprayer, as Bubba Ho-Tep, himself, and chair, went over the creek bank in a flash of moonlight and a tumble of shadows.

Elvis screamed as the hard ground and sharp stones snapped his body like a piñata. He made the trip with Bubba Ho-Tep still on his leg, and when he quit sliding, he ended up close to the creek.

Bubba Ho-Tep, as if made of rubber, twisted around on Elvis's leg, and looked at him.

Elvis still had the paint sprayer. He had clung to it as if it were a life preserver. He gave Bubba another dose. Bubba's right arm flopped way out and ran along the ground and found a hunk of wood that had washed up on the edge of the creek, gripped it, and swung the long arm back. The arm came around and hit Elvis on the side of the head with the wood.

Elvis fell backward. The paint sprayer flew from his hands. Bubba Ho-Tep was leaning over him. He hit Elvis again with the wood. Elvis felt himself going out. He knew if he did, not only was he a dead sonofa-bitch, but so was his soul. He would be just so much crap; no afterlife for him; no reincarnation; no angels with harps. Whatever lay beyond would not be known to him. It would all end right here for Elvis Presley. Nothing left but a quick flush.

Bubba Ho-Tep's mouth loomed over Elvis's face. It looked like an open manhole. Sewage fumes came out of it.

Elvis reached inside his open jumpsuit and got hold of the folder of matches. Lying back, pretending to nod out so as to bring Bubba Ho-Tep's ripe mouth closer, he thumbed back the flap on the matches, thumbed down one of the paper sticks, and pushed the sulphurous head of the match across the black strip.

Just as Elvis felt the cloying mouth of Bubba Ho-Tep falling down on his kisser like a Venus's-flytrap, the entire folder of matches ignited in Elvis's hand, burned him and made him yell.

The alcohol on Bubba's body called the flames to it, and Bubba burst into a stalk of blue flame, singeing the hair off Elvis's head, scorching his eyebrows down to nubs, blinding him until he could see nothing more than a scalding white light.

Elvis realized that Bubba Ho-Tep was no longer on or over him, and the white light became a stained white light, then a gray light, and eventually, the world, like a Polaroid negative developing, came into view, greenish at first, then full of the night's colors.

Elvis rolled on his side and saw the moon floating in the water. He saw too a scarecrow floating in the water, the straw separating from it, the current carrying it away.

No, not a scarecrow. Bubba Ho-Tep. For all his dark magic and ability to shift, or to appear to shift, fire had done him in, or had it been the stupid words from Jack's book on souls? Or both?

It didn't matter. Elvis got up on one elbow and looked at the corpse. The water was dissolving it more rapidly and the current was carrying it away.

Elvis fell over on his back. He felt something inside him grate against something soft. He felt like a water balloon with a hole poked in it.

He was going down, for the last count, and he knew it.

But I've still got my soul, he thought. Still mine. All mine. And the folks in Shady Rest, Dillinger, The Blue Yodeler, all of them, they have theirs, and they'll keep 'em.

Elvis stared up at the stars between the forked and twisted boughs of an oak. He could see a lot of those beautiful stars, and he realized now that the constellations looked a little like the outlines of great hiero-glyphics. He turned away from where he was looking, and to his right, seeming to sit on the edge of the bank, were more stars, more hiero-glyphics.

He rolled his head back to the figures above him, rolled to the right and looked at those. Put them together in his mind.

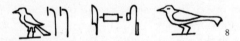

He smiled. Suddenly, he thought he could read hieroglyphics after all, and what they spelled out against the dark beautiful night was simple, and yet profound.

ALL IS WELL.

Elvis closed his eyes and did not open them again.

(THE END)
    Thanks to

(Mark Nelson) for translating East Texas "Egyptian" hieroglyphics.

NOTES

1 B YOU B B A H O TE P

2 SCRIBE LIFE R HIL-SLOPEDALE

3 CH ET W I L L I A SON MALE

4 PHARAOH GOBBLES DONKEY DICK

5 CLEOPATRA DOES THE NASTY

6 B I I THE UNWINKING RED EYE OF RA

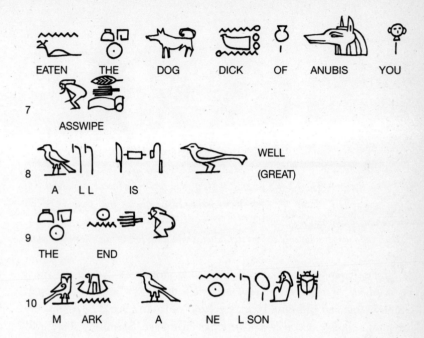

EATEN   THE   DOG   DICK   OF   ANUBIS   YOU

7   ASSWIPE

8   A   LL   IS   WELL   (GREAT)

9   THE   END

10   M   ARK   A   NE   L SON

It's no secret that The King's greatest wish was to become a movie star. Many of His biographers, from the definitive Jerry Hopkins to the reviled Albert Goldman, make much of this fact.

But who was it who said to be careful what you wish for, because it might come true?

"Elvis Pictures" are certainly a genre unto themselves—but they're not a respected one. With the exception of movies like the 1958 "musical film noirs" King Creole *and* Jailhouse Rock *(or 1960's* Flaming Star), *Elvis primarily appeared in insipid, assembly-line dreck like* Clambake, Speedway, *and* Girls! Girls! Girls!.

How ironic, then, that out of the thirty-three films Elvis did make, one of the best (yet most error-ridden) was a posthumous documentary.

Here's ROGER EBERT to tell you about it.

Ebert is the most influential film critic in America. Half of the successful TV movie review program "Siskel & Ebert," Ebert has won a Pulitzer prize and written books like Roger Ebert's Movie Home Companion *(a home video guide) and* Two Weeks in the Midday Sun *(an amusing chronicle of the Cannes Film Festival). He continues as house critic for the* Chicago Sun-Times; *Ebert also penned the script for Russ Meyer's hilarious cult classic* Beyond the Valley of the Dolls, *the type of subversive activity I wish he'd do more of.*

Now Ebert sets his sights on This Is Elvis, *a polished production which opens in Portland, Maine, as workers prepare for an Elvis concert at the Cumberland County Civic Center.*

Unfortunately, the date of this activity is August 16, 1977.

170

The same day Elvis died.
Obviously, The King didn't make this gig.
That didn't stop the filmmakers.
Or Roger Ebert.

THIS IS ELVIS

by Roger Ebert

This Is Elvis ★ ★ ★ ¹/₂
PG, **88** M., 1981

Voices: Elvis (Ral Donner), Joe Esposito (Joe Esposito), Linda
Thompson (Linda Thompson), Priscilla Presley (Lisha Sweetnam).
Directed, produced, and written by Malcolm Leo and Andrew Solt.
Featuring documentary footage of Elvis Presley.

This Is Elvis is the extraordinary record of a man who simultaneously
became a great star and was destroyed by alcohol and drug addiction.
What is most striking about its documentary footage is that we can
almost always see both things happening at once. There is hardly a time
when Elvis doesn't appear to be under the influence of mind-altering
chemicals, and never a time, not even when he is only weeks from death,
when he doesn't possess his special charisma. The movie's lesson is
brutal, sad, and inescapable: Elvis Presley was a man who gave joy to a
great many people but felt very little of his own, because he became
addicted and stayed addicted until the day it killed him.

This movie does not, however, intend to be a documentary about
Presley's drug usage. It just turns out that way, because Presley's life
turned out that way. The film is a re-creation of his life and image, and
uses documentary footage from a wide variety of sources, including
Presley's own professionally made home movies. Not all the footage is
even really of Presley. Some early childhood scenes are fiction, with a
young actor playing Elvis. They don't work, but they're soon over. A
few other scenes are also faked, including one shot following Presley into
his home on the night he died, and another showing him rushing to his

mother's sickbed (the double is an Elvis imitator named Johnny Harra). But the faked footage adds up to only about 10 percent of the movie, and is helpful in maintaining continuity.

The rest of the film's footage is extraordinary, and about half of it has never been seen anywhere. This film isn't just a compilation of old Elvis documentaries. The filmmakers got permission from Presley's manager, Colonel Tom Parker, to use Presley's own private film archives and to shoot inside Graceland, his mansion. They include footage that was not even suspected to exist, including scenes from a birthday party Elvis had in Germany when he was still in the Army (we see a very young Priscilla at the party), scenes of Elvis's parents moving into Graceland, scenes with Elvis clowning around with buddies, and shots taken inside his limousine very near the end, when he was drunk and drugged and obviously very ill. There are also sequences during which we frankly wonder if he will be able to make it onto the stage.

The documentary also includes some of Presley's key television appearances, including his first guest appearances on the old "Dorsey Brothers Bandstand" and the "Ed Sullivan Show" (with Ed assuring America that Elvis was "a real decent, fine boy . . . Elvis, you're thoroughly all right"). There is newsreel footage of Elvis getting out of the Army (and, significantly, observing "it was so cold some nights we had to take bennies to stay awake"). There is an old kinescope, long thought to be lost, of a TV special hosted by Frank Sinatra to welcome Elvis back to civilian life (and in his duet with Sinatra, Presley is confused and apparently under the influence of tranquilizers).

The young Elvis in this movie is an entertainer of incredible energy and charisma. The charisma stays, but somewhere along the way we notice a change in his behavior, a draining away of cheerfulness, a dreadful secret scourge. And in the film's final scenes, Presley is shockingly ill: He's bloated, his skin is splotchy, he's shaking and dripping with sweat, and, in one very painful sequence shot during a concert, he cannot remember the words to his songs. But he pushes through anyway, and his final renditions of "My Way" and "Are You Lonesome Tonight?" are beautiful and absolutely heartbreaking. He may have lost his mind, but he never lost his voice or his heart.

Elvis Presley should, of course, still be alive. The film interviews his former bodyguards about his drinking and drug usage, and they argue convincingly that they could not stop him from doing what he was determined to do. But an addict, of course, has only two choices, no matter how he might deceive himself that he has many. He can either continue to use, or he can ask for help.

The irony in Presley's case is that his own doctor was apparently the source of most of his drugs. Could Elvis have stopped? Sure. Would he have been alive today? Probably. But he was never able to admit his addiction and find the will to seek help. And he was surrounded by foot-kissers and yes-men. This movie shows the disintegration and death of a talented man who backed himself into a corner. He did it his way.

If you haven't read Roger Ebert's This Is Elvis *review yet, now's the time.
Don't worry about the delay—I'll wait.
All finished?
Good.*

*We're about to move from Ebert's review of a real Elvis movie to MICHAEL
REAVES's world premiere of an imaginary one. So settle back for the second
half of our Elvis Presley double feature, a Japanese/American co-production
which suggests there might have been something kind about Presley's premature
death after all.*

*Because if he'd lived, The King's career could have included something like
Elvis Meets Godzilla.*

*Michael Reaves lives in Woodland Hills, California, with his wife Brynne
Stephens, their daughter Mallory, and "a paranoid cat." He's written ten
published novels, including* Dragonworld, The Burning Realm, *and* Street
Magic. *However, Michael primarily works in television; he's done work for the
Fox Network's animated* Batman *show and has had over three hundred teleplays
produced for series like "Star Trek: The Next Generation" and "Teenage
Mutant Ninja Turtles."*

*"Elvis Meets Godzilla" is clearly enhanced by Reaves's familiarity with the
filmmaking scene. But there's more than just a million-dollar title here;
"Godzilla" also alludes to the dizzying swan dive awaiting many a washed-up
celebrity, that precipitous career decline which hurls once-sacred superstars into the
deepest chasms of the cultural abyss.*

*This showdown between the King of Rock 'n' Roll and the Big Green Guy
from Tokyo features moments of pity, courage, and moral responsibility, too.*

In Hollywood, no less.

Michael's always been good with fantasy . . .

ELVIS MEETS GODZILLA

by Michael Reaves

Lex Poldini got the call while he was hunched over the Movieola, trying to decide how best to kill the A.D. It had to be slowly, that was for sure. And painfully. The son of a bitch *had* to pay for giving him practically no coverage at all on the last three days' shoot.

Lex ran the footage past the tiny screen again, his lower back threatening to spasm as he hunched over. It looked like shit. Of course, *Deathdealer 2* was not a project from which one expected great cinematic art. But there was shit, and then there was shit. This shit was not acceptable even by the admittedly freer standards of Tandem Productions. He could live with matte fissures about as wide as the Snake River Canyon; he could even accept, albeit reluctantly, the unmistakable glimpses of the stunt man's beefy red neck under the zombie mask. All that might pass unnoticed by the beer-guzzling college students who would provide most of the rental revenue on this nine-day direct-to-video extravaganza —*if* he had been given enough cutaway footage to insert shots of Angelique's blood-splattered breasts bouncing like volleyballs as she ran. But the asshole had framed *everything* in master shots, and what the hell could he do with that?

Lex knew better than to blame the director. Joel Woodfield was providing the effects on the shoot for cheap in return for a director's credit. All he'd done by way of actually directing was to poke his head out of his trailer long enough to say "Action," and lately he hadn't even been doing that. No, it was the A.D.'s fault, and suitable tortures would have to be devised.

It was at that point that the phone rang. Marty's voice said to him, "I'm in screening. Get down here. This you're not gonna believe."

Then he hung up. Marty had an annoying habit of doing that on calls.

He wasn't being consciously rude, it was just that his brain moved at warp speed and he assumed that everyone else could and wanted to keep up. It usually put him several steps ahead of the other person in negotiations, which made up for a lot of abrupt phone calls.

Lex twisted his torso from side to side carefully, grateful for any excuse to avoid cutting this atrocity. Marty sounded excited, but that in itself meant little since Marty always sounded excited. Might as well go down and see what he had. His partner had just gotten back from Japan and the Tokyo International Film Festival. God knows what he had picked up in the land of the rising yen . . .

He headed out of the editing room and down the hall, catching the toe of his shoe, as always, in the carpet hole just outside the door. The narrow corridor was lined with framed one-sheets of films the two of them had produced over the last ten years, mostly low-budget horror, sci-fi, and action flicks with names like *Deathspawn, Star Destroyer,* and *Karate Commando.* The offices were in an ancient warehouse near Western and Santa Monica; most of the floor space had been converted into a sound stage. If strapped for cash, they could—and had, in the past—cranked out twenty-thousand-dollar quickies in a week's shooting time there.

It wasn't exactly an office suite on the lot at any of the majors. On the other hand, Lex told himself, it was his own business—well, his and Marty's—and it had paid a modest mortgage in Van Nuys and put two children through school. Sometimes looking at it that way made him feel almost good about the way his life had turned out. Not often, though.

The film industry had traditionally been recession-proof, but this latest economic dip had blown that axiom to hell and gone. He couldn't remember when it had been so hard to get financing. The books had been neon red for the past six weeks, and the banks were starting to make ominous noises about the mortgage on the building. It wouldn't be long before his house note would be teetering on the brink too.

I've never been a major player, Lex thought, *but for twenty years I've been a survivor. That counts for something in this town—just not very much.*

Twenty years could go by fast. He thought of 1972, fresh out of film school, ready to scale the heights of cinematic art. Well, not exactly; Lex had always taken a pragmatic approach to the business. Maybe that had been his problem. Maybe if he'd tried to be more visionary, taken more chances . . . After all, what did Coppola have that he didn't? Aside from a few truckloads of talent . . .

Lex pushed open the door to the dark screening room. Marty Groman was sitting in one of the four lounge chairs, sallow face illuminated by the glow of a small tensor lamp. He was swinging one foot nervously. Some part of Marty was always in motion. It used to drive Lex crazy before he decided that he had bigger things in his life to make him crazy.

"This better be good," he said, dropping his ass onto the worn nap of the seat next to Marty. "Drag me all the way down the hall from a rewarding experience like editing that lost cause." Then he took a closer look at his partner and felt a small stirring that might be excitement in his chest.

Marty was grinning. *Grinning.* An expression Lex had seen not nearly as often as he would have liked to over the years. A Cheshire-cat-acid-grin which always meant Marty had scored big-time. Lex grinned back. He couldn't help it. It was part of what made Marty so deadly across the table. Marty was a hustler with a grin that made you want to reciprocate.

"Something good?" Lex asked.

"Better than good. Better than sensational. The word hasn't been invented yet." He looked back at the booth. "Okay, Bill," he shouted. "Reel four."

"We're not starting at the top?" Lex asked, as grainy white light illuminated the screen before them. He was thinking, *Maybe it's something really good this time. Maybe it's what we need to pull ourselves out of this black hole . . .*

Mind reading was another thing Marty was good at. "Just wait," he said. "You'll see. It's a fucking green machine."

A long shot of a Japanese city filled the screen. Thudding martial music pushed the speakers toward feedback. The city was obviously a model; the whole thing seemed vaguely familiar. And then, just as Lex recognized the music, there he was on the screen, stomping his way through the Nippon suburb with ponderous glee, the coral spikes on his back lighting up as he stopped to scorch a housing tract with his atomic breath: Japan's perennial box office favorite, ol' Big Green himself.

Lex glanced at Marty, confused. "A domestic release on the latest Godzilla? This is your big surprise?" It might do okay, but hardly rake in the moviegoing public. He hadn't even known Toho was still making them.

"Keep watching," Marty said gleefully.

Lex shrugged and looked back at the screen. They were in a laboratory now. A group of Japanese scientists in ill-fitting suits talked and gesticulated animatedly, one trying to convince the others. "It'll need a new dialogue track," Lex said, the calculator part of his brain toting up costs. "We'll have to ADR the whole thing—"

He stopped. Stared. Aware that his mouth was hanging open and not caring. Aware that Marty was laughing uncontrollably beside him.

An American had joined the oriental scientists. His identity was unmistakable—the close-up unnecessary. Lex recognized the characteristic rebel sneer, softened by years of good living and lounge acts; the hair, graying now but still sporting the trademark wave. The paunch stretching the white jumpsuit. The sideburns.

"No," he said.

Marty bounced in the seat beside him like a delighted child. "Yes! *Yes!*" he howled. "And it's *ours!*"

Lex said nothing. Marty had been right; there were no words. Elvis— and he was the real McCoy, no doubt about it, this was not an impersonator—was arguing with the scientists, it seemed; insisting on something. Lex could lip-read a few words, but the King's dialogue had been dubbed into Japanese. The head scientist, a gangly sort with thick horn-rimmed glasses, shook his head emphatically. The sound track was filled with off-camera screams and the distinctive battle cry of Godzilla, which had always sounded to Lex like an elephant being butt-fucked by a diesel locomotive. Through a window could be seen a grainy rear-screen of burning pagodas and a huge green tail dragging through the shot.

He moistened dry lips. "How?" he asked.

"Found it at the festival. Seems the picture was made just before Elvis bought that big Graceland in the sky. Afterward they decided to shelve it. Dunno why; maybe they thought it would be disrespectful to release it."

On the screen Godzilla dismantled a bridge with the curious intensity of a child destroying his Erector set. Frantic extras, blue-screened into the foreground, fled.

"So what? We get domestic on this?" Christ, even sharing it with Toho this could be a fortune—

"Even better," Marty said, his face beaming in the shifting light.

"Friend of mine at Toho and I got drunk on sake, played poker. I won it."

Lex stared at him. "You mean—it's *ours*?"

"Only print in existence. We can strike an inter-neg from it, make our own copies. Can't you see it? *Elvis Meets Godzilla*! The midnight runs alone'll make us a fortune!"

He *could* see it, with blinding clarity. It was the ultimate camp classic. It could be right up there with *Rocky Horror*. Lex grew dizzy at the thought of the possibilities on sell-through video.

It was a gift from heaven, no doubt about it.

So why wasn't he excited?

Marty pummeled his arm, pointed at the screen. "This is the best part! Watch!"

Lex realized his attention had strayed; his mind had racked focus, perceiving the flickering light on the screen as abstract movements of color rather than actual images. Now Elvis was standing on some kind of raised platform and the scientists were arrayed at various control consoles around the room. The gangly one with the glasses stood behind a cannon-sized ray gun, festooned with wires and lights. Electrical arcs crackled from various terminals, VU meter needles waved like windshield wipers. Elvis stood, hip cocked, the ghost of that old insolence visible in his attitude. Lex felt suddenly sorry for him. Snatches of songs chased themselves in his brain: lines from "Hound Dog," "Blue Suede Shoes," and others. What a long strange trip it had been for him, indeed; from being a truck driver in Memphis to the height of fame and fortune, to the faded glamour of Las Vegas shows. And then to Tokyo.

An animated ray suddenly crackled from the projector, splashing over Elvis, bathing him in pyrotechnic lights. The camera angle changed to a lock-down as Elvis began to grow.

"Aw, no," Lex said softly. Marty clapped and whistled.

Elvis's image expanded, wavering slightly due to the poor matte quality. The film cut to an exterior as he burst through the roof, and Lex had to bite his tongue to keep from giggling insanely. *Elvis has left the building.*

The ray continued to play over Elvis as he grew, looking vaguely bewildered. Then it stopped. A cut to a wide angle established him standing among the ruins of the miniature city, staring across the rubble at Godzilla.

How had he come to this? Lex wondered. He could picture the King sitting alone in Graceland, alone in that Ethan Allen showroom of a mansion, staring at the jungle tapestries on the walls, chug-a-lugging Gatorade and gobbling down caseloads of Eskimo Pies, paranoid and unhappy, wondering if it was all going to end the way it began, penniless and alone. Then comes a call, an offer from Tokyo to be in a movie, and maybe they don't tell him he'll be playing opposite the tallest, greenest leading man in the Far East, or maybe they do, and he just thinks *Fuck it, I'm going,* because after all, you can never be too rich or too fat, and he jumps on the next plane, doesn't tell the Colonel or anybody, he's there for maybe a week, they block-shoot his scenes and cut them in later, and then he's back, and maybe halfway through a banana split he wonders *Jesus on a stick, what've I done?.* And maybe he gets the film shelved, or maybe they decide to put it on hold after he dies. Whatever the reasons, he did it. And now it's here.

And it's mine, Lex thought.

Godzilla lumbered toward Elvis, who crouched like a sumo wrestler, the stylized tiger on the back of his jumpsuit snarling. Godzilla had seen better days too, Lex realized. He remembered seeing the original as a kid, the one with Raymond Burr cut into it for the American release. The cheapness of the production and the black-and-white film had given a surprising power and nightmarish quality to the scenes of Godzilla ripping up Tokyo for the first time. Also, back then the Big Guy had been *scary,* despite the primitive effects. The effects had grown more sophisticated over the years, but Godzilla had not; doomed to an endless cycle of kiddie movies, fighting Mothra, Gidorah, and other costumed extras lumbering around extensive model railroad sets, he had come to look unnervingly like a gigantic Cookie Monster exiled from "Sesame Street."

And yet, Lex had loved those old movies. The Japanese monster films and Hammer Grand Guignol of the Sixties, the "giant bug" movies of the Fifties, the Universal horror classics of the Thirties and Forties. To a great degree they had pushed him toward whatever modest success he had achieved.

Just as Elvis with his music, and all the other giants of rock and roll, had shaped him. He remembered seeing the King for the first time on the "Ed Sullivan Show," remembered being dazzled by the great set and choreography of the *Jailhouse Rock* production. Remembered fondly movies like *Blue Hawaii, Follow That Dream, Viva Las Vegas* . . . plots that were little more than thinly disguised excuses for Elvis to burst into song at every opportunity, with a conga band lurking behind every potted palm and fountain.

And the music, of course. The power of that voice, sure and strong even in his later years, belting out songs like "If I Can Dream" and "My Way." "American Male." "Big Chunk'a Love." "Heartbreak Hotel." *Maybe,* Lex thought, *maybe Jim Morrison and James Dean had had the right idea.* What becomes a legend most? Death, of course. Not sweating for an audience of blue-haired housewives, or living on a diet of soft drinks, or jelly doughnuts and drugs . . .

The two giants of the silver screen collided in thunder. Godzilla's shrieks blended with Elvis's grunts. Lex, his brain having journeyed beyond astonishment into a kind of stupefied acceptance, watched as Elvis struggled with the stunt man in the rubber costume. They fell, splintering buildings and overpasses, rolled over the ground, crushing cars. Elvis stood and thrust one leg out in a decent karate kick that knocked Godzilla ass over teakettle and crushed a residential subdivision. Godzilla loosed a bolt of atomic fire at Elvis's size 910 boots and lumbered to his feet. He swung his huge spiked tail at Elvis, who grabbed it and, with improbable strength for someone even forty stories tall, began spinning around, whirling Godzilla off his feet in a huge circle. Pro wrestling had never been this outrageous.

Marty was helpless with laughter in the seat beside him. "I can't stand it," he gasped, beating one fist on the armrest. Lex watched as Godzilla flew through the air and plowed a furrow the length of a 747 runway. *Why aren't I laughing?* he wondered. Why wasn't it funny?

Elvis and Godzilla were struggling at the edge of a huge, smoke-filled fissure on the outskirts of Tokyo now, no doubt created during one of the Big G's rampages. They swayed to and fro, trading punches. Finally Elvis lurched forward, grabbed Godzilla's leg, and pulled the huge monster off-balance. Godzilla teetered on the edge of the abyss, then plunged into the misty depths with a final cry of rage. For a moment it looked like Elvis was going to follow him, but the King managed to recover his balance at the last minute.

The music swelled as he turned away from the fissure, facing the city of Tokyo which had been leveled yet again in what had to be the most spectacular long-range urban renewal project in history. Like a latter-day

Colossus of Rhodes, Elvis looked out over the devastation. Lex wondered for a moment if he was going to toss his huge, sweaty scarf down to cover a city block or two. The credits began to roll . . . and then the film stopped and the lights came up.

Marty faced him, eyes shining. "Did I tell you? Is this *gold,* or what?"

Lex just nodded. He honestly did not know what to say. Fortunately, Marty was too wired to notice his partner's mood. "I've got distributors to talk to," he said; "screenings to set up. We've got to get some prints cut. I don't want to waste a moment on this." He dashed from the screening room.

Lex sat there for several minutes. Then he got up and went into the projection booth.

Elvis had been forty-two when he had died of heart failure. Lex was forty-one as of last June. A modest success, nothing to boast of, and certainly he had produced no body of work that would live on after his death, save possibly in the minds of a few fans of low-budget, low-rent genre films. Elvis, whatever his personal failings, had been a star. He had helped shape the thoughts and minds of a generation, and would go on doing so from beyond the grave. And now here was a piece of the King's *oeuvre* that belonged to Lex Poldini. True, there would be rumblings from the Presley Estate, but nothing that couldn't be dealt with. After all, it had been Elvis's decision to go *mano a mano* with Toho's Green Meanie. They had free and clear title to the film.

But it still didn't seem right.

Bill had left; he was alone in the booth. Lex rethreaded the first reel, feeding the leader through the gate but not onto the take-up wheel. Then he turned out the lights and started the film, watching through the narrow window in the booth.

The film played, moving at twenty-four frames per second past the light and spilling from there onto the booth's floor in an untidy pile of celluloid. It was fairly easy to follow the plot, despite not knowing a word of Japanese. Elvis was playing a singer on tour in Japan who had the bad fortune to be doing a gig in Tokyo when Godzilla showed up. Lex watched, and thought about his own life.

He had made some shady deals, some questionable decisions, during his sojourn in show business, Lex knew. It was not a business where one got anywhere by being a nice guy. He had stolen a few ideas, juggled a few books, indulged in more than a little creative accounting.

But he had never robbed from the dead.

The two hatch marks in the upper right hand corner of the screen flickered by, and a moment later the last few feet of film slithered to the floor. Lex threaded the second reel.

He remembered the first time he saw *Plan 9 from Outer Space,* Edward D. Wood, Jr.'s masterpiece and surely one of the worst films ever made. The audience had been like Marty, howling with delight at such sights as the pie-tin flying saucers and the cheap sets. Which, he had had to admit, were pretty funny. But he had watched Bela Lugosi lurching through the scene, obviously stoned and dying, and kept thinking of the actor at his height in films like *Dracula, The Black Cat, Son of Frankenstein.*

Marty was right—there was no way they couldn't make money on this movie. Lots of money. More than enough to get out of debt and finance some more pictures to boot.

With luck, he would live a lot longer than Elvis. He wasn't in the best of shape, but he tried to hit the gym and the treadmill a couple of times a week and he wasn't addicted to anything worse than coffee. There was still time. Time in which he might be able to produce something of substance.

It didn't seem long at all before the second reel had passed through. He replaced it with the third.

Fame was hard to deal with; Elvis had certainly been proof of that. Even Godzilla hadn't been able to resist the temptation to sell out for an endless string of sequels. Each had been a giant in his own field; looking at it that way, Lex decided, it really didn't seem so bizarre that they had met. He indulged in a brief fantasy of Elvis and Godzilla palling around on the lot between setups, maybe going to a bar after a day's work to pick up a couple of geishas. They had more in common than it would seem at first glance; each was, after all, a creature of excess.

Lex started threading the last reel.

Marty would be very upset. In fact, the partnership would probably not survive this. Truth to tell, Lex could not feel all that sorry to see Marty go. The man was a good hustler, but only so good. Which was one of the reasons for the financial bind they were in.

He would want to know why. Why in God's name Lex had destroyed their ticket out of this endless cycle of mediocrity. And Lex would not be able to explain, would not be able to make Marty see that in this case lying down with big green dinosaurs only meant you got up covered with truly impressive amounts of shit. That there was another way to break the cycle, even if it meant declaring bankruptcy and starting over.

Fame was hard to deal with. So was success. Elvis had been happy cutting records in Nashville, Lex felt sure. It was only when he became caught up in the whirlwind of Hollywood hype and glamour that he lost sight of what was important.

The last reel, which he had already seen once, flickered to an end and snaked its way to the large pile of film at his feet.

Lex rummaged through a couple of drawers until he found what he was looking for. Then he sat down cross-legged on the floor next to the pile of film. Elvis's last film.

It was a simple choice, really. Your money or your life.

Snatches of songs were still running through his head as Lex began to use the scissors. He listened to a ghostly voice singing somewhere in the still distance. A voice sultry and powerful and young, full of promise that wonderful things could still happen, that great artists may fail themselves, but never their work. The lyrics spoke of not regretting the past, of bright futures ahead.

The song was "Don't Be Cruel."

HARLAN ELLISON's prose is like rock 'n' roll made ink.

It's fast. It's lyrical. It's in your face.

A sometimes eloquent, sometimes brutal literary musician fusing Lou Reed's acidic lyrics with Napalm Death's grindcore thrash, Ellison first burst onto the scene during the mid-1950s. His specialty was transgeneric, moralistic, blood-and-thunder short fiction. Cage-rattling stories whose adrenalized prose could skip between raging peaks of Andes-high imagination to dark valleys hemmed in by melancholy sighs.

These gems—"The Whimper of Whipped Dogs," "A Boy and His Dog" —are collected in anthologies like The Beast That Shouted LOVE at the Heart of the World. Yet Ellison also penned well-received rock novels (Spider Kiss), edited superlative anthologies (Dangerous Visions), and wrote excellent teleplays for classic television programs like "Star Trek" and "The Outer Limits."

There's more.

Harlan's won too many literary awards to count (Edgars, Hugos, Nebulas, you name it). He's now a regular editorial commentator on cable television's Sci-Fi Channel, has a new collection of short stories called Slippage coming out, and will soon see the release of a computer game (titled "I Have No Mouth, and I Must Scream"), based on one of his stories.

No doubt about it: Harlan Ellison rocks.

Yet there's a tender, sensitive side to Ellison as well, a tendency toward the evocative, which doesn't generate much press.

"The Pale Silver Dollar of the Moon" is a good showcase for those traits.

Quiet and gentle, this perceptive study of one man's existence demonstrates the riches which may litter any "normal" life.

This story is also, quite possibly, the finest work yet written on Elvis's dead-at-birth twin.

Because even though Jesse Garon Presley is buried in a shoebox, in an unmarked grave, at Priceville Cemetery in Tupelo, Mississippi—

It's finally his turn in the spotlight.

Jesse, take a bow.

THE PALE SILVER DOLLAR OF THE MOON PAYS ITS WAY AND MAKES CHANGE

by Harlan Ellison

He told them Jesse Garon had been stillborn at 4 A.M. He would have told them the same about Elvis Aron, at 4:35; but they were watching more closely. Dr. Hunt managed to get the elder of the twins away from the house in Tupelo. Jesse Garon lived. Jesse Garon lives. William Robert Hunt, M.D., died in 1952, never explaining why he had "saved" the older Presley twin. But Jesse—who had kept a book of himself—had been contacted by the old country doctor. He knew who he was. He never went back to Tupelo.

He only visited Memphis, Tennessee, once. August of 1977.

1939

Eight million were unemployed. Nazi Germany attacked Poland. The earthquake in Anatolia took 45,000 lives. No one had come to my birthday party the year before, not one kid of all the kids from my grade school who had received a personal invitation done in multiple colors with the sixteen crayons in my Crayola box. I had even laid out all my comic books with just the titles showing, line after line of them, under the piano, in case anyone wanted to read about The Human Bomb or Tom Mix or Scribbly. And I waited, and waited, and looked out the front window and waited, but no one came; no one even called to lie; and when it got dark we had dinner, with pieces of my cake for dessert.

This year, I knew there wouldn't even be a party, it was too embarrassing. I don't remember if I cried, but I think I did. But I did it in my room. And no one saw me.

188

This year, I wouldn't give them the chance.

So after school I never went home. I ran away. I crossed Mentor Avenue against the wishes of my mother and father, and I trudged down through the high weeds and sumac woods of the empty lots behind the Colony Lumber Company, and I sat on the edge of the bank that surrounded the dirty green water of the nameless pond, and I tossed stones into the thick dirty water, and I watched the skeeter bugs skimming the surface across the circular ripples, and I tried to catch one of the nasty fish that lived in the muck of the pond, using a string and a piece of bread and a stick I broke off a bush.

When it got dark, I still sat there. For hours after it got dark. Until it got so cold that I finally trudged back out of that minor wilderness, and recrossed Mentor Avenue, and went home. My mother and father were beside themselves. They had called out the police. I came into the house, muddy and cold, and still crying. And I saw they had left most of the cake with the candles unlit still on the table, along with the birthday presents they'd bought me, and if there had been any kids there, they were gone now. It looked like there had been kids there, but they were gone a long time. But I still knew my mom and dad would have had to call parents to get them to come. Henry Moore sculpted his *Reclining Figure*. Barcelona fell to Franco's troops and Loyalist resistance in Spain was ended. Polyethylene was invented, Freud died, and Igor Sikorsky constructed the first helicopter.

1947

Chairman J. Parnell Thomas called his first witness in the preliminary hearings to establish loyalty or seditious behavior on the part of Communists or Fellow Travelers in Hollywood. Just outside King of Prussia, Pennsylvania, I accepted a ride from a man in a Hudson touring car. I'd been hitching my way east and hadn't eaten in a day and a half. At a farmhouse in the outlying north of Smoketown, near Lancaster, I had gotten a dinner from a nice woman and her family by knocking on their door and telling them I could repair the old washing machine and mangle rusting away in the side yard.

She had looked at me with skepticism, but I said if I couldn't fix it, it wouldn't cost her nothing. But if I got it working, could she spare something to eat? So she asked her husband, who was working in the barn, and he came out just beyond the big barn doors, and he shaded his eyes with his hand to look at me with the setting sun behind me, and he told her *what've we got to lose,* so she let me go ahead.

I didn't know any more about fixing a washing machine or a mangle than the man in the moon, but I'd done this kind of thing about twenty times before, and once in a while I'd spot something simple that I could twist back into shape or hook up, and it'd work, and I'd eat. So I labored over them both, the washing machine and the mangle, and I sweated for a couple of hours, but couldn't get either of them to going. And it was dark, then, and the lady came out and asked if I'd done any good, and I said no ma'am; and I started putting my windbreaker back on, so I could take off down the road again; and she said *well, c'mon in, then, and have a bite with us,* which was very kind of her because she probably knew I was faking it all along, but I'd sweated for a couple of hours, so she fed me.

And that had been a day and a half ago. I got into the Hudson, and the man put it in gear, and he put his hand on my lap and asked me how old I was, and I yanked down the door handle as hard as I could, and I grabbed my stuff wrapped up in a shirt, and I jumped out of the car before he could get it into second, and I ran away into the woods. Great Britain proposed the partition of Palestine, and there were tremendous protests from Arabs and Jews.

1959

Fidel Castro swept down out of the Sierra Maestra and drove Batista from Cuba with the invasion of Havana. I was serving with the U.S. Army in the capacity of reporter for the Ft. Knox newspaper *Inside the Turret.* I was living in a trailer in Elizabethtown, Kentucky, because I was married, even though they didn't know I was separated. I hated the barracks and had taken the trailer under what they called separate maintenance. But she was back in New York, and we'd probably never see each other again, which was fine by me.

One night I went to a record store in Elizabethtown to buy a jazz record, and I met up with a bunch of teen-aged kids from the high school who knew me because they'd seen me around, and they asked me if I wanted to come to a sock hop that night.

So I went to the high school and paid a dollar to come into the dance, and I hung around and had some punch, but nothing much was happening. And then I saw a girl, maybe fourteen or fifteen, with a leg brace on. I think it was polio. And she was sitting watching everyone dance, but no one asked her. So I went over and smiled and asked her if she'd like to dance, and at first she was very shy, but after I asked a couple more times she said okay, and we got up and I was careful not to be too tricky with the steps, and we had a nice dance. It was Danny and the Juniors doing "At the Hop." She thanked me when I took her back to her seat, and during the evening we danced again half a dozen times. The Nobel Prize for Medicine and Physiology was awarded to Ochoa and Kornberg for their synthesis of DNA and RNA.

1962

Adolf Eichmann was hanged in Jerusalem as the United States Supreme Court ruled against official prayers in public schools. How I met Carl Sandburg was this: Bill was married to Lelia, and I'd met them at somebody's party, and I was staying in a small apartment down on Wilshire near Beverly Glen, and they invited me to visit their house way up in the Glen, at the end of a small street called Beverly Glen Place, and it was so beautiful up there, all private and quiet, that I rented a funny little treehouse up a steep driveway called Bushrod Lane, and that was how I came to be living just about next door (and above) Bill and Lelia's when Bill was hired for second-unit work on *The Greatest Story Ever Told*. Or maybe he was an assistant director.

One Sunday Bill called and said there was a party going on at George Stevens's mansion up in the Hollywood Hills, and did I want to come for a while? I asked if it was okay, and he said, yes, it was fine, Mr. Stevens had told him to ask anyone he thought would be interesting. So I took the directions to Mr. Stevens's house, and I dressed up in the best suit I had, which was too big on me because I hadn't been working and I'd lost a lot of weight, and I had to pin the pants tight across my waist, and I was ashamed the way the pants bagged, but I put on the jacket and it covered the excess, flapping fabric.

I was driving an old Ford I'd bought in Chicago, and it was a wreck, but it got me up into the Hills, where I took a wrong turn and got lost. Finally, I thought I'd found the private road that led up to Mr. Stevens's big house, and there was a gate with an intercom on it, and I buzzed through, and a voice asked who I was, so I said who, and I said I'd been invited to the party by Bill, and there was a moment of silence and then the voice said okay, and told me how to get up the road to the parking lot, and the gate gave a crackling noise and opened, and I drove through.

But I must have taken a wrong turn again, because I could see the big circular house above me, but I couldn't get to it; and finally I did come into an empty lot with one or two cars in it, below the house, and I figured that had to be where I was supposed to be. So I parked, and hitched up my pants, and climbed a stairway to the house.

But I couldn't find a door to go in.

The house was marvelous. Apparently, parts of it turned like a sundial to catch the sun, and the front door was somewhere on the other side. What I didn't know was that I had come up a service road, not the front entranceway, and I was lost again. So I walked around and around the back of the house till I found a door, and I went in. But it was on the second floor, and I wandered through the bedroom level till I came out on a balcony that went halfway around the central court, and I looked down into an enormous white living room, all bathed in sunshine, and down there sitting on a huge sectional sofa was Carl Sandburg. I recognized him immediately. I was thrilled.

He had been hired by Mr. Stevens to write narration for *The Greatest Story Ever Told,* and he was staying there. I could now see, through the big picture windows, that the party was actually out on the sloping lawn in front of the house. But the living room was empty except for Carl Sandburg, who sat on the sofa doing the most peculiar thing.

Propped up on one of those plastic book-holder devices used to hold open a cookbook when making something intricate for dinner, was a large book. Lying on the big coffee table that held the propped-open book, in front of Carl Sandburg, was a roll of brown butcher's paper, the kind meat markets use to wrap up lamb chops. It was partially unrolled, and Carl Sandburg was writing on the open section with a quill pen that he would dip into an inkpot. He would look at the book for a moment, and then write something on the butcher's paper. I watched him for a long time. He would look at the book, dip the quill, write a line on the paper, and then repeat the process until he'd filled the paper handily. Then he would rip off a big chunk of the paper and toss it onto a hurly-burly haymow of butcher's paper on the floor beyond the coffee table.

I watched till I couldn't contain myself any longer; then I walked around the balcony over the living room till I found a staircase that descended to the big room. I went down and walked daintily toward Carl Sandburg, because I didn't want to disturb or interrupt him. But I had to find out what he was doing. I stood there for a few minutes till he saw me, and he smiled, and he said *hello young man,* and I came over to him, and he patted the sofa and told me to sit down and take a load off. So I sat down, and watched a while; and then I asked him, *Mr. Sandburg, what in the world are you doing?*

And he said, "Did you know the typewriter was invented in 1873?"

I said no, I didn't know that. He chuckled. "Well, son, I always traveled around with a little portable typewriter in my pack. I wrote almost all of my poems on that typewriter. On cheap yellow paper. Dollar a ream. So now it seems they want to preserve all my originals in a museum or a library or something, and I'm just too embarrassed to send them all those typed yellow pages. They just don't look important enough."

And he looked into that copy of *The Collected Poetry of Carl Sandburg,* published by Harcourt Brace, that had been bought for him a few days earlier at a bookstore in Westwood Village, and he memorized a line, and dipped his quill in the inkpot, and copied the line on brown, important-looking butcher's paper, and he tore off the poem he had copied, the poem he had written years before, and tossed it onto the ever-growing mound of elegant forgeries. I stayed sitting there for a long while, and was very impressed. Aboard the Friendship VII, John Glenn became the first American to orbit the Earth and Marilyn Monroe died of an overdose and President Kennedy sent federal troops to protect James Meredith as the first black student seeking admission to the University of Mississippi.

1975

The Vietnam War ended and Francisco Franco died. There was a serious water leak through the wall of the bedroom in my house, caused by ivy that had been growing up the outside wall and penetrating the stucco. Dozens of excellent books in a floor-to-ceiling bookcase were stained and waterlogged and mildewed. I had to throw them out, and some of them have never been replaced. One of them was a book I'd first read in junior high school about people living in the mountains of West Virginia who had never seen an airplane or a radio, and who still spoke in something like old Chaucerian English. An earthquake destroyed the beautiful Great Temples of Pagan in Burma.

1980

Ex-California governor Ronald Wilson Reagan became the 40th, and oldest, President of the United States in a landslide victory in which he won 483 electoral votes. A dear friend of mine was bludgeoned to death in her apartment in Santa Monica and I spoke at her funeral. A friend I'd known for almost thirty years revealed himself to be a terrible, cold person, and I could speak to him only distantly ever after. My nephew went to work in his father's store in Cleveland; and I don't think that's what he had intended for his life's work. Zimbabwe emerged as an independent state.

1992

The Union of Soviet Socialist Republics vanished, and a menace that had clouded the mind of the world for a century, something they had called Communism, dissipated like morning fog, almost without anyone noticing. Doves have built a nest in a tree just outside the front door of my home. When I go out to put garbage in the cans, the mother bird sits among the cactus, watching me. I smile and try to reassure her that she's safe.

I go out less frequently now. Always to a 7-Eleven or Wal-Mart. I let them see me. Sometimes I hang around at a Taco Bell or McDonald's till someone begins watching me, till they start whispering to each other, till one of them seems ready to come over and ask me. Then I get up, very quickly, and I leave. I always park a block away so no one can see where I went or if I had a car or simply levitated to a flying saucer. I do it for him.

Jesse Garon came to him first in Las Vegas. He didn't need to tell him who he was, they looked at each other and saw the same face. He read to him from the book that he had kept all those years. Then he went away, telling his brother he would be with him when the time came.

He was in the bathroom, and Jesse sat with him on the floor, and cradled his brother's head in his lap, and they recited together. "Jesus, I now admit that I am a sinner, going to hell, and need You as my Saviour. I now cease to rely on myself, my church, my religion, or anything else that I might do to save or help save me. I now completely trust You as my Saviour, to pay for my sins and keep me from going to hell. Thank You, Lord Jesus."

And his younger brother's face became as sweet as it had been, and he closed his eyes, and he sighed; and Jesse Garon kissed his temple, and laid his head on the furry chenille throw rug. He took the book of his life, and went back out the way he had entered, and found his car parked a block away, and drove the long drive back to his home.

Some few years later, he began going out regularly, wearing his hair much longer and darker. Jesse Garon did not die. Jesse Garon is alive.

And Elvis is alive and well, and flourishing on black velvet.

Berlioz wrote, "Time is a great teacher. Unfortunately, it kills all its pupils."

The pale silver dollar of the moon pays its way and makes change.

While editing Elvis Is Dead *I asked contributors for short biographies, ones I could use to flesh out these introductions.*

Here's what NANCY A. COLLINS sent in:

"Nancy A. Collins was born in 1959 and raised in rural Arkansas. Her first known story was produced in 1963 and concerned the love of a taxi cab for a bus. During 1981 she lived in Memphis, where she was once hired to count the people going into Graceland on the fourth anniversary of Elvis's death.

"In 1982 she moved to New Orleans, where Collins embarked upon a series of demeaning minimum-wage part-time jobs. Between then and 1988, though, she sold her first novel, Sunglasses After Dark. *Her short fiction has appeared in* Shock Rock *and* There Won't Be War, *while her later novels include* Tempter *(1990) and* In the Blood *(1992).*

"Collins is the current writer for DC Comics' Swamp Thing *series. She also tends to speak of herself in the third person."*

What Nancy failed to mention is that Sunglasses After Dark—*a hip, outrageous vampire novel—has achieved cult status. Or that if you call the Greenwich Village apartment she shares with underground filmmaker Joe Christ, their answering machine says, "Neither the Anti-Christ or the Whore of Babylon are in right now."*

Which should prepare us for "The Sacred Treasures of Graceland." This is a droll, tongue-in-cheek tour through a very familiar landmark, complete with futuristic mirrors reflecting the slack-jawed face of contemporary bad taste.

As a note scrawled on Nancy's bio emphasized:

"The Elvis vibrator and winkie-card mentioned in this story are real."

THE SACRED TREASURES OF GRACELAND: EXCERPTS FROM THE SANCTIONED MUSEUM CATALOGUE

by Nancy A. Collins

THE LAST SUPPER
Guido
1976–2029, American
Oils and fluorescent Day-Glo paints on black velvet

While there were hosts of iconographers working on black velvet during, and immediately after, the King's lifetime, Guido was one of the first to possess an unique vision and sign his work at the same time. Born a year before the King's transcendence, the talented young artist is reputed to have first tried his hand at customizing vans, airbrushing T-shirts, and even tattooing before finding his true calling as an iconographer. His interpretations of the King's life and deeds are certainly among the most potent and memorable of the postmillennium, as witness this, his acknowledged masterpiece. Note how the King—seen here in his classic *Viva Las Vegas* manifestation—is seated among his disciples. The beatific expression on the face of the King alone would mark this as a classic. However, it is the interplay and minute detail concerning his attendant disciples that truly make this canvas stand out.

Witness the eye contact between McCartney and Lennon, Jagger's pout, James Dean's pensive frown, Bruce Lee's arcane hand gestures as he leans over to whisper in the ear of the scowling Nixon. There's the manic gleam in Mickey's shoe-button eyes, and the sweat beading on Wayne Newton's lip as he speaks to Michael Jackson—all these deft touches separate Guido's work from that of the horde of lesser iconographers. His gift for photorealistic renderings on black velvet continues to ensure his name in both sacred and secular art histories to this day.

Injection-molded plastic vibrator shaped like Elvis, circa Viva Las Vegas
American, late 20th century

This rare and wonderful object was offered to the collection by a sister of Hidden Rank in the Illegitimate Daughters of Elvis. A stunning example of Elvis as fertility god, this mass-produced sexual device has settings that include "Love Me Tender" and "Don't Be Cruel."

The King Approached by the Lesser Elvii
Billy Bob Ray
1965–2012, American
Worked about 2000 A.D., *American*
Engraving

Here we see an interesting, lesser-known scene from the Tupelo Apocrypha as illustrated by Billy Bob Ray, who—alongside fellow iconographer Guido—was one of the first to sign his name to his work. Unlike Guido, and many of the other popular iconographers, Billy Bob Ray favored the King circa "Hound Dog." Here we see the lean, swaggering King—armed with his dimestore guitar—walking along a rocky valley floor. From the shadows of the rocks and crags emerge the Lesser Elvii—pale, flawed copies of the original, such as Fabian, Frankie Avalon, and Ricky Nelson—reaching out blindly in the direction of the divine light emanating from his self.

Mama and Child Enthroned
Tempera on wood, gold on ground

A late work by the founder of Shrine of the Immaculation in Tupelo, Mississippi, datable to 2026 or slightly later. A green Kickapoo Joy Juice soda bottle is clutched in Mama Gladys's hand: a symbol of the King's reputed virgin birth.

The Coronation of the Virgin Gladys
Oils on black velvet
$46^3/_8 \times 55^5/_8$ *in.*

One of the most famous paintings of the great Hispanic iconographer Luis Pulque, this picture was painted around 2014 (shortly after Pulque's arrival in East L.A.) for Cardinal Delveccio, the reigning Elvian spiritual leader of Southern California at the time.

Mama Visited by the Holy Ghost in the Form of an Eagle
Artist Unknown, 2060s
Oil on black velvet

Here we see Elvis's blessed mother—the Virgin Gladys—being visited by the Holy Ghost in the form of an American eagle, complete with shield and arrows clutched in its taloned feet. This unfinished picture shows the descent of the eagle-god on the confused young woman as she hangs up her wash in the backyard. The composition is similar to the more popular interpretation of the Immaculation: the Virgin Gladys and the shower of gold.

2 The Immaculation
Artist Unknown, 2050(?)
Oil on black velvet

This is possibly the most popular of all the paintings to emerge from the Virgin of Tupelo sect. The moment of divine conception is captured here as the young Gladys is surrounded by a pool of golden light while hanging up the wash in her backyard. The artist stresses Vernon's complete lack of involvement by portraying him as sitting on the porch eating a Moon Pie and drinking a Royal Crown Cola.

The Marriage of Elvis and Priscilla
3-D winkie-card
late 1960s

This rare, pretranscendence artwork shows, at one angle, a three-dimensional photograph of Elvis and his child-bride, Priscilla, dressed in evening clothes typical of the era. But from another angle it depicts the King dressed in princely array, complete with ceremonial sash and saber, while his divine consort is outfitted in a voluminous bridal gown and diamond tiara. In the background is a huge coach shaped like a pumpkin with four white horses. Whether this is an actual photograph commemorating the nuptials is uncertain.

The Black Velvet Shroud of Graceland
1977(?)

Regarded as the most sacred—and controversial—of the art treasures of Graceland, little is known about the shroud and its origins. Believed by many to be the exact likeness of the King at the moment of his Transcendence, there are others who doubt its authenticity. Why—for example—would Elvis's famed Memphis Mafia drape their fallen employer in black velvet? And if this *is* the historical Elvis at the exact moment he chose to surrender his mortal shell, why is he wearing pants and holding a microphone? One hundred and fifty years after the King's Transcendence, these nagging questions have yet to be answered. Still, who can not look upon the shadowy, bejowled face reflected in reverse-negative on that aged black velvet and walk away untouched? Until its authenticity is proven, it remains one of Graceland's most impressive—and moving—holy mysteries.

"Is He really dead?"

That's probably the single most asked question regarding Elvis Presley these days, repeated countless times by legions of people.

Who can we turn to for a definitive answer?

Well, how about Elvis's lawyer?

D. BEECHER SMITH II is an attorney with an extensive probate and estate planning practice in Memphis, Tennessee. He was Elvis Presley's attorney, drafted the will of the late entertainer, and represented the Presley Estate from probate through the successful rezoning and opening of Graceland as a museum. Smith continues to serve as Special Counsel to Elvis Presley Enterprises, Inc.

But how does an attorney get into the writing game? Almost losing your life helps; a near-fatal hunting accident in 1986 not only temporarily disabled Smith but also motivated his return to writing fiction and poetry, areas in which he'd earned honors as an undergraduate at Millsaps College.

Smith's poems have been extensively published in Canada; "Return of the King" is an example of Smithian fiction. And within this urban fantasy you'll find one possible answer to the question raised at the beginning of this introduction.

You may also ask yourself another query:

Now that Elvis Is Dead, who's feeding off who?

RETURN OF THE KING (A FANTASY)

by D. Beecher Smith II

From her penthouse balcony Delilah watched the fog roll in from the river and enshroud downtown Memphis. The breeze offered no relief from the oppressive August heat.

She took a puff from her cigarette, sucked down what remained of her iced scotch highball, and fought back the tears.

Occasionally she would hold the cold glass up against the ugly bruise on her temple, where one of the fans had pelted her with a dirt clod.

For this was another anniversary of HIS death, when all THE FANS came to mourn HIM. But, hadn't she, as HIS former stepmother, been a part of HIS LIFE, too?

This was *after* HIS father had divorced her and paid a king's ransom to make her go away forever, only she wouldn't. She dared not let the press know how she had stupidly squandered her settlement on slow horses, younger men, and older liquor.

With all the dirt she had spread about HIM—to Hell with whether or not it was true, as long as it sold—she'd at least been able to convince three publishers as to her marketability.

Those first two books had done well. She had not taken royalties. This time she'd been smarter. Right when it seemed nobody had anything new to say about HIM, she'd made up some choice material. Naturally, it flattered her and made those she didn't like look bad. Very bad.

Her street smarts had told her to say bad things that weren't true only about those who were *dead*. Otherwise she might get sued.

She'd had no problem finding targets, from her late ex-husband (HIS father, whom she had met as a widower), to her predecessor (HIS real mother), to HIM (HIMSELF). All she had to do was open her mouth and the tabloids would go ga-ga, plus pay her big bucks.

Her concoctions had been more succulent than Cajun crawfish gumbo. First she'd insinuated that HE had been homosexual. Or at least bisexual. That was probably what had earned her the dirt clod in the face today. Next she had exaggerated all out of proportion HIS involvement with drugs. Then she claimed that HIS death had been a suicide.

When none of the tabloids seemed willing to pay for any more of her wild revelations, she dropped the bombshell—her assertion that HE'D had an incestuous affair with HIS MOTHER! That sent the gossip mongers flocking with checkbook in hand.

But even tabloid readers have a threshold of tolerance. Delilah's incest line transgressed it.

All the fat ladies in stretch pants, waiting along with their balding husbands and whining grandchildren at the gates to HIS MANSION, must have read her stories. When she'd tried to pose for a publicity shot —after having been refused access to THE GROUNDS—they'd booed and hissed at her.

Shouts arose from the crowd. "Judas! Traitor! Go away, you old witch!"

"But I loved HIM," she had cried.

That was when the dirt ball hit her.

Alone on the balcony of her hotel room, she wept. "Oh, why doesn't anyone think I loved YOU? If only I could tell YOU face to face!"

The fog roiled up thick, so heavy she could barely see. She heard a rushing, soaring sound across the balcony. Then footsteps—a man's.

The fog dissipated. Standing three feet away, she saw a familiar figure. When his lips curled into that trademark sneer of a smile, she knew it could only be HIM. Wearing a black jumpsuit and matching cape, with boots—traditional stage attire—HE looked so slim and trim, like HE'D stepped off the new commemorative stamp.

His familiar, husky voice warbled, "Are you lonesome tonight?"

She felt a rush of elation and fear. HE wasn't dead. His death had been a hoax! She could explain—make up a good lie—she'd been mistaken and was sorry. HE'D forgive her. Hadn't HE always before?

It shouldn't be hard. Hadn't HE always been a fool for a pretty face and a well-turned thigh? After her most recent facelift and total body liposuction, didn't she again possess the features of a girl in her mid-thirties? Well, almost!

All she had to do was *charm* HIM.

She shook her dyed blond locks seductively and lowered the zipper on her white silk jumpsuit to expose her silicone-enhanced cleavage. She flicked the burning cigarette over the balcony and slunk enticingly toward HIM.

"I always *knew* you'd come back. Remember how much I *loved* you?"

The sneer on HIS lips became more pronounced as HE spoke, in a tone of contempt, the way HE had talked to the "bad guys" in HIS B-movies. "So you knew, huh? . . . How?"

She pressed close enough to smell HIS natural musk scent mingled with the Aramis cologne HE always wore.

"You promised to take care of us—said we'd never want for anything. Then you died—so suddenly. Your will put everything in trust for your baby and cut us out. I had to make do *somehow*."

She moved to kiss and embrace HIM, but HE caught her arms and held her back. HIS blue eyes were smoldering. Was it with desire or anger?

"Is that why you sold those lies to the rag sheets?" Menace resonated in HIS voice.

She felt threatened, yet—hadn't she always been able to handle HIM before? Like all men, HE was a sucker.

Batting her eyelids, she replied, "Why, darling, I don't know what you mean!"

HE reached inside HIS cape and withdrew a periodical with her picture on the front. "This."

The headlines proclaimed "INTIMATE FAMILY SECRETS REVEALED."

She tried to recover her charm. "Dear, nobody takes that stuff seriously."

HE came close, towering over her, breathing rapidly, excitedly. In HIS familiar Southern drawl HE said, *"I do."*

"Now don't go gettin' all worked up. Trust me. I'll publish a retraction—say I had a reaction to some prescription drugs. Your doctor always did make a good scapegoat!"

She drew close. This time HE did not resist. She whispered, "Oh, it feels so good to hold you. This wasn't right when your daddy was alive, but it's *okay* now."

She could feel HIS breath against her naked throat. HE was becoming aroused.

HE panted, "Thank you very much!"

. . . And sank HIS razor-sharp fangs into her throat.

She tried to struggle, but pleasure quickly overtook the pain. Exquisite pleasure, greater than any she had ever known. Now she knew *how* HE had come back—and she didn't care.

It made such perfect sense. HE'D always loved the night, and shunned the day.

She felt the inseam of her pantsuit flood with the wetness of a torrential orgasm. Although weak, almost to the point of death, and reeling from loss of blood, she hoped this ecstasy would go on forever.

HE broke free and said with an evil laugh, "That's enough. Doc told me to watch my *junk food intake*."

HE released her. Her life force ebbing away, she fell to the balcony floor.

HE shook HIS head in mock remorse. "You shouldn't have said bad things about my momma!"

Death overtook her as the fog rolled back in and HE disappeared.

Right at the same moment the cheap newspaper HE'D left behind blew across the balcony, and settled over her face.

Like Elvis before him, CLIVE BARKER leaped seemingly full blown from the media's brow.

Barker's debut was the Books of Blood *(1984), a three-volume set of uniquely unsettling short stories; graphic, intense, and sexually explicit. Since then, Clive's generated epic fantasies* (The Great and Secret Show), *artwork collections of his own pen and ink drawings* (Clive Barker—Illustrator), *and even children's books* (The Thief of Always).

Yet Barker's best known for creating Pinhead, the S&M zombie from hell. Cult icon and movie star, Pinhead has appeared in the three Hellraiser *films which Clive has either directed, presented, or produced. Interestingly, Pinhead can also be read as a sturdy example of the two attitudes best characterizing rock 'n' roll—confrontation and rebellion.*

Does it come as any surprise, then, to discover Clive Barker is a hard-core rock fan, with a particular fondness for bands like Coil, Can, and Psychic TV?

But what about Elvis?

In the following piece, Barker takes what is perhaps the most common reaction to Elvis Presley—I've heard of the guy, but I don't worship him—and challenges that. "Notes on St. Elvis" is both a perceptive rumination on Elvis mania and a philosophical reflection on fame and transcendence, one which carries us straight to the tabernacle of the Heartbreak Hotel.

Incidentally, here's something Clive thinks you should know.

What follows is not *an essay, appearance to the contrary.*

"Notes" initially began as a telephone interview, during which I steered Clive toward a consideration of Dead Elvis's religious significance. But then I edited our talk; pulled myself out of the proceedings, and inserted the epigrammatic paragraph headings. At which point Clive looked over the result and made his own adjustments.

So what to call this thing?

An interessay? An essayview?

Whatever. If nothing else, "Notes on St. Elvis" can be seen as an exchange of ideas between two men fascinated with the theological underpinnings of a seemingly secular phenomenon.

Or to put it another way:

Dead Elvis cults, ok.

But a religion?

NOTES ON ST. ELVIS
by Clive Barker

(In Conversation with Paul M. Sammon)

A Lad in Liverpool

First, a confession—I'm not an Elvis fan. It would be far more appropriate to say that I'm familiar with him, more cognizant of Elvis's stature as a cultural icon rather than as a performer.

The reason for this is quite simple; Elvis Presley had absolutely no impact on me while I was growing up. I was a Beatles boy, born in Liverpool, where the Beatles dominated the scene. And from my perspective, the Beatles pretty much blocked out any other musicians. Including those who, like Elvis, influenced the Beatles.

Discovering Elvis

In truth, I wasn't really aware of Elvis until he was so over the hill that he was a grotesque. And I discovered him in a rather bizarre, roundabout way.

Initially, through television, I saw the grotesque performing in Las Vegas. Then I saw *Blue Hawaii*. At which point I realized Presley had been a great talent, had been a smoothly beautiful young man who could perform charismaticly.

Unfortunately, my first impressions of Elvis were those of a bloated parody, of a guy in a white suit with wide lapels. With rhinestones and sunglasses and all that shit.

My Own Private Elvis

Therefore, if I had to choose which Elvis I prefer to watch now—and this is grotesque in itself—I would select the parody, the Elvis of the end. Because:

a. it's the first Elvis that I knew, and,

b. it seems there was a drama in Elvis's final days that wasn't present in such fictionalized concoctions as *Jailhouse Rock*.

The Man

At this point a certain fascination crept in, so I quickly read two biographies on the man.

One was Albert Goldman's biography. The infamous Goldman bio, whose scurrilous reputation was actually my impetus for reading it in the first place. What finally emerged from these books—even if you didn't believe everything that was in them, as many apparently don't with Goldman's effort—was that here was a guy who was completely unprepared for fame and celebrity. Who didn't know what to do with it when he suddenly got it. A simple man who was manipulated and, finally, deeply unhappy.

This emotion is far more common among celebrities than one might think. For example, I am now acquainted with a lot of well-known names whose public faces are those of blithe and happy people. Yet their private lives are hell.

Elvis certainly was familiar with that. Think of the implicit horror in his situation. By just putting a quarter in the jukebox, or by simply turning on a radio, Elvis became public property. And later, here he was —still alive, still breathing, in the middle of his life. Yet his deification process was already complete.

Think of that! You're only some forty-odd years old, your life is not yet finished. Yet you're in the middle of this nightmarish shit where people are only printing the legend. I think that must be bloody difficult.

Thankfully—at least for me—the kind of fame experienced by an Elvis is out of all proportion to any fame ever experienced by a writer. *Any* writer, whether it be me or Stephen King or Norman Mailer. None of us has ever come anywhere near feeling the reaction engendered by Elvis's truly popular art; my books are read by a minuscule amount of people in comparison to the vast numbers who listened, and still listen, to Presley's records.

Heroes

Beyond the man and his work, however, I am also aware of Elvis's continuing cultural resonance. But only in the same way that I am aware of a whole slew of other people in whom I invest no emotional interest.

Still, the current fascination with Elvis Presley touches upon one of the things that's important about cultural landmarks. Which is that we all have heroes.

In the contract between hero and acolyte, the worshipers say to themselves, "Okay, a little part of me is with this hero; I will invest a portion of myself with this person. Their heights will be my heights, while their faults will be my faults."

Secular Elvis

Yet Elvis's impact has clearly expanded beyond mere hero worship. He now moves on two vastly different, powerfully influential planes, the secular and religious ones. Making it that much more important to differentiate between Elvis's religious tale and his secular tale.

On the secular side, one could easily slot Elvis's life into a perfectly described arc mirroring the rise and fall of the American dream. In this case, you can learn something from Presley. There absolutely are parallels between the great hopes of youth becoming empty, hollow, grotesque dreams in later life, when it's discovered that many of the early aspirations are completely worthless.

This parallel with the American dream, this lack of cultural resonance to make sense of opportunities as they come along, is essentially a secular tragedy. A *great* secular tragedy. It is also an important life lesson which can be gleaned from even the most cursory examination of the life and career of Elvis Presley.

His Divine Resurrection

Eventually, however, Presley's secular importance collapses under the weight of an even more profound event—Elvis's resurrection myth.

The religious elements associated with iconographic heroes, with rock 'n' roll heroes, absolutely fascinate me. What I find of interest is that we are basically seeing very primal stories being told here, of heroes who seem transcendent in some way but are finally brought to their knees. Prematurely.

This story has many echoes. For instance, every now and then a random American news program will disgorge a new Elvis obsessive whose life is completely devoted, like some member of an ancient religious order, to the life and works of the Dead Elvis. What's extraordinarily interesting about this ongoing obsession is that while Elvis mania is patently a substitute for a certain lack of spirituality in modern America, it is also a *mockery* of spirituality. Because there are no moral underpinnings to the life of Elvis Presley, just as there are no real spiritual lessons to be learned from this man. None whatsoever.

Elvis does not come with any true gospel. He comes with some rather middle-of-the-road movies and a majority of albums featuring sugary love songs.

This is not the Sermon on the Mount.

Still, what I think is being laid at Elvis's feet—and I use this phrase advisedly—is the sense that he has some greater significance.

Elvis and the Miraculous

One such level of significance concerns the collision of the profane and miraculous. Where this plugs in for me is in the American subculture of the *National Enquirer,* of the not-quite urban myth of the UFO conspiracy, of the child of the devil born in Detroit. Or of Elvis seen yet again in Minneapolis.

This subculture of the *Enquirer* constantly wishes to believe in the presence of the miraculous. Yet it really doesn't have anything miraculous to believe in. So it cobbles together, in a way Charles Fort would have admired, an outré stew of flying saucer tales and the sightings of dead pop stars. It then calls these events significant, calls them evidence of the mysterious or miraculous.

One such event concerns a Presley painting. This apparently is a portrait hanging in Graceland of an idealized, youthful, and somewhat beatific Elvis. A folk legend has grown up around this painting. The claim is that if you lay your fingers on it and wish for a miracle, something good will happen. Not surprisingly, this portrait has been reproduced in the American tabloid press, with further claims that it has restored the sick to perfect health.

Obviously, the Dead Elvis can now lay claim to his own fair share of "miraculous" events.

The Pantheon

However, the central question remains—why is Elvis being elevated in this manner? Why has he been transformed into myth?

The answer is that Elvis is just one of a recent pantheon of deified dead celebrities. You could add James Dean. Or JFK. Or Jim Morrison. Extending the religious metaphor a bit farther, one could even sense that our Mary Magdalene is Marilyn Monroe.

In other words, there is strong evidence to suggest one should study this strange, contemporary pantheon. J. G. Ballard has done this, in fact. He and others have shown that the American psyche is very adept at taking the formal structures of myth and then fitting people into these structures who don't really belong there. The preoccupation with pop stars other than Presley—with Jimi Hendrix, with Janis Joplin, to a lesser extent—or the fact that there are acolytes going on mystical treks to Marilyn Monroe's grave, to simply touch the place where Marilyn's remains now lie, seems further proof that these preoccupations aren't simply with Elvis Presley.

The Urge to Worship

Basically, the issue we are dealing with here is the urge to worship. And this urge is incredibly intense in our species.

We all desire, to some degree, to have something larger and more mysterious than ourselves. Something more connected with the numinous, with the holy, with the powerful, than with us. And if you don't supply this urge in quite the right way, people will go and attach those feelings to the strangest things. They will attach it to channeling, or astrology, or cults of various kinds. They will believe all manner of weird shit. And this will become, in the fullness of time, religion.

I have always cherished a scene from the movie of *Tommy,* when Arthur Brown plays the High Priest of the Church of Marilyn Monroe. The director of that film, Ken Russell, was completely onto something there. Here was the Marilyn cult taken to the extreme of religious experience, in a peculiarly American sense.

Yet I'm not certain if Elvis's religious underpinnings are an entirely American phenomenon. We in Europe have had religion in a fundamental, as opposed to fundamentalist, form for a very long time. It is very much a part of the way our state is run, very much a part of the texture of our lives. And religious needs have been answered, I think, at least up until recently, more readily in European than American society.

So perhaps the hunger to take innocent secular artists like Elvis Presley or Jim Morrison and make them objects of religious devotion is not present in the same degree in Europe because the pantheon of European saints is already fixed. Is already there, and has been there for many hundreds of years.

Suggesting that the root feelings entwining Elvis and Europe's saints may be identical. In fact, even Graceland may look a little less crass from the viewpoint of a pilgrim who has been to Lourdes, since Lourdes itself is decorated with the cast-off crutches of the devout.

The Church of Elvis

Speaking of Graceland, on the eve of the anniversary of Elvis's death, a huge candlelit vigil is usually held there. This undeniable act of worship, this commemoration of St. Elvis, strikes many as bizarre.

Yet given the fact that religion and faith are hard to find in our culture, if these qualities have to be rooted in the worship of a dead rock star . . . well, I'd rather they be rooted there than in the worship of, say, a Himmler. Although Himmler does indeed have his own followers . . .

Therefore, Graceland vigils are not such a terrible thing. But I would love to see people open their field of vision so as to comprehend that the urge which they're directing toward Elvis Presley is the same urge which brings people to the foot of any statue.

One of the problems isn't that people worship, but that they worship too specifically. My feeling is that all gods are worthy of our notice. The more gods you have in your private pantheon, then the healthier you probably are.

Rush to Judgment

Having said that, I still cannot find anything pathetic or sad about a single-minded Elvis obsession. I certainly refuse to be judgmental about this type of human behavior, because the moment I am judgmental, someone will point out that I too have these obsessions, that I too deify.

"You don't like my obsession with Elvis? Fine. Okay. *I* hate the fact that you think Poe is God."

One of the things I've learned as I get older is that the things that make life worth living are the things that make people obsess. For instance, there are people in the world who are obsessed with collecting Barbie dolls. I'm delighted by that, just as I'm equally delighted by people who are obsessed with the notion that Elvis is still alive. You must celebrate, I believe, people's passions. Celebrate the way in which they express their desires. However perverse or bizarre those passions may be.

Then again, I've never really been cornered by a fan who tried to convince me Elvis is alive and well. And a rabid Elvis fan could be dangerous. Especially when cornered.

But so could a Catholic.

I Know It's Only Rock 'n' Roll—But I Like It

Conversely, the most you can do in this world is leave other people's religion alone. For the moment you start to dabble with other people's religion, you start to fuck with their minds in a very fundamental way. What makes sense in a person's pantheon is all that really makes sense.

Therefore, I have no problems with someone drawing comfort from the possibility that the spirit of Elvis is alive and well and dwelling in Graceland. If loving Elvis gets someone through the night, good luck to them.

Because getting through the night is, today, a more difficult proposition than ever.

The End of Elvis?

Elvis mania has been building in America since Presley's death seventeen years ago. This raises a question.

Could this national obsession finally be exhausted?

The only way I can respond to that directly relates to the torrent of Elvis by-products which continue to appear with alarming regularity. There are still vast numbers of Elvis books coming out, as well as extensive tabloid coverage and numerous Elvis Sightings. Many television programs keep monotonously recounting the story of Elvis's final days, too.

So the answer to my own question is—absolutely not.

I have the feeling that the closer we creep toward the Millennium, the more we are going to need our private pantheons. The Elvises and the Marilyns and the James Deans are going to become that much more important to us.

Which is cool, as long as we remember that they are inferior gods to Jesus, Shiva, and Kali. That the Dead Elvis is *subservient* to these larger deities. Not a substitute.

My sense, then, is that Elvis will at least be with us through the Millennium. Yet I do know of those who disagree. As Paul Sammon puts it, "When I see the President of the United States *[George Bush]* talking about Elvis economics during a nomination acceptance speech, I know that the fad has passed."

As for myself, I *don't* know.

But I do think we've got a lot of weird shit coming up in the next few years.

Elvis will continue to be a part of that.

Sex and drugs and rock 'n' roll.

The phrase backbeats off the tongue. A staccato anthem, the Dionysian chant of generations.

Sex and drugs and rock 'n' roll.

Elvis Presley embodied the seductive promise of that phrase. He was the phrase, the words made flesh. Rock's metasymbol of celebrity excess.

Sex and drugs and rock 'n' roll.

Three elements KARL EDWARD WAGNER does some mighty strange things with in the following story.

One that even tops Albert Goldman's infamous "exposé" of Elvis, two-way mirrors, and girls in white cotton underwear.

Karl Wagner is a former psychiatrist who's written/edited over forty-five books. Best-known efforts include his Year's Best Horror Stories *anthologies, which Karl has edited for the past fifteen years, and three collections of marvelously crafted Wagnerian short stories:* In a Lonely Place, Why Not You and I?, *and* Exorcisms and Ecstasies.

Karl's also known for an intriguing series of works starring the enigmatic "Kane." An immortal, ambiguous antihero, Kane can appear in any century, in any guise, on either side of the law.

"Deep in the Depths of the Acme Warehouse" has Kane appearing in our own time. As the catalyst for an exceptionally graphic afternoon delight.

One which, were it a compact disc, would have stickers warning PARENTAL ADVISORY: EXPLICIT LYRICS *plastered all over it.*

Tipper Gore's gonna love this one.

DEEP IN THE DEPTHS OF THE ACME WAREHOUSE

by Karl Edward Wagner

"I think I want to be raped," Lucy touched her breast and said. She stretched slowly against the plastic lounge chair. Her sunscreen smelled hot and buttery. Her brain was clouded with sun and 'ludes.

Lucy Minx tugged her thong straps further down her hips, exposing just the shaved beginnings of her mons. She turned her head and flipped up her mirror shades, flashing her wonderful Italian eyes.

"I think I want to be raped by you." She slid back her sunglasses and shivered in the sun. Languidly she reached for her white wine spritzer, sipped from the straw.

Mina Rush chugged her beer. It was tepid and tasted like the plastic poolside cup. She glanced at Lucy, wondering: *What next?* Mina was wearing a black one-piece and wishing she had Lucy's figure and could get away with a chartreuse thong bikini.

"Say, what?"

A black man in a dark blue jumpsuit was pushing a red vacuum cleaner across the lighter blue poolside carpet. Mina stared at his crotch. Breeze fluttered across the pool, whipping false waves through the chlorine-drugged surface. A slight bit of crumpled newspaper rolled against her bare feet. Mina picked it up. Elvis had been seen in Brazil. Elizabeth Taylor was pregnant by Prince Andrew. Rock Hudson was assassinated by the CIA. Plastic extrusions from flying saucers had raped a nun in France.

Lucy examined her straw, flicked it behind her shoulder, followed it with her cup. She had a luxuriant mass of black hair with a lazy natural curl, and she liked to toss it about for emphasis, just as she liked to flash her eyes. Tossing and flashing, she pulled and twisted bits of her bikini, fussed with her bag of things, and then she left for the shower.

During all this, Lucy said to Mina: "Or forget it."

There was a dead thing in Mina's beer cup. She said: "Shit." And then she repeated it, really meaning it this time. Lucy was a nut case, but Mina had dreamed about her too many times not to have scored. She knew that Lucy knew that she wanted her, and she knew that Lucy enjoyed this sense of control. Lucy might tease and flirt, but for Mina she never gave more than a mocking smile and a brief heartless kiss. "A prick-tease," their drummer had once confided.

Mina Rush was a henna-head with expressive if narrow green eyes and a Prince Valiant haircut that did little to help her rather angular jaw. Her right upper front tooth had been broken when someone lobbed a Jack Daniel's bottle early on in her career, and she flashed a neat gold cap with an inverted pentacle when she smiled. She had long legs, boyish hips, girlish breasts, and a bad attitude. She was maybe the finest white female blues singer since Janis Joplin, but she couldn't hold a group together for more than one tour, and her next album was a year late.

On the edge of superstardom, Mina Rush made only three mistakes: She had a weakness for cocaine, she had an obsession for Lucy Minx, and she had an encounter with Kane.

Something was blocking the sun. Already testy, Mina raised herself on her elbows and glared suddenly upward.

It was not as large as a refrigerator, but only just. He wore denim cutoffs, a black Hawaiian shirt with palm trees and dancing girls, and mirror shades. He was carrying two tall frosty glasses with tiny umbrellas on top and some opalescent liquid inside. The sign at the hotel pool gate commanded: *No Glass*.

"Drink this," he said. "There's a bug in your beer."

Mina accepted the glass automatically, and he reclined upon Lucy's vacated lounge chair. The plastic and aluminum creaked, but held. Mina wondered whether he would sink in the pool like a stone. The man seemed to be a solid block of muscle and bone, very roughly hewn, and was probably in his early thirties. He had a neat red beard, slicked-back red hair, and when he lifted his sunglasses the intensity of his cold blue eyes made her want to look away.

"I'm Kane," he said. He raised his glass. "Cheers."

"*The* Kane?" Mina sipped her drink. Her record company had just recently been acquired by something called Kane, Ltd. All Mina knew about it was that it wasn't Japanese-owned, and no one knew much else about the firm that now held her contracts. Supposedly the head of the organization was enigmatic and unapproachable. Photos were rare, but *Rolling Stone* had described him as an NFL lineman turned outlaw biker. Mina thought about the foggy photographs she had seen. Yes, could be.

The drink tasted of licorice and took her breath away. "What is this?"

"Absinthe on the rocks," said Kane. "Not on the bar list here."

"I'd always thought absinthe was illegal. Even here in New Orleans."

Kane swirled his drink. "So is cocaine, Mina. Will you drink up, or call for the police? Besides, a little tincture of wormwood is good for the soul. This bottle was laid down in 1837."

"Where'd you get a bottle?" Mina knew when she was being served up bullshit, and in this case she decided it was with a glass of Pernod or Herbsaint.

"Connections," Kane told her. "You can obtain anything if you have connections."

Whatever it was, the drink had a kick to it. That plus the sun. Mina crunched a bit of ice. A small lizard crept out of the poolside shrubbery and warmed itself on the stone wall. Two children splashed about noisily in the shallow end of the pool. She could smell steaks broiling in the hotel restaurant. Lucy would be toweling off after her shower a few doors away. A sparrow was hopping along the terrace, looking for morsels.

Only now there was a shimmering haze to the air, sounds seemed too distant, and the world had moved light-years away. A crumpled pack of Camels drifted aimlessly across the patio. A radio played "Run Away" in the distance. But in the dream state, Kane remained.

"Of course," Kane said, "I now hold all your contracts. Do you fancy another?" He held up his glass.

"Another what?" Mina heard herself say.

A large black-gloved hand took her glass. Another glass took its place upon the poolside table. Mina saw a large person, wearing black biker leathers and mirror shades, longish black hair and black beard, black motorcycle boots. He hadn't been there before.

"Thank you, Blacklight," said Kane, sipping a fresh drink. "We're just talking contract."

"What's that?" Mina wondered if she were the only one here without mirror shades.

"Blacklight sometimes helps me with negotiations. And I sense that you are not happy."

"Personal matters."

"The elusive Miss Lucy Minx?"

"Is she under contract, as well?"

"Eventually, everyone is."

"I want her."

Kane considered his drink. "An admirable choice, if dicey. Anything may be obtained."

The drink was making her giddy. Mina asked: "What's the price? My soul?"

Kane seemed offended. "Worth nothing to me, Mina. All I want is your next album. The one that's so overdue. I think, once released, platinum in three weeks. I'll personally produce it for you."

"So. What have you ever done?"

"Far more than you'll ever live to guess."

"You're most reassuring."

"You can't do the album without Lucy. I'll give you Lucy. You give me the album. I'll even write some of your material. But we'll discuss this in good time."

Blacklight had reappeared. Only the three of them seemed to be at poolside. He handed Kane a glass phial with a silver spoon attached. Kane, with surprising delicacy, snorted a spoonful of white powder, paused and remarked: "Nearly there, I think." He then handed the phial to Mina. "Yours to keep."

Mina tasted a few spoonfuls. If it was coke, it was better than any she'd ever had. Perks of being a rising star. She had another couple. Kane was watching her with more than casual interest. Mina tried to say something, then felt Kane inside her mind.

"Most interesting," Kane said. "Did you know she has a thing about Elvis?"

"Obviously."

"She's a wicked twist."

"Obviously."

"You'll need a proper dildo."

"Are you through?"

"Do you remember the Plaster Casters?" Kane suddenly produced a yellowed issue of *Rolling Stone*.

"They were a joke." Mina glanced at the tabloid paper. "Jimi nearly lost his cock when they worked on him."

"Not the only joke about," Kane said. "There were more than a dozen like them. Groupies, whatever. They made plaster casts of their favorite rock stars' cocks. Messy job, if you haven't tried it. No so much the erection—the plaster is an exothermic reaction. Bad job getting it loose from the pubic hair. The fad didn't last all that long."

"I'm sure I can't relate to this." Mina's head was increasingly clouded. She tried a few more spoons to clear it.

"Well, said Kane, finishing his drink. "The deal is simply this. I have available a latex replica made from a plaster cast of Elvis Presley's cock, captured by a couple of really serious fans in 1969. I offer this to you. You and Lucy must make your own arrangements. You will then work together on the new album, material for which I shall supply. It will go platinum. Millions will listen to it. All will be satisfied. You may keep the cock. And keep the coke."

Kane held out his hand. Blacklight slapped down a cardboard container about the size of a shoe box. Kane dropped it onto the aluminum table beside Mina.

"Done. And good hunting."

When Mina set down her glass and sat up, there remained only a cardboard package, a phial of white powder, and the rumble of two Harleys receding into the afternoon sun.

Mina Rush waited until she was back in her room before opening the package. A little help from her nail file, and the seal was broken. Sitting on her bed, she dumped the contents onto the quilted coverlet.

Out tumbled one latex dildo—a perfect replica of a man's erect penis, scrotum included, fitted to a nylon and vinyl harness. The label on the plastic bag read: *One Acme Action Dildo. Elvis Presley Model. Amaze Your Friends!* Mina tore open the bag. Included was a plastic tube labeled: *Acme Action Lubricant and Fixative. Cherry Flavor, Slick and Quick!*

Kane would have his joke. Mina tried another two spoons of his coke, which blended nicely with the absinthe or whatever, and left her high enough to try anything. She examined the dildo—a device with which she was not altogether unfamiliar. This one came with a rippled latex rod inside the harness—about six inches long and designed to slide into the wearer's vagina for double delights. Mina had used a double dildo once with a groupie, and she reckoned she could handle this one without an instruction sheet. At least it didn't need batteries.

Removing her swimsuit, Mina took a slow shower, and then she phoned Lucy's room.

"Yeah?" Lucy's voice was clogged with sleep and 'ludes. Good job they didn't have a gig tonight.

"Ready to be raped?" Mina tried some heavy breathing.

"Is that you, Mina?"

"Who else loves you? I've just scored some really heavy shit. You ready for it?"

"Hang on a minute. Sure. What's your room number again?"

Mina ordered two bottles of champagne from room service, which arrived five minutes before Lucy Minx stumbled into her room, looking rather more stoned than Mina. Mina plied her with champagne and cocaine, before showing her the Elvis reproduction.

Lucy's expression showed total fascination as she rolled the dildo about in her hands. "Is it really Elvis's cock?"

"Read the label. There's probably a whole line of rock stars' cocks. Want to be raped by Elvis, or do I send out for Jimi Hendrix?"

"Let me see you wear it!" Lucy clapped her hands and bounced on the bed. It reminded Mina of a teenagers' slumber party. Back then it only took a few smuggled beers and a joint to be this giddy.

Mina had only pulled on a T-shirt and blue jeans, which she now pulled off. Lucy quickly struggled out of her black tube dress and handed her the dildo, giggling like a schoolgirl. She finished her glass of champagne while Mina worked the harness onto her hips. Opening the tube of ointment, Mina applied some to the interior rod of the harness, then worked it into her vagina. She sighed as the thick probe slid in, then snugged the harness into place.

Lucy was giggling and spilling coke down her bra. Mina took a few experimental steps. The dildo bobbed lifelike between her legs, totally confusing her body image and balance as she looked down. She could feel the interior probe rubbing maddeningly against her clitoris and vagina.

"Hunka hunka hunka burnin' love!" Lucy managed to sing between snorts and giggles.

Mina examined herself in the mirror. The effect was quite disorienting, but very exciting. She clutched the latex dildo and masturbated it, trying to imagine. Lucy was making enough raucous applause to keep the floor awake.

"Shut up, and spread those thighs!" Mina ordered, in an attempt at a masculine growl. It only evoked more whistles.

"You gotta tie me down and rape me!" Lucy had opened the second bottle of champagne. She pushed the gushing bottleneck onto Mina's bobbing dildo. "Bet you can't come like this!"

Mina had begun it all feeling a bit foolish—performing a prank for the amusement of her lover. With the drink, drugs, and sexual excitement, now she was well beyond embarrassment. Besides, Lucy had been prick-teasing her all through the tour. The concept of being prick-teased now that she had the equipment started Mina laughing. Lucy wanted in on the joke, and then they both fell about in a fit of laughter across the bed. Lucy insisted on giving the Elvis artifact head, so as not to waste champagne.

Somehow Mina got Lucy out of her bra and panties. Her protruding erection kept getting in the way as they wriggled about. Mina wondered how men ever managed to get anything done with a salami poking out of their groins, and Lucy said that that was why men had to jerk off twice a day when they couldn't get laid; that was what they really did in urinals, just so they could zip up their pants again.

By now Mina had managed to tie Lucy's wrists to the bedframe with her stockings, hoping that she hadn't made a run in them. Lucy kept chanting: "Fuck me, Elvis! Fuck me, Elvis!" until Mina stuffed her panties into her mouth and tied them in place with her bra.

Still making muffled squeals, Lucy presented a very pretty picture on the hotel bed—arms outspread, black lace strapped across her face, her long legs writhing seductively. Her pussy was very wet, as was Mina's. The friction from the harness had already brought her close to orgasm. Mina anointed the dildo with the tube of lubricant and climbed onto the bed between Lucy's legs.

"Here comes the King!"

She guided the head of the latex penis into Lucy's wet lips, then thrust forward all the way into her until the latex scrotum banged hard against her cunt.

"Prick-tease!" Mina growled, and she began to fuck her furiously.

Lucy thrashed about in abandon—her obvious pleasure serving to increase Mina's passion. Mina had been screwed enough to know the moves, and she reckoned she was doing far better than any man could. She lost count of time as she continued to thrust in and out of her lover. She was certain that Lucy had enjoyed at least three climaxes from her moans and the way her vagina clamped down on her cock. Mina's own orgasm was almost on her now, and she slammed her cock into Lucy hard enough to feel her balls slap against her bruised pussy.

Lucy was almost unconscious when Mina's long-awaited orgasm hit her. Mina screamed as she felt her ejaculation burst from her, pulse deep into her lover's cunt. Fully spent, she collapsed onto Lucy, rolled off gasping as the dildo slipped out, and after a moment fell into a stupor.

When Mina Rush awoke, it was well into the night. Lucy Minx had managed to slip her loose bonds and was sleeping with her head nestled upon Mina's breast—snoring softly, the picture of an innocent child dreaming of lollipops.

Mina needed to take a piss. Still very groggy, she disengaged herself from Lucy and stumbled through the darkness to the bathroom, where a light had been left on. She moved automatically, reacting only to bladder pressure.

Mina raised the toilet seat and relieved herself, wondering if aspirin would help her hangover and vowing never to mix cocaine and champagne ever again. Could that really have been absinthe? She was shaking the drops off her lily, when she suddenly began to awaken fully.

Mina stared.

She was still wearing the dildo and harness.

But how . . . ?

In as much panic as confusion, she tugged at the nylon and vinyl harness, peeling it down from her hips.

There was a sharp pulling sensation as she yanked the harness toward her knees, and then the latex sheath over the dildo popped free and joined the rest of the harness about her ankles.

Mina stared at the hollow latex sheath. She gaped at the living cock and scrotum that had grown into her flesh.

Elvis's cock.

Now hers.

Eventually she went back to bed, remembering to lower the toilet seat. She lit a cigarette and contemplated Lucy.

Deep in the depths of the Acme Warehouse, Blacklight sat on a packing crate watching Kane. Blacklight had a big bucket of cold KFC Original Recipe and a large bottle of warm Ripple. He munched and chugged thoughtfully, occasionally flinging a bone to things chittering beyond their circle of light.

"Kane, even for you that was one damn dirty trick," he observed. *In vino, veritas.*

"Save me a slug of that Ripple," Kane said. "This is dusty work."

Kane emerged from a broken packing crate. He studied the label on the plastic bag: *One Acme Action Dildo. Jim Morrison Model. Electrify Your Friends!*

He tossed the package to Blacklight. "Hang onto this. Should prove useful.

"And anyway. Mina Rush needs a deeper voice if she's ever going to make it big, and the King will give her a lot of soul. If there's a problem, I've got a knife. Snick, snack, and Bob's your uncle. All is set right."

Blacklight handed the bottle to Kane. "You really think we're going to find the Janis Joplin artifact down here?"

"For sure. Probably right there in that crate you're sitting on."

"Are you really a jillion years old?" Blacklight retrieved the Ripple and washed down a couple reds. He moved off the crate.

"And I owe it all to clean living." Kane ripped off the lid of the packing crate with one hand, sending nails and wood chunks flying.

"Well," persisted Blacklight, digesting reds and KFC, "it seems like a dirty trick for a man of your mature years. What's Mina Rush gonna do when she finds out she's a father?"

Kane had dug out a series of flat packages and was examining them with considerable enthusiasm. "Got it! British production. Hence the confusing label of 'fanny.' I know just the dude to lay this one on."

He finished the Ripple and turned pensive. "Blacklight. If there's one lesson you can learn in a jillion years, it's this: You can't always get what you need. But if you don't watch out, you just might get what you want."

What happened to Elvis in Germany?

True Believers know it was here that the King spent the majority of his military service. In Bremerhaven, West Germany, from late 1958 to early 1960. After being drafted into the Army on December 19, 1957.

Over the decades, other facts have emerged.

In November 1958, Elvis joined the 32nd Tank Battalion for maneuvers near the Czech border.

He achieved the rank of buck sergeant before his discharge on March 5, 1960.

The King's first exposure to drugs happened in Germany; a sergeant gave Elvis some Dexedrine to help him stay awake during night guard duty.

All fine and good.

Was there anything else?

JANET BERLINER GLUCKMAN presents one possible incident . . .

Gluckman left her native South Africa in 1961 to protest apartheid. She lives in the San Francisco Bay Area, where she works as a writer, lecturer, and consultant. Her short stories have appeared in such anthologies as Future Earths: Under African Suns *and* Ariadne's Web. *Novels include* Rite of the Dragon *and* Child of the Light *(co-authored with George Guthridge), a story of Hitler attempting to create an African ghetto on the island of Madagascar.*

For "Wooden Heart," Gluckman takes another historical incident and skews it toward her own point of view.

One involving Elvis, ballerinas, and innocuous German pop songs.

"Innocuous" till now, that is.

WOODEN HEART

by Janet Berliner Gluckman

May 1, 1959

Alicia signed her name.

She blew at the signature to make sure the ink was dry and glanced over the contract just one more time. A season with the Berlin Opera, mostly corps de ballet, except for understudying *Coppelia* . . . enough to keep her in Germany.

"See you in one week, Fräulein Marcus." The director spoke in precise formal English. He extended his hand. "Rest. Take it easy. It will be a strenuous season."

"I look forward to it," Alicia said, pleased that she did not have to embarrass herself with her high school German.

She took a taxi back to the room she had rented on Niebuhr Strasse. It wasn't much of a place, but it was clean, and her rent included breakfast. She took out a map and looked at the cities she had circled: Paris, Barcelona, Dresden—

Dresden. She reached for the porcelain ballerina that went everywhere with her, dusted off the round walnut doll stand, and tightened the metal rods that curved under the statuette's armpits and held her in place. "All right, Margot," she said. "Let's see where you were born."

She threw a few things into her duffle, ran a brush through her long tangle of red hair, and wrote a note for her landlady.

The trouble began in Frankfurt. She stood on line for her ticket, watching the minutes pass.

"Dresden," she said when it was finally her turn. "Round trip."

The ticket seller glanced up at the train board. "No train till tomorrow," he said. "Train left ten minutes ago."

She moved aside and looked up at the massive train schedule that hung from the high ceiling. The next departure was for Wiesbaden. Since she had no desire to see Frankfurt and she'd be going back to Berlin soon enough to start rehearsals, she shouldered her way back into line and bought herself a ticket.

"Better choice," the clerk said. "Enjoy yourself."

The train was filled with Czech workers. One of them shifted over to make room for her. "Such a pretty lady," he said in German. He stared at her ankles, at her shapely dancer's legs. "Don't look so sad. Come. Sit over here. I'll cheer you up."

"*Ich bin Blau,*" she said. *I'm blue.*

"*Blau?*" The man roared with laughter. "Drunk."

His renewed laughter followed her onto the platform at Wiesbaden. "Hope you sober up soon, Blue Lady," he shouted out of a window in broken English.

At the first taxi rank she found, she asked about a pension. The driver took her to an old house at the top of a steep hill. Inside the room, she watched as a very elderly woman made up a feather bed, raising long untouched layers of dust. From the window, she could see green lawns, orderly flower beds, trees carefully trimmed.

She unpacked, changed into a pale pink suit, and walked down the long, winding, tree-lined hill to a town square centered by Roman ruins. Men and women in tails and gowns headed for the casino and, at the far end of the square, narrow cobbled side streets, reminiscent of Lisbon, led to a tourist paradise: nude postcards and magazines, as openly displayed as in Berlin; Chinese-American restaurants offering a change from *sauerbraten;* elegant florists vying with corner flower sellers, and expensive jewelry stores offering lucky gamblers a place to rid themselves of their profits.

She headed for the casino—her first in Europe. Three years ago, on her twenty-first birthday, her parents had given her a ticket to Las Vegas. She'd loved it. But it wasn't anything like this. Here there were two casinos, one for the wealthy, another for small-time gamblers like herself.

Rationalizing that she might never get back to Wiesbaden, she paid the cover charge for both. In the elegant casino, she found a single blackjack table and several roulette wheels. No craps, no machines. Here, laughter seemed to be *verboten,* too distracting, she supposed, for the patrons using systems, working with pencil and paper, and playing with the intensity of stockbrokers.

Having checked her funds, Alicia picked up an ashtray from an unused table and put out her cigarette. She couldn't afford this, she thought, walking toward the door.

"I suggest you leave that here." A tall man, balding though he could not have been more than thirty, took the ashtray from her hand. "Security might think you wanted to steal it or, worse yet, attack their distinguished guests with it." His accent was heavily Texan. He had a fighter's spring to his walk. He was not ugly exactly, but there was something menacing about the flat bullet head that seemed too large for even his tall frame.

Alicia examined the man more closely. The ashtray had hardly looked worth stealing and, at five three, fragile, a hundred and one pounds, she was certainly not the assassin type. She started to say something about a novel approach to meeting a woman, but the look in his eyes changed her mind. He was serious, she thought. A serious nut case. Handing him the ashtray, she headed out of the stuffy atmosphere and toward the smaller casino.

In the small casino, laughter and noise appeared to be the order of the day. The only game being played was a form of roulette called Golden Thirteen. Judging by their clothing, the people around the table were locals. Some even wore blue jeans.

She moved closer to the table.

"I'm sorry Joe chased you away from the other casino," a voice said behind her. "He gets a little overprotective. Come on, I'll explain the game."

The voice was husky, sexual, familiar. She looked around. He grinned at her and nodded. "Don't say anything. Just pick a number."

The man was a dead ringer for Elvis. Though she was no swooning fan, she was as vulnerable as most to celebrities, and this was one very sexy man.

She pulled herself together. Just because Elvis Presley was stationed down the road in Darmstadt didn't mean she had to act like a fool over someone who happened to look like him.

"Pick a number," the man who looked like Elvis said.

"Seven."

He placed a bet for her.

The wheel sat in the middle of a long narrow table, with boards for betting on either side. It had fourteen slots—zero through thirteen.

"Sieben!" The croupier pushed chips in her direction. She waited for the man to reach for them, but he simply laughed and told her to take the money. Then he took her hand and pulled her toward the cashier's cage. They cashed in the chips, and he drew her toward the big casino.

"Joe. My bodyguard." Elvis introduced her to the man who had taken her ashtray. "Joe, this is—"

"Alicia."

"Let's get out of here, Alicia," Elvis said.

He took her arm and led her out of the casino. They wandered across a park and stopped next to a statue of Pan. An old man leaned against it playing a battered accordion.

Softly, Elvis began to sing. *"Muss i denn, muss i denn, zum Stadtele hinaus und du mein Schatz bleibst hier . . ."*

Drawn into the moment, Alicia kicked off her shoes and danced, a doll on a music box, arms flowing, feet performing a series of perfect pirouettes around and around and around . . . hardly noticing when Joe took out a small camera and snapped her photograph.

"Treat me nice, treat me good, treat me like you really should, 'cause I don't have a wooden heart."

Joe bent to pick up her shoes and to offer the man with the accordion a fistful of bills. The old man shook his head and smiled. Elvis seemed to understand. He took her arm and led her to a small café at the far end of town. Joe trailed behind them.

"How long will you be in Wiesbaden?" Elvis asked as they sat down.

"Tomorrow. I'm leaving tomorrow."

"Don't go," he said. "I like you."

"You really are Elvis, aren't you?" *No one will believe this,* she thought. She'd have to get his autograph. Not knowing why she did it, she held out her arm where he had touched it. "Sign my arm," she said, turning it over and pointing at the soft underside of her flesh. "Please."

Joe handed Elvis a pen.

"Wenn i komm, wenn i komm, wenn i wieder wieder komm', kehr i ein mein Schatz bei dir." Love, Elvis.

"When I come, when I come, when I come back again," Alicia translated, "I'll come back, my love, to you. That's lovely."

"It's from that music box love song the old man was playing. I've asked them to put it in my next movie. But not this verse. This verse is for you, my little music box doll."

He smiled at her, almost shyly . . . a Southern boy looking for love. She returned the smile, not to show him that she bought the act but to let him know that the sentiment pleased her anyway. "I have nothing to give you," she said.

"You gave me your dance," he said.

"It's getting late, Elvis," Joe said. "We have a curfew, remember. Gotta go."

For a moment, Alicia had forgotten his presence. He was staring at her intensely, almost jealously.

To her amazement, Elvis hugged her, clinging like a child.

"Keep in touch," Joe said. There was a strange light in his eyes.

He took a card out of his pocket, wrote something on the back of it, and pressed it into her hand. She watched until they were out of sight. After she'd ordered an espresso, she looked at the card Joe had given her: Joe Galgut. Bodyguard. A Los Angeles phone number.

She laughed at herself for thinking, even for a moment, that she had been handed Elvis's private phone number and flipped over the card. Read Joe's message:

"They'll never believe you at home unless you have the words tattooed into your skin."

She might not have done it had the tattoo parlor not been en route back to the pension. The next morning, when reality had replaced her celebrity high, she cursed her stupidity. But it was too late. *Wenn i wieder weider komm', kehr i ein mein Schatz bei dir. Love, Elvis* was tattooed into her flesh.

August 16, 1977

Alicia's career as a dancer was only a little less short-lived than either one of her marriages. The tattoo was part of the problem. During rehearsals, it didn't matter; as a member of the corps de ballet, a few layers of Max Factor—patted with a towel and replaced between scenes—did the trick. She might have thought about having it removed had she been given the chance to do more than understudy *Coppelia,* but she wasn't. By the time her contract with the company expired, the real problem had begun. It came out of a strange restlessness, beginning after Margot was stolen from her Niebuhr Strasse room. That restlessness, all but a physical itch beneath her feet, drove her to new places, new people, brought her to London after her second divorce.

Oh well, she thought. Forty-one wasn't all that old, and she was still in good shape. She glanced over her shoulder at the image in the Savoy's ornate lobby mirror and bent down to straighten the seams in her stockings. Good legs. She'd always had good legs. Waist a little thicker after two kids, flat-chested like most dancers . . . She faced the mirror. The gray was showing. She'd have to do something about that.

Not that Joe would notice. He didn't notice much unless it had something to do with Elvis. They had spoken to each other again right after *G.I. Blues* came out. She'd called to tell Joe to thank Elvis for keeping his word.

In the movie, *Muss i denn,* had become "Wooden Heart," with a few lines of German thrown in for authenticity.

But not her lines.

Joe did not sound surprised to hear from her and asked about the tattoo. After that, they spoke a few times a year. She'd even seen him once, after her first divorce. He hadn't changed much—same cryptic speech pattern, same ex-pugilist's set to his head and body; same strange look in his eyes. Her tattoo seemed to fascinate him. She had caught him several times, staring at it with almost sexual intensity. Disquieted, she thought again of having it removed and decided there was no more reason for them to keep in touch. She did not return his next two or three calls, but she did not have the tattoo removed. Somehow the pain and expense hardly seemed worth the effort after all of this time.

Why she'd called him after this divorce, she had no idea, but she had. She'd even agreed that, seeing they were going to be in London at the same time, they might as well spend a day together.

Now, as she ate her kipper-and-egg breakfast, she wondered again why she had agreed to see him. Boredom, perhaps? A middle-aged woman clinging to one of the more romantic episodes of her youth? She felt silly. It was not as if she and Joe had anything in common except Elvis Presley and, were it not for the tattoo, even that would not seem real.

Joe was waiting for her outside the hotel at eleven o'clock. She was hardly inside the taxi when he said, "Let me see it."

Knowing what he wanted, she showed him her arm. The tattoo was as clear as it had been the night she'd had it done.

"I can't stay," he said. Wasting no time on pleasantries, he tapped on the glass that separated them from the driver. "Take me to Heathrow, then drive the lady wherever she needs to go." He handed the driver a wad of money and turned to look at her. "Elvis called last night. He wanted me home right away. Said he was going to die."

"No sense hurrying back. He was right." The driver glanced at them in his rearview mirror. "The wife's in mourning. Says life will never be the same now's the King's dead."

Joe showed no sign of emotion, but to her own amazement, Alicia felt tears rolling down her cheeks. Not that she had really known Elvis, but rather that she was suddenly in mourning, too, not so much for him, but for her youth.

"Another one crying over him like he was her friend." The taxi driver sounded irritated.

"Don't cry," Joe said. "He's just resting." He patted her arm. "I'll be in touch." He tapped urgently on the glass. "Get me to the airport," he said. "Now."

April 27, 1979

"I've heard of that before," Dr. Greene said. "People with tinnitus who hear music inside their heads."

"The same song? Over and over again, day after day for years?"

"Forever. You'll get used to it."

"The hell I will." Alicia stood up. One more ENT man to cross off the list. She'd go to every last one in the world before she admitted defeat. Two years of *Muss i denn, muss i denn,* like a damn broken record, interfering with her life, her thoughts. As if it wasn't enough having to cover up her arm all of the time, sweating in the summer, tired of sleeves by the winter. She'd actually stopped hiding the tattoo for a while, until some Elvis freak suggested that she auction off her arm to the highest bidder. Why not, she thought grimly. Next thing she'd find a way to plug his fans into her head, then when they put her away she'd be the richest person in the nuthouse.

She lined up appointments with several more specialists, including a plastic surgeon who agreed to remove the tattoo, but the day before her new round of doctor's visits was to begin an envelope arrived from Joe. It contained an air ticket, a note, a snapshot, and an invitation to the opening of his new venture:

THE WOODEN HEART
Wiesbaden, Germany
Opening May 1, 1979

The note was short and to the point: *"Dear Alicia, Come and help me prepare for the opening. I've enclosed a ticket to Frankfurt and the snapshot I took that day in the park. Wear the dress in the picture if you still have it. I'll send a car to meet you. Joe."*

She pulled the old pink suit out of the back of her closet. Dubiously, expecting to look like mutton dressed up as lamb, she tried it on. It looked surprisingly good. On impulse, she rescheduled her doctors' appointments and, almost exactly twenty years after her first meeting with Elvis Presley, she was on her way back to Wiesbaden. A chauffeur-driven Mercedes took her straight to where the café had been. The town looked much the same. Only a McDonald's in the center of town reminded her of the passage of the years, that and the sign over the door of what had once been the café where she and Joe and Elvis had gone that night. Now the sign read: THE WOODEN HEART.

A faint light glowed inside the shop. The door was ajar, so she pushed it open and walked inside, jumping as it shut behind her. Here and there, in piles on the floor, lay guitars and sequined jackets. A life-sized picture of Elvis hung slightly askew on the far wall. In the center of the floor stood a huge round wooden doll stand, exactly like Margot's except that it, too, was life-sized. A thick black cable ran from the stand to a plug in the wall. She went up to it and flipped the switch.

The doll stand began to turn.

The music was there, inside her head; her memory supplied the voice and the words. *"Wenn i komm, wenn i komm, wenn i wieder wieder komm', kehr i ein mein Schatz bei dir."*

She moved toward the stand. Climbed onto it. Arms moving gracefully, she began to pirouette, a little clumsily at first but gaining balance as her feet remembered their lessons.

"Take your shoes off," Joe said.

She had no idea where he had come from, but she obeyed. He took the shoes from her.

"Your hair," he said.

She stood quietly, waiting for him to remove the pins. Her still-red hair flowed across her shoulders.

"Now dance."

The music played and she danced, danced until she was exhausted. "That's enough," she said at last. "I have to rest."

"You'll get back in shape," Joe said. "Tomorrow you'll be able to dance for longer, and the next day—"

"No!" Suddenly she was scared, deep down all the way to her toes. She stepped off the stand.

"You're tired," Joe said. "We'll talk about it tomorrow. Everything will look different after a good night's sleep." He took hold of her arm, caressing the tattoo. "I'll take you to the hotel," he said gently. "Are you sure you won't stay?"

She shook her head. "I don't want to go to a hotel. I want to go home."

"I understand, Alicia. Just dance for me one more time and then I'll take you to the airport."

Icy cold, she threw aside her shoes, climbed back onto the unmoving stand, and assumed a dancer's pose. She watched him walk toward the switch. As the stand began to move, he bent down and picked up a camera.

"Dance, Alicia," he said. "Then rest against the supports and let me take some pictures before you go."

He came toward her and wound up the huge pedestal music box with a massive metal key that he inserted into a hole in the side of the stand. Elvis's throaty voice filled the small shop.

"Dance, Alicia," Joe said again.

Again, she danced until she was exhausted. "Lean back. Rest," he said. "I'll turn up the lights." He walked over to a switch she hadn't noticed before and raised the camera.

She snuggled into the metal arms. Leaned back. Saw him lift his hand to flip the switch. In the split second before he 'acted, she caught a glimpse of Margot, on a shelf high against the wall. Joe, she thought. Joe stole her. She shuddered as the support's arms tightened beneath her armpits and around her ribs and the current ran through her. Her head lolled to one side. When the music began again, she heard nothing, not even the notes inside her head.

But Joe heard it. He heard it above the shocked voices of the people who streamed inside for the opening, above the sirens, above the words of the men who led him away. It was all he heard as he waited for Elvis to keep his promise and return to Alicia.

"*Wenn i komm, wenn i komm, wenn i wieder wieder komm', kehr i ein mein Schatz bei dir,*" Elvis sang. *When I return, I'll return to you.*

NEAL BARRETT, JR., is a national resource.

Author of over thirty-six novels and numerous short stories, Barrett has applied his distinctive talents to the full spectrum of literary genres—quirky mainstream fiction, westerns, mysteries, and science fiction. In fact, The Washington Post hailed Barrett's 1991 book The Hereafter Gang as "one of the great American novels." And his recent mystery novel Pink Vodka Blues will soon be a Paramount motion picture starring Whoopi Goldberg.

Neal's idiosyncratic, highly individualistic work delights in defying common category and convention. He's also damn good at what he does; in an age that worships surface flash, Barrett's gained a solid reputation as a "writer's writer."

It is with a great deal of pleasure, then, that I now present "Donna Rae." This typically unclassifiable Barrett opus is a comedy. I think. For shot through "Donna Rae's" humorous riffs on upper-class ennui and sexual burnout are some rather grim sketches of urban decadence, as well as telling little reminders of how ubiquitous Dead Elvis has become.

The King insists on popping up in the damnedest places!

Such as this rather peculiar restaurant . . .

DONNA RAE

by Neal Barrett, Jr.

His name was Charless Tomm. He was wealthy beyond a man's dreams. Every need, every passing whim, was gratified at once by a horde of retainers, young men and women with suitable degrees from Eastern schools. There were 216 retainers in all. They worked in three shifts. They sat at identical cherrywood desks on the 85th floor of the Charless Tomm Tower on Park Avenue. This is all they did. They were not allowed to smoke or chew gum or read paperback books. Though no one ever saw them, proper office dress was required. Bad breath, or unsightly conditions of the skin, were not allowed.

On each retainer's desk was a bank of white phones, a computer, and a high-speed Fax. In a matter of seconds, each young man or woman could contact agents of every sort around the world.

At a cherrywood desk a little larger than the rest sat Ms. Ortega-St. Clair. She was forty-four now, and she had worked for Charless Tomm for nearly twenty-six years. She had never worked for anyone else. She had never met Charless Tomm himself, but she knew everything there was to know about his needs. When her screen lit up with a call from Charless Tomm, she would instantly call upon one of the people at her command. Every request was to be carried out at once, every need fulfilled. If it was not, there would be an empty cherrywood desk on the 85th floor. One strike with Ms. Ortega-St. Clair and you were out.

Often, Ms. Ortega-St. Clair would simply not bother to give the call to anyone else. She had worked for Charless Tomm so long, it was sometimes easier to fill the need herself. She knew how Charless Tomm thought. He would get an idea for something new from whatever he was doing at the time. Soaking in the tub, he would see the water lap around his floating private parts, and decide to buy a boat. He would reach for his PC by the tub, and tap out his request.

I THINK I WANT A BOAT, he would write.

WHAT KIND OF A BOAT, CHARLESS TOMM? Ms. Ortega-St. Clair would write back.

WHAT KINDS OF BOATS HAVE THEY GOT?

THERE ARE BOATS THAT HAVE MOTORS, AND BOATS THAT HAVE SAILS. SOMETIMES THEY HAVE BOTH.

I GUESS ONE WITH A SAIL.

BIG OR LITTLE, CHARLESS TOMM?

BETTER MAKE IT BIG.

BIG IT IS, CHARLESS TOMM.

Moments after that, Ms. Ortega-St. Clair would search her encyclopedic mind for the section on BOATS. A call would go out to the Gulfstar people in St. Petersburg. Sloop-rigged sailboat. Sixty-two feet. Sleeps eight. First-class electronic navigation gear. Teak and mahogany, solid gold fixtures in the heads, Vermont marble for the tubs. Italian furniture from Atelier. Lamb-hide leather seating custom-made by Hermès of Paris, eiderdown bedding, Pratesi silk sheets.

When the sailboat was complete, crewed, and tied up at Charless Tomm's Southampton pier, Ms. Ortega-St. Clair would let him know that it was there. Charless Tomm might go out and see his boat. Then again, he might not.

This is the way things used to be. Up until 1983 or 1984, when Charless Tomm ran out of things to buy. Ms. Ortega-St. Clair had seen it coming. It never took her long to spot a trend. There were days, even weeks, when the staff sat idly at their cherrywood desks. And, when a call *did* come, it was frequently peculiar at best. Charless Tomm, who used to ask for Bentleys and Lagondas, now requested 1932 Fords. New. Not used. He wanted a balsa-wood flying kit, the Gee Bee racer Comet had on the shelves in '38 or '39, he couldn't remember which. Green and white tissue, a period rubber band, not the kind you get now. He wanted every Tinkertoy car, truck, or plane ever made. Brand new. He wanted a blue glass ashtray from Woolworth's, shaped like a duck. He thought about 1942.

These were trying times for Ms. Ortega-St. Clair and her crew. Nevertheless, they prevailed. If Ms. Ortega-St. Clair had learned anything at all in her years with Charless Tomm, it was the knowledge that anything you want can be had, if you (1) know exactly where to look, and (2) can afford to pay the price.

Ms. Ortega-St. Clair knew what was coming next. Charless Tomm's Second Childhood Phase, she was sure, would herald new demands for the sexually bizarre. If he was tired of his toys, and yearning for 1932 Fords, it was safe to assume that his usual carnal encounters would no longer turn him on. All the signs were there. His Playmate-of-the-Month phase had lasted two years. For a while, he was into Miss Americas who came from Southern states, but he soon tired of that. He shunned top models and movie stars. He crossed Emmy winners off his list. He no longer cared for TV weather girls.

Ms. Ortega-St. Clair was less than surprised when he asked for cheerleaders from each of the NFL teams. They had to be five feet six, and have bleached blond hair. Then he asked for fast-food girls. They had to be tall and brunette. They had to come from small towns in Illinois.

It was clear to Ms. Ortega-St. Clair that she was right. Charless Tomm was getting bored. He asked for Danish women who raised Dalmatian dogs. He asked for Scottish girls named Bea who refused to ride on trains. It wasn't always easy to meet his needs. Still, Ms. Ortega-St. Clair persevered.

More often than not, she handled the kinkier calls herself. She felt she owed him that. She felt the staff didn't need to know he collected the athletic wear of perky young gymnasts who had won international events. She felt she had to be discreet.

There came a time when Charless Tomm ceased to call at all. Some of the newer members of the staff began to nap. Ms. Ortega-St. Clair quickly put a stop to that.

Three weeks passed. Then four. Ms. Ortega-St. Clair grew concerned. Had something happened to him? Perhaps he was ill, perhaps he'd had an accident. Of course she knew it wasn't that. She would have been informed. She was head of her department. She had a twenty-five-year pin.

Then, on a Thursday afternoon, at a quarter past two, words began to appear on her screen. Ms. Ortega-St. Clair gave a sigh of relief. Every member of her staff sat up straight. Two of the younger girls fainted at their cherrywood desks.

MS. ORTEGA-ST. CLAIR? the words read.

I'M HERE, Ms. Ortega-St. Clair wrote back.

I DON'T BELIEVE WE'VE EVER MET. THOUGH I FEEL THAT I KNOW YOU, MS. ORTEGA-ST. CLAIR.

I FEEL I KNOW YOU TOO, CHARLESS TOMM. BY THE WAY, THAT'S A VERY NICE SUIT.

A pause from Charless Tomm, then—THANK YOU VERY MUCH. BUT HOW WOULD YOU KNOW IF MY SUIT IS NICE OR NOT?

BECAUSE I BOUGHT IT, CHARLESS TOMM. I BUY YOUR SUITS AND YOUR SOCKS AND UNDERWEAR. I KNOW WHEN SOMETHING'S NEW AND WHEN IT'S NOT. I KNOW WHEN YOUR TIES WEAR OUT. IF THIS IS THURSDAY, JUNE 4, AND I'M CERTAIN THAT IT IS, YOU'RE WEARING THE BLACK WITH CHALK STRIPES, HENRY POOLE OF SAVILE ROW. THE PALE BLUE EGYPTIAN COTTON SHIRT IS AR-THUR GLUCK. THE TIE IS DECASI, BLUE AND WHITE PAIS-LEY ON BLACK, THE SHOES ARE FROM POULSEN AND SKONE. I EXPECT YOU'RE WEARING THE ROYAL OAK WATCH BY AUDEMARS PIQUET.

MY HEAVENS, MS. ORTEGA-ST. CLAIR. I'M IMPRESSED.

NO NEED TO BE. I'M JUST DOING MY JOB, CHARLESS TOMM.

I BELIEVE YOU'VE BEEN WITH ME SOME TIME. A NUM-BER OF YEARS, HAVE YOU NOT?

TWENTY-FIVE YEARS.

THAT LONG.

TWENTY-SIX YEARS NEXT MAY.

MY BIRTHDAY'S IN MAY. I'LL BE FIFTY-EIGHT. AND HOW OLD ARE YOU, MAY I ASK?

YOU MAY NOT, CHARLESS TOMM.

QUITE RIGHT. NONE OF MY CONCERN. NO OFFENSE INTENDED, MS. ORTEGA-ST. CLAIR.

NONE TAKEN, CHARLESS TOMM.

YOU HAVE BEEN OF ENORMOUS HELP TO ME, MS. ORTEGA-ST. CLAIR. I WANT YOU TO KNOW THAT I AM GRATEFUL FOR THAT.

I DO MY BEST, CHARLESS TOMM.
DO I PAY YOU QUITE WELL?
QUITE WELL INDEED.
IS THERE ANYTHING YOU NEED?
NOTHING COMES TO MIND.
WELL IF THERE IS . . .
CHARLESS TOMM—
YES, MS. ORTEGA-ST. CLAIR?
I HAVE BEEN IN YOUR EMPLOY FOR TWENTY-FIVE
YEARS. IN ALL THAT TIME, WE HAVE NEVER HAD A PER-
SONAL CHAT. I BELIEVE WE ARE HAVING ONE NOW. I AM
NOT UNGRATEFUL FOR YOUR CONCERN, BUT I AM NEI-
THER DULL-WITTED NOR DENSE. WHATEVER YOU'RE
LEADING UP TO, IT MUST BE A LULU AND A HALF. IT IS
NOT NECESSARY, CHARLESS TOMM. I KNOW MY JOB. TELL
ME WHAT YOU WANT, I'LL GET IT DONE.
YOU ARE VERY PERCEPTIVE, MS. ORTEGA-ST. CLAIR.
You're very transparent, she thought to herself . . .
AS YOU KNOW—MORE THAN ANYONE ELSE, I SUPPOSE
—I HAVE PARTICULAR WANTS AND NEEDS.
Kinky appetites, thought Ms. Ortega-St. Clair . . .
I QUITE UNDERSTAND, CHARLESS TOMM. YOU'VE
DONE ABOUT EVERYTHING THERE IS. YOU'VE RUN OUT
OF HOLLYWOOD TARTS. YOU'RE TIRED OF DOING BUN-
NIES AND PETS. AVON LADIES DON'T CUT IT ANYMORE.
I AM GREATLY RELIEVED, MS. ORTEGA-ST. CLAIR. I
KNEW YOU'D UNDERSTAND. I WANT SOMEONE WHO'S
DIFFERENT . . . NOT LIKE EVERYONE ELSE. I WORK VERY
HARD. I DON'T HAVE TO BUT I DO. I HAVE TO WIND
DOWN. BALANCE IS THE KEY. I NEED SOMEONE WHO'S
ABSOLUTELY FRESH AND NEW.
YOU BETTER NOT HAVE PRESCHOOLERS IN YOUR
HEAD. I WON'T PUT UP WITH THAT.
PLEASE! I AM NOT SOME KIND OF PERVERT, MS.
ORTEGA-ST. CLAIR!
NO OFFENSE INTENDED, CHARLESS TOMM.
She decided not to bring up the gym suits, the chocolate-covered nuns.

I SIMPLY NEED YOU TO EXPLORE SOME . . . ALTER-
NATE SOURCES OF STIMULATION. OTHER AVENUES.

I'LL GET RIGHT ON IT, CHARLESS TOMM.

IT WON'T BE THE SAME OLD THING NOW, WILL IT?
CUTE LITTLE HOUSEWIVES WHO DRIVE RED TOYOTAS
AND LIVE IN NEW ROCHELLE . . .

TRUST ME, CHARLESS TOMM.

I DO, MS. ORTEGA-ST. CLAIR.

GOOD. KEEP THAT IN MIND, CHARLESS TOMM.

He arrived at the office at ten the next day, as he did every day except
Sundays and Horatio Alger's birthday. As ever, there were several important memos on his desk. The Vatican had called. The President wanted
to sell the Western states. Africa was starving again, and wanted to buy
some wheat. Ms. Ortega-St. Clair had left a message to call her when he
could.

Charless Tomm set the other notes aside, and turned at once to his
desk PC.

YOU'VE GOT SOMETHING FOR ME, he wrote. I AM CER-
TAIN THAT YOU DO.

I DO INDEED, wrote Ms. Ortega-St. Clair. HER NAME IS
DONNA RAE. YOU WILL PICK HER UP AT SEVEN TONIGHT.
WRITE DOWN THIS ADDRESS.

Charless Tomm did.

THIS IS VERY EXCITING. I SENSE SOMETHING DIFFER-
ENT IN THE AIR.

YOU'D BE RIGHT, CHARLESS TOMM.

HER NAME IS DONNA RAE.

YES, IT IS.

I AM FORMING A PICTURE IN MY HEAD.

YOU'RE WASTING YOUR TIME IF YOU DO.

SHE IS TALL AND QUITE EXOTIC. DARK HAIR. A SLIGHT
TOUCH OF GREEN IN HER EYES. I BELIEVE SHE COMES
FROM MAINE.

TAKE SOME NICE FLOWERS. BE THERE ON TIME,
CHARLESS TOMM.

Slight pause from Charless Tomm . . .

I DON'T THINK YOU UNDERSTAND. I WILL HAVE HER

PICKED UP. AT SEVEN AS YOU SAID. BUT I DON'T PICK
PEOPLE UP MYSELF. I HAVE THEM BROUGHT TO ME.

NOT THIS TIME YOU DON'T. YOU PICK HER UP YOUR-
SELF OR SHE DOESN'T GO AT ALL. TRUST ME, CHARLESS
TOMM.

Ms. Ortega-St. Clair logged out. Charless Tomm stared at his screen.
He studied the *Mona Lisa* on the wall. He suddenly understood. He was
seized by the moment. He felt a pleasant tingle at the base of his spine.
He was struck by the boldness, by the daring of the act. He would do it
—he would actually pick up this Donna Rae person himself. He would
walk up to her door. It would be like—he searched for the word—like
going on a date! The way ordinary people had to do!

He nearly laughed aloud. Leave it to Ms. Ortega-St. Clair to come up
with the really outlandish, the totally bizarre.

He canceled his Friday night poker with the Pope. He told the President to wait. He told Africa to call some other time. He left the office
early, something he hadn't done in years.

His driver found the proper address at six fifty-five. The apartment
was antique brick, a relatively modest structure, Charless Tomm
thought, but it was rather hard to judge these things, since everything
looked modest to him.

He took the elevator up to six. He was dressed in a tux from Gieves &
Hawkes, shoes from John Lobb. The orchids he carried were a delicate,
pale sea-green, a newly discovered species flown in that day from Suri-
name. He felt dizzy and intense. Eager and out of sorts. Like a kid on his
first prom night. He imagined her coming to the door. She was different, not like anyone else. She was a very spiritual person, gentle to a
fault. Yet, she had a pleasing whorish smile. She gave him a look that
said, I promise you wonders, Charless Tomm, that you've never known
before.

Charless Tomm knocked on the door. His heart beat like a Chinese
drum. The import orchids were sticky in his hand. In a moment, the
door opened wide, and there his vision stood, or if not quite a vision, a
sort of apparition or a wraith, a creature in disorder and disarray, a
female hideous and drab, the loser in a Klingon beauty contest, a woman
too ugly to qualify as plain.

Charless Tomm nearly gagged. She was gross and untidy from her head down to her toes. Her hair was a mass of brittle curls; he imagined a million cheap watches had exploded in her head. Her eyes were the color of rotten wood, set close against a veined and bulbous nose. Her mouth was a ruptured sewer line, her chin nowhere in sight. Her figure had all the charm and grace of a stack of garden tools. She wore a house dress, circa 1942, a former flour sack. Legs hairy as a bear's disappeared in red ankle socks, and Nikes with the toes cut out.

Charless Tomm stared, thunderstruck or worse, paralyzed by this awesome sight. The woman stared back, then offered him a smile, showing Charless Tomm around ten thousand dollars' worth of urgent dental needs. She reached out and grabbed the orchids from him and crushed them to her breasts, which were somewhat larger than a pair of Tylenols.

"I'm Donna Rae," she said. "I'd say you're Charless Tomm. Thanks for the flowers. I cost a hundred thousand dollars a night. You've got to treat me nice. You've got to take me anywhere I like."

"This is intolerable," Charless Tomm said. "This is some kind of joke is what it is."

"You don't find me attractive or what? That's it, I'll bet. A lot of people don't."

"I find you scarcely human. If we share the same species I'd be greatly surprised."

Donna Rae grinned. "You're just saying that, right? You figure dirty talk'll get me in the sack."

Charless Tomm shuddered. The sudden image in his mind made him want to throw up. "I've got to be going," he said. "I think I have the wrong address. Have a nice evening. Good night."

"No, you don't," said Donna Rae. "Here. Read this." She whipped a folded piece of paper from a pocket of her dress, and thrust it in Charless Tomm's face.

"Go on, read it," she said.

Charless Tomm did.

The note said:

Charless Tomm:
Don't say something like "This is intolerable. I've got the wrong address."
Trust me. Have a good time.

Ms. Ortega-St. Clair

"She said you'd try to run," said Donna Rae.

"It is fairly clear to me Ms. Ortega-St. Clair has lost her mind," said Charless Tomm. "We're going to have to have a talk."

"She said you'd say that too."

"She is a woman of great insight."

"She said the surface is about as deep as Charless Tomm can get. She said you thought you knew everything there was, but you didn't know much."

Charless Tomm felt the heat rise to his face. He was furious at Ms. Ortega-St. Clair, angry at himself that he'd let her get so close to his life. He was a very private man, and he realized that Ms. Ortega-St. Clair knew a great deal more about him than his most trusted lackeys, or any of his eight or was it nine former wives.

Still—at least up to now—her keen understanding of his needs had brought an immense amount of pleasure to his life. Maybe he should trust her, as she said. It was a horrifying thought, but he couldn't imagine that the always efficient Ms. Ortega-St. Clair had suddenly gone berserk. Which meant that she clearly had something up her sleeve. There was more to this impossible *date* with Donna Rae than met the eye. She was testing him. That was it. Donna Rae played a part in the game—though he couldn't imagine what—and when her act was done, he, Charless Tomm, would get a very nice surprise. Possibly the girl with the sort of slutty mouth and green eyes.

He turned and looked at Donna Rae. "You're going out with me, you're not going to dress like that. You have anything for formal wear?"

"I've got it on," said Donna Rae.

"Christ," said Charless Tomm. "I will have that woman's head."

"She said you'd say that."

"Shut up," said Charless Tomm.

"I've never been in a limo before," said Donna Rae. "This is really fine. You see this big old car go by about half a block long you say, 'Who's in that? Is it Donald Trump or what? I wonder how they see out. Do you get that dark glass special or it comes with the car?' My Lord, champagne and a fridge and everything. You want to snuggle up close it's okay. Just keep those hands to yourself, don't think one drink I'm going to flip right over on my back."

"Good God . . ." Charless Tomm stared and scooted away another foot. "I assure you your virture will remain intact, Donna Rae. I would far rather French-kiss a leper than touch your private parts. No offense, of course."

Donna Rae giggled. "I know what you're doing. I can see right through your manly wiles. You keep talking nasty, my hormones will get to humming good and you can get into my pants. No way. I'd like to get something to eat. I want to see some sights. You've got to take me where I like."

"Fine," said Charless Tomm. "The sooner we get this over with the better. We'll get some Chinese food. I'll take you up on the Empire State."

"Bull *shit,*" said Donna Rae. She sat up straight and poked a finger in Charless Tomm's chest. Her touch left a smudge on his white tux shirt.

"I'm not talking your out-of-town tourist trap stuff," said Donna Rae. "I want to have some *fun.* I want to go to the Derelict Derby is what."

Charless Tomm was taken aback. "Now where on earth did you hear about that?"

"That's for me to know," said Donna Rae.

"That place is a disgusting display. You don't want to do that."

"Afraid you can't get in?"

"Don't be ridiculous. I can get in anywhere I want."

Donna Rae gave him a smug little grin and leaned back against the seat. "We'll see if you can . . ."

Charless Tomm knew about the Derelict Derby. He knew all the places you could go, and everything that you could do. He knew you could live every dream or every nightmare somewhere in New York. He knew there was a place on East Forty-sixth where you could do it to a badger in a four-poster bed. In Times Square there was a room painted black, where a Turkish naval officer without any pants would shave you bald, and play hit tunes on your head. A girl in the Plaza Hotel would cover your entire body with rare Swedish stamps.

All these places were there, but that didn't mean you had to go. Fun was fun, and people were entitled to their own peculiar tastes, but you had to draw the line somewhere.

The Derelict Derby was in a large warehouse across the river in New

Jersey, north of the Lincoln Tunnel. Charless Tomm had no trouble getting in. Anyone out for a buck, legal or otherwise, could spot a man who had more money than fleas on a Singapore dog.

Tickets were five grand apiece. Hot dogs cost a hundred bucks, with chili a hundred and ten. Beer was fifty dollars. Donna Rae got two chili dogs and a beer, and a ten-dollar bag of nacho chips. Charless Tomm tried to lead her to the seats high up and way back. He saw several people he knew. Lesser tycoons, prominent gynecologists, mobsters, and priests. He hoped they didn't see him. Especially with Donna Rae hanging on his arm, dripping chili down her neck.

Donna Rae wasn't having any seats way back. She wanted to sit up close. "Just how do you think I'm going to *see* anything, you get us off in the dark somewhere?" Charless Tomm couldn't find an answer to that.

The wooden seats were set in tiers. In the circular dirt arena, a dozen BMW's were lined up around the rim, facing the center of the ring. There were numbers on the sides of the cars, numbers on the tops; some had names, like "Hound Dog" or "Suspicious Minds." Each car was waxed and polished, gleaming with a showroom shine.

In a moment, a spotlight swept to the side of the arena, and the drivers were herded in. The crowd cheered. The drivers shuffled and staggered about. One fell on his face. Uniformed attendants brought him quickly to his feet. The drivers were a sad lot indeed, alley gladiators, the worst sort of winos and bums, the lowest layer in the city's multistrata of the doomed and the lost, men without futures or pasts. They blinked at the lights, and wondered what the cheering was all about. Charless Tomm was next to certain they didn't have the slightest idea either where they were or why.

The spotlight shifted, and a tape of midshipmen singing "Anchors Aweigh" rolled through the stands. From the top of the arena, suspended in a circle of light, five cases of Thundergut Red slowly descended, then stopped six feet above the ground.

The winos came to life. All eyes were drawn to the center of the ring. Even eyes vitreous and webbed with strands of gray, eyes that could scarcely see at all, were held by the sight. Here was a thing they could clearly understand. Paradise waited, hanging by a silken cord from heaven, a gift from a God who didn't always understand their needs.

Colorful helmets hid a dozen toothless grins. Bony Andrettis were strapped into shiny new cars. Foggy Indy dreams began to drift through muddled heads.

"Gentlemen, start your engines!" a deep voice echoed through the tiers.

Powerful motors roared. A green flag whipped through the air. Twelve semiconscious heroes jammed accelerators to the floor. Twelve cars bellowed and howled, screaming for the center of the ring, rushing for the prize.

Charless Tomm turned away. He didn't care to see the race. He didn't wish to watch the show. He knew what the drivers didn't know, that the Derelict Derby was an inside joke, a droll bit of slapstick fun, a secret shared by those who had not forked over five grand to watch terminal rummies poke along at a bumper-car pace. He knew that master mechanics had finely tuned the cars, that the very slightest touch of scabby toes would race the engines up to sixty-five by the time they reached the center of the ring. That the tanks were topped off with a hydrocarbon mix that would boost a baby buggy up to Mars.

Charless Tomm looked at Donna Rae. Her mouth looked like a rupture in a vat of toxic waste. Chili and mustard dribbled past her missing chin, hung for a moment, then blotted out a flower on her dress. Her dishwater eyes were rapt with joy. Witch curls clung wetly to her cheeks. And, as a chain of thermal pleasure erupted in the ring, he saw Donna Rae's face turn ruby-crimson-scarlet, turn Hiroshima red.

He sat on his side of the seat. They had stopped at a market, at Donna Rae's request. Now she piled Beluga caviar from the fridge on a slice of Wonder Bread, added a squirt of ketchup and a strip of rat cheese.

"That was sure fun," said Donna Rae. "Lord, those old buggers can *drive.*"

"It was the most degrading, horrifying sight I've ever seen," said Charless Tomm.

"I take it you're not into sports."

"Throw that crap out the window. I cannot abide the smell."

"I thought Number Five was going to take it. That skinny little dude with no hair. He had a winner's look in his eye."

"They don't *have* any winners, Donna Rae. That's what it's all about."

Donna Rae dug a bit of caviar from her teeth, inspected it and wiped it on the seat. "Well sure. *Now* you tell me that."

"Just stop it. Right now." Charless Tomm turned on her, clenched his fists and glared.

"Don't play with my head anymore, Donna Rae. I won't stand for that. Don't pretend you didn't know what happened back there because you did. People like you don't know about places like that. You know, because Ms. Ortega-St. Clair *told* you about it. She put you up to this. Don't try and say it isn't true."

"So?" Donna Rae licked ketchup off her fingers, sucking each one clean. "So what? Maybe she told me lots of things."

"Like what?"

"Like, you're a guy who's had Bunnies and TV stars and roller derby queens from overseas. How that's all you know. You don't know anything else. You're like a spoiled little kid who's had every kind of toy there is, and you don't know what to play with next."

Charless Tomm let out a breath. He frowned at the creases on his knees. "Ms. Ortega-St. Clair has an overactive mouth. I was not aware of this until now."

"She's just trying to help," said Donna Rae. "She wants you to have a good time. See another side of life."

"I don't *want* to see another side of life. I like the side I've got. I'm a very sensitive man. I thought Ms. Ortega-St. Clair knew that. I like the things I'm used to. I have certain wants and needs."

"Uhuh. A man who saves gym suits from Minsk has got certain wants and needs, all right."

Charless Tomm was stunned. "She told you *that?* My God, this is insufferable. I happen to admire athletes. Competition is the key. I am stopping this farce right now. I don't have to put up with this."

"You don't but you will," said Donna Rae.

"What could possibly make you think that?"

Donna Rae found a bottle of Czech beer in the fridge, and snapped off the cap with her teeth. "Because you can't figure what kind of gross and crazy shit I'll pull next. You kick me out now, you won't ever find out."

"You are out of your mind. They ought to lock you up somewhere."

"What I want to do next is catch the Hangers' late show. It's in the basement on Broadway and—"

"I know where it is," said Charless Tomm. "And the answer is absolutely not. That is the most—disgusting place in town."

Donna Rae showed Charless Tomm a sly grin. "You say that all the time. Disgusting. Stuff you don't like that other people do. What you like to do is okay. Someone else, now, they might—"

"Forget it," said Charless Tomm. He leaned back and folded his arms across his chest. "Have another beer. Eat some white bread. Our evening together has come to an end."

"Bull *shit* it has," said Donna Rae.

Charless Tomm pretended he was anywhere else. He was grateful for the dark. It created the illusion that no one else was there. He tried to breathe through his mouth. The odors found him out. They clung to his skin. Eased in through his pores. Opium and Chanel. Champagne and scotch in paper cups. Fine Italian leather and dirty socks. Farts of the rich and famous, cocaine and pot. And, ever present, ever there, like the ghost of winter past, the faint icy chill of old formaldehyde.

Dead Theater wasn't new in Manhattan, the idea had caught on around 1962. Charless Tomm knew of eight locations in and around Times Square, but Hangers' had always stayed on top. Possibly, he thought, because it was the sleaziest of the lot, and charged more than anyplace else.

It was awful, a terrifying sight, but it was quite well done, you had to give them that. The play was *Our Town*. The actors, clothed entirely in black, could not be seen at all. They moved the cadavers with great skill and a feeling for their art. They made them smile and blink their eyes through the clever use of wires, made them sit and walk, touch one another with a gesture or a kiss. And, when it was over, they gracefully took their bows, accepting the dry and brittle flowers admirers had tossed upon the stage.

Charless Tomm got Donna Rae out just as quickly as he could. He breathed the fresh air, or as fresh as it was likely to get in Times Square.

"I hope you're satisfied," he said. "I'm sure I'll have nightmares for a week. I'm sure I'll have to burn my suit."

"I thought that guy played the father really put a lot into the part," said Donna Rae. "I'm starving, you hungry or what?"

"No I'm not."

"How much were the tickets, you don't mind I ask?"

"They were ten thousand each."

"Shit. They weren't even real good seats. I could hardly see a thing."

Charless Tomm gave her a look. "Why don't you save up, Donna Rae? You could sit right up front."

"I just might. If they'd do *Oklahoma!* I would. I like a play they do a lot of songs. You know what? I heard you can—you know, do stuff to them backstage if you like. But you got to pay extra for that."

"Disgusting," Charless Tomm said. "Who'd want to do that? There are women still alive who can give the same effect."

Donna Rae said she'd like to go to Poodles, the pet shooting gallery on Seventh Avenue. Charless Tomm said absolutely not. He wouldn't even discuss the Sheep Ranch, or Spa de Sewer on 59th. Donna Rae started whining and he couldn't take that. She sounded like a gut-shot duck. He gave in on Henri's if she'd promise it was over after that. Donna Rae did. Charless Tomm sulked in his corner of the seat. Donna Rae whistled tunes from *CATS*.

Downstairs, Henri's was a posh jewelry store on Fifth Avenue. In the back, down the hall, was a one-way peephole in a solid steel door. Charless Tomm slid his Visa card into a slot. Soon, a doorman dressed like an Argentine admiral let him in. He gave Charless Tomm his Visa card. Charless Tomm's Visa number was 3. The doorman seemed quite unimpressed.

Charless Tomm and Donna Rae climbed a set of stairs. The steps were heavy carpet, the walls were red velvet, the music was Bach, *Fantasia and Fugue*.

"I bet you've been here before," said Donna Rae. "That guy let you right in."

"I have not been here before," said Charless Tomm. "I will not be here again. As I've told you several times, I can get in anywhere I want, or anywhere I don't."

The dining area was small. There were only six tables in the room. Two were occupied. One held a pair of Saudi sheiks. Charless Tomm recognized the dark-skinned man by himself. He always wore green. He raised exotic roaches, and owned everything north of Central Park.

A waiter appeared by Charless Tomm's side. "Something to drink, sir?" he asked.

"Champagne," said Donna Rae.

"Buttermilk," said Charless Tomm.

Donna Rae gave him a sour look. "Boy, are you a lot of fun."

"Fun isn't all there is, Donna Rae."

"Yeah? What else?"

"Accomplishment. The satisfaction that one's life has counted for something. That one has reached his goals."

"And you've done that, right?"

"I like to think I have."

"Everything you wanted out of life?"

"I could say that, yes."

"So how come you keep running out of girls? How come you keep Ms. Ortega-St. Clair hot and heavy on the bimbo trail?"

Charless Tomm had decided, in the car, that he would not, absolutely not, let Donna Rae get to him again.

"That is an entirely different aspect of my life," said Charless Tomm, pleased that his voice remained reasonable and calm, "that is in the area of pleasure, Donna Rae. Diversity is a comfort to a man who has little leisure time. Those who like sailing do not always ply the same seas. Men who like golf do not always play the same course."

"Bull *shit*," said Donna Rae. "You got to keep proving you can still get it up. That's what this pussy parade is all about. You poke five hundred, you got to try for six. A man's only got two words in his head. One word's *limp* and the other word's *hard*. He spends his life hopping from the second to the first. You aren't any different from the rest. You just got enough money, you don't have to sniff around trailer courts and bars. But you got to keep at it, just like the poor jerks who haven't got a dime. You wake up every morning, praying that your snake isn't dead."

Charless Tomm stared. He blinked at Donna Rae. He shook his head in disbelief. "Am I hearing this right? Am I dreaming this or what? I am sitting here listening to the sister of Jabba the Hut, she's telling me all about carnal intercourse. Jesus, what the hell do *you* know about it? Mother Teresa knows more about getting laid than you do, Donna Rae."

Donna Rae showed him a nasty smile. "You don't *know* what I know, Charless Tomm, so don't say you do. You think a woman hasn't done a *Cosmo* cover, she doesn't have the right plumbing inside. I know I'm not pretty, okay? But I've got feelings like anyone else. And I might have something else besides."

"Like what?" said Charless Tomm.

Donna Rae cocked her head and gave him a bawdy wink. "That's for me to know and you to find out."

"Great God." A terrible image flashed into his head. He tossed it out as quickly as he could.

It was clear Donna Rae had a lot more to say. Charless Tomm was spared when the waiter brought menus and presented them with a flair. The menus were vellum, handwritten in a spidery script. There were four entrées on the list. Each item came without a price:

WELCOME TO A TASTE OF FAME
(EAST)
Goering Rump Steak
Leg of Marilyn
Ribeye LBJ
Elvisburger Supreme

Charless Tomm felt something soft and heavy roll over inside. He took a deep breath. He turned the menu facedown.

Donna Rae's eyes were bright. She leaned across the table and whispered to Charless Tomm. "What do you think? Ms. Ortega-St. Clair says it's on the up and up. I saw this movie, *The Freshman,* you know? Marlon Brando's cooking your endangered species for these real rich guys? And charging them up the kazoo? Except he really wasn't, he was just telling them he did."

"That was a movie," Charless Tomm said. "This is real life, Donna Rae."

"You think? Lord, I don't have to look twice. That Elvisburger's for me."

As they do in finer restaurants, the waiter suddenly appeared again, hovering at Donna Rae's side.

"And how would you like this prepared, madam?"

"Medium rare," said Donna Rae.

"You want fries with that?"

"Shoot, why not?"

"And you, sir?"

"I'll have a salad," said Charless Tomm.

The waiter disappeared. Donna Rae frowned at Charless Tomm. "You don't see anything you like?"

"No, I do not see anything I like, Donna Rae. Could we not discuss this at all? Is that all right with you?"

"Boy, I'm out on the town with Mr. Fun." Donna Rae took a sip of champagne. "Listen, you think you and me are going to hit it off? I can't help it, I'm starting to like you a lot. I think I'm getting kinda heated up. Dogs are barking in my head. Everything's singing in my you know what. How's it working out for you?"

Charless Tomm closed his eyes. He thought of Jodie Foster. He thought about moonlight in Vermont. He thought, *I'll get you for this, Ms. Ortega-St. Clair.*

The limo hurtled down Fifth Avenue. Charless Tomm told the driver to skip the lights.

"I can't remember when I've had so much fun," said Donna Rae. "I'd kinda like to seen that shooting gallery, though. Daddy wouldn't let us have a pet." She poked a sharp elbow in Charless Tomm's ribs. "Come on now, you tell the truth. You ever had a night as fun as this?"

"Truthfully, no," said Charless Tomm. "Not since they cut my hemorrhoids out."

Donna Rae grinned. "See? I feel I'm getting to know you pretty good. Like, I know you're just teasing, I can see that little gleam, don't you think I can't. Your mouth says no, but your eyes are crying out for romance."

Charless Tomm leaned forward. "Step on it, driver." He drew a wad of bills from his pocket and tossed them on the seat up front. "*Move* this goddamn thing."

"There's a lot of people out on the streets tonight, sir," the driver said.

"Run the fuckers down," said Charless Tomm.

The driver opened the door for Donna Rae. Donna Rae stepped out. She took three steps and threw up. She wiped her sleeve across her face and looked down at the mess.

"Jesus," she said, "I bet I puked up a million bucks."

"Close enough," said Charless Tomm.

"I feel real bad about that."

"Don't," said Charless Tomm. "It's been a perfect night."

"It might have been those fries," said Donna Rae.

As the elevator took them up to six, Charless Tomm stood well away from Donna Rae. Her body seemed to radiate a staggering array of awful smells. She smelled like burning trash, like a wet sheepdog, like the tigers at the zoo. She smelled very faintly of blue suede shoes, but Charless Tomm was certain this was only in his head.

Donna Rae put her key in the door, opened it, and turned to Charless Tomm. "You can come in if you want. I'm willing to hug and maybe feel around some, but I got to tell you straight right off, you're not getting in my sweet nest on the very first date. We get to know one another, we'll see what happens next."

Charless Tomm took a step back. He looked at the slag-colored eyes, at the horror of a nose, at the iron filings sprouting on her head. He looked at the flour-sack dress soiled with chili and fries, and he didn't want to think what else.

"Is that what you think," said Charless Tomm, "that I'm really coming *back*? That I ever hope to see you again in my life? Are you out of your fucking *mind*?"

Donna Rae grinned. She shot one hip out of joint and struck a pose against the door.

"Why, sure you will, Charless Tomm. You maybe think you won't but you will. Because you got to. You got to prove you can."

Charless Tomm shook his head in wonder. "What are you talking about? I've got to prove *what*?"

"That you can get it up for me," said Donna Rae. "You don't think so now but you will. You'll wake one night, and there I'll be in your head. You'll think, well sure, I can do it with those perfect little honeys got apple tits and legs up to here. Anytime I want, Ms. Ortega-St. Clair dumps a certified Barbie in my bed. So what does that make me? Am I Ken or what? Could I still get it up, I had to sweet-talk a girl, she works in an office somewhere, she's maybe got a blemish, she's maybe got a mole? See, that's what you don't *know*, Charless Tomm. Shrink-wrapped cuties aren't the same as a seminormal girl who can say yes or no. You don't know if that snake of yours'll bite, you take it out in the cold cruel world."

Donna Rae held him with her deadwood eyes. "That's what you got to find out. That's why you'll be coming back to me. If you can get it up for Donna Rae, you know you're going to make it with a Safeway girl, she's maybe got a little pimple here and there. Ms. Ortega-St. Clair did you right, Charless Tomm. You don't know it but she did. You wanted something different, and that's what you got. She's trying to make you real, Charless Tomm. She's trying to set you free."

Charless Tomm stepped back and didn't stop. He didn't stop until he reached the elevator, pressed against the inside wall.

"You are flat out crazy," he said. "You're as crazy as a goddamn loon. You are totally deranged, Donna Rae, and Ms. Ortega-St. Clair is full of shit!"

The elevator door clicked shut. She could hear the motor hum. She could hear him shouting all the way down:

"She
    may
        know
            my
                underwear
                    size
                    and
                        the
                        color
                        of
                            my
                            socks,
                    she
                        may
                        know
                            I like to
                            eat
                            in
                            bed.
                            But
                            she
                            doesn't know me,
                          she doesn't
                                know beans about
                            Charless
                            Herbertt

                        Tomm!"

Donna Rae picked a shred of lettuce from her teeth. "Like hell I
don't," she said.

We've all seen them.

They're everywhere, in fact.

Like cockroaches.

Elvis souvenirs!

Scarves. Dolls. Wigs. Books. Sideburns. Postcards. Guitars.

Even toenails, cribbed from the carpets at Graceland.

STEPHEN A. MANZI has written a story about this. A sweet, heartfelt, and ghastly little thing.

Just for you.

Manzi lives in New York. "The King and I" is his first published work. Steve tells me he's also appeared in a novel as a fictional character, "a CIA cryptographer in the 1991 book The Second Greatest Story Ever Told, by Gorman Bechard, with whom I'm currently co-writing screenplays."

Ironically, it's a fictional character's collision with reality which motivates "The King and I." An encounter that's actually a fairly unique condemnation of the way stardom objectifies people into things.

Incidentally, Steve's story title is a pun.

You'll see.

THE KING AND I
by Stephen A. Manzi

Even after all these years, the first thing I remember was thinking how lucky my brothers were to get this piece of business. It was just the kind of job their competitors killed for.

The second thing was how bad it stunk when they unzipped the bag. I mean, couldn't the people at the Baptist Hospital have spent a couple of extra minutes and hosed him down, at least? I know they're all big-time doctors and nurses on their high horses and everything, but come on. They should have had a little consideration.

My older brother Gary had called me down from my bedroom. The whole family was standing around the table: Gary, and my younger twin brothers Robbie and Don. Even Mama, propped up on her walker.

Robbie leaned over and smelled around the head. He took a couple of long whiffs, then nodded. "Drugs."

Of course, none of us believed him. The coroner had said it was a heart attack. I mean, it was on all the radio stations. And when Gary untied the hospital gown, you could see the big slice they'd made down the chest for the postmortem. So we thought Robbie was confused, even though he was almost always right. But a few weeks later, when the whole story came out, Robbie had the last laugh. You've got to give it to him. The kid's got a real talent, which makes Don jealous as all hell. I've seen the two of them come close to fighting over it.

Mama shrugged. "Just another stiff. Even if it *is* him." She turned around and kalunk-kalunked toward the doorway to the house. Typical Mama. Nothing impresses her. She slammed the door, and we all stood looking at each other. And at him.

Gary started giving orders, like he was in charge or something—which he was, since Daddy died a few years before. "Robbie, you drain him, but I don't expect there'll be much left. Don, you'll wash him down. I'll handle the juicing and the head. Both of you can help me position him." He started unpeeling the bag from around the body and looked over at me.

"Linda Sue." He smiled. "You want to take care of the mouth?"

You could have knocked me down right there. They always said I did the best mouths. Sometimes when the families first came in, and, in the glow of the peach-tinted lights, saw their loved ones lying there with the flowers everywhere, I'd hear them say things like, "You can almost see a smile." And that would give me a nice feeling that made it all worthwhile.

But, even now, I wonder if Gary wanted me to do the mouth because I did such a good job, or because he was feeling sorry for me. I mean, ever since Jimmy had left me to run off with that waitress and I'd moved back home, everyone had been treating me real different. Except Mama, that is. "I warned you about that guy." That's all she had to say, and I'd get all teary and run back up to my bedroom and shut the door. I was pretty much a weepy mess back then.

My brothers, though, they were as nice as could be. Especially Gary. "Whenever you want to get back into the business, you just say the word. We can always use the help." But the weeks went by, and thinking of Jimmy and that waitress, I just never much felt like it. Until now.

I nodded to Gary and smiled back at him. "Good," he said.

Don switched on the exhaust fan, which was a real blessing, since it pulled most of the fumes up into the hood, and we could all start breathing normally again. I sat myself on a stool next to the table, while the boys put on the elbow-high gloves and got down to work.

Looking at him lying there all naked and rubbery and pale like that, I started thinking about Jimmy again, which wasn't unusual, because I thought about him maybe a hundred times an hour back in those days.

Sometimes, when Jimmy would come home all drunk and everything, he'd force himself on me, do his business, and then fall flat asleep. And he'd lie on his side of the bed, just like this, not moving, fat breasts sinking toward his armpits, head to one side.

But as my eyes traveled up over the mountains and valleys of the body on the table, I was struck by one big difference: the face. Even dead, even with all the fat, even with the pull of forty years' worth of gravity, there was no contest between this face and Jimmy's.

In *this* face, you could still see that gentle, grinning kid who had been on the "Ed Sullivan Show" twenty years before. You could still see the generous nature that was the talk of Memphis. You could even still see the love he'd had for his mama. When you looked at *Jimmy's* face, on the other hand, all you saw was one mean son of a bitch.

The drain pump started making that gurgling sound like when you're sucking through a straw in an empty pop bottle. Robbie looked down at the clear plastic tube attached to the catheter shunt that was stuck in the leg. There was nothing more coming out. He reached over and turned off the pump, then peered into the stainless steel collecting canister. He held it so Gary could see. "You were right." Gary nodded. There was never much left after the doctors did a big PM.

Robbie took the canister over to the waste basin, turned on the water, and poured out the blood. Gary, meanwhile, had already hooked up a plastic bag of embalming fluid to the pump. He reversed the switch, and the pump started whirring again. Just as the body seemed to inflate a tiny bit, the bag emptied its last drop, and Gary disconnected the tube.

Don pulled the spray hose down from the ceiling and soaped up a sponge. Gary and Robbie flipped the body over, and Don opened up the nozzle and started in on the flushing and scrubbing. He was humming while he worked, some song by the Beatles or somebody, which seemed kind of weird, but I didn't say anything.

They turned him over so that Don could do the front. While he finished up and dried everything off, Gary went into the office and got the clothes. He came back in with them, all pressed inside dry cleaners' bags. Under one arm, he had a pair of boots, nice and polished.

Don was just done dusting the body with talcum powder when Gary and Robbie started cutting the clothes up the back. When they were finished, they brought them over to the table, and draped them over a cart.

Gary took hold of one of the arms and tested it. He made a noise with his tongue, and looked at Don and Robbie. "Pretty tight. We're going to have to do some cracking." Without any reply, Don grabbed the left arm above the elbow, while Robbie took hold up above the wrist. Don looked at Robbie. "Ready?" Robbie dipped his head. With a quick move and a splintery pop, the arm was loosened so it could be moved. They moved to the other side and did it all over again.

They dressed him, rolled him over to do the quick stitches up the clothes in the back, and then it was time to do the head and hands. Gary and I, each holding a syringe of shaping paraffin, got down to business. I tightened up the cheeks, and, with a couple of dabs of body cement, fastened the eyelids and mouth so they were closed up tight. Finally, as Gary finished the hands, and started on the hair, I moved to the lips.

I put little bitsy injections of paraffin all along both lips, then worked them with my fingers. I was surprised at how easily it was coming back to me—like riding a bicycle or something. Gary was done with the hair, and he and Robbie and Don were standing around me, watching me work. A pull here, a pinch there, a couple of quick swipes with the rouge brush. I stopped to look.

"Nice job," Don said.

I shook my head. "No, it's not right."

"But . . ." Don began.

I cut him off. "It's *not* right."

I started over, pushing the lips together, then flattening and molding them. I must have been at it close to half an hour, when Gary came over and took my arm.

"Linda Sue." He took my hand and waited until I looked at him. "He's done."

I pulled my hand away. "Just one more minute." Gary shook his head no. "Please," I begged.

He sighed and let me go. I stood for a second, stared down at the face, then realized what was wrong. I picked up the syringe, and put in one more shot. Then, with my pinky, I gently nudged the side of his mouth upward just a hair. The sneer. *Now* he was done.

I stepped back. And when I saw him there like that, all dressed and handsome, something happened. I don't know if it was me thinking about the first time I saw him on the TV, and how he was dead, and I wasn't young anymore, or if it was Jimmy again, or whatever. But I just burst into tears, and ran up into my bedroom and sat on the bed and cried and cried all afternoon, until Gary came upstairs and knocked on my door.

"Linda Sue," he called. "Can I come in?"

I opened the door, and he came in with a big garment bag over his arm. "What do you want?" I asked.

He laid the garment bag down on the bed and pointed to it. "Put this on and come downstairs with me."

I was confused, and when I realized that this was the garment bag that Mama had packed my wedding gown in five years back, I got even more bewildered. "What's going on?" I wanted to know.

Gary stood up straight, and for a minute, as I looked at him from behind the tears, he reminded me of Daddy. "Just do what I say. Come on. Get moving." He turned his back, and though to this day I don't know why, I did what he told me. Then, when I was all dressed and had put on my veil, he led me, like I was in some kind of dream or something, downstairs and through the door to the prep room.

When I stepped inside, I nearly jumped out of my skin. There he was, all alone, standing by himself—as if he had just walked off the table. But then I saw. They had rigged him up using the block and tackle Daddy had installed to help us casket the bodies. A rope came from his back, and was tied around him underneath his jacket.

Don came in behind us with a stepladder and a sheet. Behind him was Robbie with his Polaroid camera. Don set up in back of the body, then cut and hung the sheet in such a way that the rope wasn't visible. Gary led me over and handed me a bunch of flowers that he must have taken from one of the other customers' arrangements. He positioned me right next to the body then stepped away.

I looked straight up into that face. They had opened his eyes, popped out the real balls, and replaced them with one of those glass sets they use when the heads come in damaged. I snaked my wrist through the crook of his arm, and could feel the wires running along underneath that they put there to hold it in place.

Robbie peered through his camera and motioned with his hand. "A little tighter together."

I moved closer and rested my head on his shoulder. It was snug and safe, and I felt myself smiling. As Don and Gary looked on, Robbie started snapping away.

With the flashbulbs popping, it was almost like a real wedding, except that we could only do a couple of poses on account of the rope and wires. Robbie might've been a professional photographer, the way he was directing me to tilt my head up, turn a bit, and hold my bouquet higher.

Until the door flew open.

It was Mama, of course. And when she saw what was going on, she whipped into a rage, asking what Daddy would have thought if he had lived to see this, and what kind of people were we, and on and on and on. I ran back to my room sobbing, with the sound of her and Gary arguing following me halfway up the stairs.

The next day, I had calmed down. By then, my brothers had straightened him all out, shut his eyes back up, and laid him flat in the box. I went with them in the wagon when they delivered him to the mansion.

Once we got there, they set everything up real proper. His daddy came down and spent a few minutes alone alongside him, then the doors were opened so the gawkers and the peepers could have their look. My brothers stood off to one side, to make sure no one touched.

Me, I stayed in the back the whole time, just watching, and thinking, and telling myself that he and I had something special together that none of these other people did. And no matter what Jimmy had done or who he had done it with, or what Mama thought or what Mama said, they were never going to take it away.

Even now, when I see another one of those tell-all books about his life, or when I watch Priscilla in some movie, or when Dave, my new husband, slaps me around a little, or my daughter, Verlene, tells me to shut up: inside my head I say, "I've got something you'll never know."

And if I want, I can climb the stairs to the attic, and walk all the way across to the space, under the eaves, where I've hidden the small gray lockbox. And I can open that box, and look at the pictures of me and him, the true, secret love of my life. And I can take out the jar. And though the fluid inside has yellowed, if I hold it up in the dusty light and shake it gently, I can look right straight into his blue, blue eyes.

ELVIS WAS A WOMAN!

That's the sort of lunatic headline you'd expect to see on a tabloid newspaper. Right in there between LOOK YEARS YOUNGER WITH CHEWING GUM FACE-LIFT or HOSPITAL RUNS FURNACE WITH AMPUTATED LIMBS!

Still, give the tabloids their due. Papers like the Enquirer have, more than any other media, kept Dead Elvis alive. We're not just talkin' those overworked Elvis Sightings, either. Where E. was last spotted in Burbank having cappuccino with Walt Disney.

Uh-uh. I mean the good stuff.

Like the lost tribe in New Guinea that can't speak English, but can chant all the lyrics to "Suspicious Minds."

Or that two-hundred-foot Elvis statue. On Mars.

Yet the current Elvis fantasies being pandered by the supermarket press piss lots of people off. Why? Because for every relatively benign Elvis Sighting come two assassination pieces. Vile tabloid sleaze, reveling in the figurative pastime of yanking down Elvis's pants simply to gawp at His naked little weenie.

Fact is, many of these scum-sucking exposés make Albert Goldman's Elvis read like a glowing testimonial.

ALAN DEAN FOSTER's chosen to do something about that.

Foster is an extensive world traveler who used to study karate with Chuck Norris and once camped out in the "Green Hell" region of southeastern Peru. His professional credits include best-selling fantasy books, many successful novelizations of films like Alien, and the treatment for the first Star Trek movie.

Alan Dean Foster also grew up, in Los Angeles, right next door to a man who worked with Elvis Presley.

The same man who appears in "Fitting Time."

I'll let Alan tell you about that.

FITTING TIME

by Alan Dean Foster

Rohrbach was in a particularly good mood as he rode the elevator to his office. He was alone except for Spike. No mother actually named her newborn Spike, of course, and his Spike was no different. His real name was Nicholas Spianski, but at six feet six and three hundred and twelve pounds, Spike seemed a much better fit. An ex semipro tackle, he'd been Rohrbach's principal bodyguard for six years. Rohrbach had several bodyguards, of whom Spike was the only one who accompanied him everywhere.

Rohrbach needed several bodyguards; he was publisher and editor-in-chief of the *TRUTH*.

You've seen the *TRUTH*. It jumps in your face every time you check out of your local supermarket, or drugstore, or 24-hour convenience store. You've probably watched its half-hour television counterpart between ten and twelve at night. It's hard to miss, the *TRUTH* is:

Loch Ness Monster Attacks Scottish Schoolbus, Eats Six Children Before Horrified Driver's Eyes!
"I Had Elvis's Love Child . . . And He's A Serial Killer," Distraught Mom Says!
Aliens Kidnap Alabama Town . . . Two Twelve-Year-Old Girls Impregnated!

No, that last one can't be right. The *TRUTH* would never use a word as big as "impregnated." But you get the idea.

As a going commercial concern, the *TRUTH* was a roaring success. It made a great deal of money for its stockholders, its employees, and most flagrantly, its devoted editor-in-chief. Rohrbach was quite a happy man.

The only people who were not happy about the *TRUTH* were the unfortunate targets of his writers' scurrilous inventions, but there was little they could do about it. If they ignored the paper, it published even more outrageous stories about them, and if they sued and won, the paper got free publicity and several new stories out of the lawsuit. The *TRUTH* was a no-win situation for its victims, and a win-win for Rohrbach.

Life was good, if not fair, Rohrbach reflected as he sloughed off Spike and entered his private office.

It had a spacious view of the Florida coast, of palm trees and blue water and surf. Beat the hell out of working for a real paper in New York or Chicago, Rohrbach thought as he settled in behind his desk. It was piled high with paper despite the presence of a computer on one side.

It was not piled so high that he failed to see the man seated in the chair off to his right, next to the concealed bar.

Rohrbach froze. The man was tall but not thin, with blond hair and blue eyes. The publisher had never seen him before. He wore unscuffed shoes instead of sandals, freshly pressed trousers, and somewhat incongruously, a florid Hawaiian shirt. His mien was not threatening, but Rohrbach knew from experience you could never tell. How had he slipped inside the office?

The publisher's hand strayed toward the alarm button set just under the lip of the desk, and hesitated. The visitor displayed neither weapons nor hostility. Calm and relaxed, he just sat there staring back at the publisher, a serious but unintimidating expression on his face. If he had a gun or something he ought to have brought it out by now.

Rohrbach drew back from the alarm and sat back in his chair. "How did you get in here?"

The man had a strong but friendly voice. "You wouldn't believe me if I told you. I only half believe it myself."

Rohrbach glowered. Beneath that glower employees and even successful lawyers trembled. "You'll believe it when I have you arrested for breaking and entering."

"I only entered. I didn't break anything. And you can't arrest me."

"Really?" Rohrbach was intrigued in spite of himself. "Why not, pray tell?"

"Because I'm not really here, in the really here sense."

Oh brother, Rohrbach thought. A nut. Harmless, but a nut. Not even radical enough for a back page squib. He sighed. His schedule was full and he was wasting time.

"I see," he said slowly. "Well, mister, uh . . ."

"Johnny," said the visitor. "Johnny Anderson."

"Well, Johnny, since you're here, what can I do for you? Before I have you thrown out by several large people who you'll no doubt also claim won't be able to do anything to you?"

"Elvis sent me."

Rohrbach had to smile. Nothing like being visited by one of your own headlines to start the day. He checked the organizer on his desk. Nothing like starting the day with a good laugh, either, and he had a few minutes before the morning story conference.

The guy was living proof of what police and newspaper professionals knew well; the real mental cases didn't look like Charlie Manson. They were regular, ordinary folk just like you and me, which was how they escaped detection and incarceration until they did something sufficiently drastic to bring them to the notice of their fellow citizens. Like Johnny here. Well, at least he was harmless.

"I see," Rohrbach said slowly. "Why did he send you? To deliver a message, no doubt?"

The visitor steepled his fingers. "That's right. See, he's sick and tired of all these lies you've been printing about him ever since he died. You know the kind I'm talking about. 'Elvis sighted at diner in Rapid City, Iowa.' 'Elvis's adopted teenage daughter goes on rampage at mental hospital.' 'Fans steal Elvis's body,' 'Pharmacist reveals Elvis's secret drug list.' Stuff like that. He wants it to stop. He wants *you* to stop."

"Sure. Uh-huh." Rohrbach fought to repress a grin. "Tell me something, Johnny. If the King is so upset, why didn't he come tell me about it himself?"

The visitor shifted in the chair. "It's kind of hard to explain. I don't really understand it all myself. Something to do with a gig. So he asked me to help him out." The visitor smiled. "We spent a lot of time together."

"Oh, right. Don't know why I didn't think of that." Rohrbach rose. "Well listen, Johnny, I don't know about you, but I've got quite a day ahead of me." The visitor nodded and stood. "I really want to thank you for bringing this to my attention and I promise you I'll get right on it."

The visitor smiled softly. He certainly was harmless, Rohrbach thought. Have to have a talk with the people in reception, though. Couldn't have strangers just wandering into the inner sanctum whenever they felt like it.

He escorted the tall visitor out, shutting the door behind him, and returned to his desk shaking his head. It was a wonderfully wacky world, which was fortunate for him because he had pages to fill.

By charming coincidence one of the *TRUTH*'s Northern California stringers had filed a nice, juicy little rumor suitable for a bottom front page banner. Later that day, at the story conference, Rohrbach and his staff settled on "ELVIS'S GAY LOVER COMES FORTH IN SAN FRANCISCO! BROKE AND DYING OF AIDS!" for a headline. The story was accompanied by several conveniently blurry photos of some poor skeletal figure in a hospital bed.

They put the weekly issue to bed later in the week, and by the weekend Rohrbach was ready to play. There were many who firmly believed that being a bachelor millionaire in south Florida was one of the planet's more enviable existences, but you couldn't party every weekend. Bad for the constitution. So on Sunday Rohrbach settled for making a day of it with a couple of friends at Robbie Stadium, where from the *TRUTH*'s private skybox they watched the Dolphins beat the Bears 24–21 on a last minute field goal.

It was as they were leaving for the limo that the pain stabbed through Rohrbach's chest. He winced and clutched at himself. Nawani, who owned a little less than a hundred of the Sunshine State's finest liquor stores, was by his side in an instant.

"Rob, man, what's the matter?" He waved. "Hey, get a doctor, somebody get a doctor!"

Even as a crowd started to gather the pain faded. Rohrbach straightened, breathing hard, his heart fluttering from fear rather than damage.

"It's okay. I'm . . . okay now."

"You sure?" Nawani eyed him uncertainly. "Looked like you couldn't get your breath, man."

"Just for a few seconds. Felt like my shirt shrank about six sizes. But it's all right now."

"Yeah, well, you better see a doctor, Rob. Doesn't pay to fool around with stuff like that. My brother Salim passed away two years ago just like that. A quick pain and boom, he was gone."

Though still scared, Rohrbach was feeling much better. "I'll check on it, don't worry."

He did, first thing Monday morning. The doctor found nothing wrong with him, no evidence of a heart attack or anything relational. "Probably just a muscle spasm, Rob. Happens all the time."

"Not to me it doesn't," Rohrbach told him.

That night Rohrbach was sliding into the custom, oversized bed at his mansion when he abruptly shot bolt upright.

The visitor was sitting on the lounger next to the built-in projection TV. "Hello, Mr. Rohrbach."

There was a nine-shot Ruger in the end table drawer. Also, Spike was two doors down the hall. A buzzer on the end table would bring him running. The bodyguard would make chicken parts of this intruder, only . . . how the hell had he slipped inside the estate?

He was wearing white pants now, with matching white loafers and a pale yellow, embroidered shirt. Far better dressed than the average nut. The kind anyone would be proud to introduce at their next party.

Steady, Rohrbach told himself.

"Are you going to ask me how I got in here again?" the figure inquired.

"No, but I know how you're going to go out. In cuffs." Rohrbach reached for the intercom, watching the intruder warily.

"Chest feeling better?" The man seemed genuinely solicitous.

Slowly Rohrbach leaned back against the thickly padded satin headboard. "How did you know about that?"

"I told you. Elvis wants those stories to stop. I was his friend, he couldn't take care of this himself, so he asked me to step in for him."

"Poison." Rohrbach was thinking furiously. "At the stadium. Somehow you got something into my drink." The publisher recalled having downed a number of drinks, not all from the same bottle.

The visitor shook his head. "I'm a very nonviolent individual, Mr. Rohrbach. I couldn't do something like that. I couldn't poison a fly, or shoot anyone, or use a knife. I wouldn't know what to do. All I have any control over while I'm here is what I know well."

"Then how'd you hurt me like that?"

"Does it matter? I didn't enjoy it. But Elvis was my friend, and I told him I'd help out on this. Are you going to stop the stories?"

"Yeah. Yeah, I'll stop them. I promise."

"That's good." The visitor rose and Rohrbach reached toward the end table drawer. But the man simply, and quietly, let himself out.

As soon as he was gone Rohrbach leaped from his bed and locked the door. Then he was on the intercom like paparazzi on a senatorial assignation.

"Spike! Dammit, get your lazy ass up!"

A half-asleep voice echoed back. "Boss? What's the trouble?"

"We've got an intruder!"

"Intruder? But, boss, security hasn't said nothin', and the alarms . . ."

"Get your head out of your butt! About six one, blond, white male. White slacks, yellow shirt. Get *on* it!"

The intercom clicked. Spike was in motion, and Rohrbach pitied the intruder if the bodyguard found him first.

He didn't. No one did. Security swore that no prowlers had been seen on the estate, and every alarm was quiescent. Rohrbach ranted and howled but it didn't do any good. He had the mansion's security checked and rechecked, as well as warning people at the office. And he put Danziger, one of his best researchers, on to finding out anything he could about a man named Johnny Anderson who just might, just possibly, have once had some kind of peripheral connection, as a dedicated fan or whatever, with Elvis.

The next week, with grim deliberation, Rohrbach made sure the *TRUTH* printed—on the inside front page—a story about Elvis's disfiguring birthmark and the surgery that had failed to cure it. Rohrbach also inserted a follow-up on the gay housemate story that purported to show Elvis's male lover being buried in a cemetery in San Jose.

Then, with his entire staff alerted, Rohrbach sat back and waited.

Nothing happened the next day, or the day after that. He allowed himself to relax.

On the third day Rohrbach stepped out of his limo outside one of Miami's finest restaurants, where he was to meet for dinner an extraordinarily beautiful and admirably ambitious new editorial assistant, one with whom he anticipated discussing little having to do with newspaper work of any kind. Spike wasn't with him.

Bedford, the chauffeur, opened the door to let Rohrbach out. It was warm but not overly humid, a gorgeous night which Rohrbach expected to end rather steamier than it had begun. He took a step toward the mahogany and leaded-glass doorway to the restaurant.

But then Rohrbach's feet spun him around to face the sidewalk and hustled him irresistibly forward.

Rohrbach opened his mouth but nothing came out. What could you say when your feet suddenly took off with you, utterly indifferent to every mental command and imprecation? No, that wasn't right. It wasn't his feet that were running away with him: it was his shoes.

Down the sidewalk with him flailing wildly and the bewildered Bedford yelling in his wake. Off the curb and out into the street.

Straight into the path of a pumped-up, oversized, bechromed pickup truck thumping out rap music as deep as the pounding of a sauropodian heart.

Rohrbach screamed, oversized all-terrain tires squealed, Bedford gasped. A chrome pipe bumper whacked Rohrbach in the chest, sending pain shooting through his ribs and knocking him down. A trio of terrified teenagers piled out of the truck to gather around him. If possible, they were more scared than he was.

"Mister, I didn't see you!"

"He stepped right in front of you, Don! I saw him! Right in front of you!"

"I'm all right." A shaken Rohrbach climbed to his feet, brushing at his suit. His ribs ached but it didn't feel like anything was broken. "Forget it. We'll all pretend it didn't happen. It was my fault."

"Yeah, man," said the third boy, "damn straight it was your fault! You . . . !" His friends grabbed him and dragged him away, back into the truck.

Bedford was at his side, anxious. "Are you all right, Mr. Rohrbach, sir? What possessed you to dart out in the street like that."

"I'm really not sure, but I'm okay now. Forget it. Just forget it." He glanced down at his shoes. When he started back toward the sidewalk they obeyed. Why shouldn't they? They were just shoes.

Carefully molding his hair, Rohrbach pushed past the chauffeur and strode into the restaurant.

The new assistant was as lovely and eager as he'd expected. Not that she had a lot of choice if she expected to move up the ladder under him. The food was excellent and the wine made him forget the incident out in the street.

Rohrbach and the young woman were waiting for dessert when his briefs started to tighten up.

At first it was merely uncomfortable. Smiling across the table at the assistant, Rohrbach squirmed slightly in his chair, trying to loosen the kinks. At first it seemed to work.

Then his briefs tightened afresh. *Much* tighter.

Rohrbach's eyes bulged and his expression grew pinched as he jerked forward. His date eyed him with concern.

"Robert, is something the matter? Are you . . . ?"

"Be right back," he told her hastily. "Something in the sea-food . . ."

He straightened and headed for the men's room. Halfway across the floor his briefs suddenly seemed to contract to half their normal size. Rohrbach bent double, a sickly green expression his face, and fought to keep from grabbing himself. Several well-dressed diners nearby looked at him askance. Somehow he staggered the rest of the way to the hall, then slammed through the door into the elegant men's room.

Rohrbach didn't even bother to close the stall door behind him as he desperately unbuckled and unzipped his slacks and looked down at himself. So deeply had his briefs dug into his flesh that blood was showing in several places around the elastic. He pulled at the material. It wouldn't give.

The pain increased and Rohrbach slumped onto the toilet, still clawing frantically at his briefs. Just when he thought he was going to pass out the elastic finally gave. Making no effort to get up, he sat there breathing long and slow in deep, shaky gasps, waiting for the pain to go away.

How long would his conquest-to-be wait for him? How cooperative would she be later, if she thought he was desperately ill? If Rohrbach had a hope of salvaging the evening he had to get back to the table.

He rose and tugged up his pants around the torn briefs, hoping they wouldn't show. The dinner jacket should cover any lines. He stepped out of the stall and took a deep breath.

Which was cut off, as Rohrbach's tie tightened.

Wide-eyed, turning blue, he wrenched at the tie. It was very expensive, custom, blue and crimson, and it didn't fray or ravel. Staggering wildly around the bathroom Rohrbach banged off the wall, the sinks, the stalls, his fingers fighting for space between the silk and his neck.

Eyes bulging, lungs heaving, he fell to the floor and lay there kicking and fighting. Everything was getting blurry and hot, as if he'd spent too much time in the pool with his eyes open underwater.

Dimly Rohrbach was aware of the door opening, of a figure bending over him and yelling. He wanted to respond, to explain, and tried to, but he couldn't get enough air, not enough air to . . .

They let Rohrbach out of the hospital the next day, around lunchtime. It had been a near thing, and he was more fortunate than he could imagine. Not every executive in Miami carried a pocketknife to his favorite restaurant. While someone else had called 911, his savior had severed the asphyxiating necktie. The sole reminder of the experience consisted of a small bandage on the publisher's throat. It covered the tiny nick the knife had made. So constricted had the necktie been that Rohrbach's rescuer had been unable to slip even the narrow blade between silk and skin.

Rohrbach responded to every inquiry that greeted him on his return to the office, even to those from individuals he knew hated or despised him. He didn't get much work done the rest of that day, or the next.

By the third morning after his release from the hospital Rohrbach was feeling much more like his old self, and friends commented freely on his recovery. It wasn't the near strangulation that had slowed him down, he explained. Unless you've experienced something like that you can't imagine what it's like; the loss of air, the knowing that death is standing next to you, just waiting to reach down and take you for his own. It's the mental recovery, he asserted, that takes longer.

Finally, Rohrbach got back to work. Awaiting his sage perusal were stories about crop circles in Wales, a two-hundred-pound twelve-year-old in Rio, a woman who had won three sweepstakes by using astrology, a man in Bombay who claimed to grow the only genuine aphrodisiac in the world (and who had eighty-three children to prove it), a nuclear worker who glowed in the dark, and . . . a submission from a freelancer in New Orleans about a shrimper who claimed that Elvis Presley had been living in the swamps outside Lafayette and had been working for him for years, and that Elvis had married a local Cajun gal and now lived only on gator meat and red beans and rice.

The assistant editor who'd brought in the story looked expectantly at his boss. "Mr. Rohrbach? I thought maybe page five, opposite the breast enlargement ad? Mr. Rohrbach?"

The publisher only half heard him. Still fresh in his mind was the remembrance of choking, the silken garrote tight as a steel cord around his throat, the wheezing sounds, the screaming in his lungs, the . . .

"No," he said.

The assistant looked disbelieving. "Sir? It's a good story, sir. They can't check very well back in that swamp country, it just meets our possibility criteria, and the food tie-in offers some advertising possibilities."

"I said no." Rohrbach blinked. "Kill it. No Elvis stories. Not . . . now. My gut feeling is that Elvis is . . . overexposed. Get me something fresh. Cher. We haven't had a good lead on Cher for a month. Come on, get on it!"

Later, a few of the *TRUTH*'s employees eyed Rohrbach strangely after their story conference, but no one said anything. Feeling slightly queasy, Rohrbach returned to his office, speaking only to a couple of people on the way back. When he settled down behind his desk his thoughts were more than a little confused.

His researcher buzzed for admittance and Rohrbach let him in.

"What is it, Danziger?"

"Sir. You remember that man you wanted me to try and trace? Anderson?"

Rohrbach looked up sharply, his mind now crystal clear. "Don't tell me you found something on him?"

The researcher looked pleased. "Actually it wasn't that hard, sir. His connection with Elvis is more than peripheral." While Rohrbach looked on Danziger glanced down at the notepad he carried. "Apparently he's quite well known in the business."

"What business? Movies?"

Danziger nodded. "Knew Elvis real well. Did ten . . . no, eleven films with him."

Rohrbach hesitated. "He's an actor?"

"Nope. And the operative verb is 'was.' He passed away in December of 1991."

Rohrbach said nothing, just sat there behind the big desk, gripping the edge with unconscious concentration.

"In a way he was probably 'closer' to Elvis than just about anybody the King worked with." Danziger was grinning, pleased with himself.

"He was a wardrobe master. Whipped up all of Elvis's costumes on those pictures, did the fittings, took the measurements, made . . ."

Danziger stopped, mildly alarmed. "Are you all right, sir? Maybe you should loosen your shirt.

"That collar looks awfully tight."

[Johnny Anderson did indeed exist and did indeed work on eleven films with Elvis Presley. He and his family were also my next-door neighbors, two houses removed, when I was growing up in California. Johnny was a great guy, everybody loved him. When I was fourteen he gave me a pair of pants he'd made that Elvis had worn in one of his films. Dumb kid that I was, I wore 'em. Wore 'em out and eventually threw 'em away.

Johnny knew Elvis a long time.

They got along great then, and I expect they do now.]

—Alan Dean Foster

DAVID MORRELL leads two lives.

Mainstream readers know him as the author of best-selling espionage thrillers like The Brotherhood of the Rose. *In his fine 1972 debut novel,* First Blood, *Morrell also created the archetype of the disaffected Vietnam vet, John Rambo (named after the French symbolist poet Rimbaud—and an apple!).*

The other David Morrell pens psychological horror stories. Such sensitive novellas as "Blue Is for Misery, Orange Is for Anguish" and relentless novels like Totem *have endeared Morrell to the Stephen King crowd, making him that rare example of a writer reaping equal harvests from vastly different fields.*

"Presley 45" lies planted somewhere between them. This story is also something of a stylistic departure for David, as Morrell explained in the cover letter accompanying his manuscript:

"One of the things I like about working in the short-story mode," Morrell wrote, "is that I get a chance to experiment. There is no exposition in this story. No description. No speech tags. The narrative is presented solely in dialogue fragments or in dialogue-like substitutes."

"Presley 45" is a dramatization of the ongoing academic compulsion to legitimize pop culture. It shows Dead Elvis slipping away from the rock ghetto to be claimed by the halls of academe, where vaguely silly-sounding college courses like Deconstructing Elvis: Rock Semiotics in the Fifties *are taught.*

This is also a story of passion.

A fan's passion, to be exact.

And madness.

Not, necessarily, in that order.

PRESLEY 45

by David Morrell

"You want to teach a course on . . . ?"

"Elvis Presley."

"Elvis . . . ?"

"Presley."

". . . That's what I was afraid I heard you say."

"Do you have a bias against Elvis Presley?"

"Not in his proper place. On golden-oldie radio when I'm stuck in traffic. Fred, are you really serious about this? This isn't the Music Department. Not that I can imagine *them* offering a course in Elvis, either. Musical appreciation of Elvis. What a joke. So how could I justify teaching Elvis in the *English* Department? The subtlety of the lyrics? The poetry of 'Jailhouse Rock'? Give me a break. The dean would think I'd lost my mind. He'd ask me to resign as chair. Fred, you don't look as if I'm getting my point across."

"Not a literature course."

"What?"

"A culture course."

"I still don't—"

"We already offer Victorian Culture. And Nineteenth-Century *American* Culture. This would be *Twentieth*-Century American Culture."

"Fred, don't you think you're interpreting 'culture' rather broadly? I mean, listen to what you're saying. Elvis Presley, for God's sake. The department would be a laughingstock. And for *you* in particular to want to teach such a course."

"I?"

"That's what I mean. You said 'I' instead of 'me.' Perfect grammar. You're the only person in the department who speaks as if he's writing an essay for *Philological Quarterly*. Correctness of language. Wonderful. But, Fred, you're hardly the type to . . . You'd sound ridiculous teaching Elvis Presley. You're a little—how would the students put it—uncool for the topic."

"Maybe that's why I want to teach the course."

"High school. When I was fifteen."

"What are you talking about?"

"If you'll stop interrupting me, Edna, I'll explain. When I was fifteen, my high school had a student committee that selected the records for the Friday-night dances after the football and basketball games."

"So it's going to be another stroll down memory lane. Every night at dinner. Well, if I'm going to have to hear one more story, you'd better pass me the wine."

"I don't need to tell it, Edna."

"In that case, I have a phone call to make."

"And I was the president of the committee. I had three subordinates, and every Saturday morning, we went to our favorite record store."

"I thought you said you weren't going to tell the story."

"I was wrong. I do need to tell it."

"And I still need to make my phone call."

"To Peter Robinson?"

"What makes you think I'd be calling . . . ?"

"The two of you seem awfully chummy."

"Are you insinuating . . . ?"

"Just drink your wine. The record store had soundproofed booths. Customers were allowed to choose records they were interested in buying and to play the records in the booths. Each Saturday, my committee and I—"

"Fred, did anyone ever tell you you talk as if you're lecturing?"

"—would spend hours playing records there. The committee was allowed to buy only two records each week. The small ones. Forty-fives. That format had recently been introduced."

"Fred, I know. I remember what forty-fives looked like."

"But we played as many as thirty before we bought our quota of two. Strange. The owner didn't seem to mind. To me, that booth in the record store felt like—"

"Fred, how can I drink my wine if you don't pass the bottle?"

"—home ought to be. And I never had closer friends than the students on that committee. We debated each record with absolute fervor, determined to supply the best music possible for the dances. I was underweight even then. And of course, I'm short. And—"

"Fred, is there a point to this story?"

"—I didn't have a chance to be popular, as the football players and basketball players were. Come to think of it, all the members of my committee were, I guess you would say, geeky. Like me. So we tried to be popular in a different way. By controlling the music at the dances. Other students would have to come up to us and make requests. They would have to be nice to us or else we wouldn't play the records they wanted."

"Fred . . ."

"Of course, I never danced. I was far too shy. The dances were really only the excuse that allowed me to be able to go to the record store on Saturday morning. I don't think I ever experienced anything as exciting as hearing Elvis Presley sing 'Don't Be Cruel' in that soundproofed booth. I sensed that he was singing directly to me. I felt his emotion— the feeling of being picked upon, of being an outcast. What a revelation. What a sense of being privileged to listen to that record before the students at the dance could."

"Fred, I asked you before. Does this story have a point?"

"Since then, I don't think I've ever been so happy."

"Two hundred and twenty-five students enrolled in the course. I must say I'm gratified. I never expected to attract so many Elvis Presley enthusiasts."

("He's a funny-looking dude, isn't he? Check out the Coke bottle glasses and the bow tie.")

"As I emphasized on the syllabus that I distributed among you, the subject . . . Elvis Aron Presley . . . may be misleading to some. You may have concluded that this is what you call a fresh-air course, that you can expect high grades for very little work. Quite the contrary. I expect the same intense diligence that my students bring to my courses in semiotics and poststructuralism."

("Talks funny.")

"Our subject is one of those rare individuals who through talent, character, and coincidence becomes the focus of the major trends in that person's culture. In this case, a young, Southern male, who adapted black musical themes and techniques, making them acceptable to a segregation-minded white audience. It can be argued that Presley's music, bridging the division between white and black, created a climate in which desegregation was possible. Similar arguments can be made about Presley's contribution to the counterculture of the fifties and the later sexual revolution."

("That sexual revolution sounds interesting.")

"I must say, my initial instinct was not to let Fred teach the course. I'm pleased that I listened to his idea, however, and needless to say, the dean's very happy with our increased enrollment. Another martini? By all means. These receptions make me thirsty. Speaking of which, the dean I mean, look at Fred over in that corner, talking to him. Lecturing to him is probably more accurate. These days, all Fred can talk about is Elvis. The poor dean looks like he's afraid there's going to be an examination after the reception. Fred's got Elvis on the brain."

"And I was one of the few people I ever met who saw Elvis's first television appearance. No, I don't mean the "Ed Sullivan Show." Everyone knows about that and Sullivan's insistence that Elvis not move his hips when he sang, that the camera focus on Elvis only from the waist up. The incident is a perfect example of the cultural and sexual repression that Elvis overcame. What I'm talking about is an earlier television show. When Jackie Gleason went on summer hiatus, the Dorsey brothers filled in for him, and it was the Dorsey brothers who introduced Elvis, gyrating hips and all, to viewers, most of them unfamiliar with the 'Hit Parade' and most of them burdened down by conventions."

"Wigglin' his ass. Why, I never saw anythin' like . . ."
"Ought to be a law. The man's no better than a pervert."
"And look at that long hair. What is he? A man or a woman? Every time he jerks his head back and forth, his hair falls into his eyes. Them sideburns is butt ugly."
"Now he's wigglin' his . . ."
"Pa, you know what they call him, don't you? Elvis, the Pelvis."
"Shut your mouth, Fred. Go to your room and study. I don't want you watchin' this junk."

———

"It's difficult to overstate the importance of Elvis's appearance with the Dorsey brothers. Those who hadn't seen his performance were told about it and enhanced it with their own imagination. A phenomenon was about to . . ."

"Professor?"

"Please wait until the end of my lecture."

"But I just want to say, don't you think it's ironic that Elvis was introduced on television by musicians who seemed as outdated to Elvis's generation as Elvis seems to the Metallica generation?"

"Is that a question or a statement?"

"I was just thinking, maybe some day somebody'll offer a course on Metallica. [Har, har.]"

"Fred, enough is enough! It's three in the morning! I can't sleep with that noise you're making! How many times do I have to hear 'All Shook Up'? The neighbors will start complaining! There! I told you! That's probably one of them phoning right now!"

"Look at the sideburns Fred's trying to grow. They remind me of caterpillars."

"As bald as he is, that's the only place he *can* grow hair."

"Those blue suede shoes don't do anything for me, either. The next thing you know, he'll be taking guitar lessons."

"And boring us with concerts instead of lectures."

"Or making us read that book he's writing."

THE CORRUPTION OF A LEGEND
Chapter Six

The crucial demarcation in Elvis's career occurred in 1958 when he was drafted by the United States military and sent to Germany. To paraphrase a lyric from one of his best-known songs, that's when the downfall begins. The episode is rife with implications. Politically, the government has proven itself stronger than the rebel. Sexually, the shearing of Presley's magnificent ducktail-style hair symbolizes society's disapproval and conquest of his manifest virility: a metaphorical emasculation. Two years of military indoctrination have their effect. Elvis's long-awaited return to society is shocking. The constant sneer with which he signaled to his young audience his disdain for authority has been replaced by an eager-to-please grin. His "Yes, sir, no, sir" manner earlier had the hidden insolent tone of a black servant who is hypocritically polite to his white employers, but now Elvis seems genuinely determined to suck up to the Establishment. Even his newly grown hair appears flaccid. If we discount the regional Southern hits that Elvis had from 1954 to 1956, it is clear that Elvis's astonishing career remained pure for only two years, for 14 rebellious, million-selling records from 1956 to 1958. After the military interruption, the hits continued, but the self-mocking "My Way" is a far cry from the innocence of "Hound Dog."

"He did it his way, all right. He became a tool of the Establishment."

"Fred."

"The Jordanaires were shunted aside. Instead of a small, rhythm-and-blues section, he now had the equivalent of the Mormon Tabernacle Choir behind him."

"Fred."

"The songs lost all pretense of substance. That wretched remake of 'O, Solo Mio,' for example, which was called 'It's Now Or Never,' sounded so Muzak-sweet it's a wonder his audience didn't die from sugar shock."

"Fred, you haven't shut up since we started dinner. It's been forty minutes. I'm sick of hearing you talk about Elvis. In fact, I'm sick of hearing you, period. I'm certain the Robinsons would like a chance to get a word in."

"Oh, I'm terribly sorry. I must have gotten carried away. Good gracious. What was I thinking? By the way, Mrs. Robinson, did you know that your husband Peter here is fucking my wife?"

"Thirty-three wretched movies."

("Word is our prof is getting a divorce.")

"Each more insipid than the previous ones. Increasingly their only theme seems to be that its audience should take a vacation at Las Vegas, Fort Lauderdale, Acapulco, Hawaii, or wherever the film is set, as if Elvis has become a travel agent or a chamber of commerce booster."

("Maybe his wife isn't an Elvis fan.")

"Las Vegas. That symbol of excess becomes synonymous with the decay within Elvis. His anti-Establishment zoot-suit appearance in the mid-fifties changes to a parody of bikers' leather after his return from the military and finally to sequined suits with capes that rival Liberace for ostentation. When Elvis reappears on television in 1968, he looks like the Vegas act that he'll soon become."

("I hear the *Today* show is coming to do a story about him.")

"Nine years later, he'll die on the toilet."

"Professor Hopkins, what made you think that Elvis would be a proper subject for a university course?"

"If you look closely at him, he represents America."

"What, Professor? I'm afraid I don't follow you."

"Bryant, I . . . Can you hear me?"

"Yes, the remote transmission is coming through clearly."

"Bryant, you take a boy who was raised to sing gospel music at his Pentecostal church, a boy who worshiped his mother, a boy who from all accounts ought to have blended with the Establishment but who instead chose to fight the Establishment. He was only nineteen when he made his first recording for Sam Phillips in Memphis, and it's hard to imagine that someone so young could have been such a significant force in cultural change. By making Black music popular, he promoted racial understanding and was easily as important in the Civil Rights movement as Martin Luther King, Jr."

"Professor Hopkins."

"In terms of the sexual revolution, he—"

"Professor Hopkins, your remark about Elvis, the Civil Rights movement, and Martin Luther King, Jr. Don't you think that's somewhat overstated?"

"*Nothing* about Elvis can be overstated. For a brief moment in the middle of this century, he *changed* this century."

"Professor Hopkins."

"But the messenger became the victim. Society fought back. Society defeated him. Just as Elvis symbolized the rebel, so he eventually symbolized the vindictiveness and viciousness of American society. When he died on the toilet, a drug addict, a glutton, bloated, wearing diapers, he delivered his final message by showing how destructive capitalism is."

"Professor Hopkins."

"In effect, he'd already been dead a long while, and Graceland, that garish monument to decadence, was the mausoleum for his walking corpse."

"Professor Hopkins, I'm afraid we're almost out of time."

"I wore this sequined suit and cape today because in Elvis's perverted image there must be retribution. You see this pistol."

"For God's sake, Professor . . ."

"One of the most publicized events in Elvis's life is the incident in which he shot the picture tube of a television set. Form without substance. He was merely demented by substances. But television *was* his enemy, just as television *is* the enemy, the manipulator and destroyer of the American people and proper values. In Elvis's name—"

"—shot the lens on the television camera being used for the remote broadcast of the 'Today' show, shot and killed the remote segment's producer, shot several students whom he'd brought to the interview as representative of the other students in his course, went to the English Department office and shot his chairman, went to the university administration building and shot his dean, went to his former home and shot his estranged wife along with a friend, Peter Robinson, who was visiting her, and finally went to a downtown record store where he clutched an armful of Elvis CD's, put his pistol to his head, shouted 'Where's the booth? Never been so happy! Long live rock and roll!' and blew his brains out. A note in his sequined suit coat pocket said simply, 'All shook up.' Officials continue to investigate one of the worst mass murders to take place at an American university. This has been an NBC News update."

Due to its live coverage of what have been called the Elvis murders, the "Today" show last week received its highest ratings in two years. A TV movie has been announced.

NANCY HOLDER *is a friendly woman with an irrepressible wit. This sense of humor occasionally bubbles over into her fiction; witness the following.*

Holder lives in San Diego with her husband Wayne and their border collie, Mr. Ron. She's written three dozen stories and articles for Shadows, Borderlands, *and* Still Dead: Book of the Dead II. *Other Holder efforts include two mainstream novels and thirteen romances, which have received awards from* Romantic Times *and placed Nancy on the* Waldenbooks *Romance Best-Seller List. Seven times.*

Romance of a different variety powers "Love Me Tenderized." This tongue-in-cheek escapade is a direct sequel to a prior Holder story titled "Cannibal Cats Come Out Tonight" (reprinted in my Splatterpunks 2 *anthology). But not to worry—"Tenderized" is a self-contained unit. One that continues the (mis)adventures of those sexy, fun-loving, and always hungry rock stars, Dwight and Angelo.*

This story also pays a visit to the West Coast branch of a shady dining chain, one whose New York counterpart appears in Neal Barrett, Jr.'s, "Donna Rae."

Bon appétit.

LOVE ME TENDERIZED
OR
YOU AIN'T NOTHIN' BUT A HOT DOG
by Nancy Holder

Dwight was taking out the trash—they were real careful about that—when Angelo pulled up on his Harley and nearly slammed into the closed door of their four-car garage.

The mansion was cool, and just down the road from the one the Grateful Dead used to live in; and Angelo could fucking run into it if he wanted to, cuz he was forking out serious bread in rent.

"Dwight!" Angelo said, pushing down the kickstand with the heel of his boot.

"Hey, man!" Dwight put down the Hefty bag and wiped his hands on his leather vest. Dwight was stoked to see him; Angelo had been gone all day. Angelo went out a lot, working his butt off to set up gigs for the band—get them out of the Sunset Boulevard dives and into the big time. It wasn't how they thought it would be; man, this town was eating them alive.

But turnabout was fair play, Dwight supposed.

"Hey, bro," Angelo said, taking off his helmet and ambling over to Dwight and the pile of Hefty sacks. He looked so cool. He wore tight black leather pants, like Dwight's, only on him, they molded truly solid muscles. Dwight wasn't exactly flabby, but he sure wasn't buff like Angelo.

Dwight felt a rush of gratitude: Angelo had saved Dwight from getting beaten to death by his old man, dropped out of high school with him, and brought him and their band, the Tokers, here to L.A. Angelo was smart, he was rich, and he played his Stratocaster like a totally cool cat.

A cannibal cat, as Angelo liked to say.

"Hiya," Dwight replied. The two blood brothers gripped hands and shook once, hard. The sleeve of Angelo's black leather jacket rode up, revealing his wrist, slashed with pink, shiny scars that looked like pieces of baked ham. Dwight's wrist matched it, attesting to the many blood oaths they had made, and so far pretty much kept, to each other. (The only fuck-up so far being when Angelo ate their girl singer, Alice, but Dwight had almost forgiven him for that.)

"Where you been?" Dwight asked.

"You are not going to fucking believe this!" Angelo let go first. He pulled off his shades and shook his long, curly black hair.

"Believe what?" Dwight asked. Angelo was high; Dwight could always tell. There were so many great drugs in L.A., in quantities and varieties they hadn't even dreamed of back in Iowa. When you wanted into the music scene, you had to do lots of drugs with the fat cats. Not that either of them minded.

"There's this restaurant." Angelo burst out laughing. He covered his face with his hands and his shoulders shook for a good minute before he got it back together and went on. "This restaurant where they serve . . ." He snorted. "Naw, I gotta take you there. I want to see your reaction."

"Well, okay," Dwight said slowly, but the thing was, all they pretty much ate these days was human flesh. In fact, last time Dwight tried normal food, he had barfed it back up in the men's room at On the Rox.

"C'mon. Get on the bike."

They peeled out of there like a fucking orange.

Dwight lost track of the twists and turns that Angelo made. Jesus, L.A. just went on forever, streets and doughnut shops and mini-malls and all manner of shit, and then you hit another rich section where the buildings were made out of mirrors. A total funhouse, and Angelo promised that when the Tokers hit it mondo big, they'd own this entire friggin' Six Flags Over Hollywood.

Angelo zipped along without a helmet and did ninety whenever he felt like it. It made Dwight nervous but he would never say anything; that was pussy. So he closed his eyes most of the time and tried not to hang on too tight. Which was a pretty good description of his entire relationship with Angelo.

"Okay!" Angelo shouted as he swerved into a spot at the curb between a Mercedes and a Jag, and slammed on the brakes. Dwight slammed against him, hard, and Angelo laughed. Everything was a joke to Angelo. But he'd been rich all his life, and popular and athletic in high school, so laughing came easy to him.

"Get ready." Angelo ran his fingers through his own hair, then pulled out a comb and handed it to Dwight. Dwight untangled his red, permed curls while Angelo adjusted his jacket with the Tokers' rocker stitched on the back. Their logo was a big fat ganja joint, kind of like the Stones' fat lips and tongue. The Tokers had been founded in Angelo's garage in Iowa. They were pretty cool guys.

Dwight and Angelo were parked beside a glass hi-rise topped with a bunch of neon lettering that Dwight couldn't read. It was twilight and the sky was the color of nickel, too much light for the nighttime sign.

"Where are we?"

"You will not fucking believe this." Angelo burst into more laughter, hushed himself. He gestured for Dwight to follow.

They walked up to the revolving front door and Angelo swaggered inside. He was so confident; he had the attitude. Dwight lurched behind.

A bald security guard sat behind a granite-topped table. Angelo said, "We're here for a legal appointment." He whipped out a couple of bills and the guard took them and stuffed them in his pocket.

Angelo turned right and headed for a bank of elevators, punched the "down" button; doors opened, and he stepped inside. Dwight did the same.

Angelo hit "P2" and began to whistle soundlessly.

"We're going to the parking garage?" Dwight asked.

Angelo started laughing again.

The doors opened to another door. Angelo knocked on it and a face appeared in a little box in the center of it, just like in a gangster movie.

"Ed Gein sent us," Angelo snarled, imitating Edward G. Robinson. Dwight giggled; he was excited; he was getting a contact high.

He was also nervous, and he didn't know why.

The face drew back slightly, scowled at him. The little box slammed shut. Uh-oh, Angelo had pissed him off.

And then the big door opened. Dwight held his breath—

—and walked into a small but snazzy dining room—round tables, white tablecloths, paintings on the walls lit by candles. About a dozen men were dressed in suits and tuxes, and their babes—maybe six of those —wore sparkly dresses that draped over their boobs like water and tons and tons of jewelry and makeup. The air smelled of good food, but smells could be deceiving.

Dwight had no desire to hurl in the bathroom tonight.

"Smoking or nonsmoking?" asked a man dressed the same as the ones sitting down. Dudes in tuxes waiting on dudes in tuxes, how surreal, but that's how it went out here.

"Smokin', man," Angelo replied haughtily.

They followed the man to a corner table. Angelo looked midly pissed, but said nothing. He took the menu the man offered and told him they'd both have some tequila shooters and beer chasers.

"This is a shitty table," Angelo confided to Dwight once they were alone. "It means we're nobodies."

Dwight opened his menu. This is what he read:

WELCOME TO A TASTE OF FAME
(WEST)

House Specials
(broiled, grilled, teriyaki)

John Belushi (very limited supply)
John Lennon SORRY, SOLD OUT
Janice Joplin

Specialty of the Day (advance order required)
Henri has flown in from Montreal to prepare our final
offering of none other than The King, Mr. Elvis Presley. Savor
the end of an era at A Taste of Fame, and share with us a night
to
remember!

Dwight stared, too stunned to read further. "Jesus, this is a . . . a . . ."

"Cannibal restaurant!" Angelo finished triumphantly. "Can you dig it? Look around you, dude. These are Hollywood high-rollers. Look over there. Who do you see?"

Dwight craned his neck. "Where?"

"God, Dwight, don't be such a nerd! Over there," Angelo murmured, jerking his head to the left. "There's Diana Ross. And I swear that's Alice Cooper. And there's Aaron "Casey" Sonnenblum." Across the room, a short, pale man with thinning gray hair and a black goatee sat alone, sipping some wine. There was a honkin' big diamond on his pinkie.

"Wow!" Dwight half-rose. It was cool to see the famous people, but they'd been trying to get Sonnenblum, president of Day-Arts Music, to listen to their demo ever since they'd arrived in L.A. Of course, they'd been trying all the companies and all the producers—with, like, zero luck. They'd been bummed, to say the least.

Angelo pushed Dwight's butt back down in his chair.

"Be cool, dude!" he hissed.

"He's a *cannibal?*" Dwight asked, astonished.

Angelo rolled his eyes. "Dwight, these dudes are tourists. They're just acting dangerous. For God's sake, they have to freeze all this stuff, what do you think, they're eating it fresh? It's probably freezer burnt. They don't know shit."

"Do you think we can eat it?" Dwight looked down at his menu. "Wow, Elvis. *Elvis.*"

Angelo winked. "I knew you'd go for it. Whatever my buddy wants, my buddy gets. I pulled a few strings. Dwight, my man, we are dining on the King tonight. Elvis's pelvis, to be exact."

"Bitchen," Dwight said, excited.

The waiter came with their drinks and set them down, shot glasses of tequila and amber-colored Corona. The boys smiled at each other. If they'd been fags, they would've held hands and gazed at each other in the candlelight. But they were not. They were only cats.

Cannibal cats.

Well, Elvis wasn't all that great. As Dwight and Angelo had already discovered for themselves, once you killed the meat, it didn't taste half as psychedelically delicious. That's when it tasted like chicken, the way people claimed. When it was still alive, a mere nibble sent you into orbit.

They'd learned that when they'd made their first kill.

However, Elvis didn't make Dwight puke, so the evening wasn't wasted.

But what was really great was that Angelo got tanked on some tequila and beer, and, combined with whatever he had ingested previously, he became some kind of magic Prince Charming guy who just sauntered over to Sonnenblum's table and started talking to him. As Dwight squirmed and watched, Sonnenblum invited Angelo to sit down, and pretty soon they were talking and laughing like old friends.

After about fifteen minutes, Angelo waved Dwight over.

"Casey, this is Dwight. He's the co-leader of the Tokers." Dwight shook The Man's hand and managed to sit in his chair before he fell into it.

"I was telling Casey about our demo," Angelo went on.

"Yes, I might be interested in the, ah, Tokers. I mean, anybody wild enough to eat here . . ." The producer made a face. It was obvious this experience had not been a high point in his life. Dwight looked at his plate and saw the remains of a salad; he wondered if the man had consumed any protein at all. You could get sick, you didn't eat enough protein.

". . . to my place?" Sonnenblum was saying.

"Sure, man," Angelo said, clapping Sonnenblum on the back.

"Okay, then." Sonnenblum raised a hand and the waiter came over. He was pretty blitzed. "I'll pick theirs up, too."

To the waiter, Angelo said, "We want to take a bottle of tequila with us."

Sonnenblum laughed and nodded. "Good idea, Angelo."

They took Sonnenblum's stretch limo. Angelo didn't even blink in the direction of his Harley, and it was his prized possession.

In the limo, there was a TV and a phone and lots of shiny glasses and decanters. Dwight wanted to check everything out, but he knew it wouldn't look cool. They passed around the tequila bottle and Sonnenblum broke out some ass-kicking coke. Angelo pulled out the world's fattest joint and Sonnenblum said it was some primo shit. The Man was slurring and saying things like, "really innersted in your music," and Angelo winked at Dwight and flashed him a peace sign over Sonnenblum's head.

They drove and drove, and talked and joshed like buds from way back. Like blood brothers.

Then things slowed down. Dwight was too totally stoned; but even in his state of devo-ness, he could tell Sonnenblum was beginning to come down. He traded "uh-oh" looks with Angelo, but not even Angelo could snap the dude back into the joy time. Shit. He even looked like he was sorry he'd asked Dwight and Angelo back to his house.

Angelo took a deep breath and said, "Hey, Case? What's bugging you, man?"

"Gimme that bottle." Sonnenblum reached for the tequila, but the bottle was empty. He gestured toward the racks of bottles and glasses.

"Got some good scotch there. You like scotch, brothers?"

"Sure," Angelo said in an up voice. He made a "hurry, hurry" motion to Dwight, who fumbled around and grabbed the first scotch-looking decanter he saw.

"Here, dude." He handed it to Sonnenblum. The producer tipped it way back. His Adam's apple bobbed, glug-glug, and Dwight had a flash-forward of Angelo and him making up lies for the paramedics they would have to call if Sonnenblum OD'd.

"Ah, ah." Sonnenblum rested his head on the back of the leather seat. His body was small; the limo swallowed him up. Funny, how before you met somebody, you imagined they were seven or eight feet tall, could devour you for breakfast. Dwight had been scared shitless of Sonnenblum when all he knew about him was that the guy could give them a record deal.

Well, he was still scared, but the dude didn't make him quake and shake anymore.

"Case?" Angelo prodded. Dwight was constantly amazed by Angelo's balls. Shit, without Angelo, where would he be? Six feet under, probably, lying next to his weak-willed mom and his bullying animal of a dad.

"Oh, shit, guys, sorrya drag you my house," Sonnenblum mumbled. He reached for the mirror with the coke on it and dabbed at it with his pinkie. The light from his diamond danced on Dwight's face like a hypnotic message from a UFO.

"What's wrong with your house?" Angelo asked.

"Nothin'. Zwhat lives init." Sonnenblum sighed. "My wife."

"Oh, hey, your old lady's a drag? That's a real bummer, man. Huh, Dwight."

"Mmm." Dwight was embarrassed. And uneasy. He knew sometimes people told other people stuff they later wished they hadn't, and then they got pissed off about it and blamed you for listening to them in the first place.

"Such a bitch. Sleeps around. Goin' througha money." Sonnenblum shook his head. "Can' divorceher."

"Wow, that's terrible."

"So beauful." A tear slid down the man's face. He hefted the de-canter. Dwight realized he should've gotten him a glass.

They drove up into the hills, past houses Dwight had seen when he'd bought a map of the stars' homes and driven around in the Tokermobile to see them. Wow, here was where that Tarzan dude had lived. And that was where they used to film the "Beverly Hillbillies." The Playboy mansion sat behind those fences. Six Flags, dude. The lights twinkled and winkled and Dwight wanted to snort them, see how they went down.

Dwight wasn't sure but he thought Sonnenblum dozed off after a while, and then he thought he himself had. Angelo was smoking another joint and talking to the producer in a low, soft voice, and it seemed so late it might be morning.

They stopped at an intercom, and the limo guy punched in a code, and a massive white gate opened slowly toward them. Hedges rose on either side of the drive. They turned to the left, and a mansion swung into view that was more immense than the Grateful Dead's, with a kind of California sixties look to it—big stucco arches and glass balls on the fence. Three stories tall, and it just went on forever in a blur of avocado green. Like Dwight's mom's portable dishwasher.

There was green grass everywhere, and shrubs and pine trees and beds of flowers. Dwight saw all this under the bright spotlights shining down like in a concentration camp.

"Help me with him," Angelo whispered, and together they pushed-pulled the producer out of his car.

"God, Angelo, what do we do now?" Dwight whispered back.

"Thangs, boys," Sonnenblum said, gently shaking them off. "I c'n manage."

"So, here he is, with some new faggot friends," someone said with a lilting accent in the darkness.

Dwight turned around. Behind him, Sonnenblum started barfing.

Beneath the lights stood the juiciest, most mouth-watering woman he had ever seen. She had monster black hair that floated in sausage curls around her long, tanned neck and shoulders. Her eyes . . . he squinted. She was Asian. She looked like an oriental goddess in a strapless evening dress of white and silver and a collar of a bazillion diamonds.

"Well?" The woman took a few steps forward. Dwight looked away, embarrassed at having been caught staring. Sonnenblum made a wimpy sound. And threw up.

Angelo walked up beside Dwight. "He got food poisoning," he said, throwing back his hair. He put out his hand.

"I'm Angelo."

"Why do I care?" the woman shot back. Then she kind of gasped as Angelo took her hand and shook it, then looped her arm around his waist and headed for the house.

"Let's go find him some Pepto-Abysmal."

She didn't say a word. She just followed Angelo into the house.

Two weeks later, The Tokers were in the Day-Arts studios, working on a single. Sonnenblum came by and talked to Angelo a lot, alone.

During a break, Angelo twanged on his bass and said, "He knows his woman's chewing my bone."

"What?" Dwight was dumbfounded. Angelo was sleeping with his wife?

"He knows why, too."

"Why?"

One of the Tokers sauntered over and gave Angelo a beer. He swallowed half the can and handed it to Dwight. "Thanks, bro," Angelo said to the guy, who got the hint and walked away.

"You want to help me?" Angelo pulled a hair pick out of his back pocket and fiddled with his hair.

"Help you?"

"Don't be dense, Dwight." Angelo grinned, flashing his teeth. "I'm going to eat her."

"Jesus!"

"For Casey."

Dwight took a step backward. "You . . . we said we'd never tell . . . Angelo, what are you doing, man?"

"Relax." Angelo clapped him on the shoulder. "All's he knows is that

I promised to get rid of her for him. And that I swore there'd be no evidence." Angelo took the beer back and drank the rest. "It ain't no loss, dude. She really is a total bitch. Delicious to look at, but that is it. No wonder he hates her."

"But we don't eat *everything*. There'll be some stuff left over." He thought about what he was saying. God, Sonnenblum's *wife*!

"How bad you want a record deal?" Angelo asked him, and while Dwight stood there, gaping, he threw back his head and shouted, "Hey, Mikey! Throw me another beer!"

It wasn't like it usually was.

Usually, they homed in on some chick and followed her. Angelo did the picking out and the picking up; they took her someplace and had sex with her, and then they ate her.

But this time, the cannibal cats rode to the Sonnenblums' on the Harley, supposedly for sukiyaki and Jacuzzi.

Casey left on an errand in his Mercedes. It was the limo guy's night off. It was everybody's night off.

Dwight, Angelo, and Keiko—that was her name—got mucho, mondo, stoned. Keiko could really put it away. They watched *Eating Raoul,* and she and Angelo drank beer and nibbled on each other the whole time.

Dwight was reeling by the time Keiko said, "I'm turning into mush." She turned off the movie and took off her silk blouse and silk pants right in front of both of them, and swayed her bare ass around as she sauntered to the Jacuzzi room.

"You want it grilled or poached?" Angelo asked Dwight, nudging him in the ribs.

Dwight was totally freaked.

He was also very hungry. He'd been fasting for three days so he could go through with this.

He did.

The rest they packed in Hefty bags.

Doggie bags.

They got a three-record contract from Day-Arts the next day.

And time flashed forward, oh yes; within six months, The Tokers took off and Dwight and Angelo were real-life rock stars. They strutted and sang in their rock-star leathers in front of the lasers and strobes and fog banks of dry ice, shocking and virile. Cannibal cats.

Then Sonnenblum came backstage one night. He looked terrible, white face and panda eyes, gnawed by fear.

"The police. People are asking all kinds of questions about Keiko." He groaned. "My ulcer. My guts are eating me alive."

"Hang loose, dude." Angelo patted Sonnenblum's shoulder. "No one can prove anything."

Sonnenblum wiped his face with his hands. "I should never have agreed to this."

"Agreed to it? Man, you *asked* us to help you." Angelo glanced at Dwight, who was thinking to himself that Sonnenblum had never asked *him*.

"But hey, man, we owe you. Don't we, Dwight?" Angelo raised his brows. Dwight nodded vigorously. "Because of you, the world fully appreciates the Tokers. Where would we be, if you hadn't cut us a deal?"

"Yes, yes, but . . . but . . . murder . . ."

"It's cool, man." Angelo caught the man in a bear hug. "We love you, man. We're your blood brothers."

"Oh, God," Sonnenblum croaked. He pulled away from Angelo and walked out of the studio.

"He doesn't know how we did it, does he?" Dwight fretted.

Angelo shook his head. "Course not. But we gotta do something, Dwight."

We.

Six months after that, the Tokers switched record companies. MMF, their new label, poured more money into their records and videos than Day-Arts had spent on all their artists in the last two years. MMF sent them on a worldwide tour. Dwight and Angelo's band set attendance records wherever they went: Six Flags Over the Universe.

By the time they got back to Hollywood, they were the highest of the high-rollers, for sure. The other rockers and celebs dug hanging out with them, and told them they were the coolest. Which they were, those cannibal cats.

Shortly after their return, Dwight and Angelo snuck into A Taste of Fame. They themselves were so famous they had to eat in the kitchen.

A large man with a bald head and Asian features put a large plate of sushi on the table, bowing low. He poured *sake* into tiny cups in front of the two blood brothers and bowed again.

"To Casey," Angelo said, clinking cups with Dwight.

"Yeah." Dwight looked at the sushi plate and swallowed hard.

The large man asked, "Everything is okay?"

"Totally primo," Angelo told him. As usual, he was supremely high. "Please tell Nagai-*sama* we're very grateful." To Dwight, he murmured, "No freezer burn tonight, eh, Dwight?"

The large man disappeared.

"Angelo, Nagai . . ."

"Doesn't know anything except what I told him," Angelo whispered. "That Sonnenblum offed Keiko. *Alone*."

"But how—"

"Easy, Dwight. Easier than you'd ever guess." Angelo preened. "Hey, Casey should have told us Keiko's dad is a big guy in the Japanese mafia." With his fingers, he picked up a square chunk of rice topped with a glistening, pink strip.

"The *yakuza*," Dwight murmured, shuddering. "MMF . . ."

"So they own it. So big deal. Look what it got us, Dwight. We're real cannibal cats now!"

"But shit, these guys are fierce! If one of them fucks up, he cuts off his finger and gives it to his leader," Dwight said. He wiped perspiration from his brow. "And then the guy doesn't even eat it!"

"Dwight, chill, man. He thinks we're doing Casey sushi for a joke," Angelo said, his eyes shining, his hair wild and free. He was so confident, so smart, so . . . everything.

Angelo winked at him. "I guess you didn't notice Top Job over there's missing a few digits?"

"Oh, God," Dwight moaned. Man, he and Angelo were in it so deep now; God, they were fucking *owned* . . . and how could you play the guitar without all your fingers? Hell, Mr. Nagai wouldn't just cut off their pinkies, he ever found out they'd eaten his kid.

"Speaking of Ol' Three-Fingers, he's watching us. Eat or he'll get offended," Angelo told Dwight.

Dwight popped a piece of sushi in his mouth. Well, Casey wasn't much. Elvis had been tastier, even frozen for all those years.

"Hey, perk up, dude," Angelo said, filling his *sake* thimble again.

"We're safe. It's just like in the old days when people ate their enemies, ya know?"

"It's a dog-eat-dog world," Dwight replied dourly. His old man had taught him that.

"Dwight, it's the Hollywood food chain. If you want to get somewhere in life, you don't just eat the rich. You eat the powerful." He plucked a piece of sushi and chomped down on it. "I wonder what Nagai tastes like."

Dwight choked. "I don't think this is how Elvis got famous."

"But he was just as hungry for it as we are." Angelo held up his *sake* cup. "To Elvis."

Dwight sighed. And tapped glasses with Angelo, his blood brother. His fellow cannibal cat.

"To Elvis," he said. He looked at Angelo, the cool one. Angelo, who made everything happen.

Angelo, the rich and powerful one.

And suddenly, Dwight realized he was very, very hungry.

WAYNE ALLEN SALLEE is based in Chicago.

Often using that metropolis as the backdrop for genuinely upsetting fiction, Sallee is equally adept at mystery, horror, and poetry. He began his prolific career contributing to small press magazines.

Wayne now has over eighty short stories and eight hundred poems to his credit. Notable efforts include the powerful "Rapid Transit" (wherein a murder witness undergoes mental collapse) and The Holy Terror, a dark mystery novel. Sallee is currently preparing Speck Behind Bars, a nonfiction study of infamous Chicago nurse-killer Richard Speck.

Wayne, incidentally, is also a true-blue Elvis fan. With a demented sense of humor. I'd like to tell you about the hilarious, extremely odd Presley paraphernalia Sallee regularly sends me, but it's probably better not to know.

Anyway, Wayne's specialty is urban terror. Street-level vignettes, sharply (and sensitively) observed. With ordinary people confronting all-too-real horrors.

Trademarks appearing in "Elviscera," Sallee's salute to August 16, 1977.

An anniversary most people greet with grief or nostalgia.

But not the disaffected teens you're about to meet, in what is perhaps the most disturbing—and certainly the most melancholy—contribution to this book.

ELVISCERA

by Wayne Allen Sallee

Last year's ritual had gone off really bad.

The world hadn't changed; we even went to war in the Persian Gulf. A guy down the block from my folks, he's a walker at the Board of Trade, but he was also in the National Guard, he goes to Kuwait and steps on a land mine. Ba-boom. Most people would say, my heart pumps purple piss, I got enough problems. That's why we started the ritual in the first place, to get back some of the happiness everyone seemed to know when He was alive.

Nobody cares about anything anymore. There are even women serial killers in Florida now. Which is why we thought that this year, changing the ritual might help.

Mick Dunleavy said last year's went bad because the guy the Hideboys brought in was stoned. What the hell, I was thinking at the time, He was when He died. Or so I've read. That's why they got me keeping this down on paper, Mick, Sheska, Nix, and the rest. Because I read a lot, and can impress them. Keep them in awe. Personally, I don't think it was the drugs; it was the loss of self-esteem that killed Him. He might just as well as suffered through the indignities of carrying a cross on His back and having nails pounded into His flesh.

So He took drugs. You do what you can to survive another day. Like, my father's an alcoholic. And Sheska's dad licks out her cunt every Thursday night after the news. Every Thursday night, she doesn't know why. He beat her bad once for asking. Beat her and licked her cunt at the same time.

I asked my mom once, couple years ago. I was in junior high, I came home and she had on one of those exposé shows. The subject was Elvis.

I asked, what was the big deal? So He took drugs. So what? What was wrong with that, and why was everyone so bent on denying it?

Well, my mother had a shit hemorrhage, wouldn't say hello for a week. No, He didn't take drugs at all, she said. It was simple to talk ill of the dead. They couldn't talk back. And His bodyguards told all those stories because they wanted money for their own cocaine habits, and the black pussy those damn Southern boys were so pumped on. Her own words.

I didn't tell her that I actually hung with a black woman, even if Sherideen MacLareny sounds like an Irish name. But it's easy for my mother to criticize habits. She doesn't even smoke, she quit her Virginia Slims back in 1979, after all the big news reports about breast cancer.

So uh-uh. You did what you could to live that much longer. Let the man rape you, or your father perform cunnilingus. Let the homosexual killer up in Milwaukee shave your pubic hair even though you know that he is going to slit your throat when he is through blowing you. Tick tock tick tock, tickee tickee tie tie. Live a few ticks longer, then die without self-esteem. I know that Jesus only carried that cross because He knew, if He told the Roman soldiers to jazz off, they'd have gutted Him right there on the road.

Yeah, you did what those who had the advantage said. *He* listened to His fans. Did the drugs and got up on stage. Borderline insane, play the game. C.—C. C. Rider, I said see what you have done.

The reason the ritual in '90 went sour, I think, is that we all tried a little too hard, too fast.

And the guy died a little too soon.

This time, we had to stretch it out, make the guy's self-esteem even lower. He had to be a mindless machine that we could milk. An unthinking, rheumy-eyed cow. And we had to play the part of the masses, lower our self-esteem to the dankest depths.

This year, we had an electro-stimulator that was going to do some pretty impressive things. Dunleavy said it best: he didn't know what was worse, milking the victim's semen through the anal-probe electric shock, or us wanting to drink the output in Dixie cups.

We didn't end up drinking the semen, though.

It's always hard waiting for the sixteenth to roll around. August is so damn hot here, hardly ever a breeze off the lake. The ritual is about all we have to look forward to before school starts up again.

————

Skinny Minny Krejca is the one who's in charge of allocating the sacrifice. For two reasons. One being that Minny looked oldest out of all of us, and probably by next summer he'd be getting us into the regular clubs on the skank. Second, and more important, he sometimes cut the grass for a lady down his block who happened to be the precinct captain. Therefore, she had access to all types of information needed during the primaries, in the ways of voters' backgrounds and preferences.

She knew what their jobs were, the number of voting members per household, what unions they belonged, what charities they supported. Also, she knew their ages.

This time around, it was going to be a lot easier to find out which of our intended victims was forty-two years of age.

Minny got the list photocopied back in March. We chiseled down the list in terms of who would be most difficult to abduct. It didn't matter to us whether the guy was single or married and the father of three. Identity didn't matter.

We decided on Bill Ivy. Date of birth 2 May 1949, place of residence 2233 West Wellington. Worked the second shift at a factory on Goose Island. The guy was single, lived in a two-flat with the landlady downstairs. It would be a while before he'd be missed.

Just like last year, we got some money together for these two gay bruisers—the HideBoys, because of the clothing shop where they worked—who would pick Bill up off the bus stop on Armitage. The owner of Mansfield's—the place we'd perform the sacrifice—had gave Minny, Pieman, and me keys to the back door last winter, because we were leaving home so much, our parents adding to the clusterfuck of the world on a daily basis.

Pieman's mother actually talked once about filing for divorce because his father couldn't keep an erection up any amount of time. She actually told the lawyer, and this is in the court records, even, that it was her belief that if her husband watched more movies like *Girl Happy* and *Blue Hawaii* instead of "Monday Night Football," then maybe his dick would stay up longer. (I agree with Pieman, who thinks his father was having an affair with his secretary, and the whole thing is what drained him, so to speak.)

Anyway, the Hideboys would get the electro-stimulator from one of their autoerotic friends. Then they'd knock Ivy out and bring him in through the back entrance, where the beer was delivered on Tuesday mornings.

Way past easy. Like being the Man Himself. All *He* had to do was ask Jerry or Sonny or Red, any of those guys would have done it all for him. Found out who did what where, whose nuts to lay on a table and hand out hammers.

The bodyguards did it all for Him. I guess we considered the Hideboys to be our own special type of bodyguards.

I know all about this stuff, the man behind the legend. Where the exaltation ended and the exploitation began, if you'll allow me to wax poetic. He sure did, during the last concerts in '77. I heard a bootleg of Him at the Chicago Stadium that May. "The stage is bare, and I'm standing there, without any hair, aw no. Who am I talking to?" And the fans ate it up, applauding at the end like He was a stroke victim who just learned to write His name again. That's what I mean by loss of self-esteem going both ways.

After my father had his third seizure, because he mixed Miller Genuine Draft with phenobarb and Dilantin, I stopped applauding when he came out of it. That time, I came downstairs and he was vacuuming the cement back porch in his underwear, high noon on a summer weekend.

I know all of this because I read books, not like some of the other guys and girls, who learned it from their mothers and grandmothers.

I watched the documentaries. Not the films where He played a doctor in Harlem or a race car driver. Shit, that stuff wasn't real at all. One movie, He was singing underwater, in a diver's mask.

And people like our parents say that Freddy Krueger and the Terminator are all crazy make-believe shit. They are the ones who do not accept the truth for what it is. Pieman's mother mooning over His movies as if they were an aphrodisiac for her husband's schwang . . . Jesus.

He made stupid movies—the ones in color, at least—and died because He took too many drugs. But we were going to bring Him back. Get the world back on track.

We were going to bring Him back, or at least make a new one.

This year, it was Sheska's turn to be the chalice.

Once again, we performed the late night benediction at Mansfield's. It's a two-tier tavern up on Lincoln, near Diversey Parkway. Used to be a funeral parlor. Real cool place for hanging.

Mansfield's tried to make it in the area for over a year now, attempting to get the nonteen Gothic crowd in the doors. The neighborhood is gay and yuppie-mixed, though most of us kids come from middle-class families. Pieman, his parents are yuppies.

You ask yuppies about Elvis and they make a face. Ask them what's the quickest way to screw their best friends out of their life savings, they can draw you out a list, their eyes bulging like traffic lights. You ask them about Elvis, though, you might just as well ask them if they believe in werewolves.

To get the over-twentyonners in here, Mansfield's did a bang-up job in serial killer deco. Along one wall, separating parlors A and B, they have this space filled with photographs and shit.

The front page of the *Tribune* with the picture of Jayne's head—the bar's namesake—lying on the hood of her '66 coupe. The crime scene glossies of the Black Dahlia, her torso neatly severed. The headlines about Gacy being found guilty and sentenced to death.

Above a mantelpiece, there was a glass display of prescription bottles, many of them fake, no doubt. Marilyn Monroe's OD bottle. The experimental cancer drug Michael Landon was taking before his death.

Forty-seven candelabras shone down from the ceiling on this display. On the facing wall was a Body Parts chart, covering recent pattern killers. Eyler, Dahmer, and Dolenz. Two out of three in jail. The whole display brought in as much of the goshwow types as it did the Satan worshipers, and business is business, as Willy Sid might say.

But Mansfield's big money came from us underage Goths, just as it did in other north-side juice clubs like Berlin and Medusa's. All dressed in black, the guys wearing fingerless gloves to make some kind of pathetic statement. The gashes with all their talcum powder and grandmothers' sachet.

All wanting to be fucking vampires. So romantic.

It's the legends that live forever, not the men who make them.

I spent some of the dog days before the sixteenth all hyped up and looking forward to it, now that we had the electro-stimulator. Watching the old documentaries. The ones where He was on tour. The Singer

Special from 1968. My mother was seventeen, then. My particular favorite is the one where He practices His karate and they play that Kung Fu Fighting song about the funky Chinamen from funky Chinatown.

Now that scene about told it all. He was brain-dead in that one. Yet, whether they'd admit it or not—even Nubbins Montgomery's mother —all of them would have sucked Him off even if He couldn't get it up. Because of the way the drugs affected Him, I'm guessing He was limp pretty often toward the end.

I read that He even had a guy come in and dye His pubic hairs. It was fairly well known that He used Grecian in the hair on His head.

Getting it up. That was the big problem last year. Before He succumbed, last year's sacrifice couldn't get it up at all.

Man. Sucking away on a limp one. Just to say that they had His dick in their mouths. Backstage performances.

That's why we were so primed on this year's sacrifice. Optimistic doesn't cut it, we were *pumped*. The electro-stimulator was what got our little hearts thumping like bunny rabbits. The thing prolongs an erection and semen extraction through an electrical probe in the anus. The NSA's been using them for years. That's the National Security Agency. Don't fucking ask me why they use them, I sure as shit don't know.

Of course, they won't admit to it. Just like they won't admit that UFO's are real. I know a guy in Downers Grove, head of a school out there. He spoke at the Cultural Center, told the audience that our government has met with aliens from seven different solar systems. He also said that NSA gets all its funding through the gangs and drugs all over the country.

That kind of talk has to make you wonder what technology we really used to bomb Baghdad. Everything we know is wrong. We have had no control over anything since He died on 16 August 1977.

The world is a wild child these nights, as Simon the Pieman is fond of saying. Back a few years ago, the juice bars were a new thing. I was out there dancing my ass off under the el tracks in Medusa's beer garden. Dancing with a different girl each night, and I was only thirteen. I really think that's why a lot of us started dressing Gothic; it made you look automatically older. If you didn't have pimples. The talcum powder only aggravates a skin condition like that.

See, you could go to the J bars and drink Jolly Good colas till you puked if you were sixteen, the real alcohol was sold when we had to clear out by 10 P.M. Jolly Good cola and snack trays of vanilla wafers.

So a few of us started wearing the dusters and weight-lifter gloves. It caught on, the way one girl starts smoking Indonesian cigarettes, then everyone is, next thing you know. Eventually, some joker is pulling out unfiltered Camels for a show.

My older brother told tales of having to go cold turkey when the drinking age got bumped from nineteen to twenty-one back around the time Elvis died. What he'd do, he'd have a pint of schnapps with him in a boot flask. Mix it with a pony of ginger ale at the Fire Lodge at 47th and Hoyne. Went there to see the impersonators. He caught his buzz, and carried a packet of wintergreen Certs in his pocket in case the bouncers winded to his breath.

Now Dunleavey, somebody asked him about his minty breath, he'd mouth off and say how he just gargled after swallowing some goo at the Hideboys next door.

And you wouldn't see that kind of shit at Mansfield's. Reno didn't run a crooked house, and there were no bouncers there. There would be just us and Bill Ivy, come the sixteenth.

And the instruments.

The truth is, nobody needs the real alcohol. Yeah, Schnapps is pussy fuel, but I'm just making a point like I was about Mick's attitude.

We don't need to drink to get our highs, like our parents do. From everything I have ever read about Him, neither did He. Pills are a different thing. Man, everybody takes pills. Shit, the straightest joe will only take Excedrin, then up the dosage to three tablets without consciously noticing it. Then one day, he's even dry-swallowing them. And don't try to tell him that his brand of choice is Excedrin because of its high caffeine content.

Pills are everywhere. I don't know that we have a choice *not* to have them shoved down our throats, pun intended. But, since we don't smoke crack or shoot up 50/50 meth, we amount to more than the common street jimmie.

I really think that I am right in believing that He took the pills to keep going. To carry Him physically when He no longer wanted to go on mentally. He died before our generation was out of diapers, but I'd like to believe that things aren't any more confusing now than they were fourteen years ago. Except that we don't have to put up with disco music.

The only real problem with the ritual lay in the pills. The sacrifice had to be able to withstand all fourteen drugs in his body, roiling around at the same time. That's why it turned out good that the HideBoys were abducting Bill Ivy. Even though he looked like a human cockroach, he had enough weight on him to take all the injections and tablets.

Whether he could withstand the other indignities remained to be seen.

Lincoln Avenue has its share of attendant ghosts. Dillinger was gunned down outside the Biograph, Tanarsie October OD'd in the back of M.C.'s. There's even a giant cutout of Him—reflections in gold lamé—above a punk bar called the Big Nasty. It being a mixed neighborhood of gays and yuppies, the aforementioned killers whose photographs adorned Mansfield's walls went after the former demographic group while the serial killer Every Mother's Son took care of the latter.

We kept His ghost alive.

As He kept us alive. With hope for something better.

And it brought in business for the bar, let's not kid ourselves in our altruistic ways. Some of the guys who came around every August wouldn't do it if the girls didn't get off on the sacrifice so much.

And even though the ritual involved only a specific audience, the bar commemorated the anniversary of His death.

Big-screen TV's replaying the Singer Special in gels of yellow, red, and blue. I always think of the Martian tripod in *War of the Worlds*. The owner of Mansfield's didn't offer up any gimmicky drinks; the Reptile Room down Augusta Boulevard served Love Me Tender shots and Hunka Hunka Burning Tequila Chasers.

None of that here.

The anniversary of someone's death was a somber thing. If you started celebrating the death day of all the big celebrities, I mean, think about who has died since the nineties began. Sammy, Landon, Hambone, Garbo. Gardner, Granger. Danny Thomas, Jerzy Kosinski, and Dr. Seuss. There's a holy trinity for you.

There'd be a damn party every night of the year, almost. Talk about losing a sense of self-esteem, in that you had to celebrate somebody's death to make your own miserable life seem better . . .

The HideBoys dragged Ivy in just before midnight.
He was dead before the sun came up.

Even though Ivy died sooner than we expected, we were able to
impregnate Sheska. Some of the guys there still were asking what was the
point; they thought it was just a ritual slaughter and that there was
nothing mystical about it.

I tried to explain things to them in a way they could understand, kind
of like apples and oranges. Well, maybe not like that. It's just that I don't
want anybody thinking that we were sacrificing people in the name of
Satan or anything like that.

Each of us think that the baby that was inside Sheska, something
beautiful born of such ridicule, had to mean something in the eyes of the
gods. Our sacrifices had to mean something.

The HideBoys—I've kept a solemn promise to keep their names out
of this—waited for the bloated man near Armitage and Clybourn, by the
comic shop we knew he always went to on Friday nights. Everybody had
his or her rituals, and buying the new independent and adult comics
every Friday, payday or not, was his. One of the Hideboys told me that
when Ivy left the store, he was muttering to himself about a "Lost in
Space" comic still being delayed. Jesus, what a life.

Hit the sap with a sap, behind the ear. The guy tumbled, and if
anybody noticed, they certainly didn't care. The Hideboys had their
own delivery van, for when they sold crotchless leather underwear and
dog collars after the North Halsted Street bars hit closing time. Solid
black van, which just about two-wheeled it into the back parking lot of
Mansfield's.

Me and Mick Dunleavey were sitting on the delivery steps. He was
singing this new song by Robin Lee called "Black Velvet." I told
Dunleavey not to quit the day job. Meaning, he couldn't sing. Sheska
was inside, primping with a Summer's Eve spritzer; the others were
setting up the throne, and putting the needed items in the right places.
Roz Oz was getting the books ready, the ones He read while He was on
the throne in the middle of the night. Cathe Choate was putting aluminum foil over all the bathroom windows.

I fingered the needle in my pocket.

Nothing could keep a human cockroach, especially one with a greasy mustache, down for long; Bill Ivy was already coming out of it in the back of the van. The blast of air hitting him when the HideBoys slid open the van door must have shocked him like a jolt of caffeine.

They pushed him up to the back steps, the two of us sitting there, talking shit.

"Jimmie Kensit," he said with some amount of disbelief. Bastard still didn't know what was going on. Unfortunately, I knew him through my parents. From before my mom tried to kill herself drinking Pine Sol.

"Tonight, Ivy, you can call me 'Dr. Nick.' " I pulled the needle out of my pocket and jabbed him with 30 cc's of Demerol. It had been His favorite drug.

"Ah need it, Red, ah need it," Dunleavey mimicked. I shot him a dirty bird glance as Ivy tumbled once again.

Everything was in its proper order when Ivy came out of it, about thirty minutes later. I had given him a nice dose of D, but I believe that even somebody in a coma would become consciously aware of his surroundings if he had just had two pork chop sideburns stapled to his jawbone with a staple gun.

Before we'd taped his mouth shut, Dunleavey did a half-assed job of shaving the greasy mustache off, catching a few patches of lip and skin. The blood wasn't noticeable under the opaque bandage. But it made it impossible to give Ivy the other tablet-form drugs—EEzlax, Gas-X, Dolobid, Darvocet, Tylenol No. 3—because we were afraid that he would choke on his blood. In afterthought, Dunleavey even hooked a paper clip under Ivy's lip, wrapped the tape to it and gave him the patented sneer that made Him famous. The girls applauded.

At the first sign of his awareness, all of us gathered, fingering our TCB medallions. The same gold chains with the lightning bolt that His entourage wore; I took the Greyhound down to Graceland and spent two weeks' allowance on them. Taking Care of Business, it meant.

We were in the men's room, beyond Parlor B in Mansfield's. You could hear mariachi music faintly from the bistro next door, if the wind blew. I thought of *Fun in Acapulco*.

Ivy's new sideburns jiggled on his face as his breathing picked up. The HideBoys had done a good job on those, *weaved* sideburns; we all thought so when they'd showed them to us in June.

Choate injected the surrogate with a stimulant called Modrax. Another of His drugs. Though there would always be conflicting stories on exactly what He was hooked to.

The surrogate was frightened, shaking. Shit, Ivy jumped if you blew a car horn. But the room did look eerie. We'd gone all out this year, knowing we had the rectal stimulator. Blew it all out of proportion. Lived the lie, lost as much self-esteem collectively as our surrogate sacrifice would.

Eight-by-ten glossies tacked to the stucco walls, all of the characters He had played. Ross Carpenter in the black turtleneck, Deke Rivers in Technicolor cowboy suit. Rusty Wells in a Fort Lauderdale hangout. The others. Danny, Johnny, plain old Joe, who kept turning up like a bad penny.

We had Ivy in the big handicapped stall. Both arms were stretched out to the metal railings for the wheelchair riders. His arms were bound tight from elbow to wrist, his eyes quavered. There was a magazine rack next to the toilet, filled with astrological books. Cathe Choate picked up one and read from *Linda Goodman's Sun Signs,* alternating this with pulling the long strands of her black hair away from the pages.

Ivy was now dressed in powder-blue pin-striped pajamas, the pants bunched down around his ankles. As with last year's sacrifice, his dick was withered and small, out of fear. The rectal stimulator would change this.

We started with a reading from the Albert Goldman biography; a sordid tale depicting Him in His Belair mansion, secretly videotaping two Vegas showgirls going at it, and then coming out in front of the camera and jerking off onto the lens.

Amen, we all said.

Ivy's head lolled to one side. The taller of the Hideboys slapped it upright.

Dunleavey passed out photocopies of the lyrics from the closing credits of *Change of Habit.* We sang "Let Us Pray," in solemn tones. Last year, we sang "Confidence," from His movie *Clambake.*

I moved forward, letting the taller Hideboy wheel in the machine. Ivy was shivering now. A shot of Demerol warmed him up good, but not enough to put him out. Made him dreamy. While I shot him up, Dunleavey cracked from the background: "Jimmie Kensit, the guy who brings mah water and mah scarves . . ."

314 WAYNE ALLEN SALLEE

I pulled the rectal probe away from the snap-hold on the side of the monitor screen. We wouldn't be paying much attention to the readout anyways. I pried Ivy's legs further apart; the stench was disgusting. He had silently crapped himself down the inside of the bowl. Some of the drizzled shit had splattered onto his thigh.

It was a good sign. We hoped that wherever He was, He was watching.

The probe looked like a tiny awl. I shoved it up the sacrifice's anus and felt the sphincter catch hold. The sneer shivered up over the side of the bandage.

Our crowd mumbled lines from His last days.

"I actually learned to play the guitar . . ."

"Now the stage is bare, and I'm standing there, without any hair, aw no . . ."

"From Blue Hawaii, lazngenlmen."

That last was always my favorite.

I turned the machine on. The electric current ran up into the sacrifice's asshole.

Ivy did make the perfect bloated surrogate, that was for certain. The electric current made him tense, and his dick went half-hard, growing and slapping his fat, pale underbelly. Why our mothers wanted to fuck something like this, I'll never know.

I motioned for Nubbins Montgomery to get on the side of him and undo one of the arm restraints. Nubbins took a tiny stiletto out of his earring casing and cut through the left bandage as deftly as any triage nurse.

I increased the surge from the machine; Ivy's lower extremities tensed and he flopped off the porcelain bowl. The way He did on His last night. Perfect. "He's in the lateral decubitus position," Montgomery said. I shrugged, not knowing what the part-time mechanic was talking about. Looked it up in my Webster's later; found nothing.

The head of Ivy's penis was purplish-blue, and his testicles had constricted until they were bound together. It was time for Sheska to mount him.

She left her blouse on, and simply peeled off her jeans and panties, letting them ball up on the tile floor. By now, Ivy's eyes were rolling up in the back of his head, and his eyelids were fluttering. None of us were looking at Sheska's cunt or her pale buttocks as she kneeled down and winnowed up the sacrifice's body. She guided his erect penis into her, milking the urethra deftly.

Bill Ivy ejaculated twice and then died.

We then joined in prayer, asking Him to see that what we had done was good. The world had to change. Sheska got back into her clothing and Dunleavey paid the Hideboys off to dispose of the body.

We left Mansfield's, each of us continuing his wishes and prayers in private.

I am writing this on 22 October 1991. Things have not gotten better. Sheska did not get pregnant; we don't know what went wrong. A week ago, a man drove his pickup truck through a restaurant in Killeen, Texas, and killed twenty-two people.

It's on the news all the time. That, and abortion clinics being bombed in Wichita, sex discrimination in the Senate, alleged rapes in the Kennedy Compound . . .

Everybody thrives on this. The only good news is bad news. This is the world we will continue to grow up in. The world we will eventually die in.

I went back to Mansfield's, surveyed the killing scene from two months ago. Maybe the key is not in sacrificing somebody who is forty-two years of age. Elvis started losing his self-esteem when the Colonel forced him to join the Army when he was twenty-three. He started taking benzedrine in Germany, to stay awake on post.

The smaller of the HideBoys turns twenty-three next week.

I sat down on the toilet and prayed up to Him, looking for guidance. Why is it that, whenever a song of His comes on the radio or jukebox, half the place turns wistful? Everyone forgets the evil in the world, at least until "Bossa Nova Baby" plays through.

I don't know what else we can do. More people remember His death that summer of 1977 than recall the capture of Son of Sam in New York City one week before. It's no longer a question of where were you when you heard about Kennedy's assassination.

He did so much for this world.

I stood up and smoothed my jeans. Stared at myself in the mirror for long minutes, watching the veins in my forehead pulse.

And, as was often said of Elvis at the end of his concert albums, I left the building, saying to no one in particular, thank you and good night.

The death of heroes breeds legend.

Consider:

A noble King, larger than life, lives in a beautiful castle. Handsome, brave, adored by all, it is still rumored that the King is not happy. That he struggles with dark forces threatening to overwhelm him and his kingdom.

Then—The King dies. Whereupon it is revealed that these forces came not from without, but within.

Sounds positively medieval, doesn't it? Chivalric.

Like the legend of Dead Elvis.

KEVIN ANDREW MURPHY is an emerging young writer who's a regular contributor of articles and fiction scenarios to the gaming industry (TSR, White Wolf, Bard Games). He recently sold a story to editor George R. R. Martin's Wild Cards: Card Sharks anthology.

For "I'm Having Elvis's Baby!" Murphy cooks up something different. First he simmers a few traditional fantasy figures—trolls, princes, elves—over a low fire, and seasons them with a nineties update of Tam Lin, that Old English ballad featuring beautiful maidens and changeling knights.

Then—for spice—Murphy adds a dash of Elvis Presley.

The resulting dish is one damn goofy stew.

Definitely bewitched, bothered, and bewildered . . .

"I'M HAVING ELVIS'S BABY!"
by Miss Janet Carter of Pope County, Arkansas

by Kevin Andrew Murphy

I know everybody thinks I'm crazy, but I swear it, I swear it to God! Not only did I see Elvis, but I'm gonna have his baby.

Elvis is alive. I know I was jus' a li'l thing when everyone says he died, but he didn't. No he didn't. That boozy ol' thing that snorted cocaine an' went shufflin' aroun' with the potbelly weren't Elvis. Nosirreebob. That weren't Elvis at all. That was jus' a fat old troll.

But I'm gettin' ahead of myse'f.

The first time I met the *real* Elvis, I was workin' jus' outside town for Bob and Melba at the Jiffy J Diner (jus' off Route 7—Melba said I'd get a raise if I mentioned that, and you should go there anyway, cuz the food's real good, 'specially the chili, which I help make). Anyway, Melba thought it might be an idea to get some live entertainment, like a band, since we needed sumpthin' after the TV started shortin' out an' all we could get was Oprah Winfrey. Who came in all squinched and purple.

Anyway, Melba'd hardly had that "Need a band" sign out for any time t'all when the cutest li'l ol' thing came in, young, not much older than me even, an' didn't he look jus' like Elvis. (Course he *was* Elvis, but we didn't know that jus' yet—I'm gettin' ahead of myse'f again). He was dressed real nice, but simple, jus' blue jeans an' a T-shirt an' a beat-up ol' guitar. He bought a cup of coffee, then asked if me and Bob and Melba wanted to hear him sing. An' lord if he didn't sound jus' like Elvis when he did "Love Me Tender" and "Teddy Bear" and "Blue Christmas."

Then he sang "Hound Dog" an' I *knew*. He was Elvis. He was the King. Other people might soun' like 'im or look like 'im, but nobody could move his pelvis that way—not Jon Bon Jovi, not Randy Travis, not even George Michael, though he tries real good. (And certainly not that ol' troll they showed waddlin' aroun' jus' before he died—that weren't Elvis at all.) Watchin' him twitch his behind aroun' that floor of the Jiffy J, I jus' knew I'd found the real Elvis—an' I was gonna make him mine.

Anyway, he said his name was Tommy. (It was Elvis, of course, but he was workin' undercover.) Melba gave him the job right away.

After that, "Tommy" came into the Jiffy J every Thursday, Friday, and Saturday night and sang while Bob cooked an' Melba tended counter an' I waited tables. An' after we got off work, Tommy came on back to my trailer, an', well, we did what we did, y'know?

An' everythin' was jus' great until the month I didn't get the Curse. I panicked, 'cause I couldn't go to my momma, an' I couldn't tell Lori Beth, my best friend since junior high, or it would be all over town. (Lori Beth's great, but I swear, she's got that telephone attached at the ear.) So I went to Melba, an' she was real good to me an' sat me down an' 'splained all 'bout the birds and the bees an' all. An' after she was through goin' on (shoot—if I didn' know 'bout the birds and the bees in the first place would I have got myse'f into this fix?), Melba went to Wal-Mart and got me one of those little plastic things. Lordy if it didn't turn blue.

"Tommy" came in that night, an' after I spilled the third pot of coffee, Melba gave us the evenin' off. I took "Tommy" behind the diner an' laid it out to him straight.

After a li'l while, he tol' me it weren't that he didn't want to marry me, but he couldn't. I asked why not, an' he says he already was married, an' I says, "To who?" and he says, "Priscilla Presley."

I tol' him he was full of it—He may look like Elvis an' soun' like Elvis, but the real Elvis was a fat ol' geezer who up 'n croaked more'n ten years ago. An' then Tommy says, "Forsooth, fair Janet, that was not me. That was a troll they had disguised with glamour."

I wanted to know why he started talkin' so funny all of a sudden, an' who was this "they" he was talkin' about, an' did he think I was a half-wit, 'cause there weren't no way you could use no fashion magazine to make a homeless person look like Elvis.

Then he got scared, and says that "they" was the elves, an' they kidnapped him like they always did with musicians they liked. An' to keep him from being missed, they found a fat ol' troll an' let him go live in Graceland with Priscilla.

Well that sure explained a lot of things, but I still didn't buy it. Then he asked me to come with him. So we got on his motorcycle an' lit outa town. An' lordy, didn' he feed me a line! All 'bout how the elves had stolen him away, and Jim Morrison too, an' a lot of others, then let a bunch of fat ol' trolls doll themselves up with some magic makeup an' take their places. I asked if they'd done that with John Belushi, but he said no, John Belushi had croaked hisse'f good an proper with his own cocaine an' the elves didn' have nothin' to do with it. They had certain standards, y'see.

Well, I'd nearly had enough of that. But then Tommy tol' me somethin' real creepy. 'Bout how the elves had something called a tiend, which was sort of like payin' rent to hell. Near made my blood run cold, him tellin' 'bout how the elves had to send a soul to the devil every seven years. An' how he was goin' to be the next one. Either him or Jim Morrison. An' after that movie they jus' had, the elves had taken a lot more of a shine to Jim. So Tommy was goin' to have to do somethin' right quick, or get ready to shovel coal for an awful long spell.

I weren't right pleased to hear that, but what he says next were even less funny. Tommy wanted me to go to the closest crossroads an' wait for him an' his nutty elf friends to go cruisin' by on motorcycles. An' when I saw a white motorcycle with a biker with only one motorcycle glove, I was to reach out an' wrassle him to the groun', an' all the rest of the bikers would be so stoned that they would ride right on past. But if they didn', they might use their glamour to turn him into all sorts of things. But no matter what they changed that biker into, I was supposed to hold on, until he finally got all lit on fire like he was in a horror movie. An' I should then up and toss him in a mud waller an' the fire would go out an' he would be jus' fine an' them elf people would give the devil Jim Morrison instead.

I tol' Tommy that all was crazy talk, but *he* sure seemed to believe it. Then I asked Tommy why he and Jim didn't jus' up an' leave these loony birds an' let them give themselves to the devil if they were so set on doin' it. But Tommy said that wouldn' work. They'd find him, an' the only person who could save him was me.

I tol' myse'f then, "Janet, girl, you's gonna have a chil' an' his daddy's a crazy man who thinks he's Elvis an' who's got hisse'f mixed up with a mighty strange bunch. So you best watch your step or you're gonna land in a bigger heap of trouble than you already got yourse'f into." Then I spoke up an' asked Tommy if there was anythin' more he wants me to do. An' he says, well, that the next night is Halloween (which it was), an' that all the elves an' fairies an' trolls an' suchlike was gonna gather at that crossroads he was talkin' 'bout an' go paradin' by, kin' of like when we used to go cruisin' in high school. An' that's where the devil would appear, too, right there at the crossroads.

Then I says that the biggest crossroads aroun' Pope County is the 7-40 interchange, an' those elf people was gonna have a heck of a time cruisin' in the middle of a interstate with all them big ol' trucks comin' by. An' I says that even if Ol' Nick hisself decided to drop in, I'd put my money on a semi-rig.

Tommy says didn' I know anythin'—trolls don' hang out *on* bridges, they hang out *under* bridges—an' that's where they was all gonna be the next night, made up with glamour to look like a bunch of motorcycle riders. An' the devil would show up an hour later. (He didn't say what the devil would look like.)

Anyway, then Tommy dropped me off at my trailer and lit out like a rooster with his tail on fire. I went right on inside an' got on the phone to Melba, askin' for the next night off, then asked if I could borrow that there new Handycam she and Bob bought themselves las' Christmas. See, I knew it would take some convincin' for the local sheriff to believe there was a nest of Satanists hangin' out under the freeway interchange. But I'd watched the news an' I knew there weren't nothin' like a video-tape as evidence ever since them police down in L.A. beat the snot out of that colored guy.

Then I called up Lori Beth an' tol' her that I might be late for the Halloween party, 'cause I promised Tommy I'd go with him to meet some people under the 7-40 interchange. Lori Beth, nosy as always, wanted to know what was goin' on. So I let on that I thought Tommy might be mixed up with some drug dealers, and if I didn't show up at the party by one, she'd better call the police.

I knew she'd do better'n that—Lori Beth's sweet on Hank Buchanan, an' he's even sweeter on her. More important, Hank's a sheriff's deputy. An' I knew if I didn't show up, Lori Beth would have Hank and almos' every squad car on the force out there to rescue me, cuz no matter what

Tommy'd said, I didn' think his nutty friends would take kindly to me yankin' him off his motorcycle.

Then Lori Beth says I shouldn't be mixed up in stuff like that and I should drop that Tommy, even if he did look jus' like Elvis. But I says, all in secret like, an' I'd kill her if she should tell anybody, I was pregnant, an' I needed to make sure Tommy was safe, cuz I weren't gonna let my chil' grow up without a daddy like I did. That shut her up right quick. An' while I knew Lori Beth would have it all over town in the week, it wouldn't matter, cuz once I married Tom an' the baby shower rolled aroun', anybody who could count backward from nine on their fingers would know that chil' weren't conceived in wedlock. But I also knew that Lori Beth would murderize Hank if he just up and let her best friend get carried off by Satanists come Halloween.

Anyway, next day I was real nervous. But everythin' went to plan. I borrowed the Handycam from Melba, then took the bus to near the interchange an' hiked down below. I set up that Handycam in some bushes and wrapped myse'f up in my jacket an' got set to wait. An' at midnight, there they came. Biggest pack of bikers I ever seen. An' you gotta remember, I work at a diner off the interstate.

I switched on the remote control and saw the li'l red light on the Handycam come on, which meant it was rollin'. An' there came the bikers jus' like Tommy said, an' they was the weirdest-assed bunch I ever seen. Lots of leathers and chains an' all sorts of stuff like you'd only see on one of those MTV videos we used to get before Pastor Snodgrass saw that Paula Abdul dance number and shut down the cable station. An' the riders looked even weirder than what they was wearin'. But I wasn't payin' that much mind: I was looking for the white motorcycle with the guy missin' one glove.

Lucky for me, them elf people decided to cruise by a bunch of times, jus' cuz they wanted me to get a good look at them, I 'spose, all whoopin' and hollerin' an' all. Then a black motorcycle whizzed right in front of me, an' a brown one right after. An' then came Tommy on a white motorcycle. But I didn' need to look 'n see if he was wearin' gloves—Tommy had his visor up, an' I could see his face plain as day.

Well, maybe I was crazy to be there, but I still weren't going to jump no guy on a motorcycle. So instead I jus' throw my jacket in Tommy's face an' yanked on the sleeves. It worked right proper; he los' control of his bike an' went down in a tumble with the wheels spinnin' out.

Then I ran an' jumped right on top of him.

I was right, though—Tommy's weird elf friends weren't gonna let him go without a fight. An' they'd have to be a bunch of half-wits not to notice a motorcycle crash, 'specially with as many of them had to swerve to avoid it.

They all circled aroun', gettin' chains an' suchlike out, an' then the meanest motorcycle mama I ever seen pulls up an' takes off her helmet an' shakes out her hair an' it's black as pitch an' long as a preacher's sermon. An' she says, "Ware! A maid is here to challenge us for one of our company, the minstrel known as Elvis! Stand forth, bold maid. Do you truly seek to challenge Mab, Queen of Elvenlands?"

Well, that sure scared the bejesus out of me, I tell you. But I'd learned one think at the diner—it didn' pay to back down from bikers. If they sassed you, you sassed 'em right back. So I held tight to my Elvis an' I tol' that bitch damn straight I was there to challenge her. An' my name was Janet Carter, an' I was a waitress, not a maid, an' I thought it was a pretty sorry-assed sort of queen who only rented her kingdom 'stead of ownin' it.

Well you should have seen the colors she turned. Her eyes jus' about popped out of her head. But the rest of the bikers looked like they was a li'l on my side, cuz I could tell I'd struck a sore spot.

After that Mab bitch finished openin' an' shuttin' her mouth like some sorta goldfish, she looked at me an' says, "Boldly spoke, *waitress* Janet. But you cannot prevail against the Queen of Air and Darkness."

She held her arms up above her head then, like she was goin' to do aerobics or sumpthin'. Then she twitched her hands aroun' an' my Elvis started twitchin' aroun' in my arms. His face got longer, an' his ears got longer, an' his teeth got a *lot* longer. An' the next thing I knew, I was holdin' onto a pit bull jus' like that Spuds McKenzie they usta have in them beer commercials. My Elvis—he weren't nothin' but a hound dog!

One mean-assed hound dog too, cuz the next thing I knew he was snappin' an' slaverin' like he got the hydrophobia. But I held on to him tight like Tommy'd said, an' I cried, "You're my Elvis an' I love you an' I don' care what ya look like!"

Well that biker queen, she didn' look at all pleased with that. So she waves her hands again an' the slaverin' Spuds McKenzie dog in my arms starts growin'. An' his nose starts gettin' longer an' his teeth get even sharper an' he gets a long, switchin' tail, an' the next thing I knows I'm wrestlin' a ten-foot gator!

But I cries, "Elvis! Elvis! I luv' ya, Elvis!" An' that Mab queen twitches her hands aroun' ag'in, an' the snappin' gator starts gettin' one *heck* of a lot bigger, an' harder, an' more scaly, an' a hood ornament sprouts on his nose, an' the next thing I know I'm ridin' aroun' on the hood of one of those monster trucks from the fair!

The motorcycle bitch seemed to be operatin' it by remote control, cuz she's got one of them li'l boxes in her hands, an' I don' see no driver in the cab of my Elvis. Next thing I know that monster truck pops a wheelie. An' I get thrown in the mud 'n jus' about killed.

When I get up 'n catch my breath an' wipe the mud outa my eyes, I see that Mab bitch standin' over me, smilin'. Behin' her I see the monster truck sort of shift 'n melt an' pretty soon my Elvis is there. He's smilin' too, but he looks a mite glassy-eyed.

"Well met, waitress Janet," says that mean-assed motorcycle bitch. "You fought valiantly. But 'twas not enough, for you are not the first maid to challenge me for my mortal knights." She smiled again, *real* mean, an' I wonder what was comin' next. Then she says, "I knew my Elvis might betray me. So I took the precaution of exchanging his heart for a stone and his eyes for elven wood. Only I can hold them now."

Then comes the sickest thing I ever seen. Mab or Babs or whatever holds up this glass locket, an' inside was Elvis's heart an' his eyes, jus' like them creepy jars they had back in my high school biology class.

That elf queen laughed then an' so did the rest of them. But suddenly we all got hit by a floodlight. An' here comes this big voice on a loudspeaker: "THIS IS THE POPE COUNTY SHERIFF'S DEPARTMENT! PUT YOUR HANDS UP!"

It was Hank Buchanan! Lori Beth had sent 'im early, like I knew she might.

Well, them elf people didn't waste any time. But they didn't pay no attention, neither. Next thing I knew they was on all their motorbikes, an' they high-tailed it out of there faster than a hog from a sausage factory.

The police went chasin' after 'em. But they didn' catch nobody. Not that it were much of a surprise. My Elvis went with 'em too. So I sorta sighed a little an' got the Handycam. Then I let Hank take me to the hospital, an' Melba an' Lori Beth fussed over me somethin' fierce.

There ain' much to tell after that. Later on, 'bout the only thing happened was the whole Pope County sheriff's department put out this APB for a bunch of drug-dealing Satanists.

But I know better, an' I'm gonna get my Elvis back! My child's gonna have a daddy to raise him up proper, not like I did. An' I'm gonna *marry* Elvis, you wait n' see. I don' care if he *is* still married to Priscilla—mos' of those years she was jus' slobberin' on an ol' troll anyway.

And that Mab bitch—Who elected her queen anyway? An' what makes her think she can go kidnappin' people and turnin' 'em into gators and monster trucks? She may think she can brush me off, but I got it all on videotape, an' I'm gonna sell it to "60 Minutes" an' "A Current Affair"! Let's see what Mab says to Dan Rather!

That's my story, thank you much.

An' don' forget the Jiffy J Diner.

Jus' off Route 7, Melba says.

MARTIN AMIS is Britain's reigning literary smartass.

This is no small feat in a country which respects, indeed, thrives on personal eccentricities and the written word. Despite the competition, however, Martin maintains a superior position in England as both a media celebrity and serious author. One whose stinging, surgically precise wit is just as well known as his work.

In fact, when you get right down to it, Amis is the literary equivalent of a sarcastic rock star. Sort of like Frank Zappa with a pen.

Rock 'n' roll attitudes certainly saturate Amis's work. Prickly novels like The Rachel Papers, Time's Arrow, Dead Babies, Money, and London Fields (a best-seller in the United States) are mostly nasty black comedies, blisteringly mordant critiques featuring idiosyncratic young antiheroes with a horror of the sham and pretension riddling contemporary England. Amis's are also very hip books, plugged in to modern culture. Traits that prompted The New Statesman to describe Martin's satirically inclined voice as being "somewhere between T. S. Eliot and a pop video."

Which makes Amis the perfect attack dog to turn loose on Elvis, Albert Goldman's infamous 1981 "biography" of the King.

"Elvis Presley: He Did It His Way" first appeared in book form in The Moronic Inferno, Amis's witheringly ironic 1987 nonfiction survey of America's cultural landscape. A panoramic, thoughtful book I highly recommend, if only because of the droll manner with which it terminally torpedoes Goldman's controversial sleazefest, the most reviled history yet written on a public figure.

ELVIS: HE DID IT HIS WAY

by Martin Amis

At this stage in the obsequies, a genuinely "shocking" book about Elvis Presley would disclose that the King secretly gave away vast sums to charity, that he was actually very slim and healthy, and spent much of his free time working with handicapped children. But it is not to be. Following the slanderous testimonies of every hanger-on in the entourage, we are now offered a definitive summation of the grossness, egomania, and barbaric vulgarity that was, apparently, Elvis.

Albert Goldman's *Elvis,* which one is obliged to call an investigative biography, begins and ends with an eerie evocation of the mature Presley. First, the house—Graceland. It looks like a brothel or a gangster's triplex: red velour, gilded tassels, simulated waterfalls, polyurethane finish. Elvis always insisted that everything around him had to be *new.* "When I wuz growin' up in Tupelo," he is quoted as saying, "I lived with enough fuckin' antiques to do me for a lifetime."

On to the master bedroom—black suede walls, crimson carpets and curtains, eight-one square feet of bed with mortuary headboard and speckled armrests. To one side is an easel supporting a large photograph of Elvis's mother, Gladys; to the other is a sepia-toned portrait of Jesus Christ in his pink nightie. On the bed lies Elvis himself—"propped up," in Goldman's gallant formulation, "like a big fat woman recovering from some operation on her reproductive organs."

Before going to work, Elvis rings his valet and junk-food guru, Hamburger James. After a midnight snack—a hundred dollars' worth of Fudgsicles—Elvis consumes a pound of Dixie Cotton bacon, four orders of mash with gravy, plus lots of sauerkraut and crowder peas. He sleeps in diapers these days, thick towels pinned round his middle. He weighs over eighteen stone.

This is a modern biography, so we now follow Elvis from the bed-room to the bathroom. Not that Elvis can get there under his own steam: a bodyguard has to carry him. The bulb-studded sanctum is full of devotional literature, high-powered laxatives, and the King's special "medication"—i.e., his drugs. Elvis hates drug addicts; he would like to see them herded into concentration camps. He once had an audience with Nixon, offering himself as a figurehead in the battle against dope. He was stoned at the time. In fact, he is a drug addict. His doctor must delve between his toes for an unpopped vein.

In his six-door Batmobile Elvis leads the motorcade to Memphis Airport. His private plane, like his house, is a kitsch nightmare of velvet and plastic. At dawn the *Lisa Marie* (named after Elvis's daughter) lands at Las Vegas. Waiting limos ferry the party to the Imperial Suite of the Hilton International. Elvis is cranked down into sleep. "Mommy, I have to go to the bathroom!" he tells his girlfriend. "Mommy will take you." He sleeps. He is cranked awake. He eats, with a handgun beside his plate.

Bandaged and "braced"—i.e., corseted—Elvis dons an outfit embroi-dered with the crowned head of King Tutankhamun and buckles his $10,000 gladiator's belt. He stumbles and mumbles through his act, climaxing with his "American Trilogy": "Dixie," "The Battle Hymn of the Republic," "All My Trials." He comes off-stage pouring with sweat and screaming for his medication. Soon he is back in his tomb, vowing that never again will he play "this fuck'n' Vegas."

Elvis: What Happened? published just before Presley's death, was the first exposé, cobbled together by a couple of sacked goons. Since then, everyone has blabbed. Well, what *did* happen? How did Elvis's life, like his voice, turn from energy and innocence into canting, parodic ruin? Goldman's answer is that the whole phenomenon was corrupt and farci-cal from the beginning. "There is," he warns, "absolutely no poignance in this history."

Elvis's family were hillbillies, "a deracinated and restless race." Elvis's father, Vernon, "greedy and stupid," "a dullard and a donkey," was clearly a fine representative of the breed. Elvis was "a silly little country boy" who just happened to be able "to sing like a nigger," the "acne-spotted self-pity" of his early songs making a strong appeal to "the hysterically self-pitying mood of millions of teenagers."

Nursing dreams of becoming a new Valentino, Elvis's real ambition was to become a movie star. Soon "the biggest putz in the history of filmmaking" was well established as "one of the ugliest and most repulsive presences on the American screen." When this bubble burst, he settled for the Vegas routine. The audience was ideal, consisting of "a couple thousand middle-aged people sated with food and drink."

Personally Elvis was always "a momma's boy," a bully, a coward, and a fool. His career as "pervert," "voyeur," "masturbator" and so forth, was predictable as early as 1956, when Goldman pictures him "thrusting his fat tongue into the mouth of a backstage groupie." Finally, the "freak," the "pig junkie," completes his "deterioration into homicidal madness."

It quickly becomes clear—does it not?—that Goldman isn't to be trusted. In his palpable eagerness to explode the Presley Myth, he has erected an antimyth to replace it—which, in turn, is already being whittled away at by transatlantic commentators. It may indeed be the case that Elvis was no more than a horrible, and horribly uncomplicated, embodiment of American Success; but *Elvis* leaves us none the wiser.

In biography, displays of such inordinate aggression leave one wondering about the personal problems of the author rather than the subject. I read *Elvis* under the impression that Goldman was a surly young iconoclast of the *Rolling Stone* school of New Journalism. On the back flap I am confronted by a middle-aged chipmunk who used to be Professor of English and Comparative Literature at Columbia. As should by now be evident, the book is a prodigy of bad writing, excitable, sarcastic, and barely literate. It is also as exploitative as the exploiters whom Goldman reviles, and no more tasteful than a Presley pants suit.

Observer 1981

Biographical information on PAUL M. SAMMON can be found at the back of this book.

It should be noted, however, that throughout The King Is Dead *we've seen Elvis zombified and eaten, watched him kidnapped by elves, or supplanted by opera-singing twins.*

Because of these tribulations, there may be those among you who feel ye editor harbors a certain . . . disregard for Mr. Presley.

Nothing could be further from the truth.

In memory, Elvis performs under warm, amber-colored spotlights. On the happiest stage of my youth.

"The Heart of Rock 'n' Roll"—which is a rewritten, self-contained portion of a similarly titled novel-in-progress—should help confirm that.

One final note:

This one's for you, Pop.

THE HEART OF ROCK 'N ROLL
by Paul M. Sammon

Venice, California—1993

Chaz came weaving toward me, twin Corona bottles in one hand, Cuervo shooter in the other.

His thumb was curled over the shot glass's mouth. It kept most of the tequila from slopping onto the floor as he expertly threaded through a knot of moshing dancers.

They were slamming to "Tired of You." Satori's new single which was rapidly climbing the college radio charts. Right now it blared from a scruffy boom box that looked scrounged from a Salvation Army bin. The song's double-bass line *thumped*! off the apartment's hardwood floor. Bombarded the thin plaster walls like invisible cannon balls.

Whoever lived downstairs was getting an earful. No matter; this was Venice. The neighbors were probably up here slamdancing too.

Chaz caught me studying him. He nodded. Flipped long blond braids away from his eyes. Raised both bottles, in mock salute.

I waved back.

Behind bluemirrored sunglasses, my own eyes felt dry. Gritty. I rubbed one. Saw Chaz almost make it to the couch before an oblivious Kasi, arms flung wide and spinning in circles, slammed into him.

Half the tequila splashed across Kasi's T-shirted breasts.

Chaz frowned. Yelled something. Kasi didn't react. Satori's keyboard player was high, blasted on a doubledose of Ecs. Suspended in that intense, sensuous halfworld between clarity and abandon.

Kasi tried to kiss Chaz on the cheek. He ducked. Avoided her. Finally made it to my side of the sofa, doing a little dance step as he hopped over my legs.

The battered Naugahyde wheezed in protest as Chaz flopped down beside me. Without preamble, he jumped back into our conversation.

"I can't buy that," Chaz shouted over the music. "Nah."

He knocked back what was left of his Cuervo. No lime, no salt.

"Friends," he yelled, with loud finality, "fuck you up."

I sipped the club soda Chaz had given me earlier. Leaned against him so I wouldn't have to shout.

"Depends," I said, close to his ear. "It's really a matter of knowing who to trust."

Chaz took a short, sullen nip off one of the Coronas.

We'd been having this staccato conversation for almost an hour now, periodically interrupted by the boom box and by Chaz's choppy silences. It hadn't taken long to discover that Satori's lead singer was a skeptic, like most of today's intelligent youth.

He also was a realist. Shrewd enough to know a golden opportunity when he saw one. Such as me, Mick Tyler, whom the inscrutable Rock Gods had suddenly dropped into Chaz's life.

I'd first heard Satori last summer, during a low-profile, incognito recon through the local club scene. They were good. Chaz interested me.

But Amber had counseled patience.

"Wait," she'd urged. "Watch, and learn."

I had. Nearly a year passed by as Amber acquired Satori tapes and quietly investigated Chaz's background.

He was young, talented, and broke. A troubled performer barely out of his teens, who drank too much and partied too hearty.

Your basic musician, right?

Yet between the fistfights and escalating acts of self-destruction glimmered a second, more complicated Chaz. A smart, nervous kid who crafted complex songs of loss and responsibility. One who'd been born into a radical feminist commune, and never known his father.

Then, yesterday afternoon, Amber had called my estate.

"Have you seen the *Weekly*?" she'd asked. "They're playing tomorrow night. At Skank. That should do, don't you think?"

It would. So earlier this evening we'd swept into the club like the royalty we were, fully aware of adoring eyes upon us. Amber was resplendent in silks and turquoise leather; I had my hands thrust deep into the pockets of an Italian duster, trademarked mirror shades raked tight across my face.

Around me was a hot, low-ceilinged place. Skank catered to a hardcore piercing crowd, tattooed modern primitives out for their fix of riot grrrl, grindcore, grunge. And everywhere I looked were Madison's or septum rings, Earl's and labrets.

I saw punctured lower lips, laden with metal fruit. Heard the sound of tongue jewelry clicking nervously against teeth. One man had pierced himself right between the eyes; the tiny rubber form of a naked black woman hung at his browline.

Maybe his balls were festooned with *hafadas,* those scrotum piercings which had originated in the Middle East.

If so, he probably jingled when he took a leak.

Skank's fawning manager had ushered us to his own private booth. There we'd ordered Evians, and stared at the stage.

It was empty; Satori was between sets. Yet just as I'd identified the music pumping through the club as something by Skinny Puppy, the houselights dimmed, squeals of feedback split the air, and a disembodied voice screamed "Satori!"

They were a foursome. Jym on lead guitar, Kasi on synth, Jak on Gibson bass. But Chaz—ah, Chaz, he was the rock. The nexus. The flaming core who attacked his Yamaha drum kit and melancholy lyrics with the same raw, angry grace.

Satori played a blistering set. Windmilled through a unique mix of power pop, rockabilly and trance. Every tasty number was filled with licks and hooks and hot, hot rock.

But midway through their encore, Amber had tapped my wrist.

I'd stood up. Gone backstage, knowing she'd leave without me.

A few minutes later, after Satori finished their set, I'd moved in from the shadows and introduced myself. An apparently friendly aristocrat, the bigleaguer trying hard to be a fellow musician and all-round ordinary guy.

Chaz had been wary—I got him drunk. The more liquor he'd consumed, the more our conversation slipped beneath his guarded surfaces. Into life, women, art.

Getting an invitation back to his shitty little apartment had been easy. No trouble at all.

Manipulation has always been one of my natural abilities.

I got that from my Dad.

Behind us, someone changed the tape on Chaz's boom box. Satori went away; Ministry took their place, with "Stigmata."

"You dig Ministry?" Chaz asked.

"Yeah," I replied. "They're angry, but they *rock.*"

"No shit."

Chaz sipped his beer.

"I don't trust anyone or anything," he suddenly blurted out. "Except my music."

Well. That had taken awhile.

We sat in silence, listening to Ministry. Chaz was staring out an open window. I stared with him.

The window opened onto a deserted, latenight Venice boardwalk. Three stories down and a hundred yards away, an empty beach embraced curling, luminous waves.

I heard a sudden clattering. Looked up.

Above the window were the type of cheap ricepaper blinds you find in import stores. Inexpensive things—student shades. They rustled loudly in an errant ocean breeze, made a stiff, dry racket.

"Nice view, huh?" Chaz said. "Kasi chose the apartment 'cause of it. Hey. Watch this."

He casually flipped up one of the nowempty Corona bottles. Caught it by its neck. Tossed it out the window.

I waited. No delayed crash, no splintering glass. Must have fallen on sand.

"Nice shot," I said.

"Yeah."

The windowshades rattled again. Louder, this time. Chaz scowled.

"Is that fucking irritating, or what?"

He jumped up and lowered the blinds. As he did, I realized Chaz had been wanting to show me something.

Pasted on the windowshade were a number of small black-and-white pictures. They appeared to be clipped from fanzines, and were painstakingly arranged to form a crude but striking collage.

I saw animals and landscapes. Homicide scenes. The inevitable headshots of musicians.

Kurt Cobain, Exene Cervenka. Iggy. Al Jourgensen. Joey Ramone. Me. Lots of pictures of me.

I leaned closer. Touched the blind with the tip of a finger.

A spiral of photographs arced out and away from the central mass like the drunken arm of a tiny *noir* galaxy. My finger followed it, flesh through an inkandpaper maze. Ended at—

The King.

I'd stopped at a picture of Elvis Presley. He was standing in the aisle of a train, wearing a suit, and flirting with two young women. The late Fifties, early Sixties Elvis. Handsome, thin, not yet bloated by success.

I recognized this shot. It had been taken by Alfred Wertheimer during a train trip Elvis once took, from New York to Memphis. But the girls in the picture hadn't believed this really *was* Elvis—despite the fact that his arms were wrapped around a huge teddy bear.

To prove his identity, The King had invited them to a concert that night. A performance at Memphis's Russwood Stadium.

The women turned him down.

With that perverse synchronicity which will never be avoided or explained, "Stigmata" suddenly ended and the opening bars to "Hard-Headed Woman" flooded Chaz's apartment.

"Great song," I said, covering Elvis with my palm.

Chaz moved so fast he startled me. His hand grabbed my upper thigh. Squeezed painfully.

"You like Elvis?" Chaz asked. His tone was urgent.

"Uh-huh."

Chaz let me go. Squirmed excitedly on the couch.

"Guy was a genius, man. White trash, maybe, but he really had it. You know? All these other assholes"—Chaz gestured vaguely toward the collage—"compared to Elvis, they're fuckin' wankers. Pathetic nobodies." Then he caught himself. "Present company excluded, of course."

I almost told him, then. Almost let the real reason behind my visit slip. Instead, I grinned.

Chaz smiled for the first time that night. He slid closer.

"You ever see him? The King, I mean."

"Well," I responded, "that was a long time ago."

Chaz sighed.

"Aw, man, don't do that. I get enough of that shit from the band. Kasi's always telling me how retro it is to dig Elvis. But *you* like him, I saw it on your face. That's fine by me, ok? We're probably the only two people here who *do* like The King."

I wasn't prepared for this. None of Amber's researches had indicated an Elvis fixation.

And that was spooky. Because in a very real sense, Elvis Presley was the reason I'd gone backstage tonight. Just as he was responsible for Mick Tyler and the Tornadoes' brand-new nickname, the one we'd picked up last week at the MTV Awards.

The World's Greatest Rock 'n' Roll Band.

And fuck The Rolling Stones.

"It's not much of a story," I said. "More like a paragraph."

Chaz shook his head. "Tell me anyway," he urged.

I sipped my water.

"I was about six or seven years old," I began. "Living in the Philippines. That's where I first heard Elvis Presley."

Chaz's eyebrows went up.

"You heard Elvis in *the Philippines*? Man, I haven't even been to Tijuana! Hey, Kasi!" he shouted. "C'mere!"

On the far side of the room, Kasi shimmied to the King's beat. She smiled. Blew Chaz a kiss. Turned her back and kept dancing.

"I don't think she's interested."

"Yeah. Fuck her, she's ragin'. Me, I've got every one of Elvis's old records, 45's, the *dinosaur* shit! Cost me major bucks. So. Tell."

I stared at Wertheimer's photograph. On the other side of it, out there in the dark, surged the vast Pacific Ocean.

I thought of how cold its Southern California currents are, even in deepest summer. Remembered the bloodheat of the South China Sea, where the water's so warm it can melt the wax off a surfboard.

As the King sang on. *My song,* I thought. Elvis's first gold record. A tune specifically recorded for *King Creole.*

It had taken me a long time to learn that, though. Before, during my childhood, Elvis had only been a Voice. A Voice and catalyst far more powerful than anything these lost, chattering children would ever, possibly, know, as—

Cavite City, Philippine Islands—1958

—the exotic scents of sizzling *lumpia,* of fishheads and fried rice, swirled in great, invisible clouds around his head.

The boy inhaled. He loved these strange aromas. They sure were different! Not like the same old hamburgers and vanilla shakes they served at the gedunk. Uh-*uh*! Not at all!

All the sudden Daddy made a growly noise in his throat.

"Hurry," he said.

The boy did his best to catch up with the thin, curly-headed man in the Chief Petty Officer's uniform, who was marching straight-backed and stiff-legged a few paces ahead of him. He and the boy had just left the base to go into town; they were going to buy Mommy a birthday present. First, though, they had to walk a couple of blocks to get to the shops.

So the boy closed his eyes and sucked in another breath. He was playing nose detective, trying to figure out which smells were what.

Hey! He knew that one! That was *pancit,* the big noodles Fely ate!

"Goddamn it, Mick! I said hurry up!"

The boy's eyes flicked open; Daddy was farther away.

He began to run, taking in everything around him.

Cavite★ was a small, crowded place, with narrow windy streets that were noisy and smelly and busy and alive. There were crazy stores. Funny, crooked houses. Little Filipino kids wearing nothing but T-shirts, and peeing in the street.

Thunder rumbled overhead.

The boy glanced up. Grinned.

Wow! Those sure were some big, fat clouds in the sky!

Suddenly, he was shoved to one side. The boy stumbled. Nearly fell.

"Pay attention and watch where you're going," Daddy snapped. "You almost stepped in that."

Daddy had pushed him away from a mud puddle. The kind that were everywhere on Cavite's unpaved streets.

"Yes, Father," the boy mumbled. He looked away.

Welp, there went his good mood. Squashed like a bug. The boy knew better than to say anything, though, 'cause he knew Daddy was mad.

But it wasn't fair—Daddy was *always* mad.

Why couldn't they be friends, like back in San Francisco?

Back there, Daddy had read him bedtime stories. Every night! They'd played "bumpheads," too, wrestling and tickling until the boy laughed so hard it hurt.

★ Cah-VEE-tee.

Then Daddy went away to a place called the Philippines. And for a whole year the boy and his Mommy had had to wait in San Francisco, until the Navy found them a new place to live.

Finally, though, he and Mommy got transferred too. That's what the Navy called it, "transferred." They got on a big ship called the *Barrett* and spent three weeks on the ocean and finally came to a tiny place in the Philippines called Sangley, Sangley Point Naval Air Station, which was exactly one mile long. Where everybody lived in goofy little houses called Quonset huts but looked more like big tin cans cut in half and laid on their side, if you asked him.

The boy frowned.

Something bad had happened to Daddy at Sangley.

At first, Daddy tried to act just like he did in San Francisco. But one day he'd sat the boy down and said that Mick was too old for kid's stuff anymore. Just like that.

Now it was time to GROW UP. To BE A MAN. To FOLLOW THE RULES.

First off, the boy couldn't say "Daddy" anymore. Just FATHER. And he couldn't cry anymore, either. That was for SISSIES.

Even so, the boy discovered Sangley Point was kinda neat. It had maids, for one thing. Filipino girls who lived with your family and did all the cooking and cleaning.

Their maid was Fely. The boy liked her; she was nice. Fely was teaching him her LANGUAGE. The one the American kids called Tag-A-Log.

Still, the boy was awful lonesome.

Especially since he and Daddy never, ever played "bumpheads" again.

BEEP! BEEPBEEPBEEEEPPPP!

A jeepney roared past. The boy smiled.

He *liked* jeepneys. You got in the back of this like open-air taxicab and sat down on funny leather benches. All scrunched up beside six or seven other people who were holding packages or kids or even, sometimes, chickens and little pigs on their laps.

Daddy had told him jeepneys came from THE WAR. The big one everybody still talked about. American soldiers had left these jeeps behind an' the Filipinos had fixed them all up with mirrors and plastic saints and other stuff. Then they'd turned 'em into taxis.

A Filipino woman was sitting in the jeepney. She saw the boy grinning at her. The woman smiled back.

Now the boy saw some words painted on the jeepney's rear bumper: LA BOMBA.

The boy thought that was a funny name. So he laughed. Out loud.

"What are you laughing at?"

The boy turned. The question had come from over his head.

"Nothing, Father."

"Then stop it. It's weird."

The boy hid his face. Why'd he have to say *that?*

All the sudden somebody yelled.

"Mr. Tyler! Look out!"

Two men were coming toward them. One wore a raincoat over a Filipino police uniform; he was the one who'd yelled.

The second Filipino had a raincoat on too, over black pants and a beautiful silk shirt. The kind Fely called *Barong Tagalog.*

This man was smiling.

He was also tossing a great big bucketful of dirty brown water right at the boy's face.

The boy ducked. The water sailed past him in a solid sheet and splashed, full force, across Daddy's chest.

"Mr. Tyler! You are all wet!" the policeman said.

Daddy yelled something nasty at the water thrower. But the man just laughed and skipped away, swinging his bucket like a kid.

The policeman came up to them. He looked like he was trying hard not to laugh himself.

"Are you all right, Mr. Tyler?"

"Hell, no!" Daddy said. "I'm soaked! What was that all about?"

The constable shrugged. "St. John the Baptist. A feast day, Mr. Tyler. It's a town custom; you find some water, you baptize somebody. Maybe you should buy a raincoat."

"What for?" Daddy complained. His uniform was dripping wet.

"Ah, well." The policeman winked at the boy. "That man was *loco,* no? There will be more of him today—watch out!"

The boy smiled. He felt grateful to be noticed.

"This is Johnny," Daddy said. "Johnny Cloud. He's a night watchman at the Chief's Club. Johnny, Mick."

"*Mabuhay,* Mick," Johnny said.

"*Mabuhay,*" the boy replied.

"Maybe I should have read the Plan of the Day," Daddy grumbled. "Then I'd still be——"

"A *loco loco baboy!*" the boy interrupted.

"What?" said Daddy. He looked confused.

Johnny Cloud tousled the boy's hair.

"He didn't mean you, Mr. Tyler. I think he was talking about that man with the bucket. Right, Mick? Wasn't he a 'crazy crazy pig'?"

The boy nodded.

"You have a very smart son, Mr. Tyler. He is becoming more like a Filipino every day!"

"*Ay, naku!*" the boy responded.

Johnny laughed.

Daddy took out his handkerchief and wiped his face.

"That's terrific," he said.

Then, for no reason at all, Johnny and Daddy started talking about baseball.

The boy sighed again. He *hated* baseball. Just as much as he hated the way that whenever two grown-ups got together, they hardly ever talked to *you.*

The boy walked over to a nearby shop window. Looked in. Saw monkeypod ashtrays and carved water buffaloes and little ashtrays shaped like *nipa* huts.

Big deal. It was all tourist junk. Not anything cool like that old Japanese submarine, the big, rusted thing the Navy had pulled up from the bottom of the ocean and towed to Sangley the other day.

Then the boy heard music. He turned his head.

The music was close. Somewhere down the street.

The boy looked back at the grown-ups.

Still talking baseball!

Very carefully, the boy began walking sideways. As if he was still looking at the tourist stuff.

What he was really gonna do, though, was hunt for that music.

The boy *loved* music. There was plenty of it around his house. Not just kid's stuff, either, like "Eggbert the Easter Egg" or "Purple People Eater."

Nope, this music belonged to Mommy and Daddy, who played these round red yellow things called 45's all the time. Mommy liked SHOW-

TUNES and stuff from THE HIT PARADE; Frankie Laine singing "Granada," Mitzi Gaynor doing "I'm Gonna Wash That Man Right Outta My Hair," stuff like that. Daddy liked HILLBILLY MUSIC. Red Foley, Ernest Tubb, Kitty Wells, the boy knew all their names. He even knew the words to "I'm Walkin' the Floor Over You."

So him and music were friends. Good friends.

In fact sometimes, late at night, he'd sneak out of bed. Just to listen to it.

The Quonset hut would be all dark and quiet around him like it was holding its breath. The boy would tiptoe into the living room and switch on the big Philco, the one next to the rattan couch. Then he'd tune it to Armed Forces Radio and turn down the sound and pile up some pillows on the floor and get all comfy, so he could lean his head up against the vibrating cabinet and listen to songs like "April Love," or the soft and velvety "Chances Are."

But what was this *new* stuff? This song he'd heard in Cavite?

It wasn't *anything* like the records at home!

The boy inched cautiously down the block. Stopped in front of a really weird building.

The place looked like the side of a cliff. Like it was made outta big flat rocks or somethin'. There were all these long gray stone spears, too, hanging by the door.

That door was open. Beside it was a sign. A bright, electric sign, with lots of colored lights.

D'CAVE, the sign said.

The boy shifted, foot to foot. He'd heard about these places. They were called BARS, and they were for grown-ups.

But then he heard that MUSIC again!

The boy looked over his shoulder, back at Daddy and Johnny. They didn't even know he was gone.

So he swallowed. Threw back his shoulders. Walked through the door.

Inside, it was dark. It smelled funny, too. Like moldy bread.

The boy blinked. All he could see were some funny pink lights. So he blinked again.

His eyes focused. Now the boy made out another Filipino man, one who was standing across the room behind a low wooden wall. This man was polishing a glass. And staring at him.

The boy squinted.

Behind the man was a mirror. Above that . . .

The boy gasped.

It was a painting of a pretty Filipino woman. Like Fely. But *this* woman was NAKED!

The boy's gaze dropped, scorched. As it did, he saw one little word printed beneath the painting:

HONEYCOMB.

The boy felt his cheeks getting hot. The lady's titties were so big! And uncovered!

Close by, somebody laughed.

The boy turned his head. Two sailors were sitting nearby, at a small round table. Brown bottles of San Miquel beer in their hands.

"Whatcha doin' in here, kid?" the first sailor said.

"Yeah," said the second sailor. "Kinda young for poontang."

The first sailor laughed.

"You from the base?" the second sailor asked.

The boy squirmed. His heart was hammering and his palms were wet and he was having a hard time getting a breath.

The first sailor frowned. "Maybe you'd better take off," he said.

Uh-oh!

The boy timidly pointed toward a jukebox, the big old yellow/ silver thing where the MUSIC was coming from.

"What's that?" he asked.

The first sailor turned slowly around in his chair. Looked back at the jukebox.

"That's a Rockola," the second sailor said.

"No!" The boy almost yelled in frustration. "The MUSIC!"

"You mean Elvis?"

"What's an Elvis?" the boy asked.

The first sailor turned around.

"Shit, kid, where you been? Mars? That's rock 'n' roll! Elvis Presley!"

"Who?"

"Kid's outta touch," said the second sailor to his friend. "Been in the P.I. too long."

Behind the low wall, the Filipino man banged down his glass.

"You!" he yelled, pointing at the boy. "You leave!"

The boy's eyes got big.

"Aw, c'mon, Ernie," said the first sailor.

The Filipino ignored him. Shouted "Ziggy now!"

"Damn, Ernie!" said sailor #2. "Give the kid a break. Came in to hear Elvis, that's all. Hey—how 'bout gettin' us another round? And some pretzels, too. *Kasiya-siya?*"

The Filipino man said some bad words in Tagalog. Then he banged through a door behind the little wall and disappeared.

"Don't mind Ernie, kid," said sailor #2. "He thinks you're under-age."

"Not like us," laughed sailor #1.

"What's that song?" the boy asked.

The second sailor swallowed some beer.

" 'Hard-Headed Woman,' " he said.

"Shoulda been 'All Shook Up,' " said sailor #1. "Like Ernie."

"I like it," the boy said. "It's cool."

The second sailor winked at him.

"Kid, you're pretty cool yourself," said sailor #2.

The boy shut his eyes. Now that he knew what the music was, he could just relax and listen to it.

Rock 'n' roll, huh? Boy, was it *neat*! And that VOICE!

He liked it. It made him want to move. He couldn't help *but* move. So he did.

One of the sailors whistled.

"All RIGHT!" the sailor shouted. "Go, kid, go! Fuckin' A!!!"

The sailors started pounding their bottles on the tabletop. That surprised him, but the boy didn't stop. He *liked* to dance.

Anyway, all he heard now was that VOICE. A VOICE which rolled out of the jukebox in big warm waves, like the surf at Black Sands beach. A VOICE which crashed against his body and tickled the top of his head. A VOICE that ran through his neck and his arms and his legs, which, to his astonishment, were jittering faster than they'd ever moved before.

Pumping madly to the beat, he gave a KICK here and a THRUST there, as THE VOICE cried *Ah-Ha-Huhm!* and *HA-HUHM!* and *HUHH-HMMMM!!!*

"HU-HUHM!" the boy yelled back.

The sound felt punched up from his throat.

All at once a heavy hand dug painfully into his shoulder.

344 PAUL M. SAMMON

"What the HELL are you doing?" shouted another, all-too-familiar voice.

The boy opened his eyes. Looked up.

Oh no.

The breeze rattled Elvis's picture again.

"I was a Navy brat," I told Chaz. "My family was stationed on a base in the Philippines. It's not there anymore."

"Yeah?" Chaz said.

"Yes. One day, my father and I went into town. I got lost. Ended up in a serviceman's club, where "Hard-Headed Woman" was playing on the jukebox." I took a sip of water. "That's it."

Chaz's eyes were avid. "Wow! Anything else?"

"Let's see. Yeah, my first naked woman. I saw her on an oil painting, over the bar."

Chaz laughed. "Just like a western," he said.

More like an epic, I thought.

By the time I'd turned thirteen, my family had rotated in and out of any number of bases; Yokuska, Port Hueneme, Charleston. And as we moved, so did the music.

An explosion of it, like the world had never known.

The fragile innocence of "April Love" and "Bali Hai" had long been ravished by the raging hormones of "Jailhouse Rock" and "Great Balls of Fire," which in turn were washed away by surf bands like The Beach Boys, The Astronauts and The Ventures, by Surfin' Bird and Pipeline. Then came Motown—Smokey Robinson, The Supremes. "Stop, in the Name of Love."

The entire time I'd struggled to master the guitar. Learned how to strum and how to tune. How to fingerpick and flatpick. How to apply three-chord progressions to "Gloria" and "Louie Louie."

By the time I was sixteen I'd run away from home. Given up everything, just to rock 'n' roll.

At the age of twenty-one I was a session player in New York.

Ten years later, I'd placed four albums in the Top Ten.

Only to discover that the sweet kiss of fame had left ashes in my mouth.

This unhappiness wasn't due to the work, you understand. On the contrary—my business is passion, and it's passion that makes life bearable.

Music is passion's key.

Still, something deep was out of whack. My soul felt splintered. Spiderwebbed. Cracked by some vague, subterranean fault I couldn't quite put a finger on.

Gradually, it grew worse. The fame, the money, the women, the flattery—nothing left me satisfied anymore. My heart was a dry scrap of tundra, trapped within an Arctic rock. Waiting to be warmed by a freakish ray of sun.

Beside me, Chaz reached behind his ear. Pulled out what used to be known as a joint. These days, the hip-hop crowd calls it a blunt. Whatever. He lit it, inhaled, and offered it to me.

I shook my head.

"That's right," he said. "I forgot." Jets of smoke shot out of Chaz's nostrils. "These days you're straight."

I shrugged.

"Hey, man, no offense. I smoke 'cause it helps me create. You don't need it, I understand."

He didn't. Chaz was too sure of his own sense of immortality to understand how precious health could become for a burnout like myself.

"Don't stop because of me," I encouraged.

Chaz took another hit. "Must have righteously fucked up your head though, huh?" he mused. "I mean, sex and jukeboxes and Elvis. All in the same day, too. Whew."

I smiled. It *had* been important. Important enough to turn me into a walking encyclopedia. One who could tell you what Elvis hated (runny eggs) and what he liked (the color blue). And when.

"I've read about that," said a woman's voice.

Kasi was standing behind the sofa. I could read the words that were stenciled on her damp T-shirt: CHRISTIANITY IS STUPID.

"In *Rolling Stone* or *Spin,*" she continued. "Some old article by Amber Collins. Doesn't she work for you? Anway, she made out Elvis was the whole reason you got into music in the first place."

I studied Kasi's face. Behind the Ecstasy's artificial joy, her eyes were sharp. Alert.

"Cheap psychology," I replied. "Journalists love that, to analyze. Makes them forget they're writing about what they can't do."

"Maybe," Kasi said. "Didn't she also say you hated your father?"

Chaz frowned.

"Lighten up, K.," he growled. "We're talkin' Elvis, not Oedipus."

"Oh, right. The King." Kasi smiled. "Can't interrupt that. Bye."

She drifted away.

"Don't mind her," Chaz said. "Kasi gets suspicious around strangers."

He puffed on his pot. "She sort of looks after me."

Lovers, I thought. Something else I hadn't known.

Chaz smoked his skunk weed. I swiveled my head.

Kasi was dancing with Jym.

I watched her and wondered what she would have thought about my last meeting with my father.

Balboa Naval Hospital, San Diego CA—1984

The old man had been trying to get in touch with me for years.

To work things out, his letters read.

In truth, my father had never been far from my thoughts. I was old enough now to understand his hard early life, one filled with poverty and neglect. My father was also of that generation for whom certain emotions were difficult. Weaknesses, to be locked away.

Yet despite the increasing harshness he'd shown me as a boy—the beatings, the sarcasm, the relentless ridicule of everything I'd wanted or loved—I'd actually begun to make excuses for him. Had even considered some sort of surprise visit, from the prodigal son.

Then I'd realized how stupidly romantic that was.

My father had been the reason I'd run away in the first place. My mother? She was dead, gone years ago. The sole buffer between two men whose ties were twisted up in hate.

So I'd ignored my father's phone calls. Thrown away his cards. Until the day he lay dying in a Naval oncology ward.

I'd had to go then.

The sleeping old man lying on the hard, narrow bed was shrunken and wasted. I hardly recognized him. His lungs were awash in toxic secretions; too many drinks, too much anger, too much Navy lifestyle.

Then my father regained consciousness.

"Mick?" he'd mumbled.

"Dad," I'd said.

Shockingly, my father started to cry.

"The pain, Mick!" my father gasped. "I'm afraid!"

I didn't know what to do. The old man reached for my hands; I extended one toward his own. But my gesture was shaky, awkward. After these years, he still was Daddy, and I was still his little boy.

The old man sensed my embarrassment. "Goddamn it, Mick," he'd muttered irritably. "What's wrong? Touch me . . . be a *man* . . . !"

The words were like gasoline thrown on an old, smoldering fire.

I'd hesitated. Frowned. Stood up.

To tower above him, frozen and silent. Too upset to speak, and too damned petty to take the offer of an old man's trembling hand.

Suddenly, his bloodshot eyes widened in surprise.

"Tired!" he very distinctly said.

And then my father died.

We never did touch.

It was just before noon on a brilliant, unseasonably warm winter's day. I stood by the bedside of a stranger. A brusque, intimidating man who'd spent one night creating a son, and the rest of his life figuring out what to do with him.

Finally, I touched my father's brow. It was cool. His damp, curly hair felt surprisingly soft. Like a child's.

What else was I feeling?

Guilt? Shame? Loss?

A little, I suppose.

Mostly, though, I felt empty.

And that, I suddenly realized, was exactly what was killing me.

Unwanted tears trickled down my cheeks. A nurse came by, tried to comfort her famous visitor. Told him what a wonderful son he was, to come all this way just to be with his father.

Sure. That was me. The brave little soldier.

The nurse handed me a Kleenex. Led me down a corridor toward her workstation, to finish some necessary paperwork.

On our way we passed an office. A young black orderly was sitting inside it. His feet were up on a desk.

He was munching on a doughnut and listening to a radio. A *big* radio.

It was playing "Hard-Headed Woman."

And at that precise instant, the strangest image flashed through my head.

I saw two phantoms, drinking beer and listening to a jukebox. Before them writhed a small, lonely ghost, moving to a tune that would forever alter its life.

The nurse took hold of my arm; I'd suddenly stopped in my tracks. She asked what was wrong.

I didn't—couldn't—reply.

For with that ancient memory had come the unexpected.

And miraculous.

Something had wrenched loose in my chest. Something thick, and gray, and muffled. It was floating up into consciousness now, and I could *see* it. Examine it. Easily peer beneath its vague, suffocating folds. As if I'd never spent those countless nights and albums trying to dislodge this sorrowful thing in the first place.

I'd swayed. Felt dizzy. Had to sit down.

The nurse ran off to get a cup of water.

I didn't really need it. Everything was clear. Perfectly, *ridiculously* clear. Crystalline. As if I'd been hit by a thunderbolt.

Once, a long time ago, I'd been fated. Wrenched away from everyday banality by Destiny's subtle hand. And despite the subsequent adult disappointments, in spite of the bitterness and distrust and all-consuming fear of failure, a fear I now recognize as the true price of fame, Fate had never quite forgotten me.

How did I know?

Because, just now, it had visited once again.

I sprang up and ran inside the office. Swept aside the orderly's feet. Ignored his startled questions and picked up the telephone.

First I called Marty, my business manager. I ordered him to buy a mausoleum. A huge, stately thing, reeking of money and class.

Then I hung up and rang the limo driver. Told him to go home and bring me my favorite photograph.

The last thing I did was return to my father's room, where I signed away his corneas and sat with the old man's body, until they came to take it from me.

The photograph?

It was a snapshot. An old, yellowing thing. It showed the three of us— my dad, my mom, me—standing in front of a tiny house. In San Francisco. We're smiling, and looking impossibly young.

That was the picture I tucked into Dad's silk jacket. The one I bought to bury him in.

And yes, the whole time I was doing this, I knew it wasn't enough. But it was a start.

"First time I saw Elvis was on TV," Chaz said. "This dude gave me a tape of his '68 comeback concert. And, man, I could not fuckin' believe it! It was like Elvis was singing to *me*. Straight to my heart, you know?"

I nodded. I knew.

Chaz finished his second beer. Set the bottle on the floor. "Can I ask you a question?" he said.

"Shoot."

Chaz cocked his head. "Why'd you come here, anyway?"

That might have startled someone else.

"You want me to leave?" I asked.

"No! Don't get me wrong, man. We've all dug your stuff for a long time. Kasi, she *loves* your shit. Me too."

"Then what's the problem?"

"There is no problem." But Chaz was a little too drunk to stop. "Guess I'm havin' a hard time believing it. I mean, Mick Tyler! Here, in my house! That's like findin' Axel Rose in your fuckin' bathroom!"

"Thanks for the compliment."

But he wasn't listening. "Guess I'm just paranoid," Chaz said.

"About what?"

"About . . . what do you want, Mick?"

A long, long silence.

"I don't want anything," I finally replied. "I just dig your music."

Chaz considered this. Nodded. My answer seemed to satisfy him.

"There is one thing," I added.

"What?" he asked, wary again.

I raised my empty bottle.

"You got any more water?"

Chaz exploded with laughter. "Man, you are all right. Allfuckinright! Sure, I'll see what I can do!"

"Don't forget to come back," I said, grinning. "We haven't finished with those Elvis stamps."

"Yeah," Chaz chuckled. "You know, when they first came out, I put a dozen stamps on twelve different envelopes. Then I sent 'em all to phony addresses, so I'd get some back stamped 'Return to Sender.' "

"Now, why didn't I think of that?"

Chaz smiled and got up. He loped toward the darkened kitchen, passing through small clusters of people sprawled around the floor and the few pieces of furniture.

Most everyone had gone home; Satori's party was winding down.

Chaz, though, looked happy.

I sighed and turned around. Stared at the windowshade. Thought about Kasi's accusations concerning my Dad.

Then I thought about Elvis's habit of giving away Cadillacs, and finally made my decision.

Satori was about to hit a string of good luck. Little things, at first. Like being able to connect with the right agent. Or knowing which detox programs worked best.

Eventually, though, their fortunes would snowball. And the whole time, Chaz would never know what was really going on.

I'd make sure of that.

The windowshade rattled again. Lifted Elvis's picture.

Behind me, the boy I'd come looking for started to sing.

I raised my empty bottle and toasted Wertheimer's photograph. Joined in Chaz's song, humming it under my breath.

The window's drab reflection showed Kasi detaching herself from Jym. I saw her lean against Chaz. Smile. Give him a gentle hug.

Satori's lead singer *must* have been feeling lucky tonight.

But he isn't, you know.

Not nearly as lucky as me.

Unlike Chaz, I knew who my real father was.

—For Paul A. Sammon

Why in the world, you're probably asking yourself, is an epilogue not the final entry in this anthology?

Good question.

You'll have to flip ahead to the introduction preceding "The Eagle Cape" for your answer, though.

In the meantime, here's another question:

What's When Elvis Died?

Just one of the three best books ever printed on the Dead Elvis phenomenon, that's all.

(The other two—in case you're interested—include Greil Marcus's Dead Elvis *and Charles Thompson/James Cole's* The Death of Elvis, *a tough-minded nonfiction work which mixes autopsy reports with relentless investigative journalism to conclusively prove that Elvis is dead, dead, dead).*

When Elvis Died *was originally published by an obscure outfit named Communications Press, in 1980. It was difficult to find.*

It was also a serious examination of the postmortem Presley cult. When Elvis Died *opens with a fateful 1977 telephone call to a Memphis newspaper called* The Commercial Appeal; *it then spends fifteen chapters chronicling America's obsessive reaction to the loss of a legend. With all the attendant grief, greed, media circuses, and fan hysteria that went along with it.*

There was only one problem.

When Elvis Died *stopped its coverage of the King's life in the year 1980.*

Thankfully, in 1992 Pharos Books celebrated the fifteenth anniversary of Dead Elvis's transcendence by reprinting When Elvis Died *in a brand-new edition. And its authors—NEAL and JANICE GREGORY, writers and public relations professionals based in Washington, D.C.—added a new chapter,*

351

one nicely updating Elvis's tidalwave saturation on the floodplains of popular culture.

I've reprinted that chapter here.

Because I can think of no better way to summarize Dead Elvis's all-pervasive influence.

Or a better way to (almost) end this book.

WHEN ELVIS DIED: EPILOGUE
by Neal and Janice Gregory

The media and the public, their attention fixed suddenly and vividly on Elvis at the time of his death, have solidified the entertainer's place in America's cultural mythology.

In the still-chaotic early days, grieving fans continued to butt up against a puzzled establishment. More than a million people visited Forest Hill Cemetery in the month after Elvis was entombed. After an aborted attempt to steal the body, however, Vernon Presley obtained a zoning variance and permission to move the bodies of Elvis and his mother, Gladys, to the Meditation Garden near the south end of the mansion. The Tennessee State Department of Archives and History provided a historical marker for Graceland, and the family opened the grounds to visitors who came by the thousands to visit the graves.

Radio stations around the world kept playing Elvis's songs, and record sales continued unabated. Fan clubs increased their memberships and new groups were formed. Parts of Elvis's first Cadillac were melted down and pressed into heart-shaped pendants and offered for sale. Many of the custom-designed luxury automobiles he had owned toured the country as promotions for car dealers and other businesses. Memorial albums appeared. An entrepreneur tried to sell pieces of the marble crypt where Elvis had first been laid to rest. Madame Tussaud's in London unveiled a three-thousand-dollar wax effigy of the singer standing near Kojak, Marilyn Monroe, and the Royal Family; the exhibit quickly became the museum's most popular attraction.

Then came August 16, 1978—the first anniversary of Elvis's death.

Dozens of memorial events were scheduled in Memphis. The Memphian, the movie theater Elvis frequently rented for post-midnight showings for his friends, booked a festival of Presley films. Andy Warhol

353

opened an exhibition, featuring his painting *Elvis Forty-nine Times,* at Brooks Memorial Art Gallery. The Circle G Ranch, property in nearby Mississippi once owned by Elvis, announced sunset memorial services at the base of a fifty-foot-high concrete cross.

But a massive fire and police strike crippled Memphis. The National Guard was called out and a curfew imposed. Many of the Elvis events were canceled, but thousands of fans showed up anyhow, along with network television crews and reporters. In the midst of it all, a drunken electric company employee knocked out most of the city's power supply. All the side events and peculiar happenings, along with a spate of retrospective analysis and commentary, filled newspapers and television screens. Once again Elvis and Memphis were a media epicenter.

The irreverent NBC television program "Saturday Night Live" satirized the situation, interviewing the city's mayor, gum-chewing young National Guardsmen in full battle dress, and two visiting British housewives wearing sweaters with "Elvis" stitched in rhinestones across the front. Garry Trudeau's "Doonesbury" cartoon strip made light of a fan who had visited Memphis and stocked up on Elvis souvenirs of questionable taste. An editorial writer for the *New York Times* asked: "Which will seem more absurd to students of our time, the nationwide flap in the 1950s that kept Elvis Presley's gyrating hips from being televised or the hysteria with which his fans this week commemorated the first anniversary of his death?"

As the staying power of the Elvis phenomenon began to sink in, professional hands moved to respond to the public's fascination. The Las Vegas Hilton once more tapped his box-office drawing power as it renamed its giant dinner theater the Elvis Presley Showroom. It was here that Presley—and only Presley—never played to an empty seat. In September 1978, Barron Hilton, head of the hotel chain, and Priscilla Presley pulled a gold chain to unveil a life-sized romanticized bronze statue of Elvis by Carl Romanelli, a moment that highlighted an "Always Elvis" festival produced by Vernon Presley and Colonel Parker. The event *Variety* called "a big hustle" featured a multimedia production accompanied by a memorabilia display of costumes and personal effects and souvenir booths. Representatives of RCA Records presented Vernon with fifteen gold and platinum records in recognition of Elvis's record sales in the year following his death. At the Hughes Executive

Terminal at Las Vegas International Airport, fans could see Elvis's Convair 880 jet, the *Lisa Marie,* for a five-dollar admission fee.

Another year passed, and *Elvis,* the ABC television movie, attracted top ratings and critical praise. A steady stream of books about the singer appeared, written by fans, by his nurse, by his bodyguards. Then, Elvis's father died and was buried at Graceland next to his first wife and his only child. Elvis had left all his possessions to his father, his grandmother, and his daughter, with Lisa inheriting the shares of the older Presleys when they died. Vernon's will named Priscilla Presley as executrix of his estate. The media had a fresh story to pursue.

Compared with the two previous years, Memphis was relatively calm in August 1979. Thousands of fans arrived in the city for memorial services. A fiberglass model of the city's proposed statue was exhibited. Memphis State University presented a series of seminars on the man and his music to mark the second anniversary of his death. In Tupelo, officials dedicated the memorial chapel at Elvis's birthplace. A pattern had been set: the event and the date that so many people recalled so passionately were now locked into a perpetuity of remembrance.

On September 13, 1979, came the ABC television bombshell that drugs, not a heart attack, had killed Elvis. A few days later, the *New York Times* published a front-page story about the mystery surrounding the singer's death. *People* magazine ran a story about ABC's investigation in Memphis and featured Elvis on its cover. Once more the nation's media responded in ricochet fashion even though the story of drug problems had been there all along. A few months after Elvis died, the *Commercial Appeal* had copyrighted a story by Beth Tampke which said that the singer's body contained at least ten different drugs and that a private autopsy report by Baptist Hospital listed the cause of death as "polypharmacy."

Simultaneously with the airing of ABC's "20/20" investigative report, Tennessee's Board of Medical Examiners charged Dr. George Nichopoulos with "overprescribing" drugs. A sensational public hearing in January 1980, with television cameras present, revealed that Nichopoulos had prescribed "almost ten thousand tablets of uppers, downers, tranquilizers and narcotics" for Elvis in the twenty months before his death. The board suspended the doctor's license for ninety days and placed him on three months' probation. On May 16, 1980, a Shelby County grand jury returned a fourteen-count indictment, charging

Nichopoulos with "unlawfully, willfully and feloniously dispensing" ten controlled drugs. Continuing stories of drug usage, the darker side of the Presley persona, dominated much of the media coverage, but they did little to diminish the appeal of the singer. Fans kept coming to Memphis and Tupelo, visiting the shrines of the King.

In May 1980, Mrs. Minnie Presley, Elvis's grandmother, died and was buried at Graceland, leaving Lisa Marie as the sole heir to the estate. There had been sporadic discussions with the city of Memphis about a possible takeover and preservation of Graceland as a museum and historic site, but the estate's demands for concession rights and other amenities turned off local government officials. "We don't know what sort of interest will be there in the future," said Clifford Pierce, Jr., who was the city attorney at the time. "The crowds may continue to come, or he may wind up like Rudolph Valentino with one rose on his grave."

But the crowds continued to show up year after year, seeking more details about the man/myth and those whose lives were intertwined with his, however tangentially. The book market exploded, with dozens of new titles appearing each year. Picture books and serious rock criticisms appeared, with Dave Marsh providing an excellent retrospective analysis of the good and the bad in a photo history appearing in 1981. Relatives, casual acquaintances, and hangers-on produced books about the man's "secret life." *Are You Lonesome Tonight?* was the story of Lucy de Barbin, a Louisiana teenager who said her love affair with Elvis produced a child, Desiree. Elvis's stepmother, Dee Presley, and her three sons, Billy, Rick, and David Stanley, told of life at Graceland in *Elvis, We Love You Tender*. Observations were published by his cook and his maid and his hairdresser. In *Elvis and Gladys,* writer Elaine Dundy explored Elvis's ancestral roots, tracing his mother's line to an Indian who married a soldier in Andrew Jackson's army.

The most devastating assault on the Presley memory was a mean and tawdry book by Albert Goldman, who thoroughly trashed the Presley myth. Showing contempt for Elvis's background and anything Southern, Goldman added kinky sex to the stories of drug use in a 1981 bestselling blockbuster. His efforts generated defensive outcries from fans of the King, fueling new public fascination concerning all things Elvis.

The ultimate focus of that interest centered on ex-wife Priscilla and heiress Lisa Marie. The tabloids followed Lisa's every move as the child grew up—her schooling, kidnap threats, her marriage to Danny Keough in a Church of Scientology ceremony. When Lisa's child Danielle, Elvis's granddaughter, was born in May 1989, the news was a page-one story in countless newspapers and an exclusive cover photo in *People* magazine.

Priscilla modeled and promoted hair-care products, and for five years she starred on the hit CBS television program "Dallas." She wrote a steamy book, *Elvis and Me,* which stayed atop the best-seller lists in 1985 and was broadcast on ABC television as a two-part movie, with Susan Walters as Priscilla and Dale Midkiff as Elvis. The production became the highest-rated TV movie of the 1987–88 season.

A sometimes reluctant keeper of the Elvis flame, Priscilla told the *New York Times* that there seemed to be no end to the Elvis phenomenon: "When I wrote my book, I thought it would be the end of the chapter. But if you open a newspaper, a supermarket tabloid or a magazine, he's there. I changed my name for a while. I tried using Priscilla Beaulieu. But I can't fool the public even by saying I'm Priscilla Jones. I still have his daughter. The curiosity will always be there. If they talk to me, they're somehow tapped into Elvis."

Gradually, order was brought to the management of the Presley estate. In her role as executrix, Priscilla announced that there would be no change at Graceland following Vernon's death. But lawyers were concerned at the enormous financial drain created by maintenance and security costs as thousands of fans filed by the gravesite. They wondered if anything would be left for Lisa Marie to inherit. Meanwhile, the Internal Revenue Service increased its appraisal of the estate from $5 million to $22.5 million and imposed new taxes.

In 1980, Memphis probate court appointed Blanchard E. Tual as guardian *ad litem* for Lisa Marie. After reviewing all the singer's business contracts, the lawyer was shocked to discover that Colonel Parker was receiving 50 percent of Presley's income (compared with the 15 to 25 percent that was common for management of most artists) and that no one had ever conducted a royalties audit of RCA Records. Tual concluded in his court-ordered report that Colonel Parker "violated his duty both to Elvis and to the estate." The probate court then ordered attorneys for the estate to file suit against Colonel Parker and the record company. A complex series of legal proceedings ensued in California, New York, Tennessee, and Nevada. Settlement was reached in 1983, with Colonel Parker turning over Presley assets to the estate in exchange for a cash payment of over $2 million from RCA. The record company paid the estate $1.1 million in royalties owed on recordings made after 1973. A state court later extended Lisa Marie's trust, originally set to expire in 1993 on her twenty-fifth birthday, until 1998.

Elvis Presley Enterprises, Inc., established to ensure stability of the estate, for the first time registered Presley trademarks (such as the "TCB" symbol and "Graceland") and started legal moves to protect rights to the Elvis persona. Jack Soden, brought in to provide professional management, says the estate has been so successful in its enforcement actions against souvenir sellers that most Elvis merchandise is manufactured by authorized licensees. The estate has also made its peace with RCA Records, renewing its ties in 1990 with the release of *Elvis's Greatest Performances.* Elvis Presley Enterprises receives record royalties from all of the album's songs, including those recorded before 1973.

Estate financial worries were effectively eliminated for good with the decision to grant public access to the mansion. Since the house was opened on June 7, 1982, it has drawn more than 600,000 visitors a year. Of all the homes in the United States, only the White House attracts more people. Ninety-minute tours of sixteen to eighteen persons start every few minutes, with shuttle buses carrying visitors to the mansion's front steps. Inside, guides tell stories about each room, relate anecdotes about Elvis, and answer questions. The tour takes the paying guests through the first-floor den, living room, dining room, and music room and to the basement TV and pool rooms. Visitors also see the recreation facility where Elvis played racquetball and the large trophy room where the gold-record collection and dazzling stage costumes are on display. The tour concludes at the Meditation Garden, where the graves of the singer, his parents, and his grandmother are located.

In the intervening years, the corporation has acquired the entire area across Elvis Presley Boulevard from the mansion. Now called Graceland Plaza, the central feature of the former shopping strip is the ticket pavilion, a large assembly point where the sounds of Elvis recordings are frequently interrupted with announcements of tour departures and reminders to "enjoy your stay at Graceland." One can easily spend a full day at the growing theme park. In addition to the mansion and grounds, there are restaurants, record stores, Elvis's tour bus, a movie theater, gift shops stocked with licensed souvenirs and merchandise, and other royal attractions. Fans can tour the *Lisa Marie,* the luxuriously outfitted jet aircraft that was moved to Graceland from its Las Vegas exhibit site, and a smaller JetStar, which Elvis christened *Hound Dog II*. The public can walk up to the gravesites at no charge each morning from seven-thirty to nine-thirty. The exhibits and gift shops of Graceland provide two thirds of the $15 million annual income of Elvis Presley Enterprises.

The newest addition to the entertainment complex is the Elvis Presley Automobile Museum, featuring twenty vehicles associated with the singer, including the pink Cadillac he gave his mother. When it opened in 1989, a reporter for the *New York Times* said the question was not whether the museum would succeed: "The question is whether there is any limit in sight for the empire built around America's obsession with an entertainer who died twelve years ago."

Jack Soden clearly has other projects in mind that will test the reporter's query. Among his ideas is "a pop version of the King Tut exhibit"—traveling museum shows that will take Graceland to the world.

The estate has more than enough material on hand to outfit such attractions. The way has already been paved by dozens of private entrepreneurs outside Memphis who have been drawing huge crowds and making a lot of money from Elvis memorabilia. A sixty-million-dollar theme park about Elvis and America in the 1950s is planned in Japan. Collector Vince Everett and three other fans sold their homes to raise 1 million pounds to create an Elvis museum and theme park in the Welsh village of Bwichgwyn, near Wrexham. Leading auction houses frequently offer Presley jewelry, automobiles, or other artifacts; two Elvis stage costumes fetched forty thousand pounds in a 1988 sale in London. Two years later, Sotheby's offered Elvis's 1962 Memphis Public Library card and his first driver's license, while Phillips auctioned the electrocardiogram tape that was running on Presley when he died. Hard Rock Cafés pay top dollar for guitars and other items associated with Elvis; rock memorabilia is central to the decor of the ever-expanding worldwide restaurant chain. Jimmy Velvet, with Elvis museums in Nashville, Orlando, and Honolulu and traveling exhibits touring the nation's shopping malls, told *USA Today* that he expected to gross $5 million in 1989. Ron Cade sells over a thousand different items from his all-Elvis store, Memphis Memories, in Levittown, Pennsylvania. Paul McLeod and his son, Elvis Aron Presley McLeod, have outfitted an antebellum mansion in Holly Springs, Mississippi, as a museum/shrine that they call Graceland Too. There, VCRs constantly monitor TV stations, capturing all programming involving Elvis.

The vast archives of Graceland were significantly increased in the fall of 1990 when the estate acquired the lifetime holdings of Colonel Parker. The collection weighs 70,000 pounds and includes many items of limited value, such as office furniture, a collection of elephant bric-a-brac, and letters from fans thanking the Colonel for his Christmas cards. Some cynics think the Colonel, in receiving a payment in excess of a million dollars, may have had the last laugh once again. The estate, however, points to "treasures" like the mint-condition 1976 Cadillac Seville that Elvis gave the Colonel and Elvis's gold lamé suit, possibly the best-known performance costume in entertainment history. The collection also includes thousands of original photos and negatives that span Elvis's entire career, 90 percent of which have never been seen by the public. Graceland has already started marketing limited edition reproductions from this nostalgia lode. Its first offering is a framed advertisement—"made from Colonel Parker's original poster artwork, negative and materials"—promoting Elvis's Honolulu benefit concert for the USS *Arizona* Memorial.

The transformation of Graceland from a mysterious fortress to a well-managed festive shrine has given the Elvis legend a new foundation. The many fan clubs and associations are linked by its newsletter/magazine, *Graceland Express,* which provides a forum for pen pals and for those seeking Elvis items and offering memorabilia for sale. At Christmastime, the estate replicates the spectacular lighting of the grounds, a holiday custom that Elvis originated. A birthday tribute is offered in January, with cake served to the fans on the Graceland Plaza. But the midwinter weather in Memphis deters most fans, who instead prefer the summer vacation time that coincides with the anniversary of Elvis's death.

Elvis International Tribute Week is the formal name for the occasion in August that grows larger each year. Graceland hosts a luncheon for fan club officers and sponsors concerts, video shows, and art contests. Tours to Tupelo are arranged, and other Memphis organizations stage events. A key feature of the annual gathering has become an evening vigil in which thousands of fans with lighted candles walk up the mansion's driveway to the gravesite, hold a brief ceremony, and return.

"Gentle on My Mind . . ." was the theme for the celebration in 1991 when activities included the thirteenth annual memorial gathering at Memphis State University, the eighth annual Elvis Presley Memorial Karate Tournament, the ninth annual Elvis Presley Memorial 5K Run for United Cerebral Palsy, the third annual Elvis Presley Memorial Dinner for the Make a Wish Foundation, the twelfth annual Elvis Presley Memorial Auction to benefit LeBonheur Children's Medical Center, and the tenth annual Elvis art exhibit by Betty Harper. Also available were fan club meetings plus a fifties dance at the Circle G Ranch, a theatrical show at Libertyland, an "Elvis: Legacy in Light" laser concert at the Pink Palace Museum Planetarium, a Carl Perkins concert sponsored by the *Elvis International Forum* magazine, plus tours of Sun Recording Studio, Humes High School, and the MED Elvis Presley Memorial Trauma Center.

Jack Soden thought that 1987, the tenth anniversary of Elvis's death, would be the peak year for attendance at Graceland. But crowds increased the following year, perhaps influenced by monumental reports of "sightings" of Elvis throughout the country.

The new psychic phenomenon apparently was first reported by homemaker Louise Willing, who is absolutely certain that she saw Elvis standing in checkout line Number 2 one Sunday at Felpausch's Supermarket in her hometown of Vicksburg, a town of 2,800 people in southwestern Michigan. Her story was ignored by editors of the town's weekly newspaper, but the supermarket tabloid *Weekly World News* picked up the news in May 1988 with the headline "Elvis Is Alive! The King admits his funeral was faked and tells of secret life in Michigan." The paper added that Elvis had also been seen eating a Whopper and drinking a milkshake at a Burger King in Kalamazoo, some ten miles away.

The *Detroit News* picked up the story, and the Associated Press relayed the article to its subscribers. Other media followed. Radio stations began offering rewards for anyone who could bring Elvis in for a live interview. Around Kalamazoo, signs appeared proclaiming "Elvis rents his movies here," "Elvis tans here," and "Elvis worked here." *USA Today* published a map showing sightings in forty states. Elvis was reported listening to a rock band in a bar in Riverhead, New York, on a parachute ride at a carnival in Denton, Texas, in a '69 Plymouth with Colorado tags in Tennessee, and living in a secluded cabin near Orlando, Florida.

The sightings came on the heels of a book by journalist Gail Brewer-Giorgio, *The Most Incredible Elvis Presley Story Ever Told,* which posed questions about events surrounding the singer's death and suggested that the coffin at Graceland in 1977 contained a wax dummy. The book was released with a sixty-minute cassette purporting to present telephone conversations with Elvis recorded four years after his death. On August 14, 1991, independent television stations aired *The Elvis Files,* a special based on the book. Narrated by Bill Bixby, who had co-starred in two Elvis movies, the program suggested that Elvis had faked his death after being recruited by the FBI to help convict a reputed Mafia chieftain. The special was broadcast live from the Imperial Palace Hotel in Las Vegas, site of the "Legends" stage show where three impersonators portray Elvis in various stages of his career. A majority of viewers casting ballots via a 900 telephone number said they believed that Elvis was still alive. Bixby returned in January 1992 for another broadcast that partially explained or rebutted some of the earlier rumors. But new reports were presented, unexplained photographs were displayed, "unsolved mysteries" were related. The new genre of programming, dubbed tabloid television by the critics, continued to reach larger audiences.

Many in the media reported the Elvis-is-alive stories with tongue in cheek, providing the proper cynicism for stories that won't go away. For many, it was a way to acknowledge the potency of the continued fascination with Elvis without having to embrace it. Writers for Johnny Carson, Jay Leno, and David Letterman found a new source of material for their monologues. Doug Marlette, in his comic strip "Kudzu," reported Elvis miracles in the fundamentalist church of the Reverend Will B. Dunn. The syndicated cartoon "Far Side" showed fugitive novelist Salmon Rushdie and "his roommate Elvis" peering through a closed blind, awaiting discovery. Graceland began logging telephone calls for the singer. "Elvis Tour '88" sweatshirts appeared, with a chronology of dates and sightings detailed on the back. National Football League coach Jerry Glanville announced that a pair of tickets in Elvis's name are held at the box office for every Atlanta Falcons home game.

One tabloid headline said "Elvis is impersonating himself," suggesting that the aging singer has joined the thousands of Presley imitators who make a living by performing or who just live in a fantasy world of their own. Leading British TV personality Jonathan Ross marked the fourteenth anniversary of the rock legend's death with a program on Channel Four that included El Vez, the Mexican Elvis; Janice K, the female Elvis; Clarence, the black Elvis; and Bruno, the four-year-old Elvis who prays before every performance of "Heartbreak Hotel." *I Am Elvis,* a talent directory published in 1991, chronicled the lives of some two hundred such people, ranging from look-alikes to a Pakistani whose repertoire includes such songs as "Who's Sari Now?"

While questions will always remain about the circumstances of 1977, any doubts about the singer's passing ought to have been thoroughly resolved with publication of *The Death of Elvis* by Charles Thompson and James Cole in 1990. Thompson, a television producer who had first hinted that drugs killed Elvis on ABC-TV's "20/20" in 1979, and his brother-in-law, a former *Press-Scimitar* reporter, spent a decade tracking down the autopsy report and other evidence of a cover-up surrounding the cause of Elvis's death. Through a series of lawsuits and hard digging, the two investigative reporters produced a book that is grisly in detail and unsparing in its criticism of the Memphis medical establishment and the *Commercial Appeal.* It decisively documents that Elvis is dead.

As humorists poke fun at the legend, the music lives on. Elvis undergirds a massive enterprise that touches many facets of American life. The records keep appearing, now through compact disc. A new generation discovers the music. Collectors buy the new formats and the new packaging to complete their collections. In 1990 the rare, elusive first song of Elvis's—his amateur rendition of "My Happiness," recorded for his mother at Sam Phillips's studio—surfaced. Bootleg tapes of his many concerts abound. Rumors persist that other songs exist—rejected tapes from his many recording sessions.

The video market has barely been tapped. Tapes of his TV appearances have been packaged. The Presley movies continue as staples of late night television, even though all are available for sale in the world's video stores.

A very successful syndicated television program of the eighties, advertised as the first time that cameras were permitted inside the mansion, featured Priscilla Presley hosting a Graceland tour. The videotape continues to sell well in Graceland gift shops, but the estate's venture into new television formats has not always fared so well. "Elvis: Good Rockin' Tonight," based ostensibly on true stories in the life of Elvis before he became famous, premiered on ABC Television in February 1991. Starring Michael St. Gerard as Elvis, the program received near-universal critical praise for its scripts, acting, and production values and for the new ground it broke in television. *TV Guide* said this very likely made it the most expensive half-hour on television. Priscilla Presley and Jerry Schilling were co-producers of the series, but the program did not attract viewers. Some faulted its Sunday night time slot or the sanitized version of the singer's life; others said it needed more music. Canceled after eight episodes, the series enjoys success overseas and will be available for home-video audiences. In April 1992, with Priscilla Presley as host, CBS Television recycled concert footage, home movies, and other film into a two-hour special, "Elvis: The Great Performances."

Other efforts were made to dramatize Presley's life as various producers hoped to capitalize on the success of the 1979 ABC-TV movie starring Kurt Russell. The estate lent its blessing to Touchstone Films's 1989 movie *Heartbreak Hotel,* a fictional story featuring David Keith as Elvis. In 1981, an NBC movie, *Elvis and the Beauty Queen,* focused on the stormy affair between Elvis and former Miss Tennessee Linda Thompson. Don Johnson, who later achieved stardom in NBC's pastel-hued television series "Miami Vice," put on forty pounds to play the role of a drug-dependent Elvis. That same year, with the cooperation of the estate, David L. Wolper produced a feature-film documentary entitled *This Is Elvis.* A ratings success on Home Box Office cable and NBC Television, the film had a limited theatrical run and featured home movies and concert films. Four unknown actors reenacted scenes from Elvis's life where no film existed.

When Elvis died, colleges and universities rapidly ensured some permanence to the Presley phenomenon. *The Southern Quarterly,* a journal of the arts published by the University of Southern Mississippi, called its fall 1979 issue, "Elvis: Images and Fancies." With an Andy Warhol painting on the cover, the publication featured a dozen essays examining various facets of the man and the myth, including music, religion, Southern identity, and Elvis's international appeal. Academicians continue to analyze the impact of the man and his music.

Linda Suzanne Allen, in a doctoral dissertation at the University of Oregon, presented research showing that Graceland creates mystification about Elvis through paradox: Presley is absent/present; ordinary/extraordinary. Graceland is ethereal/material; secular/sacred. For her doctorate at the University of Pennsylvania, Julia Aparin explored working-class response to Elvis through ethnographic interviews. Valerie Fox's dissertation at the State University of New York at Binghamton was a collection of poetry entitled *Sex with Jesus,* featuring voices striving to attain an intimacy with iconic figures such as Jesus, the Virgin Mary, Elvis, Emma Goldman, Margery Kempe, and Byron.

At Georgetown University, Jo Ann Thomas Nolen drew parallels between celebrity worship of Elvis and the veneration of individuals by the medieval faithful: There are pilgrimages to his shrines, relics are collected, marvelous things are done in his name. Her master's thesis, *St. Elvis of the Guitar,* suggests that Elvis is "precisely the haunting and ever present embodiment of the underside of our least acknowledged and most potent ancient and modern myths." History professor Allen Rushing, Jr., of East Tennessee State University, contends that Elvis has achieved a priestlike status in death because he reconciled conflicting ideals of mainstream America. According to Ray Browne of Bowling Green State University, the nation's leading academic authority on popular culture, the Elvis phenomenon is alive and well. Browne estimates that more than three hundred college courses center on Elvis, his music, or the sociology of the fifties.

Scholars attending the 1992 meeting of the Chicago Art Association were treated to the opening of the second annual All-Elvis Art Show. Images of the King were silk-screened, sculpted, cartooned, and painted on velvet. Marilyn Houlbert, an associate professor of art and anthropology at the School of the Art Institute of Chicago, exhibited a multimedia shrine decorated with paper palm trees, Halloween skeletons, and three hundred pounds of sand. By means of a slide projection on the mirrored back wall, Elvis appeared to levitate over the sand. A painting of Elvis on stamped tin wearing Mickey Mouse ears was entitled "American Icon." Wendy McDaris, an independent curator, told *The Chronicle of Higher Education* that the singer is an ideal iconic figure. "He tends to be the embodiment of both positive and negative aspects of American culture," she said. "He started out radical, and he ended up weary, confused, wanting to get out."

The Library of Congress has catalogued 160 books about Elvis, including titles in German, Spanish, Swedish, Finnish, Danish, and Czech. Its collection even includes books and stories about Elvis printed in Braille, especially tailored for junior high school blind children. The most popular souvenir in the gift shop of the Richard M. Nixon Presidential Library in Yorba Linda, California, is a T-shirt showing "The President and the King." The photograph of the December 21, 1970,

White House meeting of Elvis and Nixon is also available on buttons, refrigerator magnets, and postcards.

In 1980, U.S. Representative (now Senator) Barbara Mikulski of Maryland introduced House Joint Resolution 488, "authorizing and requesting the President to issue a proclamation designating January 8, 1981, as Elvis Presley Day." Other members of Congress from North Carolina to California signed on as co-sponsors, but the resolution died in committee. The idea was revived in March 1992 when Representative Glenn Anderson of California, joined by fourteen colleagues, introduced legislation to establish Elvis Presley Day. Arkansas Governor Bill Clinton knows the entire Elvis catalogue. As a presidential candidate in the 1992 New York primary, he sang "Don't Be Cruel" during an interview on public television's "The Charlie Rose Show."

The original legislative efforts to designate Graceland as a national historic landmark also languished in committee. But in November 1991 the National Park Service placed the home on its National Register of Historic Places because of its "exceptional significance." Twenty-two-year-old Jennifer Tucker of Memphis had requested the listing as part of a project for her bachelor's degree in historic preservation.

Meanwhile, Elvis fans kept turning up in high places. Edward Margolis, chief of the organized crime section at the Justice Department in the Carter administration, hung an Elvis poster on his office wall. So did Edward P. Beard, member of Congress from Rhode Island. Larry Speakes, President Reagan's press secretary, was an unabashed admirer of the King, sometimes opening his media briefings with Elvis recordings. Queen Sirikit of Thailand is an Elvis fan, as is Robert Mugabe, who became Zimbabwe's first president after Rhodesia's bloody civil war. The Marxist theoretician and holder of six university degrees likes to relax by listening to Elvis records. So does Russian president Boris Yeltsin. As communism collapsed in the Soviet Union in 1991, he plotted the revolution as he listened to the music of Elvis. According to Tatiana Uretzkaya, his personal physician, "Yeltsin plays 'Are You Lonesome Tonight?' all the time, and he knows all the words."

From the time of Elvis's death, fans began seeking the likeness of the King on a postage stamp, an honor accorded the singer by West Germany, Tanzania, and two Caribbean states, Antigua-Barbuda and St. Vincent. Their suggestion stirred opposition from critics who called it "a hound dog of an idea," and charged that Elvis's personal life overshadowed his art. After all, said *Washington Post* columnist Richard Cohen, Elvis's personal life, drug abuse, and obesity "accounted for his premature death." In a 1988 *New York Times* op-ed piece, Ben Kamin, a rabbi in Cleveland, said no stamp should honor someone whose life and death were "anathema to what we want kids to believe and practice." Outraged fans countered that stamps have honored other American artists who were substance abusers, citing as examples Hemingway, Faulkner, Steinbeck, Jack London, and Eugene O'Neill. More than sixty thousand letters and hundreds of petitions supporting an Elvis stamp were received by the Postal Service.

In February 1992, Postmaster General Anthony M. Frank finally said yes, making his announcement in a press conference via satellite from the Las Vegas Hilton, which had been the site of 839 Elvis sell-out performances. In an unprecedented move, Frank unveiled two stamp designs and said the public would be permitted to make the final decision between younger and older renderings of the singer's likeness. Five million postcards were distributed to the nation's post offices to be used as ballots in a month-long election. The *Commercial Appeal, USA Today,* the *Washington Post,* and other newspapers conducted their own poll. *USA Today* said the choice was between "raw and rockabilly" or "slick and sequined." Once again Elvis was a source of humor as TV stations predicted that millions would see the King—on postage stamps in 1993. Some commentators questioned the legality of the move, noting that postal statutes require that persons appearing on stamps must be "demonstrably dead" for at least ten years.

Many changes have come to Memphis in the years since Elvis died. The city's establishment more and more has accepted the Elvis phenomenon as a major part of its artistic and commercial well-being. Images of Elvis are a major part of the city's tourism and convention advertising. In 1990, all fifteen of Elvis's guitars from the estate inventory were exhibited in the lobby of the Vincent de Frank Hall of the Convention Center. The occasion was a pops concert by the Memphis Symphony Orchestra; the Graceland promotion guaranteed a sellout. Lloyds of London insured the items for $5 million as the collection made its first-time-ever trip outside the mansion.

The graceful statue of Elvis was finally built, and it draws tourists to the Beale Street entertainment complex, where rock music competes with jazz and blues near the Peabody Hotel. A massive glass pyramid now dominates the downtown skyline, although its construction has been plagued with financial difficulties. This symbol of the city's ancient namesake includes a sports arena where Memphis State University plays basketball and where developers still hope to feature Elvis memorabilia as part of a music museum that is planned within the structure. Some fans even propose that Elvis's body be moved to the massive building. After all, the purpose of a pyramid is to enshrine the remains of a king.

Tupelo, too, has come to terms with Elvis. A major new furniture manufacturing industry has developed in the last decade, yet Tupelo maintains a small-town ambience that draws a steady stream of tourists to the memorial chapel, the youth center, and the state park that bear Elvis's name. The chapel has been the scene of 458 weddings. Some sixty thousand visitors a year visit the Presley birthplace. The numbers are expected to grow significantly with the addition of a major Presley museum being built by the Graceland estate and the Tupelo Development Foundation. The building will house the personal collection of Jannelle McComb, who spearheaded construction of the chapel following Elvis's death. Because she knew Elvis as a friend and not as a celebrity, McComb's collection is special. "I own everything from the hammer that built the birthplace to the last picture of him walking off the stage forever," she said.

Elvis has carved a unique niche in the nation's psyche, emerging as a presence not only in music but in comedy, conspiracy theories, and almost every other subgroup of the popular culture. According to a Yankelovich survey of one thousand Americans, taken for *Time* magazine in September 1991, fully 16 percent of the public believes that Elvis is alive. Another 4 percent are not sure.

Elvis is routinely mentioned by characters on major television programs. For a Halloween plot on "Roseanne," actor John Goodman dressed up like Elvis. Ted Danson's character on the top-rated show "Cheers" sought Elvis's advice on marriage. The characters of "The Golden Girls" and "Designing Women" discussed trips to Graceland. The star of "Miami Vice" lived on a boat with his pet alligator named Elvis. In an episode of "Murphy Brown," star Candice Bergen wondered if the male secretary with the Southern accent outside her office could really be Elvis.

The rock legend appears in the lyrics of more than 150 rock, folk, and rap songs, from Paul Simon's "Graceland" and Frank Zappa's "Elvis Has Just Left the Building" to Laurie Anderson's "Hiawatha."

President George Bush evoked the King's name in his 1992 State of the Union address, suggesting that soldiers in the Gulf War who scrawled "I Saw Elvis" on Kuwaiti walls were comrades in spirit to the men who wrote "Kilroy Was Here" in previous wars. The president earlier staged a press conference at the Grand Canyon, only to have Senator Albert Gore, Jr., of Tennessee denounce the tactic with a speech on the Senate floor: "Anybody who sees George Bush as the environmental president at the Grand Canyon ought to watch for Elvis, alive and well, rafting by on the Colorado River." A week later the senator received a photograph taken at the Arizona event. In the media contingent alongside the president was a Knight-Ridder reporter, wearing a baseball cap with "Elvis" emblazoned across the crown.

Elvis has entered into the dialogue of the nation, with no explanation needed. No single theory can explain the reaction to his death and the continuing interest. When he burst on the music scene in the fifties, Elvis became a catalyst for the new worldwide youth movement. He was someone who belonged exclusively to those who faced adulthood with economic depression and global war behind them and the nuclear age ahead. One wonders if anything after 1957 really made any difference. The fuse had been lit, and Elvis would have remained the symbol of that youth movement no matter what else occurred.

But other things did happen. In the midst of the low quality of his music after his military service, Elvis moved with his generation. Like them, he shifted from rebellion into the mainstream of American life.

When pressed to explain why the President of the United States felt that it was right and natural to issue a statement on the death of Elvis, the speechwriter who penned President Carter's tribute suggested, after some thought, "because he unified popular culture both here and around the world."

The comment was echoed by Raymond Fletcher, a member of the British Parliament, who told the Council of Europe that Elvis had done more to unite the youth of the world than any political figure. Cognizant of the theory that political happenings are often influenced by a people's music, Fletcher observed that Elvis arrived on the scene just as Europe's young people sensed that something new was about to happen. On a continent that was just beginning to grope away from old hatreds, Presley had greater significance as a common focus for European youth than he did in his own country.

Elvis offered country ballads and great hymns and soft lullabies and an undemanding patriotism. But he also never lost the capacity to convey the rebelliousness and the unremitting, driving rock beat that had been his first trademark.

At Graceland, among all the gold records and other tributes, hangs the entertainer's high school diploma. Friends say that he was prouder of that simple, framed document than all the other awards. He was the first member of his family to finish high school.

This is the dichotomy—distinctly Southern—that arrests the imagination and holds one's attention: A white boy who drew on black music without affectation; the catalyst for rebellion who never himself rebelled; the quintessentially polite youth who took no gaffe; the religious man who might backslide on Saturday night; the no-nonsense musician who laughed at himself and the myth he had become.

While the paradox of Elvis challenged the mind of an entire generation, the hearts of millions were won by the hero who never forgot his people and his roots. He was not just the poor boy who made it to the top. He symbolized the ultimate rebellion of all common folk against all forms of restraint: He showed it was possible not just to be somebody, but to do it in a distinctly American way—to be somebody and to have a good time doing it.

With the last story in this book, we take our final bows.

And sing an epiphany.

VICTOR KOMAN wrote the critically acclaimed 1985 novel The Jehovah Contract *(winner of the 1988 Prometheus Award). He scribed the 1989 medical thriller* Solomon's Knife *(another Prometheus winner) and was the voice of Drowsy, the narcoleptic deer, for the animated short film "The Buck Stops Here." Victor's currently at work on a "space thriller" trilogy; he lives in Southern California with his wife and daughter. Koman's favorite Elvis song is "Flaming Star."*

As to why Victor's story is the final entry in Elvis Is Dead—

Dead Elvis's resurrection has produced many harsh by-products. Relentless merchandising, vilifying posthumous biographies, cruel lampoons, merciless jokes.

Yet He remains a charged, potent myth. A contemporary deity whose nearest historical antecedent is Janus, the two-faced Roman god. For like that ancient divinity before Him (closely identified with doors, gates, and all beginnings), Dead Elvis unlocks new legends for us.

He also presents twin visages.

One radiant with youth, the other ravaged by corruption.

Somehow, I think I know which face most of us prefer.

So does Victor Koman.

Despite its moments of domestic brutality, then, "The Eagle Cape" is an affectionate and hopeful effort. One primarily concerned with strumming the emotional chords which so perfectly encapsulate our memories of Elvis.

The loving, nostalgic ones.

The ones I now leave you with.

Plus these final, fitting words.

Ladies and gentleman—

Elvis has left the building.

THE EAGLE CAPE

by Victor Koman

She owned no Elvis collector's plates. She possessed no photographs of the King. She had never attended an Elvis impersonator contest. She had never even read a book about him or known that the tabloids continually reported on persistent sightings of him in rural America.

All she knew was his music. And how he had saved her life, and her daughter's.

Bobbie Jean reeled from the blow. As she fell to the ground, she wondered groggily what she had done to get Jimmy Joe all mad again. He bent over her, hairy left fist balled up tight.

"Please, Jimmy Joe," a voice cried from behind his skinny, whip-snake body. "Please don't hit her agin. Hit me. I'm a one did it."

Jimmy Joe gazed down at the cringing little girl for a moment, then swiveled to backhand the woman behind him. "You two better just learn from this," he said levelly, "or I'll be sorry I wasted my time on you." He flopped down in the easy chair, its stuffing bulging out from tears in the plastic like meat from beneath the torn skin of a sausage.

Carrie Lynn picked up her weeping daughter and walked into the kitchen. "He didn't mean it," she murmured to the ten-year-old. "He's just all drunk agin." She sat the child down on the red step stool and gazed at her face. "Lemme git some ice."

Bobbie Jean watched her mother open the fridge, a cigarette-smoke-stained old thing that rattled incessantly at night in the cramped kitchen. The freezer compartment was mostly frost, and it was this that Carrie Lynn chipped at with a blunt supper knife, catching the chips in a dirty dish towel.

Bobbie's left eye was swelling now, hot and throbbing. The ice felt cool and good when her mother applied it. Her mother stood in front of her, holding the ice and singing a song soft and low. She recognized it: "Are You Lonesome Tonight?"

They did not own any Elvis albums. They did not own a record player. Whenever an Elvis song would come on their tinny old clock radio, though, her mother would stop what she was doing and sing along. At those moments, Bobbie Jean noticed, her mother's face would lose all the pained lines it possessed and she would just seem to drift away. It did not matter whether the song was slow or fast—it transported her.

"Carrie Lynn!" her husband shouted from the living room. "Bring a beer back when ya done in there!"

"See?" she said to her daughter. "He ain't mad no more." She pulled a can of beer from the wilting contents of the fridge and padded back to him, leaving Bobbie Jean alone in the kitchen.

Bobbie Jean was ten years old and already beginning to show the signs of leaving girlhood behind. Daddy said she was growing up too fast and the boys would soon be sniffing around their front yard like hound dogs.

She looked through her right eye at her reflection in the night-darkened kitchen window. Her hair, brown and straight, hung past her shoulders over the plain, sacklike dress draping her thin frame. In profile, she could see that her chest parts were starting to grow. She didn't know whether to be pleased or wary—she did not want to attract anyone remotely similar to Daddy.

When her mother walked back in, she asked, "Momma—was Elvis ever married?"

Carrie Lynn gazed at her daughter with a puzzled expression. "Why, sure, honey. He married a girl named Priscilla. And they had a baby they called Lisa Marie."

"Did he ever hit them?"

Carrie Lynn stared at her daughter, at her swollen left eye. Suddenly, her chest heaved with a sob and she crouched beside the girl, hugging her and swaying her back and forth.

"No, baby, no. Elvis never hurt a soul."

In the living room, an empty beer can bounced against the wall. A moment later, the front door opened and shut, the screen door creaking on its single rusted spring to slam with reassuring finality.

Carrie Lynn glanced over her shoulder, waiting for the sound of the truck. Engine rumbled, gears ground, tires kicked up dirt and gravel. Jimmy Joe was gone to town, maybe not to return for the rest of the night. The hot August air achieved a comforting silence.

"Bobbie Jean honey, can you keep a secret? From your daddy? From everyone?"

The child nodded. If she could keep secret what Daddy did once when she was eight, she could keep anything.

Carrie Lynn took Bobbie to the bedroom, a dank and musty place with sheets that were always changed too late, though one night was usually too late considering how her husband sweated his liquor out. She smoothed out the blanket and her daughter jumped up on it, ice and all. The bedsprings squeaked and grumbled.

Bobbie watched her mother dig deeply into the bottom of the closet, searching for something. She knew right where it was, apparently, but had to remove a lot of old clothes and fishing gear to get to it. Then Carrie Lynn pulled out something that had been rolled up and placed in an old Winn Dixie shopping bag.

"Now," she said, sitting back on the bed and speaking in a conspiratorial whisper, "I told you that I once saw Elvis sing, right? I mean in person?"

"Yes, Momma."

"Now, what I didn't tell you was that I saw him sing in *Hawaii*! Even yo' daddy doesn't know that."

Bobbie Jean stared in awe, saying nothing; her mind raced, though. She had never imagined that her mother had been *anywhere* in her life, least of all to *another country*!

"Yep, Hawaii. See, this was years before I met your daddy, back when *my* daddy and momma were still alive." Carrie Lynn clutched the Winn Dixie bag close to her. The paper had lost any semblance of stiffness and was almost as soft as velvet from repeated crinklings. She gazed off into space, transported into another world by her reverie.

"Your grampa was a fine, fine man. Back then, he was still working for the *Memphis Star* even though he was sick with his cancer. Well, he got a pair of press tickets to go to an Elvis concert they were doin' for TV. In Hawaii! Well, he was goin' to take Momma because the two of them were just so much in love it was amazing. But she said no sir! She said you take Carrie Lynn because she loves Elvis and she'll love Hawaii. At first, though, Daddy thought it would be too much trouble taking a fifteen-year-old girl along. But soon he kinda warmed to it 'cause he just loved me to death and spoiled me to pieces."

Bobbie Jean stared in awe at her mother, then at the mysterious bag. Her heart beat wildly inside her. She hung on every word. Carrie Lynn described the plane flight to San Francisco, the jumbo jet flight across the ocean to the Hawaiian Islands, and the incredible concert by Elvis Presley called *Aloha from Hawaii.*

"I was only a few rows back. He was up there all in white leather and fringe. When he sang it was like I could hear an angel singin'." She smiled and blushed. "Well, a devil or angel, depending on what song it was." Her grip on the bag loosened slightly. She let it slide into her lap. "He looked so good, he looked so happy to be back on top again. He looked so . . . so . . ." Carrie Lynn shook her head. "It was the most incredible night of my life."

She reached out to touch Bobbie Jean. "But that wasn't all of it. Toward the end of the show, he took off the cape he was wearing and threw it into the crowd." She started to open the bag. "I saw it whip through the air as if it was some kind of slow-flying bird. I saw it coming toward me, coming straight toward me as if Elvis had seen me, had felt my love for him, and had sent this"—she withdrew something from the bag that looked like parchment and smelled of clean, pure nature—"as a token of his caring."

Bobbie Jean lowered the ice-filled dish rag from her face. She could not believe her eyes.

Her mother unrolled the leather cape. It looked huge. Age had turned its white color yellowish. Fringe lined its edge, long leather strings that slapped and rustled like rain against a windowpane. On its back a red, white, and blue eagle made of bugle beads spread its wings wide and proud. Bobbie Jean had never seen anything so beautiful.

Carrie Lynn said, "It sailed out to me and I caught it in my fingers and pulled it close. Some other people grabbed at me and tried to take it, but your grampa stood them off. He stuffed it under his coat when the concert was over and he wrote his article about the concert without mentioning it and he told me never to tell anyone I had it because it was worth a fortune and you never knew what someone else might do to have something that Elvis wore."

"Is that why you never told Daddy?" Bobbie Jean asked.

Her mother looked sad for a moment, then nodded. "I thought he'd make me sell it. And I couldn't. I'd just die if it were gone. I swore that the only person I'd ever give it to would be Elvis, if he said he wanted it back." She ran a hand over the smooth leather. "I never read or heard about him wanting it back. And then when he died . . ."

She picked up the cape. "When he died I swore I'd give it up in an instant if it would just bring him back. Just for a minute, so I could tell him how much I loved him. How much we all loved him."

She draped the cape gently over her daughter. Bobbie Jean's small shoulders bent under the amazing weight of it. She felt warm and strong.

"Someday, baby," her mother said, "when you're all grown up and ready to leave this place, I'm going to give it to you."

The girl threw her arms around her mother and held her tightly. The eagle cape meant that Bobbie Jean *would* grow up, that she could escape from Daddy and the squalor and the pain and everything else. Her blackened eye no longer throbbed. She would grow up, then, grow up as fast as she could.

"I'll take you with me, Momma, when I go."

"I love you, honey." Mother held daughter as close as she could. The cape wrapped around both of them like an Indian tepee. Within its folds, Carrie Lynn felt renewed, as if she could go on for years, endure any hardship, conquer every doubt. She felt the same strength radiate from her daughter and she knew that Jimmy Joe could never crush them.

The screen door slammed open, slammed shut.

"God damn' son of a bitch bastard asshole!" Jimmy Joe bellowed.

Carrie Lynn balled up the eagle cape and handed it to Bobbie Jean. "Hide it!" she hissed on her way out of the bedroom.

"Sugah?" she called out as she ran to the living room. "Honey, you okay?"

"Damn' truck hit the damn' culvert over by the Millers'. I had to walk out ass-high in kudzu and you ask if I'm okay?" The back of his hand lashed out at her face, hitting her cheekbone with cracking force. "How the hell I'm supposed to get to work tomorrow?"

Carrie Lynn rubbed at her face. She was starting to cry and no longer censoring her thoughts. "Too bad you can't call to tell Miss Vaseline you're gonna be late for—"

"Her name," Jimmy Joe said with savage force, "is *Abilene!*" He seized her by the arm and shoved her through the bedroom door and onto the bed. He worked at unfastening his big brass belt buckle. "I'm gonna get from you what I shoulda got from her."

Carrie Lynn looked around the bedroom and saw no sign of her daughter. As he threw her prone and hitched up her dress, she saw that the closet door was closed.

Inside the closet, all Bobbie Jean could hear were the sounds of struggle. Wrapped up in the eagle cape, all she could feel was the heat of her breath and the tangible darkness that surrounded her. She cried for her mother, she cried for herself. Hot tears spread across her sweating face, pooled at her nose, and dripped onto the inner lining of the cape. She heard and felt the force of several more blows her father gave her mother.

Suddenly, she felt something. Something in the closet with her. Not bugs or a rat. Something bigger. Her breath seized up in her chest. She sat absolutely still.

It brushed past her. The closet door burst open. Two loud thuds and then silence.

Bobbie Jean pulled the eagle cape from her and peered out of her sanctuary. Her fearful gaze sought her mother.

And saw her, naked, turning over to stare dazedly off into a corner of the room. On her face lay a look of uncomprehending awe.

Bobbie Jean crawled silently from the closet to follow her mother's gaze. At the foot of the bed, his pants down around his ankles, lay the crumpled form of her father. He had never looked more unconscious, even at his drunkest. She wondered if he was dead. Then Bobbie looked in the corner of the room.

Standing there was a tall man dressed all in white. White leather and fringe and beads, like the cape in the closet behind her. Only this leather still had the bright, fresh whiteness it must have possessed more than fifteen years ago in Hawaii.

The man did not say a word. He simply bent at his knees, laid an arm on his thigh, and gazed at Bobbie Jean with a warm smile.

The child said nothing. Her mother pulled her dress back down and sat up in bed. After a moment, she said, very softly, "He's come for his cape, Bobbie Jean. Give it back to him."

Then Carrie Lynn gazed at the figure in white and said, "Why now? Why didn't you come sooner?"

He reached out his leather-gloved hand to touch the tears on Bobbie

Jean's cheek. Bobbie looked back at the cape. On the eagle lay a small, wet stain. She turned to her mother.

"Because I cried on it!" Bobbie said. "Did you ever cry on it?"

Her mother shrugged weakly. "I don't know. It always made me so happy to hold it. I don't think I ever did."

Bobbie Jean stood and walked to the closet to pick up the eagle cape. It felt light, now. She felt stronger than she ever had in her short life.

The dark-haired man with the soft, compassionate eyes stood as she approached. He towered over her.

Bobbie Jean glanced back at her mother. Carrie Lynn had stepped off the bed, around her fallen husband, and approached her daughter's side.

"Are you sure, Momma?"

Carrie Lynn nodded, gazing into the man's eyes. "I made a promise to him, a promise deep in my heart. For just one minute more. One minute to tell him how much I love him."

Elvis smiled.

He reached out to lay a hand on her shoulder. All the love of the world was returned to her in one blissful instant.

Bobbie Jean extended her small arms upward to offer him the cape. Gentle, huge hands lifted it up, wrapped it around his shoulders, and fastened it on. The yellow leather shone to pure, eye-searing white again. The eagle scintillated with actinic flashes of light that seemed to come from somewhere deep within.

His smile grew. With a gesture toward the door, the man ushered the pair outside. There, in the steamy hot Decatur night, the sky glowed with a million stars.

The man bent down and kissed Bobbie Jean on the top of her head. "Always love your momma," he whispered in her ear.

He rose up tall and happy, happier than Carrie Lynn had ever seen him in pictures. He waved at both of them and then turned. And as he walked northwest into the night, toward Graceland, Bobbie Jean saw a flaming star over his shoulder and knew that she could never be hurt again.

A FINAL MUSICAL NOTE

During the nearly four years it took to compile this book, The King Is Dead *was assembled to constant background music. In a very real sense, that music shaped* Elvis's *text.*

Therefore, I feel it equally important to credit the many songs and records which inspired this anthology.

First and foremost comes the King. Various Elvis singles and albums I listened to while editing this book included:

Elvis: The Definitive Rock & Roll Album, *"Reconsider Baby,"* The Complete Sun Sessions, *"All Shook Up," "In the Ghetto,"* Aloha from Hawaii Via Satellite, Back in Memphis, *"Blue Hawaii," "That's All Right,"* The Complete 50's Masters, *"Mystery Train," "Blue Moon of Kentucky," "Return to Sender,"* A Date with Elvis, *"I'm Left, You're Right, She's Gone,"* Elvis *(1956 original LP),* Elvis—A Legendary Performer, Volumes 1 & 2, Elvis Aron Presley, *"Jailhouse Rock,"* Elvis's Gold Records, Volumes 1–5, *"That's Someone You Never Forget," "Heartbreak Hotel,"* Elvis in Nashville, Elvis in Concert, *"Teddy Bear,"* Elvis Presley *(his first LP),* For LP Fans Only, Essential Elvis—The First Movies, *"Blue Suede Shoes,"* A Golden Celebration, He Touched Me, *"Viva Las Vegas,"* How Great Thou Art, On Stage—February 1970, Singer Presents Elvis Singing Flaming Star and Others, Something for Everybody, *"Hound Dog," "I Got a Woman,"* That's the Way It Is, This Is Elvis, *"Shake, Rattle, and Roll," "Don't Be Cruel,"* You'll Never Walk Alone.

And, of course, "Hard-Headed Woman."

I also listened to numerous soundtracks, a hundred or so classical works, and

379

far too many other rock, blues, jazz, rap, rockabilly, grunge, R&B, industrial, hip-hop, DIY, and country records to list here.

But the point of all this is a simple one:

The King Is Dead *specifically concerns one man and His music.*

However, its secret subject was rock 'n' roll.

Which is why ye editor compiled, and now recommends, the many Elvis-oriented singles and albums listed herein.

As "The Heart of Rock 'n' Roll"'s protagonist put it, "Passion makes life bearable: music is passion's key."

May all your locks be opened, then.

And passion touch your life.

—*Paul M. Sammon*
Los Angeles, February 1993

ABOUT THE EDITOR

PAUL MICHAEL SAMMON was born in Philadelphia. He grew up in Asia, where he enjoyed such amazing local talents as Chito Bertol, The Original Elvis Presley of the Philippines.

However, Sammon's gleeful pursuit of the rock 'n' roll lifestyle soon brought him perilously close to burnout. At which point he was saved by The Love Of A Good Woman.

Since then Sammon has consistently surprised himself by actually making a living as both a writer and a professional filmmaker. His film studies have appeared in *Omni*, The *Los Angeles Times*, the *American Cinematographer, Cahiers Du Cinéma*, and *Video Watchdog*. Sammon edited the controversial 1990 *Splatterpunks* anthology, and is film critic for *the Sci-Fi channel* magazine.

Paul Sammon has also produced/edited/directed many commercials and documentaries for virtually all the major film studios. He provided various services for *RoboCop, Blue Velvet, F/X,* and *Platoon,* and was the Computer Graphics Supervisor for *RoboCop 2*.

Now Paul M. Sammon works almost exclusively for Japanese television, on weekly entertainment programs like *Hello! Movies, The 21st Century Theater,* and *Let's Go See Movies!*

Sammon's distinctive career was recently profiled in Stanley Wiater's 1992 book *Dark Visions*. He likes listening to *Ministry*, Etta James, surf music, and sound tracks, and recently completed the same training program Linda Hamilton used to buff herself out for *Terminator 2*.

He also plays rhythm guitar and loves everything Elvis Presley ever did.

That is, before Gladys died and the Army got him.